THE FIRST STEP TOWARD LOVE

"Loralee," Jesse said, regret and sadness in his eyes. "I think it would be best if I just . . . stayed away from you."

She nodded. "I guess I should go back inside." She *knew* she should go back inside. And still, she stood before him, reluctant to move.

Jesse studied her, wondering why fate was so cruel. She was the loveliest woman he had ever seen. "I guess so," he said.

She stood looking at him for a long time, as if she wanted to postpone their separation until the very last minute. "Do you think it would be possible to consider ourselves . . . no longer enemies?"

Jesse smiled and stepped closer to her, fighting the urge to pull her into his arms. Holding out his hand, he said, "No longer enemies."

She didn't hesitate; she put her hand in his and grasped it in a firm handshake. "No longer enemies." It was only after the handshake that she hesitated, and when the silence between them became unbearable, she turned and walked slowly up the path and around the corner of the house.

He shoved his hands into his pockets and watched her go . . . .

BOOK YOUR PLACE ON OUR WEBSITE AND MAKE THE READING CONNECTION!

We've created a customized website just for our very special readers, where you can get the inside scoop on everything that's going on with Zebra, Pinnacle and Kensington books.

When you come online, you'll have the exciting opportunity to:

- View covers of upcoming books
- Read sample chapters
- Learn about our future publishing schedule (listed by publication month *and author*)
- Find out when your favorite authors will be visiting a city near you
- Search for and order backlist books from our online catalog
- Check out author bios and background information
- Send e-mail to your favorite authors
- Meet the Kensington staff online
- Join us in weekly chats with authors, readers and other guests
- Get writing guidelines
- AND MUCH MORE!

Visit our website at
http://www.zebrabooks.com

PROLOGUE

Avondale, Pennsylvania
September 6, 1869

"Fire! *Fire!*"

"*Ta mianach guail ar tine!*" The coal mine is on fire! The call echoed down the narrow tunnel, and Sam Fedosh snapped his head up, his senses tingling. He forced himself to remain still while he tried to determine the point from which the shout had come, but in the murky darkness of the mine, the word bounced down the gangway and ricocheted in every direction.

"*Tine! Feuer! Tan! Ohen!*" Most of the miners were immigrants, and the call went out in several different languages—Irish, German, Welsh and Slovak. Everyone heard it.

Sam dropped his tools and ran toward the gangway. "Where? Where is it?" he shouted to anyone who could hear him. They had to seal it off, smother it and contain the danger.

"The shaft!" someone shouted. "It's the whole goddamned shaft!"

Sam's footsteps slowed. The shaft? It was the only way out!

Men were pouring out of the entries and into the gangway. The mules, each harnessed to a small cart full of coal, stomped the ground frantically. Even they were aware of the danger.

The men ran from every chamber within that mine, down the gangways toward the shaft—the one and only way of getting out.

The smell and the brightness reached them, and they knew, before they even saw.

"Oh, God in heaven . . ." Sam's feet stopped moving. He watched as sparks fell from above and landed in the bales of hay that filled the cage at the bottom of the pulley ropes. Hay, to feed the mules, as flammable as the very oil they burned in their lamps, maybe more so.

One hundred and ten men stood frozen, helpless as they watched the flames crawl up the ropes toward the surface.

One of the men who stood closest to the blaze shouted, "It's the breaker! The breaker's on fire!"

"Oh, God help us!"

"The breaker, the breaker . . ." Word spread from man to man, the severity of their situation blanketing them all.

"The breaker? My boys are in there!" Griffith Reese rushed toward the cage that had, just that morning, lowered the men into the mine. He peered up at the breaker, which housed the machinery to clean the coal and crack it into uniformly sized pieces. At ages nine and seven, both boys worked as slate pickers. They sat on wooden slats, straddling the chute and discarding the slate that was mixed in with the coal as it ran between their legs. They each earned forty-five cents a day for ten hours of grueling work hunched over the endless parade of anthracite.

Griffith craned his neck to look up the shaft, but from five hundred feet below the surface, Sam knew he would see nothing. Nervously, Griff moved from place to place, as though by looking at it from a different perspective he might see something he'd missed.

Sam grabbed his arm and pulled him back, away from the burning hay. "Griff, c'mon, buddy, move back."

Griffith shook him off. "They're my boys, Sam! I have to do something!"

"You're right, and that something is to look out for yourself! You can't get up there to help them, and you'll be no use to them if you get yourself burned up! The chutes are far enough away; I'm sure all the boys are out by now."

Griffith stopped to consider this, willing, Sam knew, to hold on to any shred of hope he could find. "Yeah . . . yeah, you're right. They're probably runnin' home to their ma right now."

"I'm sure they are, so now let's think about us, all right?"

Griff only nodded his head, his eyes glued to the orange glow above them.

At Avondale, the breaker had been built on top of the shaft to save the expense of hauling the coal from the mine. And above their only means of escape, it burned out of control, showering sparks upon them.

All around, desperate men pressed closer to the flames, their eyes trained on the spot of brightness above. Suddenly, Sam snapped to his senses. "Listen! *Listen to me!* Everyone get down the gangway and back down the entries!"

"What? Are you crazy?" someone shouted. "This shaft's the only way out! And you want us as far away from it as possible?"

"Listen, will you? That fire is sucking all the oxygen out of here! We've got to build a wall and seal ourselves off from it. When they put it out, they'll come get us!"

Around him, the men stopped to consider his words. Every minute they wasted, more air was sucked out of the mine, and with it, the amount of time they could wait to be rescued.

Griffith spoke up. "Sam's right! It's the only thing we can

do. Go back as far as you can and start hauling timbers out here!''

''I'll need some men to stay here and lay the timbers!'' Sam said.

Cries of ''I'll stay!'' and ''Count me in!'' went up. Fifteen of the tallest men were chosen, and by that time, they already had a pile of timbers to work with.

''Anyone who can't pull timber, find some rocks to fill in the holes. This wall has got to be as airtight as we can make it!'' Sam started to help drag the bulky lengths of wood toward the spot where a wall was already taking shape. These were men who worked surrounded by the possibility of accidents every day of their lives. They weren't the type to buckle under to their fears. They had a good plan, and they feverishly labored with faith that it would work

The wall was almost half up when the first bit of burning debris fell.

''It's the breaker! It's falling into the shaft!'' someone shouted. Sam looked up and saw another piece fall. Around him, the men stopped moving. They stared at the spot where the burning embers had fallen onto the floor of the shaft. The hay and the cage had long since burned themselves out. There was nothing else that would catch fire.

Someone shouted, ''Let's get moving!'' and the activity began again. The wall went up, faster than before. Rocks were piled, ready to fill gaps.

The wall had almost reached the ceiling. Another row of timbers was all it would take. From the floor, some of the men had started to fill in gaps. They lifted young boys to reach the higher places, urging them to ''get a good fit.''

The space through which the oxygen in the mine was being pulled toward the fire had been drastically diminished. Air was still being pulled out, but it was being forced through a smaller area. It was moving with enough speed that it created a breeze, and that convinced Sam that he'd been right to block off the rest of the mine. Without the wall, they'd suffocate in no time. With the wall, they had a chance.

"All right, send it up!" One of the men was standing on an overturned wagon, wedging the last timber between the wall and the ceiling, when, from the other side, there rose an incredible *whoosh!*

"Jesus! What was that?" asked Griffith, instinctively ducking his head when he heard the sound.

"Oh, my God! Oh, God . . ." Atop the wagon, Hugh Morris had stopped moving. He stood staring out the small hole into the shaft on the other side. "Oh, God, no!"

"What is it? *What is it!*" Sam shouted, already climbing up onto the wagon.

He stretched to look over the side. "Oh, my God . . ." he said, defeat and fear sounding in his voice for the first time.

"What?"

"What, Sam?"

"What do you see?"

"Let me up!"

The men had started to panic, and Sam could not find the energy to stop them. He turned and said, "The breaker crashed down into the shaft. The whole shaft is blocked with it."

Like a tidal wave, the men piled up onto the wagon, each one disbelieving, each one needing, for some reason, to see. Sam was pushed over the edge and onto the floor, where he stayed, his mind reeling . . . *We're trapped . . . trapped! . . . Mary, will I see you again? . . . my babies, will I see you? . . . Jesse . . . my boy . . .*

Someone fell into him, knocking him out of his private thoughts. He looked up to see that the hole had not been filled. He got to his feet and shouted, "Seal up the wall!"

The men turned to look at him. "You heard me! Seal it up! It's our only chance!"

Everywhere, men scrambled. The last timber was banged into place. Rocks were piled against gaps, dirt was packed around the rocks, until, finally, the miners were completely sealed off from the fire that raged on the other side.

"Okay," Sam shouted, "Let's walk through. Gather up all your things—lamps, pails, tools—as we go along. If you see anything we might need, grab it and bring it along, too. Because once we get back up to the wall, we're gonna have to turn out the lamps. We'll only use them in an emergency 'cause the flame eats up oxygen, and we need all we can get."

He paused, looking into the faces of the men he had worked with for years. "And while we walk, you might want to say a prayer."

One hundred and nine grim faces looked back at him, men who were staring down death and knew it. Slowly, they turned and filtered down the gangway, into the entries and into the rooms themselves, picking up tools here, discarded lunch pails there. They picked up everything that might help them.

When they were through, they gathered at the wall, waiting for Sam's next order. Although they spoke several different languages, his message somehow got through to them all.

"Okay, everyone!" Sam shouted, "Find a place, set your stuff around you and make yourself comfortable. We're likely to be here awhile." Sam looked at the men, some of whom he'd known since emigrating here with his parents. He was twelve when they left Wales, and he'd been living and working with most of the same people since. He felt the need to say something, but he wasn't sure what. They weren't a demonstrative bunch. It wouldn't do for him to get sappy now. But still . . .

He cleared his throat and waited a few seconds. "I just want to say, I think we all worked as a team gettin' this wall up. If anyone thinks of anything else we might be doin' to help our situation, please speak up." He looked down at the toes of his boots and said softly, "Let's turn out the lamps."

The oil lamps, which individually threw very little light, had, collectively, illuminated the mine more brightly than it ever had been before. Perhaps it was because of the unusual brightness, but when the lamps went out, Sam thought he had never before seen such darkness.

He settled down to wait.

Had it only been this morning that he'd stood in line, waiting for the sound of the breaker whistle's piercing scream? The high-pitched shrill of the whistle signaled the start of the work day for Sam and every other miner, laborer and breaker-boy in the anthracite region.

He'd stood in line countless mornings waiting for the wail of the whistle to cut through the stillness of the dawn. And when it did, small groups of men would climb into the cage, a makeshift elevator that was lowered into the shaft. By pulley, they would descend over five hundred feet to the bottom of the mine.

Sam thought about this morning's descent. He'd ridden the entire five hundred feet into the earth looking up at the light from above, enjoying the few precious moments of daylight that he'd see that day. He'd watched the light growing smaller and smaller until it had remained only a pinprick of white against the oppressive blackness.

Sam had worked in his own "room," a tiny chamber of solid anthracite coal, barely five feet high. He'd spent the morning chiseling, blasting and, with Griff, Sam's assigned laborer, loading coal into the carts which ran on the rails.

It was dirty, dangerous work, and still, Sam was grateful for it. For he was a "miner," the highest ranking in the hierarchy of all underground workers, except for supervisors and mine inspectors. As such, he earned the highest pay, seventy cents for each four-ton car of coal he filled. Most days he filled five or six cars.

He and Griff had worked side by side, talking to pass the time, as they always did. Griff talked about his boys, and how much it killed him to bring them to the breaker to work. Sam talked about his own boy, Jesse, who was able to go to school because of the "generous" compensation that was given to the miners proper.

Sam and Griffith had laughed about Griff's neighbor, who had the dubious honor of being the only one in the four-family dwelling able to afford an alarm clock. It then became his responsibility to see to it that all the other men were awake in time to walk to work.

Sam had talked about Mary, and the girls, and he'd told Griff that he hoped this next child, due in about two months, was another boy, a brother for Jesse.

Had it really only been this morning that he'd bantered so freely, laughed so easily? Here, on the floor of the mine, surrounded by darkness, it seemed a lifetime ago.

Sam shifted his legs and propped his elbows on his knees. He folded his hands and rested his forehead against them and said a prayer, thanking the good Lord for his family, and asking Him to look out for them in the event he, himself, was unable to do so. He asked that rescue efforts be swift and successful. If that was not to be, he prayed that death would be quick and painless.

He tried to think of important things, things he should be discussing with God, things he should be thankful for, issues he needed to resolve in his head. But he found his prayers rambling, going first in one direction, then another. He noticed that his conversation with the Almighty seemed casual, much like his nightly prayers before he dropped off to sleep. Nothing at all like he would have imagined his prayers would be during the last moments of his life on earth

Maybe that was good. Maybe that meant these were not to be his last moments on this earth. Maybe the men would be rescued and he'd be home tonight, looking in on his babies as they slept, his arm around Mary's shoulders.

Sam closed his eyes and thought about what he would do when he got home. He'd fill the big wooden tub with water. Nice hot water, fresh from the stove. He'd have Mary sit in the big rocker and he'd kneel down and give the girls a bath. One by one, he'd soap up their tiny bodies, washing hair, rubbing backs, tickling toes. He'd take them out and wrap them in a towel and send them off to their mother, who would dry them and dress them in long, white cotton nighties.

Then it would be Jesse's turn. He'd be waiting, holding the tiny wooden boat Sam had whittled from the trunk of their Christmas tree this past year. In his other hand he'd have a fistful of treasures to pile into the tiny vessel. Round pebbles, miniature pine cones, twigs stripped of their bark.

Sam would add some more hot water, and Jesse would get in, not even minding the bath, as long as he had his boat to sail.

Sam would wash his blond hair, and scrub his back and wonder what kind of a man his son would grow up to be. Would he have willing arms and a strong back? Would he be able to stay in school long enough to get a job somewhere other than the mines? Would he have a wife who'd kneel beside the tub and scrub his back, teasing him with loving fingers? Would he, someday, have children of his own to hold in his arms?

Sam would wash his son, and the girls would come to play with the boat, and their sleeves would get wet, and Mary would shoosh them away, and they'd run, giggling and chasing each other.

And when the water got cold, Jesse would get out, and his mother would help him dress for bed. Sam would kiss them all good-night and tell them how much he loved them all. As Mary tucked them into bed, he'd stand in the doorway, his shoulder propped against the jamb, and he'd listen to her lead them in their evening prayers, and when she turned down the lamp, he'd tell her, "Not all the way," and she'd leave it barely burning, and, together, they'd stand and watch their children fall into the deep sleep of childhood.

And then they'd go back into the kitchen, and, as Sam

stripped out of his clothes, Mary would add more hot water to the tub. He'd climb in and watch as the water crept slowly toward the brim, inching its way higher as he lowered himself into the steamy warmth. When he was seated, his limbs folded all around him, he'd take a deep breath and feel the aches melt away. Mary would pull the rocking chair close to the tub, and she'd take her boots and stockings off, and she'd hike her skirt up above her knees, and she'd soak her feet in his bath water. And he'd soap them all up and rub them until she said "Ahhh," the way she always did.

She'd lean over and wash his hair, pouring the water over his head with a pot, being careful not to splash too much onto the floor. And then she'd take her feet out and dry them in the towel the kids had used. She'd go to get a dry towel for Sam. And he'd scrub his fingers with a brush trying to get all the black off, but he never would.

When he finished, he'd stand, and she'd wrap the towel around his shoulders, then stand on her tiptoes and kiss his wet mouth. And he'd tell her to be careful of the wet floor.

After he'd flung the bath water into the garden, he'd hang the tub on the hook behind the stove. They'd peek in on the kids one more time, then climb into their own bed. He'd hold her, and kiss her, and she'd fret about how big she was, and he'd lay his hands across her belly and tell her, "No, you're beautiful." And he'd keep his hands there until he felt the bump of a shoulder or an elbow or a knee. And they'd laugh and wonder whether this one would be a boy or a girl.

And, wrapped in each other's arms, they would sleep.

Sam's thoughts drifted for hours. He sat up and arched his back, stretching the cramped muscles, twisting side to side to unkink the knots in his spine. He was so tired. Around him he heard sounds of snoring and thought, yes, it must be nighttime.

Settling back into his little spot against the wall, he drew up his knees and folded his arms over them, making a pillow upon which he rested his head. He'd sleep, and, surely, when he woke, they'd be rescued. He yawned and fell into a deep, dreamless sleep.

His very last thought before drifting off was, *I can't wait for the new baby to get here.* Then with the warmth of his family's love surrounding him, he slept.

Two days later, they were found.

CHAPTER ONE

Hazleton, Pennsylvania
June 1888

The child would not live, she knew. But neither would it die anytime soon.

Loralee Vander leaned over the tiny body of Maggie O'Toole and rested her hand against the girl's forehead. Her skin was so dry from the fever that her lips had cracked. And, though the babe cried pitifully, she could shed no tears. The vomiting had purged Maggie's body of every drop of liquid her mother painstakingly dropped between her parched lips. She had nothing left over to make tears with.

"She is calmer today, no?"

Loralee looked up at the girl's mother and saw desperation. Kathleen O'Toole was waiting for one encouraging word to help her get through another day of her daughter's ordeal. But it was not necessarily good for her to be calmer, and Loralee kept herself from giving that one word of encouragement, fear-ing that she might be offering false hope. "Did she cough last night?"

"Not much. Maybe she's keepin' down enough of the medicine?"

More likely it meant Maggie was too weak to cough, though Loralee could see no reason to burden the mother with that knowledge.

"A lot of people survive whoopin' cough," Mrs. O'Toole said, as though to convince herself of that fact.

"That's true," Loralee said without conviction, for it was also true that many of its victims died. She looked up at Kathleen O'Toole, already swollen with her second child, and wondered if there was anything she could possibly say to help ease the hurt.

But Loralee had seen too many children succumb to whooping cough, some who hadn't suffered nearly as long and who appeared far more likely to survive the disease than little Maggie did right now. And so, wisely, she said nothing.

Both women were squeezed into the tiny back room of the O'Toole house, a parlor, which, for the winter months had been converted to a bedroom to keep the couple and their daughter nearer the coal stove that heated the house. Though it was now early June, the parlor remained a bedroom. With Maggie's illness and Kathleen's advancing pregnancy, it was simply more convenient.

The furnishings were sparse—a wooden box frame that held the bedding off the cold floor and a simple bureau, both hand-made. Wedged between the bed and the wall was a tiny, child-sized cot, really nothing more than two planks cut to bridge the distance and hammered into place. It held a straw mattress, upon which Maggie had lain for most of the past four weeks.

A knock sounded from the front room, and Kathleen excused herself to open the door. Loralee watched her as she moved through the doorway, waddling with the ungainly gait of a woman who is soon to birth a baby.

The O'Tooles were better off than most. The house they rented consisted of four rooms, two up and two down, and, with Kathleen's warm touch, the small rooms somehow managed to appear more cozy than cramped. The braided rag rug which covered the floor beneath the kitchen table, the simple, yet colorful curtains that were tacked above the windows, a carved wooden cross that hung from the kitchen wall, rubbed with oil until the wood gleamed—all of these softened a life wrought with hardship.

Loralee was roused at the sound of a male voice. She peered through the doorway and saw a stranger standing inside the door.

He was dressed in blue jeans and a flannel shirt. The worn jeans hugged his body as though he'd been wearing that same pair for years. The shirt—with the top two buttons left undone, and the cuffs rolled up to reveal forearms that were taut with ridged muscles—stretched tightly across shoulders that seemed too broad for his frame.

He glanced up at Loralee, and she saw the most startling blue eyes she had ever seen. Her breath caught in her chest, and she could feel the blush slowly creeping up her cheeks. He'd caught her!

Loralee quickly turned back toward Maggie, mortified to have been discovered gawking. Her heart was hammering and, though she was breathing rather quickly, there seemed to be not quite enough air in the small room. She reached into her satchel and tried to focus her attention on the baby that needed her care.

Jesse Sinclair stepped through the door and reached up to swipe his cap from his head. He was hoping to hear some good news about the O'Tooles' little girl, though if Kathleen's appearance was any indication of the child's condition, he was hoping in vain. There were dark circles beneath her reddened eyes, her hair looked as if it hadn't seen a thorough brushing in days, and the apron she had slipped over her dress hung, untied, over the bulk of her protruding stomach.

"Is there anything you need?" he asked.

"Nothin' 'cept prayers."

He reached for her hands, which were constantly bunching and twisting her apron strings. "You've already got that." He rubbed his thumbs against the backs of her hands. Though the gesture was offered purely in friendship, Jesse could feel Kathleen stiffen. Such intimate contact was generally frowned upon, and though Jesse was a man who enjoyed indulging in the simple pleasure of touching a woman, he had no desire to make Kathleen uncomfortable. He dropped her hands. "Has she seen a doctor?"

She nodded her head. "Loralee's here from Dr. Farley's even as we speak." Kathleen turned and looked into the small back room. "She comes ever' day, even when there's nothin' to be done but wait."

Jesse looked through the doorway at the woman from the doctor's office. She was looking up at him, and when her gaze caught his, she froze, while the seconds ticked by and neither one of them seemed able to look away. A telltale pink flush crept up her cheeks, and she turned her head and began searching through the bag beside her. She'd blushed!

Jesse was seized by an almost uncontrollable impulse to haul her to her feet and kiss her breathless. Right there, without either of them having spoken a word to the other. He stayed where he was, squeezing the life out of the cap he held in his hands.

Pale blond hair hung down the middle of her back in a tight braid. Around her face wisps of hair had broken free, and they curled and floated on the breeze of the nearby window.

His gaze was drawn to her hands and the confident way they moved over the child. She held a small jar into which she dipped one slender finger. Then, bending over, she rubbed her fingertips gently on Maggie's chest, whispering to her all the while.

Jesse couldn't hear the words, but he knew they were meant to comfort and calm the sick child. He felt a strange thickness in his throat, and he swallowed several times before he was able to speak.

"Has she been able to keep anything down?"

"A bit of the medicine, I think, 'cause she hasn't been coughin' nearly as much."

"That's good, isn't it?" he asked, just as Loralee walked into the kitchen.

She had blushed earlier, but when the talk turned to Maggie, Loralee seemed to have been imbued with certitude. She looked straight up at him, and though they had not been introduced, she said, "It could be good, yes." She took a deep breath and let it out slowly. "Unfortunately, we can't take that as a sure sign of recovery for another day or so. She still has a fever."

Her voice was lilting and light, with no discernible accent. A second-generation American, Jesse thought, unlike the O'Tooles, whose English was heavily laced with the Irish brogue of their homeland.

Loralee began imparting last-minute instructions, as though nothing at all had passed between her and Jesse. He watched her as she spoke, impressed by the clear, precise terms she used to explain what needed to be done.

" . . any liquid you can get into her will help. Keep giving her the medicine at the regularly scheduled times. I left a jar of ointment on the bureau. Rub it on her chest every two hours. It might help her breathe a little easier."

Kathleen stood ramrod straight, a stoic expression on her face, accepting Loralee's orders without question, the way a soldier obeys his commander.

Jesse watched the exchange and caught a brief flash of pity in Loralee's eyes. It was gone so quickly, he wondered if he hadn't imagined it. Suddenly, and with absolute certainty, he realized that Loralee expected the child to die.

Normally, Jesse was a quick decision-maker. When faced with a problem, he rifled quickly through his options, chose one and acted on it without hesitation. But this was not a normal situation, and faced with the imminent death of a baby, he felt as though there should be something he could do. His mind came up blank.

"I'll check back in the morning," Loralee was saying. "And, please, try to rest. You won't be any use to Maggie or that little one," she said, gesturing toward the obvious lump under Kathleen's dress, "if you fall over from exhaustion."

Kathleen nodded. "I know. I'll try." She opened the door, and with a heavy sigh said, "Thank y', Loralee."

"You're welcome." With her satchel clutched in her right hand, she hurried down the two steps and across the street.

Kathleen closed the door, and Jesse's view was cut off. He blinked his eyes several times, as though to do so would clear his mind, and searched for something to say. "She seems very knowledgeable," he finally managed.

"Yes."

"And she works for Dr. Farley?"

"Been trainin' with him for the past six months or so. Gonna be a doctor herself, soon."

Jesse raised his eyebrows, but said nothing. A woman physician?

The women he knew were groomed to want only one thing out of life—a husband, preferably wealthy. He couldn't imagine a single one of them tending a child who was dying from whooping cough. And he couldn't believe that any of them had ever been as pretty as Loralee, even in her plain dark blue dress and sturdy, black-ankle boots, which he'd noticed as she lifted her skirt to step down into the street.

Jesse cleared his throat, embarrassed to find himself thinking about Loralee's ankles. "I'd better leave you to Maggie."

"Thank y' for comin'. It's good to know Colin has an employer who cares about his little girl."

"Colin's been a hardworking employee for nearly six years. We care about him and his family."

"Some wouldn't."

"But Valley does," Jesse said, referring to the Railroad company his father owned and operated. "Stephen remembers too well his own hard times to look lightly on the troubles of others."

It was true that many of the employers in the area exploited their employees in much the same way they did the land they robbed of its treasure of clean-burning, energy-producing anthracite. Fate had placed them on top of the richest coal fields in the world, and they meant to take advantage of it.

It was also true that Valley Railroad owed its very existence to the need to transport anthracite coal to the city markets of New York and Philadelphia. But with uncommon conviction, Stephen Sinclair steadfastly refused to do business with those landowners who, by their actions, proved time and again that greed was the mainstay of their ambition.

Wealth was nice, and the Sinclairs had grown accustomed to it, but not—as most of the town knew—at the expense of strong beliefs that some things are right, and others are undeniably wrong.

And doing nothing, or worse yet, penalizing an employee whose child lay on the brink of death was one of those things that would have been unforgivably wrong.

Jesse shifted his feet, anxious now to be free of the O'Toole home and its all-pervasive sense of impending doom. He reached for the doorknob. "If you need anything at all . . ."

Kathleen only nodded, and Jesse opened the door and stepped out onto the porch. He forced himself to walk away slowly, until he heard the door close behind him. He walked from Green Street along Church, down to Broad, crossed the main thoroughfare through town, continued south and turned left to follow Mine Street to the train station, where Valley Railroad maintained a small office.

Jesse kept his eyes peeled for a girl in a blue dress with a blond braid hanging down her back, but he made it all the way to his father's office without catching a glimpse of her.

He opened the door and found Stephen himself behind the counter.

"Hey, Dad." Jesse looked around the deserted office. "What did you do?" he asked teasingly. "Scare everyone away?"

"Yeah, I'm such an ogre," Stephen joked back. "How's Maggie?"

Jesse came around the desk, stopping to pick up a sheet of paper with his name and a hastily scrawled message on it. He read it quickly, tossed the paper back down and leaned his hips against the countertop. "Not good."

Stephen put down his pen and pushed away from the desk where he had been working. "No change at all?"

"She's coughing less, and Kathleen seems to think that's an improvement, but . . . there's still a fever."

"A thing like this can't be easy on a woman in her condition."

"No, it's not. I could see that she's all played out."

"Let's hope it's over with by the time the little one arrives." Stephen looked somberly at his son. "It'd be horrible for them to lose two children to it. Colin's working like a man possessed. I guess it helps to keep his mind occupied, but he might not be around if Kathleen needs him. Keep an eye on them, Jess."

Jesse nodded, his thoughts having already jumped in a new direction. "Did you know Doc Farley's training a new doctor?" he asked abruptly.

"Well, it's about time! We could use more doctors."

"She'll be a lot different than all the others."

"She?" Stephen asked incredulously.

"Yup. She."

Stephen's eyes opened wide. "A woman?"

Jesse just nodded his head and rubbed his chin, knee-deep in the myriad images he'd collected in the few minutes Loralee'd been in his presence.

"Who is she?"

"Name's Loralee. Kathleen never did get around to introducing us, and it didn't seem the time or place to do it myself."

"A woman doctor," Stephen said, shaking his head. "Imagine that."

"Yup."

Both men were pondering that unusual bit of news, when the door was pushed open and seven employees, fresh from their noontime dinner break, filtered into the room, filling the air with friendly chatter and breaking up the private father/son talk.

People began working, but for Jesse, the usual excitement he felt for his work was dulled by thoughts of the tempting Loralee. He moved at a snail's pace the rest of the afternoon, unable to concentrate on anything except the fact that, if he kept a close eye on the O'Toole family, as his father had requested, he just might see her again.

He could hardly wait for morning.

Friday meant payday at the office of Vander Holdings. And, as he did every payday, Edward Vander stood at the rail of the balcony he'd had constructed especially for this purpose. He looked down on the men who stood in line, eager to collect their wages from a week of backbreaking, dangerous work deep in his coal mines.

He looked hard into the faces of the few who dared to cast a glance upwards. He watched them as though they were criminals who couldn't be trusted. He watched them and intimidated them.

And it worked. Edward was always amazed at how well it worked.

As each miner stepped forward, he was read a list that recorded the amount of coal he'd produced that week. Each four-ton car of coal was worth sixty-six cents. From that total, the clerk read a list of deductions. Oil for lamps, blasting powder, ground rental (for the company homes in which they lived), groceries (from the company store, which they were forced to patronize), even coal to heat their homes. All of these were deducted from the miner's paycheck, leaving little, if any, payment due.

Because of their lack of language skills, Vander's employees could be very easily confused. Add to that the fact that they were desperate for any type of employment, and Edward found himself with a labor force that he was able to control with little effort.

Of course, there will always be that one employee, that one big-mouth who will spout off against his employer, claiming unprovable injustices. Frustrated men who reached that level of desperation were fired on the spot, serving as an example to all the others, who would then stand in silence, accepting their situation because they saw no way to improve it or escape it.

Edward looked down on the heads of his employees, and found it very easy to be repulsed by them. They wore filthy, tattered clothing, had coal dirt permanently embedded beneath their fingernails and walked hunched, the result of long hours spent underground in tunnels that were rarely more than five feet high.

Edward knew he was better than those men who stood below him. He just wanted to make sure they knew it, too. And, so, he'd had his office constructed to drive home that very point.

From the separate doorway through which they entered, they stood in line on bare plank floors. Not a single luxury was awarded them, not even that of light, for Edward had chosen to place all the oil lamps behind the counter, illuminating his domain brilliantly, while his workers stood in the gloom of a dark hallway.

And his office employees, whom he regarded as a necessary evil, were required to wear their very best clothing on payday. They were also instructed not to ever touch the filthy hand that was held out before them. They were simply to drop payment into the outstretched palms, being sure to stop often to wipe their pristine fingertips with a wet cloth. They were encouraged to do this in plain view of the men waiting for their pay.

Miners were to be addressed by their last name only, no courtesy title preceding it. Mr. John Smith became simply, Smith.

The men who had propelled him to wealth were herded in like cattle to the slaughter.

From his perch, his marble and gilded tower, wearing his finest custom made suit, Edward Vander watched. And at the end of the day, after the lot of them had gone, and their entryway had been scrubbed, Edward would smile.

Life was good, indeed.

Loralee turned the page of a small notebook that she used to recount each visit to each patient she had seen that day. "Ernest Petri. What can I say about Mr. Petri? His gout is improving, but he still wants you out to the house," she said to Doc Farley.

"Well, I can't go. I don't have time to run all over the countryside visiting people who are not sick!" He was a big, burly man, with bushy gray hair and silver-rimmed glasses, and he plunged his fingers into his hair and rubbed his scalp briskly, in an unconscious movement that Loralee now recognized as a signal that his mind was overloaded.

"Don't worry, he's getting used to me," she said with a smile. "I got him to take off his shoes, didn't I? Sure, it took three visits, but I wore him down."

Her humor hit its mark, and Doc couldn't help a wry chuckle. "His wife has him spoiled. He's used to getting everything he wants, the old coot, whether it makes sense or not, just because he wants it. The big baby."

"Speaking of babies, I stopped by Mrs. Wysinski's place. Her daughter is *not* bleeding from her privates. What the child has is diaper rash. Diaper rash so severe that her little bottom is bleeding."

"She hasn't been changing her?"

"Oh, she changes her diapers quickly enough. But she replaces them with diapers the child previously wet." When she saw that Doc wasn't following, she explained more clearly. "If a diaper is just wet, she takes it and hangs it out on the line to dry, without washing it first. Then she uses them again and again."

"Well, you can't do that!" Doc shouted.

"I know that, and you know that, but she didn't. She speaks almost no English. She interpreted 'Put a dry diaper on the baby' as dry the wet one and put it back on."

"D'ya get through to her?"

"Not until after I had scrubbed an entire tub full of diapers."

Doc chuckled. "But, again, you did it."

"I did it," Loralee said with a smile of satisfaction. She was determined to stamp out the ignorance that led to so many preventable illnesses, and her dogged persistence always entertained Doc Farley, who had taken her on as an apprentice six months earlier, as a result of that very determination. She'd pestered him till he couldn't stand it anymore, and he'd given in out of sheer desperation and the hope that she'd give him some peace.

"Anything else?"

Loralee stood up and started replenishing her satchel with items she would need for tomorrow's work. "Only Maggie."

"And?"

She stuffed a roll of gauze into the black bag. Then a bottle of castor oil. Then a bottle of Winslow's baby syrup.

"Loralee?"

Her hands stilled and her shoulders drooped, and she suddenly lost the battle with her tears. She dropped her face into her hands and sobbed as though she had been holding back the emotion until she simply burst. Doc stood up and rested his hands on her shoulders, waiting.

"She's not going to make it," Loralee whispered.

"Still burnin' up?"

"Like a wildfire. She hasn't kept anything down for two days," she said sadly. "And she's not coughing."

"Ah," Doc said, nodding in understanding. "It'll be soon, then."

"It's just so unfair!" she cried. "That child has done nothing wrong. Nothing! Why did she have to be born at all? She never even had the chance to live! Her parents . . . her parents—" She broke down into tears again, and Doc finished her sentence.

"—will be thankful to've had a year of her. Of course they don't want Maggie to die, and they're probably good 'n steamed at the Almighty themselves. But if you'd ask them if they'd rather never had her at all than have to bear the pain of losing her after just one year, you can guess what their answer might be."

Loralee sniffed and wiped at her nose with a handkerchief. "I know," she whispered. "It's just so hard to see that hope in their eyes. They look to me to guide them—"

"—and you have."

"But I failed!" she cried, as she spun around to face him, holding her hands out to him as though she was imploring him to understand her pain. "I failed," she whispered, dropping her arms lifelessly to her sides.

"Did you try every treatment you know?"

"Everything."

"Did you check her progress regularly?"

"Every day."

"Did you pray?"

"Fervently."

Doc paused a few seconds, allowing her to come to terms with something he had accepted long ago. Finally, he said, "You are not God. You did everything you could have done, and then some."

Loralee stood with her head hanging. She took a deep breath and nodded almost imperceptibly. "I know," she whispered.

"Be a little easy on yourself. This has been a tough one," Doc said, pulling her into his big, grandfatherly embrace. She accepted his consolation gratefully, for he was the only person who could truly understand what she felt. "Go home, take a good hot bath, and maybe even a little brandy. It's been a grueling week, and it's not over yet, so try to get some rest."

She dropped her arms from around his waist and backed away from him, swiping at her eyes with the back of her hand. "I want to go there first thing in the morning."

"Of course."

She nodded her head, as though they had agreed on something very important. "I guess I'll see you tomorrow." She untied her apron, which by now was stained with splatterings of who-knew-what, and rolled it into a little bundle.

"And listen to me," Doc said, wagging a finger under her nose. "I do know what I'm talking about every once in a while." Loralee smiled and huffed. "And this is one of those times. A little pampering will do you good."

"Pampering! Who has time for pampering?" she asked as she moved toward the door and stood with her hand on the knob. "We're having twelve guests for dinner tonight, and I have a command performance," she said disgustedly. She opened the door and stepped down onto the sidewalk.

"So, come down with something! I'm sure you can think of something convincing, something that will provoke ample sympathy while you retire for some much deserved peace and quiet.''

Loralee paused and looked up at the doctor. The thought of spending the evening alone in her quiet room was tempting. Very tempting. A mischievous smile tugged at the corners of her mouth. ''Not a bad idea, my friend,'' she said as she began to walk away. ''Not a bad idea at all.''

Behind her, she heard Doc chuckle and then close the door. Another day closer to her dreams.

With a sigh, she began the ten-minute walk home, thinking as she went what she would wear for tonight's gathering.

It had been her father's final edict when he'd relented and allowed her to take the job with Doctor Farley: If she failed in any way to meet her social obligations, she would have to quit her job. No questions, no arguments.

After earning a degree in chemistry from Cedar Crest Women's College, Loralee had wanted to put her knowledge to use. What good was the education she'd fought for if she wasn't allowed to use it? And so, she'd agreed.

Loralee didn't remember ever having so many social engagements tossed her way. But, though she was often asleep on her feet, she went. She kept up her end of the bargain.

Loralee Vander was no quitter. People had called her a lot of things—stubborn, rebellious, defiant, demanding—but no one had ever called her a quitter.

By the time she reached home, she had a plan hammered out. A quick dinner, an instant headache, and she'd be free for the evening.

And, though she'd been too busy today to give much thought to the handsome stranger who had come to check on Maggie, he'd been on the back of her mind all the while.

Tonight, after her obligation was fulfilled and she was sent off to bed, she'd pull from her mind the image of the broad-shouldered, blue-eyed visitor that she'd kept tucked safely away all day. She'd turn it around, she'd run her hands over its solid bulk, learning every variation of the many textures that made up the whole. Warm skin, coarse hair, fuzzy flannel and rough denim. She'd commit to memory every nuance of that amazing gaze, every subtle distinction of the colors that made up his sandy-blond-almost-brown, much too long hair.

And when she had examined him completely, she'd store her findings away for safe-keeping, a cache of joy to sustain her through the loneliest, most difficult days and nights. For she'd already learned that the private life of a doctor could be sorely lacking in personal relationships. There simply wasn't enough time to do it all.

She walked through the wrought-iron gates that separated the Vander property from the rest of town and followed the brick sidewalk up to the front porch. She paused for a few seconds, then took a deep, deep breath. With resignation in her every movement, Loralee opened the front door of her home and stepped into her other life.

CHAPTER TWO

At five minutes past nine the following morning, Jesse stood on the porch of the O'Toole home. He raised his hand and knocked, and Colin opened the door.

"Ah, he managed to convince you, then," Jesse said with a small smile, referring to Stephen, who had insisted at the breakfast table that if Colin showed up for work, he was going to order him home.

"He'd have it no other way. Stubborn as an ox, that man is when he gets hold of an idea. Didn't even have the decency to argue with me. Just kept sayin', 'Go home, Colin, your wife needs you. Go home, Colin, your wife needs you.' Till finally I said, 'I'm goin' home!'"

Jesse laughed at the picture of his father badgering one of his favorite employees.

"Come on in," Colin said, stepping back into the room.

Jesse stepped over the threshold and swept his cap from his head. "Doc here?" he said, nodding toward the back room, where a sheet had been hung to cover the doorway. *Please say yes. Please say yes.*

"Here and gone already. Said she'd be back tomorrow before church."

Jesse's heart plummeted. "How's Maggie?"

Colin shrugged. "No different, that I can see. She's one sick little girl."

"And how about Kathleen? How's she holding up?"

"She's tired. She fights it, but it's beginnin' to show. I sent her back to bed. Said she didn't need it, but her eyes was closed even before her head touched the pillow."

"The rest'll do her good," Jesse said. "Do you need anything?"

"I need a miracle, that's what I need, and I don't suppose y' got any of those lyin' about."

Jesse shook his head. "Ah, Colin . . . It's so unfair, an innocent baby like Maggie is hangin' onto her life by a thread, and everyday I see men who are meaner than dirt—they neglect their families, they abuse their bodies, and they just keep right on living with barely a trip in their step."

Colin nodded at the floor. "I know it . . . I know it."

The two men stared at each other's feet, unsure of how to proceed in these uncharted waters where feelings were laid bare.

Finally, Jesse said, "Listen, you need anything, send someone to the office or to the house. Anything. Anytime, day or night."

Colin looked up. "Thank y', Jesse. You Sinclairs, you're good men, the whole lot of y'."

Jesse opened the door and stepped onto the porch, uncomfortable with being praised for something as inconsequential as giving a few minutes of time to inquire about a sick child. "I'll stop back in the morning."

Colin said nothing. Just waited until Jesse clomped down the steps before pushing the door closed.

Jesse walked down the street, berating himself as he went. He shouldn't look forward to visiting Maggie just because he might run into Loralee.

But, he did.

He should be thinking about helping Colin and Kathleen, not about seducing Loralee.

But, he was.

He barely knew the girl; he should stop this ridiculous fantasy!

But, he couldn't.

Thoughts of her had kept him awake most of the night. He felt like a schoolboy with his first crush.

You're too old to be behaving like this!

Jesse walked up the hill on Pine Street and turned onto Mine. He looked up and, as if his thoughts had conjured her up, he saw Loralee climbing gracelessly down from a shay. He stopped and stepped back around the corner, not wanting to be seen, hoping only to watch.

Loralee gathered her full skirt around her, hiked it up almost to her knees and threw one leg over the side. Jesse watched as she balanced precariously on the narrow step, then hauled the other leg over and plunged down to the ground, all in one swift jump. She landed on both feet, but stumbled enough that she had to brush the dust from the hem of her dress.

She stood close enough that Jesse could see her lips moving, and somehow, he just knew that whatever she had muttered had not been the least bit ladylike. He smiled, thoroughly amused by her mile-wide independent streak.

As he watched, she reached back into the carriage and hefted her black satchel over the side. It slipped free, and its weight almost yanked her arms from their sockets before it settled against her legs with a soft *whump*.

Loralee let fly with another string of what Jesse was sure were swearwords. She threw the satchel down into the dirt and kicked it with all her might. Then, she straightened her skirts, adjusted the bonnet on her head and picked up the damnable bag before marching up to a small house just off to her right.

With great difficulty, Jesse managed to hold his laughter until the front door was opened and she stepped inside. He laughed so hard, he had to hold his stomach.

So! The lady had a temper! No little wallflower, this one. She'd stand up to any challenge and probably win most.

He leaned back against the rough, red brick building that housed Hazleton's post office and wondered what ailment she was treating this time.

She sure was pretty. And real tiny. He was partial to small women, probably because he only reached about five feet ten inches himself. She would fit nicely against him.

It was only as he imagined Loralee pressed beneath him that he came to his senses. What the hell was wrong with him?

Jesse pushed away from the wall and swallowed hard. He was a grown man. His time for gawking at women from afar was long since past.

And his reputation with the ladies was such that mothers warned their young daughters against him, which was fine by him, because, truth be told, he preferred his women slightly more experienced than the average debutante. Jesse made no apologies for it; he liked women, and they liked him right back.

So, what was it about this one that had him lurking around corners?

Annoyed with himself for his uncharacteristic behavior, Jesse strode around the corner of the building, not even bothering to glance toward the house Loralee had entered, until he was almost past it.

Finally, he looked up.

Other than her horse and buggy, the street was empty.

Jesse kept right on walking, and no one who saw him would ever have known the disappointment he was feeling.

He looked like a man with a purpose, and he was. His mother had planned a party for tonight, and his home would be filled to overflowing with women. Beautiful women. Sexy women. All kinds of women who would be willing to do all kinds of things.

Jesse was a man with a purpose, all right. He'd been working too much, and, if his unusual reaction to Loralee was any indication, it seemed the old saying must be true. All work and no play . . .

Tonight, his home would be turned into a playground for grown men. There would be women everywhere. Some to sample, some to feast upon.

Jesse intended to take part in the feast.

The green ribbon in her hair was the same exact shade as her dress, which was *almost* as green as her eyes.

It was Saturday night, and, after a long day of work, Loralee was preparing for a party. This was the first time in a long time that she had been out. Work with Dr. Farley kept her so busy that the only social events she attended were those that her father arranged. And they were sheer drudgery to endure.

But tonight was different. Tonight's party was a twenty-fifth birthday celebration for one Mr. Jesse Sinclair, the ruggedly handsome, but very cocky, too-charming-for-his-own-good, most eligible bachelor in Hazleton.

Loralee had twice been in Jesse's company. And though both occasions had been years ago, she remembered them vividly.

He'd never even looked her way.

She had lacked the experience necessary to attract the attention of a world-class rake like Jesse Sinclair. He favored women his own age or older. The wide-eyed eighteen-year-old was not in his league and had never even turned his head.

His exploits with women were legendary, and the entire time Loralee had been at school, her best friend, Suzanne, had kept a running commentary on the love life of Romeo Sinclair.

None of the women in town seemed able to resist his charms.

Old women thought he was sweet. Little girls flirted with him. Married women feasted on him from the safety of their husbands' arms.

Even Loralee, who thought she'd be impervious to his perfectly tuned charisma, remembered well those two glimpses of him (they could hardly be called anything more). Was it that she'd been warned her entire life to stay away from the Sinclairs? Was it simply the lure of the forbidden?

Whatever it was, she'd felt an undeniable tug toward him.

And he'd never even noticed her.

And now, rumor had it, he was on the hunt for a wife. Well, she'd go to his party, she'd even dance with him, if he asked. What she would not do was fall blindly into his trap. She'd dressed tonight with the sole purpose of getting Jesse to notice her. And when he did, he'd find out that not every female of the species found him irresistible.

A soft knock echoed from the door. "Loralee?" her mother called. "May I come in?"

Loralee walked to the door and opened it wide. "Certainly, Mother. Come keep me company."

Fiona stopped in her tracks. "Oh, my . . ."

Loralee smiled and spun around slowly.

"You're missing something."

Loralee's eyes flew open. Suzanne and her parents would be here any minute! "What? What's wrong?" She twisted around trying to get a view of her backside, thinking that her maid must have missed a button.

"It's not the dress. The dress is exquisite. But you're missing these." She held out a triple strand of pearls, the betrothal gift Edward had presented at the announcement of their engagement, almost thirty years ago.

"Oh . . . Mother, I . . . are you sure? Are you sure you want me to wear them? They're . . . they're . . ."

"They're just jewelry. You are the jewel," she said, turning Loralee around and wrapping the pearls around her neck. She fastened them with the diamond-studded clasp, and said, "There."

Loralee turned to the mirror and touched her throat, where the pearls rested. "They're beautiful. Thank you."

"You're welcome."

"Won't Papa be upset if I wear them?"

Fiona's smile faded. "Edward isn't very sentimental. I haven't worn them in so long, he's probably forgotten he ever gave them to me," she said sadly. "But, what he lacks in sentiment, he more than makes up for with stubbornness." Her voice held the hint of a warning. "Wearing those pearls wouldn't upset him. His daughter socializing with the Sinclairs would. It would *infuriate* him."

"Oh, Mother, please—"

Fiona held up her palms as though to fend off Loralee's argument. "I know my giving you the pearls to wear makes it seem as though I approve of your going tonight. But, that's not at all true. I *disapprove* completely. Saying yes to that invitation was a reckless decision."

Loralee closed her eyes and sighed heavily. She didn't want to stir up this old hornets' nest, but maybe, if she tried one more time, she might finally be able to put the thing to rest. She spoke quietly, slowly and clearly, as though to do so would make her meaning easier to understand.

"I know Valley Railroad has long refused to do business with Vander Holdings, and I know there's some sort of a long-standing feud between the two families, as there are with Papa and a lot of families, though none that's he's held on to with quite as much tenacity. I know I was forbidden to ever speak to a Sinclair, even as a child. But I assure you, I have absolutely no interest in the business dealings of either Vander Holdings or Valley Railroad. Suzanne asked me to go, I've had a very trying week at work and I need a distraction. That's all this is."

Fiona looked at her daughter as if trying to decide whether

or not she should believe her. "I know I can't change your mind—I'm not even going to try. But before you leave for your 'distraction,' there is something else you should consider. What about Charles?"

"What about him?"

"What will you tell him? What will you say if you should happen to run into him? The two of you are practically engaged—"

"We most certainly are not!" Loralee said, planting her hands on her hips.

"But your father—"

"If Papa thinks he's such a good catch, he can marry him himself! I, for one, find Charles Korwin to be a spoiled, self-indulgent know-it-all."

"Oh, Loralee, he's not that bad," Fiona said, slapping her own hands onto her hips in a perfect mirror image of her daughter's posture.

"Well, he's not much good, either!"

The two women stood not more than a foot apart, one glaring at the other and neither one willing to back down. They held their pose while the seconds ticked by, until they realized how ridiculous they looked and how silly they sounded.

Fiona was the first one to start laughing. They giggled like a couple of schoolgirls swapping secrets until Loralee finally got herself under control. She reached out and took Fiona's hand in her own.

"Look, Mother, I'm only going because Suzanne invited me. She's my best friend, and I don't get to spend as much time with her as I'd like. Besides, everybody in the world will be there. I heard his mother issued an invitation to almost everyone in town."

Fiona stared at her daughter, all the merriment gone out of her. "Your father knows you're going with the Beckers for the evening. But," she said, looking off into the distance, "he has no idea where you'll be. If he finds out, you'll be on your own. There will be hell to pay, and I won't do it this time.''

Loralee knew what her mother was saying, and she remained silent, giving the moment of shared intimacies the reverence it deserved.

Just then, their maid knocked and stepped quickly into the room.

''The Becker carriage is here for you, miss.''

''Thank you, Marta,'' Loralee said, flustered and distracted by her mother's words. She reached for a small reticule made of the same green fabric as her dress and adorned with hand-sown beads.

''You look lovely tonight, miss.''

''Thank you,'' Loralee said quietly, pressing a hand to her heart. ''Did you see the pearls?''

''Of course. Your mother's betrothal gift.''

''How did you know that?'' Loralee asked, looking from Marta to her mother and back again.

''I been here a long time, miss. Even longer than you!'' she said with a smile. ''There's a lot I know.''

Marta's delicate phrasing left much unsaid, as did Fiona's. The wheels in Loralee's head were already beginning to spin as she tried to decipher exactly what they both had been trying to say . . . without, of course, actually saying it.

''Marta, please tell them Loralee will be right down.''

''Yes ma'am.'' She executed a swift curtsey before backing hastily out the door.

''Remember what I said.''

''I will.'' Loralee said. She leaned over and pecked Fiona on the cheek. ''Thank you for the pearls. Good night, Mother.''

Loralee had gone with the Beckers before Edward had even been able to inquire about their plans for the evening. But they were decent people, and Edward was sure that Penelope Becker would see to it that Loralee was properly chaperoned. He supposed he should be thankful for that. It had been at least fifteen years since he and Fiona had attended any of the parties that were thrown by Hazleton's elite during the summer months. If Edward left it up to Fiona, his daughter would die an old maid.

It was well after nine o'clock, and he hurriedly finished his work, eager, now, to be on his way. He opened the heavy door that sealed his private office off from the rest of the house and stepped out into the foyer, where he retrieved his hat from the hat stand.

"Are you going out tonight, Edward?"

He turned and saw Fiona sitting in the front parlor, working on another piece of needlework. The woman did enough of the damn stuff to supply every household in Hazleton with more pillowcases, napkins and tablecloths than they would ever need.

"Yes." He went out every Saturday night, though he never gave a single clue as to where he might be going. He knew she wouldn't ask.

"I'll see you in the morning, then." She turned back to her needlework.

It was a dismissal, he knew, but try as she might to treat him like a subordinate, she couldn't stop the red flush that crept up her neck and over her cheeks. Despite her humiliation, she never let him walk out the door without throwing in his face the fact that she knew where he was going. She called him on it every time and then turned him loose as though he wasn't worth the effort to keep him home.

It was the fact that she knew and said nothing to stop him that disgusted him. She knew, and didn't care, and it was that realization that drove him to the cruelty.

"You know, Fiona," he said, pausing until she looked up at him, "being with her makes it almost impossible to come home to you." He held her gaze until she was forced to look away. Then he turned and walked out, never looking back.

CHAPTER THREE

Jesse had been snagged by the town's official purveyor of gossip.

He listened with little interest, scanning the crowd that had shown up to celebrate his birthday. His birthday, for God's sake! A completely insignificant day to almost every person in the room, with the exception of his immediate family. And yet, the guests had overflowed from the ballroom out onto the perfectly manicured lawns.

His gaze passed quickly over the large crowd, a gathering of socially prominent families heavily peppered with the area's many miners and railroad workers. Those two groups alone comprised almost the entire work force of Carbon, Luzerne and Schuylkill counties.

But miners, and their families—for all their hard work—lived in near poverty. Life, for them, was a study in survival. There was rarely any cause for celebration, and, even if there was, there would be no money to celebrate with.

Elizabeth Sinclair had solved that problem by throwing a

twenty-fifth birthday party for her son, the likes of which the town had never before seen. Jesse had been adopted by the Sinclairs when he was five years old, and, each year, the birthday celebrations that Elizabeth planned grew more and more elaborate. This one, however, topped them all.

She had issued invitations to everyone she knew, with the instructions that they were to invite everybody they could think of. She wanted the entire town there, the wealthy, the poor, the neighbors, the strangers, the haves, and the have-nots. And it seemed as if she had succeeded.

". . . think you'll have problems?"

Reluctantly, Jesse pulled his gaze away from a beautiful young woman who was standing nearby.

"I'm sorry, Victor," Jesse said, a guilty smile pulling at the corners of his mouth, "my mind was . . . elsewhere. What were you saying?" He turned his full attention toward Victor Henshaw, who'd worked behind the counter of Evans' General Store for as long as Jesse could remember, and who knew the comings and goings of everyone in Hazleton and the surrounding patches.

"I 'spect she's a tantalizin' sight," Victor said, turning to look at the spot over his shoulder that was holding Jesse's rapt attention. "But, bein' the gentleman that I am, I'll refrain from askin' about her."

"Her? What her?" Jesse asked with feigned innocence.

"Jesse, I've watched you grow up from a little boy, and when you've got that look in those baby blues . . . well, God help the woman you've got in your sights this time. She's settin' up for a heartache for sure."

Jesse threw back his head and laughed, thumping Victor on the back. "Ah, Vic, what can I do? My father's wearing himself ragged, worrying about a grandson to carry on the Sinclair name. And my mother . . . well, you know what this party is all about, don't you? Now, tell me, what kind of a son would I be to ignore my parents' wishes?"

"Okay, Jesse, you just worry about producin' the next Sinclair heir, and the rest of us will handle the labor unions."

At the mention of an issue that was on everyone's mind, Jesse sobered, the astute businessman in him winning out over the randy flirt. "I don't know, Victor. I'm not sure our men are too eager to join up. My father's a good man to work for. His employees have always been treated well. Do you know that in the three years since I've been back home, we haven't had a single employee leave? Not one in three years!" Jesse shook his head, marveling at the loyalty of the people his father employed. "Yet, not a day goes by that we don't have at least a dozen inquiries about openings. I'd say our employees are happy with things the way they are."

"I tend to agree with you, Jesse. Employees of Valley Railroad are a lucky bunch. Plenty 'round here not so lucky." Victor looked off into the crowd, his gaze hopping from head to head as though assigning lots in life. Lucky, unlucky, lucky, unlucky . . .

Around them, the guests filled every corner of the room, a mixed crowd, if ever there was one. To Jesse's left stood a man, probably no more than thirty-five years old, hunched and crooked and looking like he could have been seventy. A miner. He stood next to his wife and their eight bedraggled children, each of them holding a plate onto which had been piled a week's worth of meals. They ate in silence, shoveling the carefully prepared food into their mouths so fast it was a miracle none of them choked to death. Their lack of manners could be easily overlooked, Jesse thought, looking at the children's bony arms, which protruded from the cuffs of shirts long ago outgrown. Starvation had a way of trampling over the table manners of those it inflicted.

Quietly, Victor said, "You hear they lost two more men over in Vander Number Three last Thursday?" Shaking his head he said, "Now, there's a hellhole to work in if I ever saw one."

At the mention of Edward Vander's name, Jesse stiffened imperceptibly. He had his own personal reasons for hating the man, and hate him he did, with a fury the strength of which frightened him. But now was not the time to let dark thoughts invade.

He touched Victor's arm. "Excuse me, Victor, but my mother is standing next to that monstrosity of a cake and motioning for me. I guess it's time for the main event." He drained his glass and set it on one of the many trays placed around the ballroom for that purpose and moved through the crowd toward his mother.

Jesse was a natural-born charmer, and he paused several times, flirting outrageously with his female guests. Tonight, especially, he took advantage of his God-given ability to attract the opposite sex. He kept the promise he had made to himself just that morning. Tonight's affair was a banquet of beautiful women, and he intended to feast. But he was, above all, a gentleman, and men and women alike succumbed to his disarming manner. Thirty minutes later, he slid up to his mother's side.

"I thought you'd never get here," she chided gently.

"It would have been much easier if you hadn't extended an invitation to the entire town," he teased.

"Well, it's not every day my son turns twenty-five. It's a momentous occasion!"

"Mother, it's a birthday. I wasn't elected president, I haven't found a cure for yellow fever. I simply had another in a long line of birthdays."

She shrugged. "So indulge me. I felt the need for an enormous social gathering. And since I haven't any weddings to plan . . ."

Jesse laughed and wrapped his arm around her shoulder. "Well, you'll be happy to know that on my way over here, I stopped to dance with a good half-dozen young ladies."

Elizabeth's eyes brightened. "Anyone interesting?"

"Not in the least."

Her face fell. "Jesse, every woman in this town is here, you know, and some from neighboring towns! Why, there must be three hundred eligible girls here tonight! Surely you must find someone attractive?" she asked hopefully.

"Oh, there are plenty who are attractive, plenty I'd like to get to know better, some I already have—"

"Jesse!"

"Sorry," he said, without a trace of remorse. He shared an unusually close relationship with his parents and had always felt comfortable telling them anything. He looked at his mother, who was fifty-three, and still one of the prettiest women in the room. She had a wonderful marriage and wanted the same for both her sons.

"I have a confession to make," Elizabeth said. "Your birthday was a convenient excuse, but the real reason for this party was to get you interested in finding a wife." She hung her head, looking embarrassed to have been caught, but not the least bit remorseful.

"I have a confession to make, too," Jesse said with a smirk. He leaned over and whispered in her ear, "I've known that all along."

"And all this time I've been feeling guilty for deceiving you," she said with a chuckle. She looked up and saw the serving staff approaching. "It's time to serve the cake," she said, touching Jesse's arm. "Let me find your father first. Wait here!" she commanded while she hurried into the crowd.

He leaned back against the wall. The heavy draperies over the windows nearly blocked him from view. He took a moment to enjoy the solitude and examine the crowd.

It seemed that his mother had indeed invited the entire town of Hazleton. Everyone, from the many men his father did business with, to the neighbors all along the street, to the employees of Valley Railroad, complete with their large families. There were old men smoking cigars, weary mothers trying in vain to keep their children from wandering, stuffy society matrons standing around refusing to let themselves have any fun, and more young women looking for husbands than Jesse had ever seen assembled in one room.

But the face Jesse had been looking for, though he would have adamantly denied it, was nowhere to be found. He'd been working the crowd, and, if Loralee was here, she must certainly be hiding because he hadn't seen her anywhere.

He watched his parents approaching. Stephen guided his wife through the crowd with a hand at the back of her waist. He stopped to say something to Elizabeth, and, as she stretched herself taller to hear, she placed her hand on his shoulder for balance. Then they looked into each other's eyes and smiled as though they were the only two people in the room.

They loved each other so much that the simple act of touching brought joy.

But most marriages weren't like theirs. Among the wealthy, marriage was often seen as a way of solidifying two already prosperous families. And among the poor, it just seemed the most practical way to live.

Jesse looked across the room at a scrawny man standing next to his equally scrawny wife. They were surrounded by children of varying height like so many steps on a staircase. The husband and wife stood beside each other, resigned to the life they were living.

Yet, for them, marriage made sense. She needed someone to provide for her, he needed someone to cook and clean and do his laundry. And if it meant having another baby every year, when they could scarcely afford the ones they already had, they accepted that.

Both the wealthy and the poor endured their situations without protest. You might say some of them were content. But were they happy?

It was all so depressing. And that's why Jesse had, years ago, stopped looking at women as potential wives and started looking at them as pleasant diversions. Very pretty diversions, he thought, as he looked at one of the miners' daughters, dressed in a clean but faded dress that had probably been worn by three sisters before her. Her hair was as black as the coal his father's trains transported into the city, and her skin as fair and smooth as any he had ever seen.

His pale blue eyes shifted to Rita Santaro, her voluptuous body nearly spilling out of the form-fitting pink dress she wore. A very soft, very warm diversion, he thought, remembering the nights he had held Rita in his arms.

He drew a deep breath and looked away. His father loved his mother. *Loved* her. He knew that, and he envied it. And though he had only just this morning promised himself he would stop thinking about Loralee, he wanted nothing more than to leave this party, hunt her down, hold her in his arms and feel that same consuming sense of love that he knew his parents felt. He hadn't wanted to admit it to himself, but he had the feeling Loralee could become much more than a diversion. There was something about her that—

"There you are," Elizabeth said. "I thought you'd get tired of waiting for us. Your father is quite a popular man. I had to drag him away from his admirers."

"You exaggerate," Stephen said with a wave of his hand. "What have you been doing?" he asked his son.

Jesse pushed himself away from the wall. "Just hiding out behind the cake. Watching."

"And what have you seen?" Stephen asked.

Jesse looked at his father then let his eyes roam over the crowd once again. "Nothing that interests me," he said honestly.

"You're sounding very cynical for someone of your tender years."

Jesse grunted and shrugged his shoulders. "I don't mean to be. But you can only kid yourself for so long. I know what I've had, and I *know* what I'm looking for." He held out his hands and put one on his mother's arm and the other on his father's, forming a circle between the three of them. "I'm looking for what you two have. Because the life I've been living just isn't enough anymore."

Elizabeth's eyes filled with tears. "Oh, Jesse," she said, "you'll find it." She reached up and caressed the side of his face with her hand. She smoothed back his hair from his eyes, just like she had done through countless childhood illnesses. "When you least expect it, you'll find it."

Jesse looked into his mother's eyes and willed himself to believe, with all the unconditional faith of a small child who takes as gospel truth every word his mother speaks. He nodded his head, and with the wisdom of an adult, offered a small prayer to help her wishes become reality.

Please, he prayed, *please let her be right.*

"Have you ever seen so many people squeezed into one house before?" Loralee asked Suzanne as they made their way through the almost impenetrable crowd in the Sinclair ballroom. The din was deafening, and she had to shout to make herself heard.

"Never. Have *you* ever seen such an impossibly mixed crowd?"

Loralee let her gaze wander around the room. "Never," she answered back.

Small groups had formed, and they steadfastly refused to intermingle. One could see a group of proper society women hovering near the elaborately papered wall casting disparaging glances on the group of young mothers who were taking advantage of all the free food by seeing to it that all their many children ate to their fill and beyond.

On the other side of the room, the gentlemen had converged near the temporary bar that had been set up for the occasion, but they, too, held separate camps. The group of slouched, suspender-wearing mine workers feasted on the Sinclairs' brandy, which was more than a few steps up from the swill they usually guzzled. And on the other end of the bar, being careful to stand a goodly distance from the riffraff, a group of businessmen shook their heads and wondered *whatever* could Elizabeth Sinclair have been thinking when she'd invited such people into her home.

And Loralee thought that she might be the only person in the room who was caught between the two worlds. She'd been working with Dr. Farley for six months, and everywhere she looked, she saw former patients. But she'd been raised among the upper crust her entire life, and she couldn't discount the fact that she also knew most of the town's more prominent citizens.

It put her in a very awkward position, for neither group wanted to associate with the other. That meant that if she'd like to be friendly with *everyone* she knew (and she did), she'd spend most of the night scuttling from gathering to gathering, and being the object of scrutiny and disdain, no matter who she chose to speak with.

It was this unsettling fact that had Loralee so preoccupied that she nearly pushed right past two girls she and Suzanne had been friends with since childhood.

"Suzanne! Loralee!"

Loralee turned and saw Eleanor Campbell and Mary Stewart waving frantically.

"Eleanor! Mary!" she said. "How are you?"

"You'd know if you kept in touch," Eleanor teased.

"You never go out anymore," Mary added. "No one ever sees you."

"I tell her that all the time," Suzanne said with a shrug.

"I know," Loralee said, looking at the floor. "I've been so busy, and I've been awful about keeping in touch."

"You sure have," said Eleanor. "You've been so awful at

it that I've gotten engaged since the last time I saw you, and I bet you didn't even know it!''

"Engaged!" Loralee gasped. She turned to Suzanne. "You didn't tell me!"

"I didn't know!" Suzanne said, obviously irritated at having been deprived of this bit of news.

Eleanor laughed. "Suzanne's not to blame. It just happened yesterday. I just wanted to tease you for ignoring all of us.''

"I'm not ignoring you!" Loralee protested.

"We know. But you're so busy all the time," complained Mary. "First you went away to school, and you no sooner got back than you started working with Doc Farley. Are you sure you want to be a doctor?"

Loralee laughed. "Yes, I'm sure." She looked into her old friend's eyes. "*You* haven't gotten engaged, have you?"

"I wish," Mary said with a scowl. "That Eugene had better work up the nerve to ask me soon! Why, doesn't he know I've been waiting *forever*?"

The girls laughed as they thought about Eugene Forester, who'd been smitten with Mary since the two of them were in diapers. He blushed furiously whenever she showed the least bit of interest in him and then backed off, apparently too shy to ever proclaim his love.

"I think what *you* should do, Mary," Suzanne said, "is show a little bit less interest in Mr. Forester, and a little bit more interest in another man. Oh, . . . say, maybe the birthday boy?"

Mary gasped and pressed a hand to her heart. "Suzanne! I could never do that! Jesse is . . . well, he's just not . . . what I mean to say, is—"

"What she means to say is that Jesse Sinclair is not at all the kind of man she's interested in," Loralee filled in.

"Yes!" said Mary, nodding her head emphatically.

"He's a flirt—"

"He is!" Mary interrupted.

"—a rake,—"

"Most definitely," Mary agreed.

"—and unforgivably, much too sure of himself." Loralee concluded.

"Well," Suzanne said, with one raised eyebrow, "you've certainly given the man a great deal of thought."

"I most certainly have not!" Loralee said, straightening her back. "His lack of scruples is a well-known fact, according to *your* letters!"

"I'm not at all sure it is fact," Suzanne said, tilting her head to the side. "We've all heard stories." The group nodded as one. "But do any of you actually know a young lady on whom Jesse has pushed, shall we say, unwelcome advances?" Suzanne fixed each of the girls with an inquiring stare.

"No . . . but—"

"So, it's all hearsay, isn't it?" Suzanne said. "Or, maybe . . ." She let the thought dangle.

"What?" asked Eleanor.

"Yes, what?" seconded Mary.

Suzanne looked pointedly at Loralee, the only one in their group not to express an interest in her theory.

"Oh, all right, already! What?"

"Maybe the tales we hear are embellished by Jesse himself. Sort of to pad his image, so to speak."

"Oh, Suzanne!" Loralee said, rolling her eyes. "Wherever did you come up with that ridiculous notion?"

"I'm not sure it's so ridiculous."

"Don't you think the women involved in his little imaginative romps would have a thing or two to say about their reputations being slung in the mud?"

"Not necessarily," Suzanne said, holding up her palms to silence Loralee's objections. "Now, just hear me out. The women you hear the most juicy tidbits about aren't likely to be too worried about their already tarnished reputations. And the others . . . well," she held her hands up to her sides, "honestly, don't you think being associated, in some vague, not-too-damaging way, with Jesse's exploits rather adds to a woman's appeal?''

''Oh, Suzanne!'' Loralee cried. Mary and Eleanor, shocked at what Suzanne was proposing looked at Loralee, then back to Suzanne, awaiting her response.

''Now, don't tell me you don't think he's handsome!''

''That's not the point—''

''And you don't think other men would be a little more intrigued by you, wondering what it was about you that Jesse found so irresistible?''

''Suzanne! What you propose is practically . . . well, it's . . .'' she stammered. ''It's practically . . . It's underhanded, that's what it is!''

''So, now you're saying he's above such behavior.''

''I did not say that!''

''Then you agree that he might . . . enhance the details just a bit?''

''I have no way of knowing that—''

''Ladies,'' Eleanor hissed, with a hand on each of their arms, ''keep your voices down! He's coming this way!''

Loralee looked up and saw Jesse walking toward them, and, suddenly, it hit her. ''Why . . . he's . . . I know him!'' she said.

Eleanor looked at her and giggled. ''Well, of course you do!''

Loralee shook her head. ''No, I mean I *know* him. He's been visiting one of my patients. But, I didn't realize . . .'' Her voice trailed off as she thought back to the strikingly handsome man she'd seen visiting Maggie. The tight blue jeans and soft flannel shirt were a sharp contrast with the formal dark brown suit he was wearing tonight. The cream-colored ruffled shirt was buttoned tightly to his neck. Then, his flannel shirt had left a vee of skin exposed.

Loralee swallowed nervously as Jesse approached their little group. She'd spent most of the night before thinking about him, though she'd had no idea that the man she'd been dreaming about was a Sinclair.

Which one would he ask? Which one? She ducked behind Mary, who was at least six inches taller. She wasn't sure why, but she wasn't ready to face him.

"Excuse me, Miss Becker," Jesse said, holding his hand out to Suzanne. "Would you permit me the honor of a dance?"

Suzanne smiled her most charming smile. "I'd be delighted." She batted her eyelashes outrageously.

Jesse smiled the smile that broke hearts, and, as Loralee watched her best friend place her hand in his, she felt a tight knot in her chest. Breathing was out of the question.

"Would you look at the way he's holding her," Mary whispered.

"Suzanne's father will have a fit if he sees that," Eleanor answered.

They watched in fascination as Jesse spun Suzanne expertly around the dance floor. She leaned toward him, and he bent his head near. She said something, and he raised his eyebrows and smiled.

Loralee watched Jesse's hand on Suzanne's back. His fingers were spread across the bright yellow satin of her gown. Loralee wondered what those fingers felt like. Would they feel warm, even through satin? Was Suzanne enjoying the feel of Jesse's fingertips pressing into her skin?

Loralee's breathing was shallow, and she could feel her face begin to burn.

Do something! she told herself. Do something!

"Excuse me," she muttered to her friends, turning quickly and hurrying to the ladies' sitting room.

She raced through the door and stopped to lean back against the wall. She pressed her hands to her stomach as though to ease the queasiness that had come from nowhere. With her eyes closed, she tried to steady her breathing.

What on earth had gotten into her? She'd never felt like this before! For a minute, she'd been afraid that she would faint. She'd never fainted! Never!

As her breathing slowed, she began to feel somewhere near normal. She walked over to a pink velvet upholstered bench, and carefully lowered herself onto it.

It was then that Loralee realized what had happened. She'd been struck by jealousy.

For a moment, she sat perfectly still, then she shook her head and said to herself, "I am not jealous."

But from somewhere in the back of her mind, she could hear a voice taunting her. You are too jealous, it said.

Loralee spoke out loud. "I don't even like the man."

But she'd liked him plenty when she'd thought he was simply a neighbor of the O'Tooles. She'd thought about the handsome, caring stranger much too much. She couldn't deny that.

She sat staring at the floor, trying to sort out the puzzling emotions that were clamoring for her attention. Jealousy? Sexual attraction? Plain old female envy? These were new and foreign feelings, and Loralee was overwhelmed at having to deal with all of them at the same time.

Suzanne burst into the room. "There you are! I was looking all over for you. No one knew where you went."

Loralee looked nervously around the room. "I got awfully warm, and, and, I felt . . . I was a little, uh, lightheaded."

"Are you all right?" Suzanne asked, clearly concerned. "Do you want to leave?"

"No. No, really," Loralee said with a smile. "I'm fine. I think I just need a little fresh air."

"Perfect!" Suzanne exclaimed. "Let's take a walk."

She put her arm around Loralee, and the two girls left the quiet of the sitting room and stepped into the almost overwhelming noise in the ballroom.

"Let's go out that way," Suzanne said loudly, pointing to a set of tall French doors that had been propped open to allow the summer breezes indoors.

Loralee followed her friend through the crowd and out onto the flagstone patio, which was holding the overflow of guests. They stepped down onto the garden pathway and walked in the direction of an intricate, maze-like rose and herb garden. The further they went, the thinner the crowd became, until they were, finally, mercifully, alone.

"That was certainly an ordeal," Loralee said, fluffing the skirt of her green dress, which had been pressed against her legs as they walked through the throng of bodies.

"I'd do it again in a minute, if it meant dancing with Jesse just one more time."

Loralee felt a strange chill shoot up her spine. She was going to hear about this dance with Jesse whether she liked it or not. She was Suzanne's best friend, and, as excited as Suzanne was, she would want to rehash every second of their encounter.

"He's a good dancer?" Loralee finally managed.

"Oh," Suzanne said, rolling her eyes and pressing a hand to her heart, "he's so much more than just good. I've danced with him before, you know."

"I know." Loralee struggled to maintain even breathing. For some perverse reason, she wanted to hear every detail of the two minutes Suzanne had spent in Jesse's arms. And in the next heartbeat, she wanted never to hear one agonizing word of it.

What had gotten into her?

"He is absolutely the most handsome man I've ever seen, and I do mean *ever.*" Suzanne widened her already huge brown eyes. "And he's even better close up. You know," she said, glancing quickly from side to side to ascertain their privacy before she hiked her skirt and removed from the top of her stocking one tiny cigar, pilfered just that morning from her daddy's humidor, and one long matchstick, "if you take him apart, he's really not at all exceptional. He's not very tall. His hair is the color of mud, and much too long, besides. And, except for those eyes, and some *very* well developed shoulder muscles, which I could feel right through his jacket," she whispered conspiratorially, "his features are rather ordinary. But, put them all together, and, ohhh . . . he is one fine-looking man."

Loralee was still stuck on Suzanne's hands running over Jesse's well-muscled shoulders. It took a few seconds for her mind to catch up to the conversation. "He—he does have very blue eyes," she muttered.

"Blue? Blue doesn't even begin to do them justice," Suzanne said, puffing on the cigar until it was lit, then drawing in one long, steady drag. She held the smoke in her lungs for a few seconds before blowing it out in one even stream. She handed it to Loralee, who snatched it from her fingers gratefully.

She'd never much enjoyed Suzanne's occasional booty. Mostly, the cigars made her sleepy. But tonight Loralee thought she could use their calming incense to subdue her jumpy nerves. She filled her lungs twice, rapidly, with the smoke it gave off. She didn't want to hear any more about Jesse's eyes. She'd already fantasized about them enough.

"And, I swear, Jesse held me tighter than I've ever let any man hold me."

"Don't you think we should be getting back?" Loralee asked loudly. The smoke had gone to her head, and she was feeling a bit more mellow, though not mellow enough to discuss how tightly Jesse had held her best friend. Loralee took one more puff, for good measure, then handed it back to Suzanne, who took a quick drag before dropping it onto the gravel and grinding it out with the toe of her boot. She bent to pick a sprig of wild mint from the garden, chewed on the fragrant leaves then spit them out in the gravel.

Loralee followed Suzanne's lead. She chomped on a few leaves of mint before spitting them out onto the ground. "I don't think you should let yourself get too taken with Jesse Sinclair, Suzanne. He goes through women like there's a fresh shipment of us comin' in on his daddy's train every week!"

"Oh, Loralee—"

"Well, it's true," she said, holding her hands palm up to her sides. "And I'll tell you something else. If he asked me to dance, I'd refuse him!"

"Sure, you would."

"I would!" she said, knowing that she would not be able to refuse him.

The girls had reached the open doors by now, and as Suzanne stepped over the threshold, she asked, "By the way, how are my skirts?" She spun around quickly, and Loralee looked down at the bright yellow ruffles that were floating softly into place.

"They're fine." She eyed the dress enviously. "That color looks stunning on you, with your dark hair. I'd look like a giant dandelion."

"You can't have everything. I would kill for hair the color of yours." She reached out and lifted a curl from the middle of Loralee's back. "It's a perfect mixture of silver and gold strands. And curls to boot! I'll tell you, I had those irons in my hair for an hour before I could coax the tiniest wave into it." She dropped the hair, and both girls moved into the room, just affected enough by the cigar they had shared that their surroundings seemed a little more intense than they had a few minutes before.

And, within Loralee's heart, the gentle stirrings she'd felt for the handsome stranger were beginning to pound against her insides, demanding that she release them.

She had no idea what would happen if she let them take over. But, for the first time in her life, she was almost willing to take a chance, and find out.

Jesse used his fork to scrape every bit of remaining icing off the plate. He looked up to see his mother watching him with an amused grin.

He smiled and shrugged. "I can't help it. I have a sweet tooth."

"I remember when you boys were little. Dessert was always your favorite part of the meal. One day, Cook told me that she always knew which dessert plate was yours because it came back to the kitchen clean enough to put right back in the cabinet."

"At least I never snuck into the pantry and made off with an entire pie!" Jesse said, remembering his younger brother's thwarted attempt at thievery. "I didn't put you through half the things Johnny did!"

"Now what did I do?" said a voice from behind Jesse. He looked over his shoulder to see his brother, John.

"Well, he finally makes an appearance! You know, your only brother is celebrating a milestone birthday, and you barely take the time to say happy birthday before you rush out into the well-wishers!" Jesse teased.

"Yeah, so. Happy birthday, old man." John faced his brother, trying in vain to keep his face straight. "So what exactly was it that I did?"

"We were just thinking about that blueberry pie that 'no one' ate. As I recall, your stomach wasn't a very good accomplice," Elizabeth said.

John hung his head. "All right, all right, I'll admit, an eight-year-old boy probably shouldn't eat an entire pie by himself."

"So where have you been hiding yourself this evening, brother?"

"I haven't been hiding. I've just been very busy keeping our female guests occupied. There seems to be a shortage of male dance partners and a glut of single, young women," he said, raising an eyebrow in his mother's direction. "Very odd, don't you think, Mother?"

"I wouldn't know about that. Excuse me, boys, I'd better go check on the kitchen staff." She hurried away from the two young men who were smiling and shaking their heads.

"She is unbelievable," Jesse said affectionately.

"She can't help herself, Jess. She wants you married off, and that woman is determined!"

Jesse laughed. "Determined or not, she'll have to wait. I haven't found what I'm looking for yet."

"That's fine, but just know, Mother's not going to let you hold out forever."

"Well, she'll have to— Oh, my God! She's here!" Jesse's eyes were glued to a spot somewhere behind John's head.

"Who?" he asked, turning around to follow Jesse's stare.

"By the doors," he motioned with a nod. "In the green gown."

John found her and said, "The blonde?"

Jesse nodded. "The blonde." He watched, mesmerized, as Loralee stepped in through the doorway then spun around, talking with someone just outside his view. And then a young lady in a yellow dress stepped through the door. It was Suzanne Becker.

As he watched, Suzanne reached out and took a lock of Loralee's pale blond hair in her hand. She let it slip through her fingers, and they began to laugh as they headed into the crowd.

"I have to dance with that girl, Johnny!" he shouted as he took off through the crowd.

"Go to it, Jess!"

Jesse made his way through the crowd, bumping into people and elbowing his way through the human maze. And finally, he reached them.

An arm on Suzanne's elbow stopped her in midsentence.

"Well, hello again, Miss Becker! Are you enjoying the party?"

She glanced at his hand on her arm and raised her eyebrows slightly. "Why yes, Mr. Sinclair, I am."

He dropped his hand. "I'm glad to hear that. And please, call me Jesse. Whenever I hear 'Mr. Sinclair' I want to turn around and see if my father is standing behind me.'' He smiled his most charming smile and struggled to hide his rapid breathing.

Suzanne smiled back, a captivating smile that Jesse knew could snare men both young and old.

''I don't believe I've met your friend,'' he said, holding out his hand to Loralee. She hesitated for a moment then held out her right hand. He raised the tiny hand to his lips and dropped the gentlest of kisses upon it as though she were royalty.

''This is Loralee . . .'' Suzanne began, her voice trailing off as she watched Jesse press his lips against Loralee's fair skin.

Loralee pulled as though to snatch her hand back, but he held fast, refusing to relinquish possession.

''It's a pleasure to meet you, Loralee. Would you like to dance?''

Without waiting for a response, he led her toward the dance floor.

Jesse looked down into the brightest green eyes he had ever seen. They were the color of emeralds, and they sparkled, just like the gemstones themselves.

''You are, without a doubt, the loveliest young lady here tonight.''

Loralee's eyes widened. To say that they sparkled was a grave injustice. They fairly flashed like lightning, and he felt her fingers grip his hand more tightly.

He squeezed back, and her eyes shot to his hand then back to his face, where they remained boldly fixed, not even bothering to look away when the blush began to creep up her cheeks.

''I love it when a woman blushes.''

''From what I hear, you love just about everything about women,'' Loralee said bitingly.

Jesse smiled and raised his eyebrows. ''She speaks!'' he said, thrilled that he might have found, not only the most beautiful woman in the world, but one who had the spunk to stand up to his teasing.

She couldn't help chuckling, but despite her amusement, she looked away.

"You're the girl who's taking care of Maggie O'Toole," he said.

"Yes, I am."

"I thought it was you. You look very different."

Her eyes skittered over him, from the top of his head to the center of his chest. "You look very different, too. I didn't know it was you, until—"

"Until . . . ?"

"Until . . . you asked Suzanne to dance."

"If I had seen you, I would never have asked Suzanne," he said seriously. His heart was pounding. She felt so perfect in his arms. He tightened his grip on her. She shot a look at him that was clearly questioning his intent.

He returned her steady gaze without loosening his hold on her one bit. He wanted to hold her. He wanted her to know it.

"Why were you visiting Maggie?" she asked.

"Colin works for my father. He's been with us a long time, so, of course, we're concerned about his family."

"Oh."

And then he asked a question he never meant to ask. "She's not going to live, is she?"

Loralee looked up at him, and opened her mouth, but looked away without saying a word when tears began to fill her eyes.

"Oh, God . . ."

She looked up sharply. "Miracles happen."

Jesse hesitated, then he nodded his head, afraid that the lump in his throat would prevent him from speaking. "You work for Doc Farley?"

They swirled halfway around the room before she answered. "I'm in training to become a physician. I have a degree from Cedar Crest Women's College, and I started working with Dr. Farley a few months ago. It keeps me busy."

So, that explained why he hadn't seen her out before.

She was beautiful. Jesse had to keep reminding himself to speak. He could have very happily spent the entire night watching her without saying another word.

They had danced straight through two songs, and Jesse knew that he would have to let her go. He looked up and saw his parents near the open doors, watching him.

The song ended, and he turned Loralee toward the patio. "I'd like to introduce you to my parents," he said, propelling her through the crowd.

"I—I really should be getting back. Suzanne will think I've abandoned her," she stammered, trying, and failing, to hold her ground.

"Suzanne will be fine for a few more minutes," he said as they approached his parents.

"But—"

"Mother, Father, I'd like to introduce you to Loralee." He turned toward her to ask her last name, but his mother spoke before he could.

"Loralee! What a very pretty name!"

"Thank you."

"I'm Elizabeth Sinclair, and this is my husband, Stephen."

"It's very nice to meet you both."

Jesse looked directly at his father, his blue eyes dancing as though to impart an important message: *this is the one!*

Stephen's eyebrows lifted slightly, and Jesse smiled.

Stephen cleared his throat. "It's getting awfully warm in here, and we were just about to step outside for some fresh air. Would you care to join us?"

Elizabeth looked at her husband, questioning, and Jesse saw the confusion on her face. Suddenly, she seemed to understand it all. "Oh! Yes, please, join us outside," she said

With a smile, Jesse said, "We'd love to."

The foursome made their way out into the cool night air. Jesse reached for Loralee's hand, boldly twining his fingers with hers, and followed his parents out the door. Again, she made a move to pull back her hand, but he held fast. She wouldn't protest any further, he knew, for fear of causing a disturbance and offending her hosts.

"Do you like roses, Loralee?" Elizabeth asked.

Loralee glanced up at Jesse as if demanding an explanation for her abduction. He walked along as if he hadn't a care in the world. She looked away. "Yes. Yes, I do."

"Oh, good! We have a beautiful rose garden, and the first batch of blooms is at their peak. The moonlight will be just enough to see by," she said, turning down one of many curving paths.

Elizabeth babbled inanely about the roses, their different colors, their fragrance, climbers, bushes—anything to avoid an awkward silence. Jesse thought he wouldn't have cared if she had suddenly started to speak in tongues. He didn't care what she said, as long as he was able to continue holding Loralee's tiny hand in his own.

They had been outside for a good ten minutes and had managed to make several turns along the path so that they were now completely blocked from view of the house.

Suddenly, Stephen said, "Elizabeth, dear, we've been away from our guests long enough. I'm sure Jesse wouldn't mind finishing the garden tour without us."

"My goodness! I didn't realize we'd been out here so long!" Elizabeth said. "Loralee, dear, it was wonderful meeting you. Take your time and enjoy the rest of the roses!" she said, already hurrying toward the house.

Loralee stood watching her hosts rushing away so quickly they might almost have been running! "Well!" she said softly.

"I think my mother liked you."

Loralee blinked her eyes and turned toward Jesse. "Pardon me?" she asked.

"My mother. I think she liked having a woman fuss over her roses."

Loralee stared at him for a moment then turned and looked

at the retreating backs of Elizabeth and Stephen Sinclair. "Well," she said again.

Jesse took Loralee's hand and wrapped it around his elbow, beginning to walk along the garden path again. "She would have enjoyed having a daughter, but, instead, she's stuck in a house full of men. She was so happy to have a woman's company here in the garden that I'm afraid she got somewhat scatterbrained," he said, knowing full well that his mother had never been "scatterbrained" a day in her life. He turned toward Loralee, taking both her hands in his own. "She left you unchaperoned," he said.

Loralee looked up at Jesse's face, just inches from her own. He was offering her an escape. At her word, they would be rushing back toward the guests. Back toward the safety of numbers.

She looked toward the house, then back at him, and her expression indicated that she was caught firmly between conflicting desires. She wanted to stay, but knew she should go. She couldn't make the choice, and when next she spoke, Jesse was sure that her words were intended to force him into making that choice for her.

"I'm well aware that we are alone, Mr. Sinclair, and, I must wonder, why would a man with your reputation need to resort to kidnapping? Surely there must be someone in that crowd who would be only too willing to stand in the rose garden and be kissed by you."

Jesse raised his eyebrows, taken aback by her candor. "Is that what you think I want?"

"Isn't it?"

He examined her closely, the wide green eyes which picked up the moonlight and threw it right back at him, the cocky little curve of her mouth which all but dared him, Go ahead! Kiss me! And most of all, the way her tiny hands were now gripping his forearms as though *she* were the one holding *him* in place. She *wanted* to be kissed!

Her curiosity had been piqued. Somewhere between the dance floor and the rose garden, she'd decided to find out what the fuss over Jesse Sinclair was all about.

And he'd be happy to oblige her.

"You're willing to stand there and let me kiss you?"

"You're asking permission?" she taunted. "My goodness, by the way you nearly *drug* me to the dance floor, I'd have bet you didn't know the meaning of the word *ask.*"

He leveled his blue eyes on her. "You're a smart-mouthed little thing, aren't you?"

She glared back at him, silent, refusing to jump to the bait.

"Well," he said, pulling her closer, "let's see if you can put that mouth to better use."

He leaned forward, and she looked up. He meant to make this kiss one she would not forget.

He touched his lips to hers, softer than the whisper of a feather. Again and again he brushed his mouth over hers, and with each momentary contact, the heat spread throughout his body. Loralee stood stiffly, allowing him to kiss her, but not allowing herself to kiss back, and *that's* what Jesse had come out here for. Not simply to kiss her, but to drive her to the point that she kissed back—could not stop herself from kissing back. That's what he wanted.

He released her arms and settled his hands on her hips, brushing her tightly closed lips with his own until he felt her soften. She rested her hands on Jesse's shoulders, and her fingertips lazily rubbed against the jacket he was wearing, teasingly caressing the muscle beneath it.

At her touch, Jesse began to lose himself in the kiss. His tongue slicked against her lips, coaxing them to open, and he felt her draw back. He opened his eyes

She didn't know! She didn't know what he wanted her to do!

He lightened his pressure against her lips and whispered against them, "Open your mouth, Loralee."

He heard her draw in a breath, and, as she did, her lips parted. Jesse's tongue slid inside, caressing, rubbing, sucking, persuading. He explored her mouth thoroughly, gently coaxing her to respond. He plunged his fingers into her silky hair and held her head firmly within his grasp. Suddenly, he felt her tongue stroke his. She was mimicking his movements, kissing him back the way he had just kissed her.

Desire shot through his body, and Jesse slid his hands down her back. He pressed one hand between her shoulders, the other below her waist. He held her hard against the full length of himself, plunging into her mouth and taking what he wanted.

The heat between them was becoming unbearable. Jesse trailed soft kisses down her neck, and Loralee put her hand into his hair and pressed his mouth against her throat. His tongue flicked back and forth over her slippery skin, and she cried out, looking for his mouth with her own. Jesse'd wanted her to respond, and she had, haltingly at first, but with increasing ardor.

This couldn't go on. Jesse's mind started to function, and as he felt himself being pulled deeper into the vortex of desire, he knew he had to stop now, or drown.

He wrapped his hands around Loralee's waist, his fingers meeting both in back and in front, and pulled her flush against him once more. She went willingly where he led, opening her mouth to let him explore however he wanted. Her heart beat furiously against his chest, and, as she struggled for breath, her breasts rubbed seductively against him.

Unable to stop himself, he stretched out his fingers and caressed the fullness. Loralee jumped back.

"No!" she cried, pushing at his shoulders.

Jesse's breath was coming fast and shallow. He looked down at the front of her dress, and he could see her chest rising and falling as she struggled to slow her breathing. Slowly, he straightened, running a hand through his hair and letting out a long, slow gust of air.

"Loralee, I'm sorry—"

"Please, Jesse, I'm not like those other women you've known! I've never—" She held up her palms as though to fend him off. "Just take me back to the house . . . I-I don't know the way." She turned away from him.

Jesse thought he saw tears in her eyes, and he reached out for her, but she backed away, wrapping her arms across her breasts as though to hide them from his view.

"Loralee—"

"Please don't touch me again," she whispered. This time, he knew there were tears.

Dropping his arms to his sides, he watched her struggling with what they had done together. She had antagonized him earlier, chastising him for his behavior with women while almost begging to be added to their ranks. Now, shame and fear were mirrored in her every feature.

He couldn't let her leave thinking that she had done something wrong. But he couldn't think of anything to say that wouldn't make it worse.

He planted his hands in his pockets, to assure her that he wouldn't try to touch her again. "I'll walk you back to the house," he said softly.

She whispered, "Thank you," and turned away from him, anxious, he knew, to put distance between them.

As he watched her rushing away from him, he cursed under his breath. Following her up the garden path, he muttered, "Nice going, Jesse."

Stephen and Elizabeth moved hurriedly toward the patio, but once there, they leisurely mingled with the guests they had only minutes before passed without so much as a greeting.

They wandered lazily among the couples gathered outside, stopping first here, then there, sharing a little bit of their own happiness with everyone they met. The Sinclairs had not been handed their fortune, nor did their loving family come easily to them. Stephen had started with little, invested wisely, worked diligently and risked it all for something he believed in—rails being the way of the future.

And for Elizabeth, the sons she loved so dearly had only come after years of agonizing over her inability to conceive. The Avondale disaster, which had killed 110 miners, among them Jesse and John's natural father, had provided a roundabout path to parenthood.

Because they remembered their own hard times, they never looked lightly on the troubles of others. They were friendly, caring people, and everyone who knew them liked and respected them.

This was evident by the way they were greeted as they moved among their guests, most of whom had been invited by the friend of a friend, and not by Elizabeth Sinclair herself. And yet, her cheerful demeanor shone through to everyone she met, making each and every guest feel equally welcome.

Stephen was the first to spot Jesse and Loralee returning to the house, and he courteously excused himself and ushered his wife to Loralee's side.

"So, then, did you see the rest of the garden, Loralee?" Stephen asked.

"Yes, sir. It's quite lovely," she murmured, her eyes searching for a place, anyplace to rest comfortably. Her cheeks were flushed, and she clasped and unclasped her hands nervously, as though she was telling herself not to, but couldn't help herself.

Stephen's eyes shot curiously to his son, questioning the reason for the young lady's obvious distress. He was quite sure Jesse was a gentleman. He would not have allowed Loralee to be alone with him otherwise. But Jesse's tightly controlled features gave nothing away.

The foursome made their way into the ballroom. Loralee had barely set foot inside when she seized her escape.

Turning quickly toward Stephen and Elizabeth, she blurted out, "It was so nice meeting you, but I'm afraid I've been terribly rude to my friend. She's been left alone this whole time, and she's quite shy," she lied. She then turned toward Jesse, but could not quite meet his eyes. "Thank you for the dance, and I hope you enjoy the rest of your birthday." She spun and hurried into the crowd.

Staring after her for several seconds, Elizabeth turned slowly toward her son. "Jesse Sinclair, whatever did you do to that girl?"

Jesse looked at both his parents. "Nothing!" He held his hands palms up as if offering them for inspection. "We walked in the garden, and I kissed her. But not before she had every opportunity to come back to the house, if that's what she wanted to do!" He was starting to resent the implications being made. He had never forced himself on a woman. Never!

"Well, she certainly seems as though something happened."

"Yeah, something happened," Jesse said to his mother, almost daring her to do something about it. "She was kissing me, and she was loving it."

"Jesse!" his father admonished harshly.

Jesse closed his eyes, drawing in a deep breath and struggling to get himself under control. His anger was directed inward. Loralee was a completely inexperienced girl. She hadn't even known how to kiss! She certainly could not be blamed for the desire raging through him. He opened his eyes and reached for his mother's hands.

"I apologize, Mother. That remark was totally uncalled for," he said quietly. "Excuse me." He turned and went into the crowd with the intention of apologizing to Loralee as well.

But he couldn't find her. He looked everywhere. She had disappeared as completely as a dream disperses upon awakening.

His heart was heavy with something heretofore unknown.

He had never before experienced longing for another soul. Physical yearning was easily dealt with. But, this . . .

He kept his heart heavily guarded, the childhood memory of his first family too painful to relive. And, with the exception of Stephen, Elizabeth and his brother John, no one had ever penetrated his armor. Jesse Sinclair was the ultimate untouchable.

But, I have so many friends, he silently argued with himself. I'm smart, I'm fun, I'm kind, I'm rich. I'm always surrounded by people, and I strive to make those who know me like me.

After an hour he still hadn't found Loralee. Jesse thought about his life, all that it was and all that it could be, and he realized that, in order to paint an accurate picture, he'd have to add something.

Jesse Sinclair was lonely.

Loralee rushed through the crowd, desperate to reach Suzanne.

What had she been thinking? She had never behaved so . . . wantonly before! What must Jesse think of her?

Tears began to fill her eyes, and the crowd before her blurred into one big swirling mass of color. Surely, he'd never speak to her again. She had provoked him into kissing her. *Teased* him until he had done the only thing possible—he'd kissed her the way no man had ever kissed her. Touched her the way she ached for him to touch her.

But, then, somehow, she'd gotten control of her senses and realized that she was playing a dangerous game. Jesse Sinclair was a well-known playboy. He wouldn't put up with a tease. She'd offered herself, and he would have expected her to deliver.

She stopped walking and leaned against a pillar, too overcome by tears to continue her search for Suzanne.

Oh, God, everyone will see . . .

And from across the room, someone did see. Charles Korwin, the coddled, pampered youngest son of a successful banker, watched as Loralee hurled herself back into the ballroom, fresh from Jesse Sinclair's arms, he was sure.

Charles's anger began a slow simmer. He stepped down from the spiral staircase where he'd perched to watch Loralee and began to make his way through the crowd.

He had been pursuing Loralee for close to a year, ample time for her to grow tired of her ridiculous notion of becoming a doctor. Meanwhile, he hadn't wasted one second inveigling himself into Edward's good graces.

Charles had been searching for a father-in-law, more than a wife, and he'd found the prize with Edward Vander. Edward's empire was enormous, and, best of all, Loralee was his only child.

Charles had done such a good job with Edward that four weeks earlier, he had agreed to a betrothal contract. Loralee's father had grown tired of her independence. At twenty-two, she seemed in no hurry to find a husband, let alone provide Edward with an heir.

Charles was a good catch! And, when Edward had wanted to inform Loralee of the contract immediately, Charles had stepped in, on her behalf, of course, and asked that Loralee be permitted a little while longer to, perhaps, arrive at that same conclusion for herself. After all, he argued, he wanted as his wife a woman who would gladly leave her former pursuits in order to take on the role of Mrs. Charles Korwin. He didn't want a reluctant bride.

Edward had relented, setting a time limit of six months. At the end of that time, Loralee would be told, and whether she accepted her new role willingly, or fought him every step of the way made no difference. She'd be legally bound to Charles for life.

But right now, the thing he had to do was get her away from this house, before Jesse found her and apologized for something that was undoubtedly Loralee's fault. She was as naïve as a baby and had probably given Sinclair mixed signals. Still, the thought of Jesse's hands on Loralee's body started a reaction in Charles that could not be ignored. Loralee was his property!

He placed his hand carefully on her shoulder, and she jumped.

"Loralee, are you all right?"

"Oh, Charles," she said, pressing a hand to her heart. "You scared me."

"I'm sorry, I didn't mean to. I happened to see you from across the room. Is something wrong?" He used the most gentle tone of voice he could manage.

"I—I'm not feeling very well. Would you mind very much taking me home? I came with Suzanne and her parents, and I'd hate for them to have to leave on my account."

"Of course, I'll take you home," he said, leading her with an arm around her shoulders toward the front door. "Bring my carriage 'round," he said to a liveryman standing just outside the door.

"Certainly, Mr. Korwin."

Charles turned to another servant and said, "Would you please see to it that Mr. Robert Becker is informed that I escorted Miss Vander home, due to a sudden illness."

"Of course, sir." The man beckoned another servant, who was given the message and hurried off to deliver it.

"Thank you so much, Charles," Loralee said.

"No need to thank me," he said. His control over his anger was slipping a notch.

She looked up at him suspiciously. "Is something wrong?"

Aware that he was walking a precariously thin line, Charles only said, "We'll discuss it later, Loralee." He stared at the front door, watching for his carriage to arrive. The second it did, he stepped out the door, his hand on Loralee's elbow. Her shoes made an unusually loud clatter on the front porch as she struggled to keep up to Charles's pace.

"Charles, you're hurting my arm!" she whispered as she

was removed from the Sinclair house and propelled toward the waiting carriage.

"So help me, Loralee, you're lucky that's all I'm hurting," he muttered, stopping to throw open the carriage door. "Get in."

"Charles, what's wrong? Have you been—"

Grabbing her arm once more, he hauled her roughly into the carriage, tossing her against the seat so hard that she toppled sideways, banging her shoulder against the edge of the seat.

"I said, get in."

Loralee scrambled back into the furthest corner of the carriage. But there was no place to escape Charles's scorn. She had gone from a bad situation to a worse one, and she had no idea how to help herself.

He cracked the reins against the horses so sharply that they took off much faster than they needed to. They turned onto Diamond Avenue at breakneck speed, racing past the Vander mansion and out of town toward Stockton.

"Where are you going?" Loralee asked.

Without glancing her way, Charles said, "You'll speak, Loralee, when you are spoken to. Is that understood?"

She had never seen Charles behave this way before! She felt like she was being spoken to by her father. That women should be seen but not heard was one of his well-known beliefs.

Charles turned toward her, his eyes blazing. "I said, is that understood?"

She nodded her head, dropping her gaze to the floor. What in the name of heaven had gotten into him? She was afraid to say anything, lest it set him off again.

Charles drove the horses mercilessly over the uneven ground, turning at the end of the Diamond and following a trail obviously not meant for carriages. They jerked so violently Loralee thought they'd surely tip over. They climbed higher and higher till they reached a small clearing. He slowed the horses and eased them into a smooth spot on the side of the mountain, turning the carriage skillfully so that they were looking down on the town.

"Take a good look, Loralee. See those breakers?" he asked as though he was speaking to a two-year-old. "Do you see them?"

She could see two of her father's breakers from here, a faint illumination from the gaslights providing a backdrop in the otherwise dark landscape. She nodded her head, afraid to say a word.

"Well, good," he continued, seemingly totally calm. "Now, you see, those breakers are sitting on top of some of the richest coal mines in the world. They are the reason you live in the fancy house you do. They are the reason for the pretty dresses you wear." He reached out and rubbed the shimmery fabric between his fingers, then dropped it as though in disgust.

"Your father has the misfortune of being married to a woman who only managed to birth a daughter. Because he has no sons, it is extremely important that you marry well, since your husband will eventually have charge of the company."

He looked at Loralee and gloated over the fact that she hadn't known about her father's plans. "Before Edward and I were able to agree on a betrothal contract, we had a little chat."

At the mention of a betrothal, Loralee's head jerked up. She stared at Charles, and from the look on his face, she knew that it was true.

"Didn't know about that, did you?" He grinned evilly at her.

Loralee's heart was racing. "I don't believe my father would promise me in marriage without discussing it with me first," she said, although the fear that he had, indeed, done just such a thing was beginning to strangle her.

"Oh, but he did. We'll be married in six months' time. He also made his position on independent women very clear. He doesn't think you, or any woman, for that matter, is smart enough to run an operation the size of Vander Holdings."

He reached for her hand, holding her wrist tightly in his left hand and running the fingers of his right hand up the inside of her arm to her elbow. He looked at her with eyes as cold as ice. "In fact, there's really only one thing he thinks women should be used for." His fingers passed her elbow and continued upward, his left hand grasping her wrist more tightly. Boldly, he brushed his knuckles against the side of her breast.

Loralee recoiled from his touch, bringing her free hand in front of her as though to protect herself. But Charles's arm shot out like lightning, entrapping both her wrists, pinning her arms to her sides. She started to struggle, but soon realized that she wouldn't be able to move until he wanted her to. With tear-filled eyes, she looked up at him, pleading.

"Please, Charles . . ."

"Please, what?" he shouted. "Please kiss you the way Jesse Sinclair did? Please leer at you in front of a room full of people the way he did?" He leaned forward and whispered into her ear, "Please touch you the way he did?"

"Charles, he—"

"Don't deny it, Loralee!" he said, yanking her arms tightly around her back, where he could easily grasp both tiny wrists in one of his much larger hands, leaving one free to roam. He set it at her waist. "Don't tell me he didn't kiss you." He moved it slightly upward, resting at her ribcage. "I know the look of a woman who has been thoroughly kissed," he said menacingly, spreading his fingers until they touched the fullness at the side of her breast. "And when you came back into the ballroom, you were wearing that look." His words were a whisper, but they chafed against her like sandpaper.

Loralee began to cry. She turned her head to avoid Charles's piercing gaze.

"No, my love, don't turn away from me," he said, reaching up to turn her face back to him. "Look into my eyes. Look!" he demanded. She raised her eyes, terrified, that her father had chosen this madman to be her husband. He held her wrists firmly enough that she could not escape. She looked into his eyes and saw raw hatred.

"Did he kiss you, Loralee?" He pulled slightly on her arms, commanding her to meet his gaze. "Did he?"

She gathered her strength and looked into his eyes but refused to answer.

He smiled a smile that would frighten the devil himself and whispered, "Well, let's see."

He pulled her forward, releasing her wrists, but wrapping his arms so tightly around her that her arms were still pinned to her sides. Roughly, he pressed his lips against hers. None too gently, he slid his tongue along her lips, forcing them to open, and thrusting inside when they did. He plundered her mouth, growing more furious with each passing second.

He pulled away from her, his breathing labored, and looked at her contemptuously. "So, he did kiss you." Once again, he held her arms firmly behind her back, his gaze roving over her breasts. "What else did he do, Loralee? What else!" he shouted, pulling her arms viciously.

"Nothing!" she screamed. *How could he tell?* "Nothing, Charles, please! You're hurting my arm! Please stop!" she begged, as the tears rolled down her face.

But her tears did nothing to calm his jealousy. Again, he placed his hand perilously close to her breast. "Did he touch you, Loralee?" He filled his hand with her breast, refusing to let her squirm away. "Did he rub himself against you?" he said, leaning back against the carriage and pulling Loralee against his erection, delighting in her humiliation. "Did you want to touch him?" he said, pulling one small hand to the front and pressing it against the bulge in his pants.

She pulled her hand back as though she had touched fire, her fingers clenched into a tiny fist. The tears flowed freely down her face; she did nothing to hide them.

"Go ahead, Loralee. Touch me the way you touched Jesse,"

he said, rubbing her tightly fisted hand against the front of his trousers. "Did you get excited? Did you want more?"

Sobbing, she shouted, "No, Charles ... please!" before being overtaken by emotion. She cried like she hadn't cried since she was a child.

He flung her away, glaring at her like an unwanted pile of rubbish. She buried her head in her hands and cried uncontrollably. Charles waited until her tears slowed to a trickle.

"You are going to be my wife, Loralee. And I will not have my wife behaving like a common whore. You are not to go near that man again. Is that clear?" He sat back on the seat, seemingly unaffected by the whole ordeal.

"Answer me, Loralee."

She was unable to speak, and so nodded her head. The crying had stopped, and in its wake, she was left in a quiet desolation.

"Clean yourself up, for God's sake. You look a mess." Charles took the reins of the horses and started moving them down the steep grade. He descended the mountain and headed for the Vander mansion.

"I think tonight we'll set a date for the wedding," he said, as the breakers faded from view.

CHAPTER FOUR

Today would not be a good day to be Edward Vander, Loralee thought as she whipped open her bedroom door and stomped down the stairs to the dining room.

Last night had been a nightmare. An absolute nightmare. Loralee couldn't think of anything that could've made it worse.

She'd sneaked off to a party in the home of people whom she had been warned against her entire life.

She'd allowed a complete stranger with a well-known reputation as a ladies' man to kiss her.

She'd been harassed and humiliated by Charles, who would most assuredly run straight to Edward with a detailed report of his errant daughter's whereabouts.

Worst of all, she'd found out that her father had promised her in marriage to a man she neither liked nor respected!

Loralee had spent a restless night waiting to demand an explanation from her father, and with each passing second, her agitation had increased to the point that, by morning, she was shaking.

Loralee stepped into the dining room, dropped her black satchel onto the floor and stood beside the table with her hands planted on her hips.

"Did you honestly think, Papa, that you could barter me away in marriage and I wouldn't even notice it?"

Edward lowered the newspaper he had been reading and looked at his daughter. He glanced over at his wife as if she were somehow responsible for Loralee's outburst, but Fiona continued her attack on her grapefruit. Edward looked away. "What in God's name are you wearing?" he asked Loralee, completely ignoring her question.

Loralee fought to retain control. "I am wearing a work dress because I have work to do this morning."

"On a Sunday? We attend church on Sundays, Loralee."

"I'm well aware of that, Papa. Unfortunately, people can and do get sick on Sundays. I have a visit with a patient this morning that can not be put off."

"I think it's going to have to be put off—"

"Until when?" Loralee shouted, holding her hands out to him. "Until *after* she dies? I won't be much use then, will I, Papa?"

Edward raised his eyebrows. "Kindly lower your voice, daughter. The entire household can hear your shouting."

Loralee struggled to reign in her anger. "You had no right agreeing to a marriage contract with Charles Korwin. I had no knowledge of it, and I will not honor it."

"Oh, really?"

"Really."

"You have no choice in the matter. I've waited long enough. You're twenty-two years old, and you are no nearer to finding an appropriate mate than you were when you finished school."

"I'm not interested in finding a mate! I'm interested in becoming a doctor!" Loralee's heart was pounding. How dare he! She marched to the table, snatched two warm muffins from a basket, wrapped them in a napkin and deposited them in her pocket.

When she looked up at her father, she was sure the look on her face was mutinous. "Understand this right now," she said. "I will not be marrying Charles Korwin or any other man until I am good and ready." She picked up her bag and stormed out of the house.

She was so angry, she couldn't stand still long enough to wait for the stable boy to harness a shay. She walked all the way from Diamond and Church Streets to the O'Toole home on Pine Street.

The walk did her good. By the time she arrived, she had calmed down. She stepped up onto the porch and steeled herself for what she would find inside.

She knocked and waited, and a few seconds later Colin answered the door. His eyes were red and glassy.

"Colin." At the sight of him, Loralee's heart fell. "Oh, Colin, no."

He couldn't speak. He stood with his mouth clamped tightly closed. Loralee pushed past him and stepped into the front room, where she heard the crying immediately. In the back room, Kathleen sat on the bed, rocking back and forth, a small bundle in her arms.

"Oh, God . . ." Loralee felt a wave of nausea sweep over her, and she closed her eyes and took a deep breath, trying to steady herself. She walked into the room.

Kathleen looked up at her. "This mornin' . . . when I woke up . . ." She turned her tear stained face into the blanket. "My baby . . . my sweet, sweet baby . . ."

Loralee set her satchel on the floor and moved to sit beside the two of them. "I'm so sorry Kathleen. So very, very sorry."

Kathleen nodded, unable to speak.

Loralee heard a sound and turned to find Colin in the doorway. "Thank y' for that. Me and Kathleen, we know y' did ever'thin' y' could."

"Oh, Colin," she said, standing and wrapping her arms around him. "I'm so very sorry. I wish there was more I could've done. I—I wanted . . . I tried everything . . ." She dropped her arms from around him and struggled to contain her tears. She couldn't even begin to imagine how the girl's parents must feel.

A knock sounded at the door, and Loralee stopped Colin from answering it with a hand on his arm. "I'll see who it is. You stay with Kathleen," she said.

Colin nodded, grateful, it seemed, for someone to tell him what to do. He sat down beside his wife and wrapped his arms around her and their little girl.

Loralee stepped into the kitchen and opened the door a crack.

Jesse Sinclair stood on the porch. Jesse Sinclair, in all his blue-eyed, broad-shouldered splendor, and all the tumultuous feelings Loralee had experienced the night before came crashing back down on her.

And for reasons that even she did not understand, when she saw him, the tears she had been so valiantly holding back suddenly spilled.

He knew before she even spoke. "Oh, God . . ."

Loralee nodded her head. She stepped out onto the porch and closed the door behind her. A sob escaped her, and Jesse's arms flew around her.

"Shhh . . . I know, honey, I know," he murmured into her hair. He clutched her tightly against him, one hand cradling her head, the other wrapped tightly around her shoulders.

Their embrace was entirely inappropriate. After what had happened between them last night, she should have sooner spat at him than looked at him. Loralee knew that, but right now, she needed comfort. So she stood on the O'Tooles' porch wrapped in his arms and took whatever solace he was able to provide.

"When did it happen?"

Loralee swallowed before she answered. "Kathleen found her this morning."

"Oh, Jesus . . ." His arms tightened around her, eliminating the small space that had been remaining between them. Loralee's cheek rested against his chest, and she closed her eyes.

Who was she kidding? It was not just comfort she was taking from him. She breathed in the scent of him through a soft, flannel shirt. He smelled spicy, almost minty, as though he had just washed and shaved. And his chest, his hard, muscled chest heaved beneath her ear, much the same way it had last night when—

Loralee's eyes flew open. What in the name of heaven was she doing indulging in such decadent thoughts? She sniffed and pulled herself away from him. "I'm sorry. I shouldn't have . . . It's just that, Maggie's been . . ." Her thoughts came out half-formed, and she couldn't seem to find the strength to make more sense of what she was saying. How could she make sense of a baby dying, no matter how much strength she'd been able to find?

And how could she fight this attraction she was feeling when all she wanted to do was fly right back into the warmth of his arms?

She looked down at his hands grasping hers. He rubbed his thumbs against her skin, and Loralee thought about those same hands pressed against her back, buried in her hair, touching and caressing.

"I have to go back inside," she said hurriedly, yanking her hands out of his grasp and wiping her wet cheeks with the back of her fingers. He made her think of things she had absolutely no business thinking about. The smartest thing for her to do would be to put some distance between them.

She couldn't afford a reckless love affair with a playboy who'd probably already forgotten about the few kisses they had shared. She would not jeopardize her future by falling for a man who would love her then leave her. She would not jeopardize her future by falling for any man. Her dreams were too important to her.

The trouble was, she'd never before been tempted. And, having been tempted by a taste of the feelings Jesse was able to stir in her, she had to keep reminding herself not to think of his kisses as an appetizer; they were not a sample of the full-course that would follow. They were just kisses. Kisses she'd do well to forget about.

"I have to go," she said again, turning her back to him and reaching for the doorknob.

"I'll wait here for you. Offer my condolences."

She stopped in her rush. He'd wait for her?

What did he mean by doing a thing like that? Loralee stared at him while her mind raced. What did it matter, anyway, what Jesse's motives were? The question was, what were her own motives? Why was she willing to risk her heart to this man? What was it, exactly, that she felt for him?

The answer came quickly. She felt an undeniable pull towards him, had felt it even before she'd known who he was.

He would wait for her? How else could she answer? What else could she say?

"I won't be long." *What are you doing? That man is danger-ous to your heart!* But she pushed the thoughts aside, knowing that, danger or no danger, she wanted to find out just exactly how strong his hold over her was. It was only a matter of a minute or two before she reappeared.

In silence, they stepped down off the porch and began walk-ing, side by side.

"Let me carry that for you," he said, reaching out for her bag. "It looks heavy."

She handed it over without any protest. "It is heavy." Their fingertips brushed as she slid the handle off her hand and onto his. "Thank you," she said.

Loralee looked down and watched the toes of her black work boots as they kicked out from beneath the hem of her solid blue dress. Beside her, Jesse's feet, wearing black engineer boots, moved slowly, taking one step for every two of hers. "How are you holding up?" he asked.

"Better than Maggie's parents."

Jesse shook his head in understanding. "It's hard."

She waited a few seconds before she asked the question that had been on her mind from the minute she'd opened the door and found him standing on the porch. "Why did you come?"

"My father asked me to keep a close eye on them. He's worried about Kathleen, what with her being so close to her time."

"Oh." An honest answer. Honest, but disappointing.

"And I was hoping to see you."

"Oh!" she said again. He was hoping to see her?

"I wanted to apologize for my behavior last night. I was completely out of line, and I'm very sorry."

Loralee could feel her cheeks beginning to flush at the mention of last night. She glanced up at him quickly, but he was looking straight ahead. "Your apology is accepted, and I offer one of my own."

"What for?"

"What for? Any number of things. You're not the only one who was out of line last night." Loralee thought about the way she had taunted him. She'd *wanted* to be kissed. She just hadn't been prepared for the way a few stolen kisses could make a person feel. She shook her head as if to dispel the troubling thoughts from her mind. "Suffice it to say that we're both sorry it happened. Let's put it in the past."

"That would make you feel better?"

"It would."

He turned his head and stared down at her. She could feel his eyes on her, but she would not, *could not*, meet his gaze.

"I can try to put it in the past, if that makes you feel better about what happened," he said. "And I deeply regret that my actions caused you any misgivings. But I *won't* say that I'm sorry it happened.''

Her heart pounded, but she kept her sights straight ahead, and after what felt like an eternity, he looked away.

''Can I ask you a question?''

Loralee struggled to find her voice. ''Of course.''

''Do you believe in God?''

Of all the questions he could have asked, this was one Loralee was not expecting. ''Of course I believe in God,'' she said, shocked that he would even ask such a thing. ''Don't you?''

''I do,'' he said, nodding his head, as though he had to convince her. He paused before going on. ''I have to believe in God, because I believe in heaven, and there wouldn't be a heaven without God, would there?''

''No, I don't suppose there would be.''

''And, no heaven . . . well . . . there just has to be heaven. There has to be.''

She looked up at him surprised by the intensity she heard in his voice. He was staring off into the distance, thinking about something all together different than what they were discussing, she was sure.

''Why do you suppose God would take away such a tiny baby?'' he asked absently.

''I don't know.'' It was something Loralee had asked herself many times, being, as she was, involved with so many sick children. ''It seems senseless, but maybe it's not. Maybe if we could have seen into Maggie's future we would have seen even greater suffering. Maybe He took her now to spare her that.''

''I never thought of it that way.''

''I tell myself that whenever I lose a child, and, unfortunately, that happens quite often.''

They had walked from Pine all the way down Chestnut Street, and now stood in front of St. Gabriel's church, where the congregation was already filing in. By some unspoken agreement, Jesse and Loralee joined the other worshipers and entered the church together, even though Loralee hadn't intended to attend Mass. St. Gabriel's was not the church to which the Vanders belonged.

Loralee took great comfort in having Jesse by her side. She had never been to Mass so soon after losing a patient and found the experience to be very healing. She felt closer to Maggie, as though the bond between them was not completely severed.

When the Mass ended, and people were beginning to fill the aisles, Loralee and Jesse followed the flow of people out onto the sidewalk.

"I'd better get back," she said, holding her hand out for her bag.

"Me, too." He deposited the heavy bag onto her hand.

"Thank you for the shoulder," she said, with a weak smile.

He was looking at her, studying her face with those incredible blue eyes of his, but he said nothing. Finally, Loralee took a step backwards, increasing the distance between them, and he blinked his eyes. The spell was broken.

" 'Bye," she said.

" 'Bye."

She turned and started walking away from him. It was odd, but she didn't feel the least bit uncomfortable. Only this morning, she'd been mortified at the thought of ever having to see him again.

But now, she was thankful that she had. He wasn't a horrible person. He was actually a caring, sensitive man.

She walked slowly toward Doc Farley's office. She wanted to tell him about Maggie, if he was there, or leave him a note, if he was not.

Then she'd go back home to face her father.

Twilight in June was possibly the most perfect time of the most perfect days of the year. And Sunday evenings, in particular, were the best. Sunday was the day most people spent with their family and friends, wandering through the woods to pick huckleberries, gathering in fields for games of baseball, relaxing on the one and only day they didn't have to work.

This Sunday evening, however, the front porch of the Sinclair home was a decidedly gloomy place to be.

"I just keep thinking about Kathleen finding her," Elizabeth said, dabbing at her eyes. "She must be absolutely heart-broken."

"It's not right that a mother should have to see a thing like that," Stephen said, staring blankly at the floor.

Jesse listened to the conversation, but had hardly spoken at all since coming out to join his parents a few minutes earlier. A child dying of whooping cough was a common incident. In fact, half of all children born never lived to celebrate their second birthday, and everyone knew someone who had lost a baby to some dread disease. Jesse himself could easily count at least a dozen families he knew that had lost a child.

So why was this particular loss affecting him so deeply?

He shifted in his chair, trying to find a comfortable place. Stephen and Elizabeth's voices filtered through his thoughts, but Jesse's mind was somewhere else.

His thoughts had leapt back in time twenty years, to the day Samuel Fedosh, Jesse's natural father, had been killed in a mining accident. Jesse'd only been five years old, but he could still hear his mother's heart-wrenching cries when she'd heard the news. Like Kathleen, she'd been close to delivering a child.

Not close enough, however, and the child Jesse and his two sisters had helped her deliver three days later was small. Too small, the neighbor lady had said, when Jesse had finally gone to fetch her.

But his mother had been determined to save that child. It was all she had left of her husband. The boy, Jesse's brother John, had lived.

But his mother had poured every ounce of her strength into making sure that that baby survived. In the end, she just hadn't possessed enough strength to sustain two. Jesse remembered standing beside her coffin as it was lowered into the ground, and hearing one of the women say that his mother had died of a broken heart.

He hadn't known what that meant, and by the time he was old enough to figure it out, he and John had been firmly ensconced in the Sinclair family. Thinking about his parents' deaths had hurt too much, and, besides, he had a new family who loved him very much. With a child's uncanny sense of self-preservation, he had pushed the few memories he had of his first family as deep inside as he could. Remembering was too painful.

And this was the way Jesse had found to survive. He never let his memories surface.

Today's events, however, had shattered his resolve. Jesse'd been thinking about Sam and Mary Fedosh all day. The people who had given him life. The man his mother had loved too much to go on living without.

"Now I believe it is possible," he murmured.

"What's possible?" Elizabeth asked.

Jesse looked up at her, disoriented and wondering how she had known what he was thinking.

It wasn't until she asked, "Now you believe what's possible, Jesse?" that he realized he'd spoken out loud.

He pushed himself up in his chair and cleared his throat. He hadn't ever told the Sinclairs what he'd overheard at his mother's burial. He examined their faces now and wondered if he should.

"Are you all right?" Stephen asked.

"Yeah," Jesse said, nodding his head. "I just . . ." He didn't want to cause these two people any pain. They *were* his parents, and he chose his words carefully. "I've been thinking about Sam and Mary today."

He watched as Elizabeth's eyebrows lifted and her shocked eyes filled with tears, as though she was afraid, after all these years, that she might lose Jesse after all. Stephen reached out and rested his hand on her arm, and she looked at him, blinking quickly.

"What have you been thinking about them?" Stephen asked.

"I just . . ." He hesitated, not wanting to hurt Elizabeth with his words.

"You can tell us anything, Jess," she said, and this time, Jesse was sure that she had read his thoughts.

He nodded his head and took a long, deep breath before he spoke. "I don't remember a whole lot about them, but I do remember some things. I remember her crying when they came to tell us about the . . . about the fire. I remember Johnny being born. I remember standing at her graveside. And I remember hearing someone say that she had died of a broken heart. She'd mourned him until her heart broke from the pain of it. And then she died."

"Oh, Jesse," Elizabeth said. Her eyes had welled up with tears again, but, although Jesse was profoundly sad, his own eyes were dry.

"I was never sure before that that was possible. But after talking with Colin this afternoon, I believe it could happen."

Colin had come to the house to say that he would be back to work on Wednesday. He'd been in a hurry to return to Kathleen, whom, he said, was in a bad way. He'd had a hard time taking Maggie away from her, and when he had left, she'd been in the rocking chair, holding the child's empty blanket in her arms.

"She'll pull through," Stephen said.

Jesse nodded. "I think she will. I think the new baby will be good for her. I know it won't replace Maggie, but it'll be a baby for her to love."

"I want you to see to it that Maggie's doctor bills are paid. Anonymously, if possible."

Jesse looked up at his father and nodded his head. "I'll take care of it." He looked at his parents for a few seconds. He'd been lucky to have been loved by them, and he loved them just as much in return. But still, they hadn't given him life . . .

He pushed out of his seat. "I'm gonna go in," he said. "I have some work to do." He wanted to be alone.

"Don't work too late," Elizabeth said.

Jesse bent to kiss her cheek. "I won't. Good night, Mother. 'Night, Dad."

He walked into the house and into the library, closing the door firmly behind himself. He had no work that could not wait until tomorrow.

He did, however, have some thinking to do. He sat down in the cool leather chair that was behind the desk. In the silence of the library, the creaks and sighs that escaped the chair as he settled his weight into it were as loud as the rumble of thunder. He rested his head back, he closed his eyes, and he dug into his past.

Jesse dug down far enough that he replayed memories he hadn't even known he had. He let his guard down long enough that the feelings came rushing back in, so new, and so overwhelming, that he felt he might drown. He opened his heart just enough that he was sure all the love Sam had for Mary was flowing through his own veins.

He sat in the library, in the fading twilight, and he remembered.

He remembered.

And he cried.

"How could you have done such a thing? *Why* would you have done such a thing?" Loralee shouted.

"It's done all the time, Loralee," Edward said, with a wave of his hand. "Parents know what's best for their child—"

"I'm not disputing that fact, Papa, but I am not a child anymore!" She was so angry she felt like stomping her feet, childish reaction or not.

"Charles comes from a good family—a family with plenty of money of their own. I don't have to worry that he's marrying you to get his hands on Vander Holdings."

"He has money," she said flatly. "That is not a good enough reason for me to marry him."

"No? And what would be good enough for you?"

"What about love?" Loralee shouted.

"Love?" Edward spat the word at her as though it disgusted him. "That just proves how little you know about marriage. Love hasn't got a thing to do with it." He looked at Fiona, who sat on the sofa doing needlepoint, seemingly oblivious to the shouting match going on. His glance seemed to say, "See? I married *her*, didn't I?"

Loralee bit back her response, knowing that it would hurt her mother to belabor the point. "What about the fact that I don't want to marry him, Papa?" she asked softly, thinking about Charles's behavior the night before. He'd been mean. He'd been downright frightening. "Forget about loving him. I don't even like Charles." She considered mentioning his attack, but quickly decided against it. Edward might only use it as an opportunity to question her own integrity. And he'd be furious to know that she'd been at the Sinclairs', something that, miraculously, he didn't seem to know.

"How can you not like him? He's well educated, he's close to your own age, and I would imagine there are plenty of eligible young ladies out there who would even say that he's handsome!"

"None of that means anything to me," Loralee whispered, laying her hand on her father's arm. Maybe a little sensitivity would get through to Edward. "I haven't met anyone yet that I'd—"

She stopped midsentence as she thought of Jesse, as he'd been this morning. Strong, caring and good-looking. And waiting for her. *Waiting for her.* Loralee took a deep breath and tried not to think about how good it felt to be held in his arms.

She amended her wording. "I'm not ready to get married. And, when I am, I'd like to choose my own husband."

Edward looked at his daughter before he spoke, and, for a few blissful moments, Loralee thought that perhaps she had gotten through to him. But when he spoke, her hopes were dashed.

"You have been promised in marriage to Charles Korwin. I'd suggest you begin getting used to the idea." He turned and walked out of the room and out of the house.

CHAPTER FIVE

"Hey, kid, wanna earn a nickel?"

The boy jerked his head up. A whole nickel. Jesse could see how badly the child wanted it.

Suddenly, the kid turned suspicious. "What do I gotta do?" He eased back a step and planted his hands in his pockets, adopting a stance that said he didn't care one way or another about that nickel. Smart kid.

But Jesse had already seen the hunger in his eyes. "All you have to do is take this envelope across the street to Doc Farley's office. Give it to the girl who works there, then meet me around the corner."

"That's all?"

"That's all."

The kid gave Jesse a good once-over. "Why can't you take it over there yourself?"

Jesse chuckled. "I just can't. Let's leave it at that." He held out his hand, palm up. "Look, do you want the nickel or not? Because I can get someone else—"

"No! No, I'll do it." He licked his lips, eager, now, for his adventure to begin. He held out his hand and waited.

Jesse hesitated a few seconds, for good measure. The kid was so excited, he looked just about ready to pee in his pants. Finally, he put the sealed envelope in the boy's outstretched hand. "Now, remember, give it to the girl, then get out of there. She's gonna want to know who gave you this," he said nodding toward the tightly held package. "You don't know, got it? Got it?"

"Got it."

"I'll be right around the corner waiting with your nickel," Jesse said, pointing to a spot where he could watch without being seen. "Go on."

The kid nodded his head, and took a deep breath, as though he was getting ready to do battle. He scooted across the street, and Jesse moved toward their arranged meeting place. From just around the corner of the building, he watched as the kid entered Doc Farley's office and rushed back out, not ten seconds later. His hands were empty. Jesse smiled.

The door opened again, and Loralee stepped outside. Jesse jerked his head out of her view. "Wait!" she called. "Wait!" But the boy ran like he was being chased by the devil himself. He rounded the corner and slammed into Jesse.

"Whoa!" Jesse said, steadying the child by the shoulders. "Slow down!"

The little boy started to twist away, but then realized who held him. "I did it, where's my nickel?" he asked, thrusting his hand out.

"She say anything?"

"Not before I ran, she din't. Where's my nickel?"

"Hold on, hold on." Jesse fished in his pocket and withdrew a single coin. When the boy would have grabbed it, Jesse yanked his hand away.

"Hey!"

"Now, listen, here. A whole nickel is an awful lot of money for a boy your age."

"I'm nine years old!" the boy said, obviously insulted to be thought less than a man.

"Even still," Jesse said, "a nickel is a lot of money. Let's make a deal—"

"I din't agree to no deal!"

"Pipe down! I'll give you the whole thing. But I think it would be an awful nice gesture if you took a penny or two home to your ma. That would be the manly thing to do, you know." Jesse knew his last comment wasn't really fair. That the boy wanted to be thought of as a man was clear. And by the condition of his clothing, it was also clear that his mother would welcome extra pennies.

The child looked at Jesse, assessing the situation. Right now, he had no nickel. But if he agreed to the deal . . . It didn't take long for him to reach a decision.

"I'll only spend three cents."

"You sure, now?"

"Yep. No mor'n three cents."

"All right." Jesse dropped the coin into the boy's hand. "You make sure you tell your ma you earned that money fair and square."

But the child was already running. "I will! Thanks, mister!" His feet pounded the dirt roadway, sending up a trail of dust.

What a thrill the boy would've had if he'd known that inside the envelope were fifty one-dollar bills. Fifty dollars and a note instructing that the money be put toward Maggie O'Toole's bill.

Maggie was being buried this morning. Jesse'd left the house early in order to take care of his "errand," and had arranged to meet up with Stephen and Elizabeth outside St. Gabriel's Church. He glanced back toward Dr. Farley's door, but Loralee was nowhere in sight. He turned and began walking toward the church.

It was almost nine-thirty, and downtown had suddenly come alive. The farmers hauled their fresh produce to the various corner stores each morning, and the street was full of their carts. Of course, this early in the season the pickin's were still mighty slim. Summer in northeastern Pennsylvania never took a firm hold until the beginning of June. Plant too early, and you'd lose your crop to frost. The fields had not yet yielded much, but the farmers brought what they had, eager to put an end to another long winter with no income.

Jesse crossed Broad Street offering ''hello's'' and ''good morning's'' to everyone he passed. He'd grown up in this town. It was his home, and though the population had recently swelled with immigrants as the need for miners and laborers increased, he still knew most of the faces.

Part of Jesse's job was to ensure the continued good reputation that Valley Railroad had always enjoyed. Stephen had laid the groundwork through years of proving not only that he provided good service, but also that he cared about his employees.

And now that Jesse was being groomed to take the reins of Valley, Stephen put him out among the workers whenever possible. Sometimes that meant that Jesse shoveled coal into a firebox all day in order to cover for a sick employee. Sometimes it meant standing alongside a new hiree and training him personally. And when shipping schedules had to be rearranged and they found themselves shorthanded, it meant that Jesse operated a train.

In the three years since Jesse had graduated from Lehigh University, he'd worked virtually every job at Valley Railroad. Willingly. Eagerly. He didn't do it to learn the workings of the company he would inherit. That part was easy. He did it to prove to himself and to everyone else that twenty years ago, Stephen Sinclair had not made a mistake.

He rounded the corner and saw his parents standing on the church steps.

"Sorry," he said, running his hand through his hair to push it out of his eyes. "You waiting long?"

"Just got here," Stephen said. "You missed your friend, though."

"Who?"

"Loralee. She's inside already."

"She's inside?" Jesse asked. He turned to look back at the way he had just come. "But I left before she did."

"You walked. She came in a carriage."

"And she wasn't dropped from a carriage," Elizabeth said excitedly. "She *drove* a carriage. By herself!"

Jesse smiled as he thought about Loralee leaping from the side of the carriage unassisted. He wondered if she had kicked anything upon landing.

"What's so funny?" his mother demanded.

Jesse shook his head, still smiling. "She is a very determined young lady. I do believe she could accomplish anything she set her mind to."

Elizabeth raised one eyebrow. "Even, dare I say the words, spark *your* interest?"

Jesse didn't answer. His mother knew him well.

"My, my, my," she said, as she turned and began making her way up the stairs.

Jesse and Stephen followed her, sobering as they stepped into the church. They took a seat about midway back, and Jesse found that he had a clear view of Loralee.

She was sitting next to Kathleen. The women kept their heads close together, murmuring quietly to each other.

The priest began to pray, and Jesse looked toward the altar. But try as he might, he could not keep his gaze from wandering to the back of Loralee's head. She'd been so upset the day Maggie had died. He wondered if she had anyone to comfort her, the way she was so clearly comforting Kathleen.

Jesse thought about Sunday morning and the way Loralee had turned to him for comfort. He'd wanted to stand on that porch all day, just holding her, and rocking her and whispering soothing words into her ear.

I want to be the one she turns to. Not just this time—every time. And for as long as she needs it. The realization hit him like a blow to the gut. His heart began to pound.

He barely knew the girl! And, yet, he was as certain of his instincts as he had always been.

The service ended, and the mourners left the pews, moving slowly out of the church and around back to the cemetery where Maggie would be buried.

The crowd huddled together while the priest prayed over Maggie's tiny casket. It was over quickly, and Colin and Loralee, their own eyes tear-filled, led Kathleen away.

Jesse watched them leaving, and he was sure every person there shared his thoughts: please don't let all this grief hurt the baby.

After taking Elizabeth back home and changing into jeans and a clean shirt, Jesse headed back to work, distracted by thoughts of Loralee. Now that he knew this was more than a mild flirtation, he wanted to make his intentions known. He wanted to stake his claim right now!

But he didn't even know where she lived. Didn't know her full name. Knew nothing about her at all.

How had she come to be at his birthday party? With nearly the entire town invited, it was hard to say. She'd been with Suzanne Becker, but since Robert Becker owned the local apothecary, that made sense. Dr. Farley probably ordered all his supplies through Becker and, with Loralee as his apprentice, it followed that she would know Suzanne.

Jesse didn't know much about Loralee, but he did know where she worked. He swore to himself that he'd give it a few days before he approached her.

Truth be told, Jesse needed a little time to sort out the feelings she stirred in him. He climbed the steps to the building that housed his father's office determined to concentrate fully on his job. Lose himself in his work. Push Loralee out of his mind, at least for a few days.

Sure, Jesse, he thought to himself with a chuckle. Push Loralee anywhere? He thought again about her tiny foot lashing out at her damnable black bag. That was one girl who would refuse to be ordered to do anything.

He swung open the door and hopped up into the lobby with a new spring to his step that hadn't been there before. And even though he felt positively *ridiculous* walking around with a big, goofy grin on his face, he couldn't seem to stop himself from smiling.

He'd finally found The One.

By nine o'clock Monday night, Loralee was ready for bed. It had been an emotionally draining day. As if attending Maggie's funeral hadn't been difficult enough, she'd also been trying to determine Jesse's reason for avoiding her.

She knew that he was responsible for paying Maggie's bill. After opening the package and discovering its contents, she had hurried to the door, hoping to catch the little boy who had delivered it. And as she passed the window, she had seen him cross the street and hurry toward a man standing in the shadows halfway down the block.

Jesse.

Why had he felt compelled to pay Maggie's bill? And why hadn't he done it in person?

It was upsetting, both the fact that he had intentionally avoided her and the fact that it bothered her so much.

Loralee had been so worried about it that she'd stopped at Suzanne's on the way home. The girls made plans to meet for a picnic supper way out by the sand spring the next day. Loralee wanted privacy when she told her friend about what had happened in the rose garden with Jesse.

She changed into her white nightgown and climbed between the cool sheets. She was tired enough to fall asleep on her feet. But Maggie's cries and Charles's anger and Jesse's kisses kept her from finding slumber.

She pulled the covers up and turned onto her side. Suzanne would know what to do. She'd think of some way to straighten things out. At least, Loralee hoped that she would.

Her life was a shambles. And Loralee didn't know if she could pick up the pieces by herself.

Monday night was clear and bright, with what was left of the full moon washing everything it touched with a luminescent, blue glow. It spilled in through the windows and cut a swath across the bed, where two lovers lingered.

"You'll come to the party, won't you?" she asked, tracing lazy circles from his bare chest to his navel and back up again.

"How can I?"

"You have the connections. It would make perfect sense for you to be here."

"That's not what I meant, and you know it. What I meant was, how can I come here and watch you with him? How will I be able to stand that?" His voice reflected every bit of the pain he felt.

"You'll be able to stand it for the same reason I'll be able to watch you with her. You'll do it because we're both willing to take what little we can of each other."

He knew what she said was true. But still . . . to watch his hand on her back all evening? To be so close as to be able to imagine what they did when they were alone in this house? The thought of it almost killed him.

"So, you'll come?" she asked, interrupting his thoughts.

He looked down at her, resting her head against his chest, and, again, he cursed the fates for keeping them apart, when it was so right that they be together.

What could he say?

"I'll come."

CHAPTER SIX

Jesse lifted his jacket from the back of a chair and pushed his arms through the sleeves. It was Friday night, and he had promised to join his brother at a party being hosted by Zachary Tyler, a financier who was looking to invest in Valley Railroad's proposed passenger line. But, Jesse wasn't exactly in a party frame of mind.

He'd managed to stay away from Loralee all week, which was exactly what he had set out to do. Jesse hadn't realized, though, just how obsessed he'd become with Loralee until he faced attending a party without her.

It was something he'd done hundreds of times, usually with great relish. Parties meant women, and even though most of the social functions he attended had, in some way, something to do with business, Jesse always managed to find time to enjoy the women.

Jesse loved women They had some indefinable quality that perfectly complemented everything he was. They were the exact opposite of everything that was male. Soft, where men were hard. Smooth, where men were rough. Shy, where men were bold. The differences were intoxicating.

And, it wasn't simply about lust. It was the very essence of womanhood that delighted him. Not only the way they looked the first time passion took control of them, but the way they looked with a baby on their arm and a toddler hiding in their skirts. Not just the way they felt beneath a man's body, but the way they felt light in your arms when you helped them down from a carriage. It wasn't only the way they smelled when they dabbed rose water behind their delicate ears. It was the way they smelled after kneading bread dough on a warm summer morning. Slightly yeasty, slightly perspired, and one hundred percent woman.

And he'd never before prepared for an evening out, and known with absolute certainty, that his hunger for the fairer sex would be left unsatisfied at the end of the night.

Because the only woman he wanted wouldn't be there. The Tyler party would be exclusive. A working girl like Loralee would never have been invited, and, even if she was, she'd never be able to afford another gown.

No, her one night as Cinderella had come and gone. And Jesse didn't feel like playing Prince Charming to anyone else.

With a sigh of resignation, he checked the time on his pocket watch, looked in the mirror and pushed his hair out of his eyes one more time. It fell forward almost instantly.

He stepped out into the hallway and met John.

"Hey, Jess. Ready?" he asked, rubbing the palms of his hands together in sweet anticipation of the adoring attentions of his female fans.

Jesse smiled halfheartedly.

"What's wrong?" John asked.

"Nothing, really. I'm just not in the mood to go out."

"Not in the mood? Zachary Tyler throws some of the best parties in town. The man might be old, but he knows how to have a good time.'' John stood looking at Jesse as if he thought his brother must have lost his mind.

"I know. I'm just . . . well, the person I really want to see won't be there.''

"So? The place will be overrun with women, Jesse. Beautiful, eligible women. I'm sure you'll see something else that might appeal to you.''

Jesse looked at his brother, who obviously didn't understand. Somehow, he didn't feel like explaining it to him. "I'll just talk with Zachary about our plans and then leave. I trust you'll manage to find your own way home?'' John would be surrounded by a throng of women in no time. He'd watched his older brother and learned well. And, at age twenty, Jesse knew John couldn't imagine ever wanting anything more.

"I'll manage. But you're gonna miss out on a good time,'' he warned.

"I'll take my chances.''

The two brothers turned and made their way down the hall, one bursting with anticipation over the evening, the other downright dreading it.

Charles held out his hand, ever the gentleman. Loralee took it and climbed down from the carriage, managing, as she did, to avoid acknowledging his presence in any way.

"Didn't you listen to a word I said to you on the way here?'' Charles barked the words at her, his mouth locked into a deceptively charming smile. He squeezed her hand hard enough to make her wince, and still, he held the smile in place. "What did I say, Loralee?''

She hesitated long enough to be awarded another bone-crushing squeeze of her hand. "You . . . you said you wanted a pleasant partner for the evening,'' she whispered.

"So, you were listening,'' he said, his voice dripping sarcasm. "Do you think that ignoring me qualifies as being pleasant?"

"I'm not ignoring you, Charles," she said quietly, as he led her toward the Tylers' front porch.

He stopped her in the middle of the path and turned toward her, holding both her hands in his own and looking down at her with the smile he had perfected. It was the one that looked sincere to everyone except the person it was bestowed upon. It was the smile with which he allowed the veil to drop from before his eyes. Loralee looked away.

"We will be married soon," he whispered. "After our wedding, I will do whatever needs to be done to teach you to display the proper respect for your husband. I think it would be in your best interests to use your reprieve to regain my favor."

Loralee looked up at him to find that he had been smiling at her the whole time he was delivering his threat.

"I had every reason in the world to be upset with you last weekend, Loralee." He looked at her as though she were carrying some dreadful disease. "Dancing with another man . . . kissing him. Tonight," he said contemptibly, "try to act like a lady." He turned away from her as though he could no longer stand the sight of her and began walking.

Charles didn't want a lady. He wanted an ornament, a plaything. Loralee bit her tongue, and hoped that she'd spot Suzanne. After all, it was because of her that Loralee had come to this party at all.

At their picnic, Loralee had spilled the entire story to Suzanne. Everything, from Jesse's kisses in the garden to the secret betrothal agreement to Charles' terrifying behavior in his carriage to her grief over losing Maggie. She'd reiterated her stance on marrying Charles, confessed the surprising strength of her feelings for Jesse and despaired over his avoidance of her.

And, as usual, Suzanne had come through for her friend. She offered just the right amount of light-hearted envy over

Jesse's attentions, undying support in Loralee's fight to free herself of Charles, and genuine tears of sadness as they spoke of the tiny baby who had died, despite Loralee's best efforts.

But, most of all, she had come up with several very good reasons why Jesse had avoided seeing Loralee. Perhaps he gave the money anonymously, she'd said, because he knew the O'Tooles would refuse it otherwise. And maybe he hadn't been avoiding her at all, but had just been very busy. In fact, Suzanne had said, maybe he would even be at the party tonight!

And that was the only reason Loralee had finally given in when her father insisted that she attend this party with Charles.

He led her in through the main doors, pausing long enough to scan the crowd and locate the host.

"Mr. Tyler, how are you?" Charles asked. He held out his hand, offering basic politeness, but none, Loralee noticed, of the charm he usually exuded.

"Charles! Well, how nice to see you," he said, ending the handshake and peering around the young couple. "Isn't your father with you?" Charles's father and Zachary Tyler had been friends and business associates for the past twenty-five years.

"No. I was invited to the Vanders' for an early supper, and I left from there. Father should be here shortly." He turned toward Loralee, pushing her forward a bit as though offering her for inspection. "And this lovely young lady is Miss Loralee Vander, my fiancée."

Zachary raised his eyebrows. "Fiancée?" He looked at Loralee, his gaze unabashedly sweeping her entire body. He looked long and attentively, lingering where it was obvious he found the most pleasure. "Congratulations, my boy. She is lovely . . . very lovely indeed," he said quietly. His eyes sparkled as he boldly looked at Loralee's breasts. He spoke to Charles, while he continued to admire Loralee's curves. "I've found marriage to be a wonderful institution." His gaze wandered to a beautiful young woman standing about ten feet away.

She was engaged in an animated conversation with a strik-

ingly handsome young man. The man reached for her hand and
continued talking, and the woman threw back her head and
laughed, a deep, throaty sound.

"If you will excuse me, I need to greet some other guests.
Charles," he said, reaching out for another handshake. "Miss
Vander." Zachary reached for Loralee's hand and bent to press
a kiss upon it. His eyes devoured every inch of her young body
on the way back up, and then he looked directly into her eyes.
"A most lovely young lady, indeed," he said. Then he turned
and melted into the crowd.

"Charles! Did you see what he did?" Loralee demanded,
her face burning with embarrassment.

"No, Loralee. What did he do?" he asked.

"Well, he . . . when he kissed my hand . . . he looked at
me," she stammered.

"He looked at you? Well, of course he looked at you. It
would be rude not to look at someone to whom you are being
introduced. Don't you agree?"

"But, it was the *way* he looked at me. Didn't you notice
it?" she asked, turning towards him.

"Loralee—"

"He was *leering* at me, Charles. He was looking at me like—"
She turned her head just in time to see Zachary Tyler place
his hand on the young woman's waist. And, if that wasn't
enough, he dropped his hand into the folds of her skirt, making
no pretense of the fact that he was fondling her bottom.

"Charles!" Loralee whispered, her hand flying to her mouth.
"Did you see that? He just . . . just . . . touched that woman!"

Charles watched Zachary, and the look on his face was
murderous. "He has every right to, though I don't think he
needs to be so blatant about it."

"What?" Loralee demanded. Charles must have lost his
mind. Or maybe he hadn't, she thought, since she now knew
firsthand about his lack of respect for women.

"That's Abigail Tyler. Zachary's wife."

Loralee turned back toward the beautiful young woman. Zachary had removed his hand, and they now stood side by side, their backs toward Charles and Loralee.

"But she's so young."

"I know."

"But ... how old is he?" Loralee asked quietly. "Why would she marry someone so old? Why would her father let her do such a thing?" she asked.

Charles hadn't taken his eyes off of Abigail. "He's seventy-two. She's twenty-two."

"Seventy-two!"

Charles nodded his head. "And, as for her father," he looked down at Loralee, "he's a miner, works for Vander Holdings, as a matter of fact. He was never quite able to understand the fact that rutting makes babies. He's got ten mouths to feed." He looked back toward Abigail. "She could have married Attila the Hun for all he cared. A daughter who marries means one less person around the dinner table. And a daughter who marries into wealth could very well mean a little prosperity."

Loralee watched Charles as he spoke. "You seem to know a lot about her."

He pulled his gaze away just long enough to glance at Loralee before it drifted back to the beautiful Abby. "Her family belongs to our church. We had Bible school together from the time we were old enough to read." He left it at that, apparently unwilling to divulge anything further, though Loralee could easily see that Charles and Abby had more than a passing acquaintance with each other.

"I could use a drink," he said abruptly, ushering Loralee through the heavy crowd.

They passed Frank, one of Charles's long-time friends, who called out, "Charles! Hey, Charles!"

Charles and Loralee turned to find Frank standing with a giggling girl on either side of him, which, in light of the way he was swaying, was probably a good thing.

"Hey, Frank. Having fun?" Charles asked as he stared at the ample-breasted girls that were supporting his friend. His gaze was rude, insulting even.

"Damn straight, I'm havin' fun!" Frank yelled, oblivious to the smirks and smiles of the women standing nearby.

The blond girl standing on his right poked him in the ribs. "Frank! Watch your tongue! Why, Mr. Tyler will have you thrown out if he hears you talk like that!"

"Sorry, honey," Frank drawled, drooling over the full curves that filled out the top of her dress. "I'm just no damn good."

"Fraaaank!" she said, rolling her eyes.

"All right, buddy, I'm headed for the bar." Charles turned toward Loralee, and said, "Stay with him till I get back, and don't let him get thrown out." It wasn't a request. It was an order. He glared at her until, nervously, she looked away. Only then was he satisfied.

Charles walked toward the bar, pausing occasionally to swap greetings with friends and acquaintances. He loved a good party; he rarely turned down an invitation, and he knew just about everyone there.

He'd almost sent his regrets for tonight's affair, but at the last minute found he couldn't do it. Looking without touching was agony, as he'd known it would be. But, at this point, he was so hungry for her that he was willing to settle for whatever crumbs he could get.

As if he had willed her to appear, she suddenly materialized in front of him.

"Hello, Charles."

He drew in his breath, and his eyes locked with hers. Seconds passed where neither of them uttered a word, and yet, volumes passed between them.

"I've missed you," Abby said, her dark eyes filling with tears. "I can barely tolerate standing next to him when I know you're in the room. I never thought it would be this difficult."

Her fingers brushed his arm, fleetingly. She hesitated, as

though she wanted to say more, then silently turned and made her way through the crowd, and he watched her go, out through the foyer doors and toward the large staircase. His heart hammered with each step she took. One step up onto the stairs. Then another. He imagined her slippered feet touching the cold marble stairs. The third step. The fourth.

And then she turned and looked across the crowd, directly into his steel gray eyes.

He was bound to her, as he could be to no other. And as she turned and continued up the stairs, Charles slipped from the crowd. His drink, and Loralee, were completely forgotten.

Jesse was listening to one of Hazleton's biggest braggarts. William Tanner was one of those people who might just as well have been standing in front of a mirror extolling his own virtues. He'd seized upon Jesse when he'd found him standing alone, waiting for his turn to speak with Zachary.

Jesse took another swallow of the brandy in his glass. Maybe if he drank enough, he wouldn't realize how bored he was, or how irritated that he had to act as a sounding board for this self-important idiot Tanner!

Jesse's only reason for coming tonight had been to talk over some business plans with Zachary. So far, he hadn't been able to get near the man, and his patience was wearing thin.

"—and, so you see, it was rightfully mine all along!"

Jesse looked at Tanner blankly. He had no idea what the fool had been ranting about. "Uh-huh," he muttered.

"Some people had doubted that I was the one who . . ." Tanner's voice droned on and on. At this point, Jesse knew he no longer had to feign attentiveness. An occasional "uh-huh" could sustain this conversation for hours.

He looked beyond Tanner's bald head and scanned the crowd. Off to his right were several other local businessmen, each one, like himself, waiting to speak to Zachary. The man had more money than he could spend in ten lifetimes, and having him as an investor in any project guaranteed a cash flow that would virtually ensure a good return, eventually, if not immediately.

Out on the dance floor, couples whirled around the room. The music was lively; Zachary liked to whip up the crowd, and he avoided anything that might subdue his efforts, from the music that was played to the food that was served.

On the left side of the dance floor, he spotted Johnny and several of his friends bombarding a group of young ladies with so much charm and flattery that their blushes could be seen clear across the room. Jesse smiled. John would find his own way home tonight.

And just a little to the left of Johnny's crowd, two very well-endowed girls were trying to support a guy who'd obviously drunk more than he could handle. Standing a few feet away from them, as though she didn't want to be associated with such riffraff, was—

Loralee!

Jesse nearly knocked poor Tanner over with the strength of the pat on the shoulder he gave. "Excuse me." He tossed back the rest of his brandy and took off after Loralee, leaving a sputtering William Tanner in his wake.

He pushed his way through the crowd, never once taking his eyes off of Loralee. He'd wanted to come to grips with what he felt for this girl. He couldn't wait to touch her again.

When he was about twenty feet away from her, she looked straight at him and her eyes lit up.

"Jesse!"

"Hey," he said, coming to a stop in front of her. He ran his hand through his hair, pushing it out of his eyes. She was absolutely beautiful, and the urge to kiss her right here in the middle of the ballroom was almost too strong to fight.

He reached out and took her tiny hand in his much larger one. "Come with me," he said, pulling her past the dance floor, through the foyer, and out the front door.

They slipped around the side of the house, and were lost among the shadows of the towering trees. Thunder rumbled in the sky, promising the rain that had been threatening all day. The air held a certain expectancy, as though all of creation were anticipating the release of cool rain as it burst from the clouds.

Jesse backed her against the trunk of a hundred-year-old oak, his hands diving into her shimmering blond hair. He held her face in his hands, taking in every detail while he moved slowly toward her. "I can't believe you're here," he said.

"I can't believe I'm here, either," she whispered. She was breathing hard from their race through the crowd. He was breathing heavily, too, and it had nothing to do with the speed with which they'd left the house.

His hands still buried in her hair, he flexed his fingertips against her scalp and pulled her forward. Loralee's head dropped back and her eyes slid closed. She wanted to be kissed as much as Jesse wanted to kiss her.

He wasted no time. His mouth came down on hers, and she met him eagerly. Their kiss deepened, binding them together. It fanned the flames of desire, creating an inferno that seared both their hungry souls.

She reached up and held his head with her tiny hands, trapping him in this place where nothing beyond their mouths mattered.

She broke away, kissing him on his cheek, his ear, down his neck. He groaned and pulled her tightly against his chest, his hands roaming freely over her back, his fingers searching out the warmth of her bare skin at the nape of her neck, beneath her hair.

With his thumbs Jesse tilted her head, exposing the sensitive skin of her neck. He bent to gently rub his lips from her ear toward her shoulder, stopping when she drew in her breath. Hovering just above her skin, he teased her with his breath.

He touched her skin with the tip of his tongue. He licked; he nibbled. She was delicious.

The wind in the trees sent the leaves trembling, their edges rustling against one another, the urgency in their dance increasing as the storm moved closer. But the lovers in their arbor took no notice.

She ran her hands across his chest, and Jesse strained toward her.

"Loralee," he whispered, between sips at her mouth. "I need to touch you. Please don't be afraid. Say I can touch you." His voice was ragged, tortured.

Slowly, her fingers slid down the length of his arm until they reached the edge of his sleeve. With the slightest of pressure, she guided his hand to her breast. Her heart pounded against his palm.

Jesse drew back, his eyes taking in her face, her neck, her shoulders. He looked into her eyes, holding her captive, while his hands brushed lightly against the swell of her breasts, the curve of them filling the palms of his hands.

The lightening flashed, a brief warning of the loud crack of thunder that would follow.

Jesse's fingertips moved slowly over the fabric of her dress, and her nipples hardened beneath his touch. She dropped her head back to rest against the tree.

"Oh, Jesse, this is . . ." She breathed deeply, abandoning the rest of her thought. Reaching up, she covered his rough hand with her own, and arched her back away from the tree, leaning further into him.

Loralee reached up and pulled him down for another intoxicating kiss. His hands left her breasts and spread across her back, holding her tightly against his chest. They kissed until their hearts hammered and their breathing became labored.

Jesse pulled away, cradling her head against his chest. "I have to stop," he said, fighting to gain control of his breathing.

She nodded her head against him. "This scares me," she whispered.

"I know." He ran his hand down the back of her head, smoothing the silky hair into place.

"No, I don't think you do. The last time we were together . . ." She pushed against his chest, and he loosened his hold. "It frightened me very much—that's why I ran. But, it wasn't you that scared me. It was the way I reacted to you. I don't even *know* you!" She looked up into his eyes as though looking for answers.

He examined her fair, smooth skin, now flushed to a pink glow. The sparkling green eyes, now wide with the passion she felt. The soft mouth, now bruised and swollen from the pressure of his kisses. She was a beautiful, passionate woman, and Jesse wanted so much more than a kiss.

She dropped her head and buried it against his chest once more.

"Why do I feel like this? I've never felt this way before. I've never *behaved* this way before!" she added, obviously embarrassed by her lack of modesty.

"I know."

"But I've never even—" Her hand flew to her mouth, and she backed away from Jesse. "Oh, no!" She moved beyond his reach.

"What's wrong?" he asked, reaching for her, but she avoided his touch.

"I have to go back!" she said frantically. "He'll be looking for me!" She closed her eyes. "Oh, what have I done?"

"Who? Loralee what—"

"I have to go back, don't you understand? He'll be furious!" She looked around as though searching for an escape.

"Okay! Okay, we'll go back in." He reached for her hand, squeezing it tightly. "Just calm down. You can't go back in there like this." He bent down so that he was closer to eye level with her. "Look at me." She looked into his eyes, and he held her gaze. "Take a deep breath. Everything will be fine. You've done nothing wrong." Loralee did as he commanded.

"There you go. That's better," he said, smiling at her. "You go back in the way we came out. I'll wait a few minutes and follow you."

She looked up at him, hope dawning in her eyes. "You don't think anyone will know we were out here together?"

"Of course not," he said smiling at her gently. "Say you needed some air."

She nodded her head, nervously chewing on her bottom lip. "Okay. He won't know. He won't know."

"No, he won't. Just go in and mingle, and I'll be in in a few minutes." He smiled at her, hoping to reassure her.

"Thank you," she whispered, reaching out to lay her hand upon his cheek. Then she turned and disappeared into the darkness.

Sounds of the party drifted out into the night. Loralee peeked around the corner of the house, and when she found the front door propped wide open, she slipped around the corner, through the foyer and back into the crowd, no one the wiser that she had ever been gone.

A waiter bearing glasses of cold lemonade passed, offering her a drink.

"Thank you," she said, taking the frosty glass and sipping the refreshing liquid from it. She sighed with relief, smiling, now that she was safely back inside. But how long had she been gone? And would Charles have missed her? How long would Jesse wait outside before coming back into the party? He couldn't stay out there much longer. The lightning flashed ever closer.

With that thought, she turned toward the foyer. She was just inside the throng of the crowd, but still had a clear view out through the double doors. She looked toward the front door, which stood propped open, just as it had a minute before when she had passed through it. No one had, as yet, followed her through it.

She stood still, thinking what to do next about finding Charles, when, from the corner of her eye she saw a motion.

From the top of the staircase, a figure had emerged. He paused at the top, as though to ascertain that no one stood in the foyer below. Then he hurriedly descended the stairs, adjusting his necktie and smoothing his hair.

Loralee drew in her breath with surprise. She watched until he had almost reached the bottom of the stairs. She stepped back further into the crowd, then turned and hurried to the other side of the ballroom, bumping elbows and nearly colliding with a waiter in her haste. She offered a muffled "Excuse me," and rushed on.

Something was wrong. Something was terribly wrong. That staircase led upstairs to the private rooms of Zachary Tyler and his wife. No guest should have been up there.

But the man she'd seen hurrying down the stairs was most definitely a guest.

That man was Charles.

Jesse stayed put, watching as Loralee hurried toward the front of the house and disappeared around the corner. He watched for a few more minutes, and when she didn't reappear, he sauntered toward the carriage house, where many of the partygoers' rigs had been hitched.

He found his with no trouble and walked straight to his team, coming up along side the near horse, making much ado about checking on her.

"Good evening, sir," said the stable boy. "Are you wanting your carriage pulled around front?"

"No, no," Jesse said, with his hand resting on the horse. "She was a bit skittish on the way over," he lied. "Just wanted to check on her, what with the thunder and all.'' What he really wanted was some excuse for being outside during a thunderstorm, in the event anyone caught him on his way back in.

''She's been fine all evening, sir.''

''Glad to hear it. You'd better get yourself under cover. Storm's real close,'' he said, gesturing toward the sky.

''I will, sir. Thank you.''

Jesse nodded to the boy and walked back toward the party, wondering how Loralee had fared. Had her father noticed that she was gone? And, if so, had he believed her excuse about needing some air? Jesse hadn't seen her ushered out by an irate parent. She was probably safely back inside watching the other couples spin around the dance floor .

He walked slowly, allowing as much time to elapse as he dared. The lightning flashed ever closer, and the rain would not be far behind. He could barely wait to get back inside so that he could find Loralee, introduce himself to her father and begin courting her properly. She was a charming young lady who deserved better than to be groped while hiding behind a tree. His treatment of her was unforgivable.

He shoved his hands into his pockets, shaking his head and wondering what the hell had gotten into him.

Jesse had rarely been without female companionship since turning sixteen. His years away at Lehigh University had been filled with a parade of beautiful young women. He'd even visited the occasional whorehouse, treating the girls who worked the place more respectfully than their occupation called for.

So why couldn't he keep his hands to himself when he was kissing Loralee? He barely knew her, but he felt a connection to her that he'd never felt with any other woman.

Jesse paused on the front porch before going in, peering up at the sky and wondering if what he felt for Loralee was the something wonderful his mother so wanted him to find.

Strangely enough, the idea didn't terrify him as it had in the past.

With a deep breath, he walked quickly into the foyer just as the clouds burst open, releasing torrents of water.

Jesse's heart pounded as loudly as the thunder as he scanned the crowd, his eyes searching for the woman he was beginning to believe might very well be his future.

Loralee raced through the crowd toward the spot where she had left Frank. She rushed headlong into Suzanne.

"Hey! Slow down!"

"Where's Frank?" Loralee asked breathlessly.

"What?" Suzanne asked, straining to hear. The crowd had doubled in size in the few minutes since the rain began, and the chatter was deafening.

"Frank!" Loralee said, grabbing Suzanne by the arms. "Do you know where he is?"

Suzanne eyed her friend warily. "I have no idea. I haven't seen him. Loralee, what's wrong?"

"There's no time! Come on!"

The two girls forced their way through the seemingly impenetrable wall of people until they finally reached the spot where Loralee had been standing when she'd spotted Jesse. There, on a chair against the wall, sat Frank. Or rather, slept Frank. He'd apparently been abandoned by his two companions, who, no doubt, were looking for someone with a little more pep than Frank was exhibiting, slumped forward as he was.

Loralee hurried to his side, throwing orders at Suzanne. "Hurry up! Pull him up in the chair, he's sliding off."

"Loralee, if you think—"

"Suzanne! Just do it, now! I'll explain later!"

Suzanne hesitated for a second, then shaking her head, helped Loralee boost Frank up into the seat. He didn't even stir.

"There—"

"I am so sorry."

Loralee spun around to find Charles hurrying toward her, an apologetic expression on his face.

"Charles!" Loralee exclaimed, pressing a hand to her heart. It was beating so hard from her race across the ballroom that there was no way to hide it. She was breathing entirely too fast, and she couldn't stop it.

"What's the matter? You're all out of breath," he said, looking from her to Suzanne and back again.

"Well, of course we are!" Loralee exclaimed, looking toward Suzanne and silently urging her to play along. Suzanne began fanning herself and breathing loudly.

Charles looked at both girls, and the suspicion he always felt whenever Loralee spent time with Suzanne registered clearly on his face.

"Frank is not a small man, you know," Loralee said, making a great show of trying to regain her composure. "Where on earth were you? He started sliding out of the chair," she gestured toward Suzanne, "and it was only with Suzanne's help that I managed to keep him from crashing onto the floor!"

"Really, Charles, you should speak to your friend about his overindulgence," Suzanne threw in. She might not have known exactly what was going on, but she knew enough to see that Loralee had the upper hand.

Charles glared at her then turned back toward Loralee. He held out his hand and took hers, squeezing it gently. "I'm so sorry. I had no idea that he'd drunk that much. What happened to the other two girls?"

"They left when it became clear that Frank would not be any more fun this evening," she said, figuring that her guess was probably very close to the truth. "Where were you, anyway? You were gone for ages!"

"And you've been here this whole time?" he asked, his eyebrows raised.

"Well, of course," she lied. "We couldn't very well leave

him here by himself. Mr. Tyler would most assuredly have had him thrown out.''

She could almost see Charles visibly relax. The tension went out of him, and he assumed some of his usual arrogance. ''I was detained by another one of my father's business associates. We were standing over by the doors leading in from the foyer.'' He gestured toward the other side of the ballroom.

''Well, no wonder I couldn't see you from here,'' she said, drawing him deeper into her trap. ''The room has gotten so crowded. My neck is strained from stretching to find you above all these other heads.'' She rested a delicate hand along the back of her neck. ''If only I was a few inches taller, I probably could have seen you the whole while.''

Charles smiled. ''If you were taller, you probably could have.'' He turned and pointed toward the large double doors leading out of the ballroom. ''See those big doors? I was leaning against the left one the entire time, trying desperately not to fall asleep. Mr. Johansen can be such a bore.''

Loralee smiled back. ''Poor Charles.'' She looked back toward the spot he had indicated, knowing that he had not been standing there for even two seconds of his absence. And then she saw another figure descending the staircase. She watched just long enough to see who it was before she turned away.

''I'm sorry to say this, Charles, but I think you're going to have to take Frank home. He's your friend, and friends always help each other out.'' Her eyes shot to Suzanne, sending a silent *thank you, my friend*. Suzanne's lips curved into the fleetingest of smiles.

''You're sure you don't mind leaving early?'' he asked, slipping his arm under Frank and jostling him awake.

''Wha-'' Frank struggled to focus his eyes. ''Wha's goin' on?'' he slurred.

''We're taking you home, buddy. Come on,'' Charles said, helping him to his feet and leading him in the right direction.

''Bu' I'm not ready t' go,'' Frank said.

"Oh, yes you are," Charles said, holding him by the shoulders and propelling him forward. He stumbled along, and, miraculously, the crowd parted to let them pass, where before, Loralee had practically had to run these same people down in her effort to put as much distance as possible between herself and Charles.

Loralee grabbed Suzanne's sleeve. "Are you staying?"

Suzanne nodded. "My parents are here. What's going on?" she demanded, her eyes like saucers.

"One second." She turned back toward Charles and called out his name. He turned and she said, "I think I'll stay. Suzanne's parents are here. They won't mind taking me home if you get detained."

He looked at the two girls, the refusal to allow Loralee to stay already on his lips, but Frank chose that moment to begin slumping toward the floor. Quickly, he bolstered him back up again. Charles really had no choice, unless he wanted to make a scene. He could hardly yell at her from fifteen feet across the room.

With disapproval showing clearly on his face, he raised his left hand in acknowledgment then turned and continued out of the room.

Loralee spun back to her friend. "I have to talk to you."

"Why, what—"

"Where is the ladies' sitting room?" Loralee said, almost more to herself than to Suzanne as she spun around looking at the doorways leading out of the ballroom. From about twenty feet away, she saw two older women emerge, engaged in a quiet conversation. That was probably it.

"Come on," she said, grabbing Suzanne's hand.

"But—"

Suddenly, Loralee stopped in her tracks She looked at Suzanne, and said, "Wait. For this we need a drink."

"I don't want a drink," Suzanne said. "I just want to hear what happened."

"Believe me," Loralee said, lifting two glasses of bubbly, pink champagne from a passing waiter, "you'll want a drink after this!"

Jesse wandered through the crowd, stopping to chat with friends and acquaintances along the way. But his mind was set on one thing. Finding Loralee.

A hand on his arm stopped him.

"Hey, brother."

Jesse turned and smiled. "Hey, John. Where have you been?"

"Watching the storm through those windows," he said, indicating a bank of windows off to the one side of the foyer. "For some reason, the ladies seem compelled to watch the lightning, even though it frightens the daylights out of them."

Jesse smiled. "Of course it frightens them. But they have big, strong John Sinclair to protect them, which is why they feel compelled to watch. If they're not afraid, you can't protect."

"Smart man," Johnny said. He raised his glass and took a swallow. Casually, he said, "We looked out right before the rain started. Just in time to see you loitering among those very secluded, very dark trees in the yard." He smiled at Jesse's obvious surprise. "So, who was she?"

Jesse chuckled. "You know, you were a pain in the ass when you were little. Always following me around, always asking questions. I would have thought you'd have outgrown that habit by now."

"I haven't. Who was she?"

Jesse looked at his brother, then held up his hand. "Let me get a drink."

He walked to the bar, watching for Loralee as he did, and was back next to John in five minutes, brandy in hand.

He helped himself to a healthy drink of it, then said, "You know how Mother goes on about how wonderful it is to be in love, how it changes your whole world. How true love cannot be denied . . .''

Johnny nodded his head. "I hear it, too, though you get the brunt of it, being, as you are, almost beyond the marrying age," he kidded.

Jesse looked down into the dark amber liquid in his glass. "The thing is," he said, his dark lashes lifting slowly, "I think she may be right."

Johnny's eyes widened, but he said nothing.

Jesse took a deep breath and let it out slowly, his smile growing to a full fledged grin. "I think she might be right about not being able to deny true love. It's there whether you want it to be or not."

Johnny stood up straighter. "All right, I'll say it again. Who is she?"

Amused by his brother's impatience, he laughed and said, "Loralee."

"Who's Loralee?"

"You remember, the girl in the green dress from my birthday party. The blonde," he added when Johnny showed no signs of recognition.

"Oh, her!" he said, the realization dawning on him. "She was beautiful."

"She is beautiful."

"Well, where is she? When do I get to see her up close?"

Jesse raised his brows and looked out over the crowd. He waved his hand and said, "She's out there somewhere."

Johnny shook his head. "Wait a minute. I'm a little confused. You don't know where she is?"

"Uh, no. I don't."

"But you're in love with her," Johnny said, sarcastically.

Jesse looked at his brother, all humor gone. "Yes, John, I think I am."

Johnny held up his hands. "All right, all right, I'm just sayin'—"

"You're just saying that she's like all the rest. And I'm telling you that she's not."

"Jesse, you don't even know this girl! You can't seriously think you're in love with her."

"I can. And I do." Jesse's eyes blazed as he looked at his brother. Johnny was twenty years old. What did he know about love?

"Jess," Johnny reached out and squeezed Jesse's arm. "I'm on your side, here. I'm just . . . surprised. So let's find her, and you can introduce me, and I'll probably say, heck, Jesse, if you weren't in love with her, I'd be in love with her myself!"

Jesse shook his head and rolled his eyes, his anger fleeing as quickly as it had flared. He couldn't stay mad at the brat.

"Okay, little brother, let's find her. She's wearing a light pink dress. And, well, the hair. You saw the hair."

"Yeah, yeah, the hair," Johnny said, already sifting through the crowd. "I'll take the right side of the room, you take the left. We'll meet back here in ten minutes," he said, checking the time on his pocket watch.

Jesse did the same then turned to his brother and said, "If you find her first, just remember, she's mine."

And with a smile, they were gone.

"I still can't believe it," Suzanne said, as they stepped back out into the party.

"Well, believe it, because it's true," Loralee said, giving the bustle of her dress one final fluffing. "I have to think of a way to get out of this wedding! How can I marry Charles? He's having an affair with a married woman, and I'm in love with another man!"

"Don't worry, we'll come up with something." She reached for Loralee's arm and pulled her close to whisper, "I think we should have more champagne!"

"No! My head is spinning as it is," Loralee laughed. "Now

I know why drunkards are always falling down. Why, the stuff makes me dizzy!''

Their laughter caught the attention of a gentleman standing a few feet away. Suddenly, he was standing in front of them.

"Excuse me, ladies," he said politely. Both girls stopped laughing immediately.

There was something vaguely familiar about this man, Loralee thought. She struggled to remember a name, but could not recall one.

"Are you, by any chance, Loralee?"

Stunned, she said, "Well, yes. Yes I am."

He smiled. "Finally!" He held out his hand. She looked at it then held out her own. He raised it to his lips and dropped a brief kiss upon the back of it. "My name is John Sinclair. I'm Jesse's brother."

Loralee opened her eyes in surprise. "Where is he?"

"If you'll follow me, I'll take you to him."

Loralee nodded, and Johnny turned and led them across the room. She followed eagerly, anticipating the moment when she would be near Jesse again. She pressed her hand to her heart as though to calm it. From somewhere in the back of her mind came the thought *What are you doing?*

But Loralee knew exactly what she was doing. She was hurrying toward the man, the very thought of whom, could send her heart tripping over itself.

And suddenly, she saw him. Pacing a small spot near the bar. Hands in his pockets, hair slightly mussed. And she smiled, knowing that he had been worried about not finding her again.

"I got the prize!" Johnny called, and Jesse's head shot up.

"Loralee!"

"You were looking for me?"

"Of course I was looking for you!"

She smiled shyly and said, "I'm glad you found me."

They stood smiling at each other until Johnny said, "Ahem. I don't mean to be rude, but we haven't been officially introduced. Jesse, you forget your manners."

Jesse smiled and, never taking his eyes from Loralee's, said, "Yes, I do."

She blushed outrageously! She could feel the heat rising in her cheeks but could do nothing to stop it.

Jesse turned and placed his hand on Johnny's back. "This is my brother, John, the younger of the Sinclair boys." He held out his hand toward Suzanne. "This is Miss Suzanne Becker."

Johnny took one look at Suzanne's mischievous eyes, and Loralee thought, Oh, no, here we go again.

Jesse reached out for Loralee's hand and pulled her around to his side. "And this lovely young lady is Loralee."

It was only with great difficulty that Johnny tore his gaze from Suzanne and tried to be polite. "Loralee," he said. "It's so nice to finally meet you. My brother has told me a lot about you."

"Oh, has he?" she asked, raising an eyebrow in Jesse's direction.

Jesse tried to hide his smile as their eyes locked, and between them, the sparks flew.

"He has no manners," Johnny quipped to Suzanne. "Our mother would be horrified." Looking at his brother he said, "Does Loralee have a last name, Jesse?"

Jesse didn't even blink. "I would imagine she does." He smiled. "But I don't know it," he said to Johnny, with a shrug.

John opened his eyes wide. "You don't know it?"

"Nope."

Loralee laughed. "It's Vander. Loralee Vander."

The mirth and merriment that had been bouncing between the four of them suddenly fled as though it were the oxygen being sucked out of a burning building. Jesse's face sobered instantly. "Did you say Vander?"

"Yes, I did," Loralee said, confused by his sudden change of mood.

Jesse was looking at her as if she was a ghost in a bad dream.

John reached out and touched his brother's arm. "Take it easy, Jess. It doesn't necessarily mean anything." Jesse glanced at him and then back at Loralee.

"Are you, by any chance, related to Edward Vander?" he asked quietly.

"I am. He's my father."

Jesse rolled his eyes toward the heavens, muttering a quiet, "Oh, God . . ." He stepped back, looking at her with an emotion Loralee couldn't quite pinpoint. Anger? Disgust? Hatred?

"Jesse, what's wr-"

She started to reach out for him, but he yanked his arm away from her. "What's wrong?" he said quietly. "I'll tell you what's wrong." He took a step toward her until he was looming over her. She looked down and saw that his hands were shaking with a rage she did not understand. He clenched and unclenched his fists in an effort to still them, but nothing worked. In a voice that was ominously quiet, he said "Your father killed our father."

"What? What are you talking about? I met your father just two weeks—"

John interrupted. "Stephen and Elizabeth Sinclair are our adoptive parents. Our father was killed in a mining accident before I was born. Our mother died shortly afterwards." He spoke quietly, sadly, but with none of the anger that was so evident in Jesse's voice.

Loralee shook her head. "I don't understand."

"Well, let me paint you a picture," Jesse said, grabbing her arm and hauling her out onto the front porch, John and Suzanne following. It was deserted, the wind from the thunderstorm still whipping through the trees.

He had barely stepped through the doorway when he turned on Loralee. "Have you ever heard of a little thing called the Avondale Disaster?" She shook her head. "No? Well, let me tell you about it. Twenty years ago, 110 men were killed in a mine owned by Vander Holdings. The reason? The breaker above the mine's entrance caught fire and crashed into the shaft, blocking the one and only exit. Every man in that mine died, my father among them.''

"But that sounds like an accident!" Loralee cried. "How can you blame my father for an accident?"

Jesse looked at her with disgust. "You've been pampered every moment of your life, Loralee. But I remember very well the first five years of my life. I remember the days when we had only boiled onions for supper. I remember my father coming home from work covered in filthy black coal dust. And I remember him coughing that same coal dust out of his lungs.''

Loralee looked away. She was beginning to see where he was going with this story.

"Miners work twelve hours a day, six days a week. Did you know that? And even then, they can barely afford to feed their families. While the owners of the mines live in complete luxury." He pointed a finger at her. "My father died because your father was too greedy to spend the money on a second entry way into that mine for the safety of his men!"

Johnny put his hand on Jesse's shoulder. "Jess, come on, it wasn't her fault.''

Jesse flung the hand off and turned on his brother. "You don't know, Johnny! You don't know what it was like. Stephen has *never* treated his employees the way Edward Vander did. The way he still does.''

Jesse turned back toward Loralee, his eyes blazing with a hatred so strong, it terrified her. "My father died because of Edward Vander's greed. Plain and simple. And I will *never* forget that. I sure as hell won't forgive it.''

He turned and stormed off the porch, leaving Loralee, Suzanne and Johnny staring after him.

CHAPTER SEVEN

Another dead end. Loralee huffed her way back from the carriage house to the main house, disgusted with the answers she'd been given.

It had taken a few days for the pain of Jesse's accusations to dull. But when it finally had, Loralee's spunk had fought its way to the surface. Even if her father had done something wrong, how dare Jesse find Loralee guilty by association!

And so, she'd come up with a plan. She'd made a list of all the people in the Vander household who had been in her father's employ in 1869. But, in the past two days she had spoken with all six people on her list, and she wasn't any closer to knowing the truth about the Avondale Disaster.

She had, however, heard one interesting thing. Apparently, Dr. Farley had been training up in Wilkes-Barre at the time, and had been part of the rescue efforts. Maybe he would be able to shed some light on the events of that fateful day.

She stepped onto the front porch, where her mother sat in a wicker chair pushed far into the shadows. Fiona sat as straight as ever, the only outward sign that she was even remotely bothered by the heat was a painted paper fan which dangled from her right hand.

"Hello, Mother," Loralee said, dragging a chair closer to her mother and plopping down into it. "Mind if I join you?"

"Oh, Loralee, must you sit down that way?" Fiona said, rolling her eyes. "I know that you know how to sit like a lady because I taught you myself."

"I need to ask you something." Loralee said, ignoring the reproval. She took a deep breath and held it for a few seconds before blowing it out. "It's about the Avondale Disaster."

Fiona closed her eyes and shook her head. "Oh, Lord. Now, what?"

"It's just that . . . well, I . . . I have some questions."

"Loralee, it's ancient history. Why in the world would you want to dredge it up now, after all these years?"

"Because I was speaking to someone the other night who made some horrible accusations concerning the incident. He accused Papa of being negligent to the extent that he caused the death of those miners. If that's not true, then I want to be the one to put those rumors to rest. I want to be able to confront that person and say, I've checked into the incident thoroughly, and my father did nothing wrong.

"The trouble is, I haven't been able to find anyone who would come right out and say Edward Vander did nothing wrong. No one that I've spoken to is willing to talk very much about it."

"And just who have you been speaking to?"

Loralee hesitated. She knew how her mother disapproved of mingling with the help. "Just some of the staff."

Fiona made a *tsk-tsk* sound with her tongue. "Loralee, you know you are not to discuss anything with the hired help! It just isn't proper."

"But, Mother, I want to know what happened that day!"

"Why is it so important to you? Who have you been discussing this with?"

Loralee hesitated a moment, knowing that the name she was about to say would undoubtedly bring recriminations. Finally, she said, "Jesse Sinclair."

Fiona raised her eyebrows. "Do you see what comes of reckless behavior? Do you see, now, why I didn't want you to go to that party?"

"Do you know if it's true?" Loralee asked, ignoring her mother's words. "Was Papa at fault?" She held her breath, waiting.

Fiona stared at her daughter long and hard before answering. "Why do you care about this Jesse Sinclair so much that you are obsessed with proving him wrong? You are an engaged woman Loralee. If Charles found out about this fascination you seem to have for another man, why, he'd likely call the whole thing off!"

"Fine. Let him."

"Loralee, don't even—"

"I've told you before, I don't want to marry Charles. I won't marry him!"

"Your father will never let you call it off. Never!"

"He has to! I won't do it! It's a mistake, I know that as surely as I know my own name," she said, imagining Jesse's face when he'd heard the Vander name. Tears sprang to her eyes, and she turned away, avoiding her mother's penetrating gaze.

"How can you be so sure of that?" Fiona lamented.

Loralee thought about Charles, and the way he had forced her to touch him. Her cheeks reddened. Would Fiona understand the fear he had struck into her with that single act? Would she understand the repugnance Loralee felt at the thought of being made to touch him so intimately again?

"How, Loralee? How can you be so sure that it is a mistake?"

She was desperate to escape Charles's grasp. Desperate

enough to tell her mother at least some of what had happened with her intended and pray that she would understand and support the decision not to marry Charles.

"Mother," she said, in a voice that was barely above a whisper. "Charles has . . . done . . . things."

There was a brief moment of hesitation before Fiona asked, "What kind of things?"

Loralee took a deep breath, but released it without saying a word.

"Loralee?"

With her eyes closed, Loralee whispered, "He's touched me."

Fiona's eyes widened, and she gripped her daughter's arm tightly. "Oh, dear God, you haven't let—"

"No!" Loralee cried.

"What, then?" Fiona whispered.

"I haven't *let* him do anything," she said quietly. "But he has touched me. Against my wishes and amid much protestation, he has . . . touched me in private places." Their heads were together now, and they both spoke in the most hushed of whispers. "That's why I've been avoiding him."

"He touched you against your wishes?"

Loralee nodded.

"And you're very sure that you made it clear to him that you did not wish to engage in such activity?"

"Oh, he knew, Mother. He knew I wanted him to stop." She closed her eyes and took the plunge. "But that's not even the worst of it."

"What could be worse? Unless you've—"

"Charles is having an affair with Abigail Tyler! I know it because I've seen them together," Loralee blurted out. Talking about this with her mother was more difficult than she had thought it would be. But it was the only thing she could think of that might get this wedding canceled. And she had come this far, she might as well have done with it.

"Don't be so naïve, Loralee. All men have affairs."

Loralee looked at her mother, horrified. "What? That's not true, Mother!"

"Well, maybe not all, but most. In any case, an affair is no reason to call off a wedding," Fiona said.

"It's not? Okay, Mother, how about this for a reason? Charles . . . he took my hand . . . and he . . . he forced me to . . . to touch him. *There*. He made me put my hand right on it, and I . . ." Tears filled her eyes, and she dropped her head into her hands. "He said that after we're married . . ."

Her words were muffled, and she had begun to cry in earnest now. "It was humiliating. And he enjoyed it! He enjoyed making me feel . . . dirty." She sobbed harder, her whispered words blending with her tears. "He . . . called me a . . . a c-common whore."

Fiona's fingers gripped the arms of the wicker chair so tightly, her knuckles were white. With wide eyes, she watched her daughter sobbing.

"He's mean, Mother! He *wants* to make me feel bad. He said things that were intentionally meant to hurt me." She rubbed her wrists, thinking of the way Charles had so easily held her hands behind her back. "He held my arms . . . he's so much bigger than I am . . . so much stronger." She wiped at her tears with the back of her hand. "I couldn't even fight back," she whispered, rubbing her wrists again.

Fiona's face had blanched. She watched her daughter's tiny fingers rubbing reed-thin wrists. Loralee was a very small girl, much like her mother. And Charles was a much larger man.

"I can't do it, Mother! I just can't marry him knowing that whenever he wants to he can make me . . ." Loralee looked into her mother's eyes for the first time since divulging the awful shame she felt. "What can I do?"

"I don't know. Edward is a stubborn man, but surely . . ." Her voice trailed off, and the words hung there between them.

Fiona licked her lips and pulled herself up, ramrod straight.

"I'll speak to your father. I'll make it perfectly clear to him that I am no longer in favor of a marriage between you and Charles." She reached out and drew her hand along Loralee's tear-stained face, in an uncharacteristic show of emotion. "You deserve better."

Loralee threw her arms around her mother's neck. "Oh, thank you, Mother! Thank you. You can't imagine the weight of carrying something like this all by yourself. I was so afraid to tell anyone. You can't imagine."

"Oh, yes," Fiona said, gently squeezing her daughter's tiny hand. "I can."

Conversation between Fiona and Loralee remained stilted all afternoon. Now, the two women sat across the dinner table from each other, looking anywhere except at each other. Fiona was so embarrassed by what Loralee had told her that she couldn't even look her daughter in the eye. Because of this, Loralee decided to tell her father herself. As if her thoughts had beckoned to him, the front door opened and Edward strode into the house.

At his approach, Fiona gave a discreet nod to a woman standing next to the door leading to the kitchen. She tugged on the tasseled pull-cord that would signal the kitchen staff that the servers were to bring the first course and she began pouring minted iced tea for the family.

Edward sat down. "Loralee. Fiona."

"How was your day, Papa?"

"Hot."

The servers set down salads of crisp greens, and Edward plunged his fork right in. He never did care much for dinnertime conversation, and Loralee struggled to find some topic with which she could get him talking.

"Mother and I spent most of the day on the porch trying to catch a breeze."

"Mmm."

"But the air was deathly still. Not a breeze to be found."

"Mmm."

"Even for this time of the evening it's still very warm."

Edward looked up at his daughter. "Was there something you wanted to discuss, Loralee?"

She looked nervously at her mother then back to Edward. "It'll keep till dessert."

"Good. Then perhaps we can enjoy a little quiet with our meal?" he asked pointedly.

"Of course, Papa," she said.

She poked at her food, eating halfheartedly, while her stomach churned. Somehow, she managed to get through the salad and the main course.

Facing her father was terrifying. Maybe this hadn't been a good idea. Maybe it would have been better to—

"Now, Loralee. What is on your mind?"

She hesitated a few seconds, glancing at her mother for support. Finally, she said, "The wedding, Papa."

"I don't know the first thing about weddings. Talk to your mother about it." He pushed back his chair to rise.

"Perhaps I should have said the marriage. Surely you know something about that."

Edward stopped in his tracks and fixed his daughter with a look of outrage. "You'd better watch the tone of your voice, young lady."

"I'm sorry, Papa. I didn't mean for it to come out that way."

"Charles won't put up with that kind of back talk from you."

Loralee took a deep breath and let it out slowly. She gnawed her bottom lip. And all the while she looked at Edward and wondered what she could possibly say that would get through to him.

"Well, come on. Out with it. I don't have all day." He stood behind his chair with his fingers drumming incessantly on its backrest.

"I don't want to marry Charles. I want to call off the wedding," she blurted. There! It was done!

"That's out of the question. Plans have already been made," he said, turning to walk out of the room.

"But, Papa, I don't love him!" Loralee cried, as she sprang from her chair and grasped at his arm.

"And what has love got to do with the making of a marriage?"

"But, Papa, I don't want to marry him! I *can't* marry him!" she leaned over clutching his coat sleeve.

"You can, and you will," he said, removing her fingers from his arm.

"I *can't*! It wouldn't be right! I'll never love him! Never!" As usual, give her a fight, and Loralee would rise to the occasion.

Edward glanced disdainfully at Fiona. "What do you know about this?"

She struggled to look him in the eye. "She doesn't want to marry him. He's been . . . forceful with her." She blushed bright red.

"Forceful?" Edward looked back at Loralee. "What does that mean?"

Loralee looked at her mother. *No! Don't say any more!*

"What does that mean, Loralee?" he asked, pushing for an answer.

She couldn't meet his eyes. "Charles has . . ." The silence stretched out.

"Charles has what?"

"He touched me," she whispered, flushed to the roots of her hair.

"He touched you?" he asked quietly.

Loralee nodded her head but kept her gaze glued to the floor. He seemed to considered her words carefully before he spoke because it felt as though hours had passed. Finally, he said, "I'll speak to Charles, and, if it is agreeable to him, your wedding date will be advanced to mid-October."

Loralee's head shot up. "What?" she cried.

"Mid-October. I don't want this situation getting out of hand. The next thing you know, we'll be shuffling you off for a private ceremony. I won't have that shame brought down upon this family. The wedding will take place in October."

"Didn't you hear anything I just said?" Loralee shouted. "I won't marry him! I won't!"

"Why not, Loralee? Because he touched you? You should be more careful of your behavior around Charles. A man can only take so much temptation."

"I've been tempting him? I have done no such thing! I will not marry that—that beast!"

"He's not a beast, Loralee. He's simply a man. Your mother should have warned you about a man's needs," He glared at his wife, who seemed unable to utter a single word.

"But I don't love him! And I don't care what you say, love does matter. And I know that because I love someone else!" She was breathing rapidly and having no trouble looking him in the eye, now. This was her future they were talking about, and she had no intentions of giving it up without a fight!

Edward sat back down in his seat and waited until Loralee had done the same. "You love someone else? And who might this someone be?"

"It doesn't matter. Even if—"

"Who is it, Loralee!" he demanded, slamming his fist onto the table and sending the silverware up dancing into the air then crashing back down.

"Edward!" Fiona said.

"Stay out of this!"

"I'll not have my daughter manhandled!" she shouted. It was the first time that Loralee could ever remember her having defied him.

"I said, stay out of this!" He jabbed his finger toward Fiona, and she backed down quickly, her fleeting courage vanishing.

He turned back to his daughter. "I want to know who's been filling your head with such nonsense. Who is it?" His tone was deceptively soft.

Loralee knew when she wasn't going to win. She hesitated only a few seconds before she looked up at him and said, "Jesse Sinclair."

"Jesse Sinclair," he repeated to himself, almost as though he should have known.

"Did you know that he and his brother were adopted by the Sinclairs?" she asked.

"The whole town knows that, Loralee."

"I didn't. And did you know that his natural father was killed in the Avondale Disaster?"

"Loralee, I don't even own that mine anymore."

"But you owned it then, didn't you?"

"That fire was not my fault!"

"Jesse would disagree with you."

Edward pounded his fist onto the table again, setting the silverware back in motion. "I don't give a God damn what that little fortune-hunting liar would do!"

"Edward!" Fiona held her delicate fingers to her throat, as though she were struggling for breath.

Edward glared at his wife, pounding the table again and roaring, "Fiona, God damn it, stay out of this!" He lunged toward her as he spoke, and she recoiled, the fear plain on her face.

"Papa! There's no reason—"

Edward pushed his chair back and towered above Loralee, pointing his finger in her face. "You stay away from Jesse Sinclair, you hear? Do you hear me?" he thundered.

Loralee could not bring herself to look at him. She kept her face turned to the side and nodded quickly.

Edward stalked toward the doorway, turning just as the servants outside scurried away. ''You *will* marry Charles! And I don't want to hear another word about it!''

He stormed down the hall and into his private study, leaving his terrified wife and daughter behind.

CHAPTER EIGHT

On Tuesday morning, Loralee arrived for work early, so eager to avoid contact with Edward that she'd skipped breakfast entirely. She was checking through the contents of her black bag when Dr. Farley arrived.

"Good morning," he said, struggling to hide a yawn. "Sorry. Not awake yet." He walked past her and unlocked a window, jiggling it until he managed to raise it a few inches. He propped it with a stick that rested on the sill for just that purpose.

"I've been awake for hours," Loralee said quietly.

Doc glanced over his shoulder as he walked into the waiting room and raised the front shade. Sunlight came pouring in, illuminating the dust motes that floated through the stuffy air. It wasn't even nine o'clock, but already, it promised to be another unbearably hot day.

Doc and Loralee had been working together for a while, and with the familiarity that so often grows out of close working conditions, they had learned to read each other's moods quite accurately. After letting some air into the place, he stepped in front of her and said, "What's wrong?"

Loralee closed her eyes and rubbed her forehead with one hand. "What isn't wrong might be the better question."

Doc reached out and pulled a chair across the bare wooden floor. It screeched as its legs scraped against the age-worn planks. He pointed at it. "Sit."

Loralee dropped wearily into the chair. "Do you have a few minutes? Because this is—"

"You're of no use to me the way you are now," he said, mopping at his forehead with a handkerchief from his pocket. "If you've got something to talk about, you may as well spit it out." He leaned back against the wall and crossed his big arms in front of his chest, waiting.

Loralee looked at him for a few seconds, then nodded, as if agreeing with him. "I have a few questions I think you might be able to answer."

"Ask away."

She took a deep breath and held it, then blurted out, "I've been looking into the events which occurred in Avondale, back in '69."

He raised his eyebrows, and asked, "Why?"

"My father owned that land when the accident occurred. It has since been sold, but he refuses to talk about what happened there."

"What do you want to know?"

She cleared her throat. "I've been talking to some people, trying to determine the cause of the accident. I would just like to know what happened there, and no one will tell me. I heard that you were part of the search and rescue crew, and I thought that you might be willing to discuss it."

He eyed her warily, as if making a very important decision about her. "Some of it might be upsetting to you," he said simply.

"Dr. Farley, I can deal with upsetting. It's the not knowing that's driving me crazy."

He thought about that for a few seconds then nodded his head. "What do you know so far?" he asked.

"Well, I know, or at least I've been told, that there was a fire of some sort. The entrance was blocked and 110 men were trapped inside. I was told that there was not a single survivor, and that the reason for that was my father's neglect in providing an alternate way out of the mine." She sat perfectly still, knowing that the next words he spoke might condemn her father for those many deaths.

Dr. Farley leaned back against the wall with his head tilted back as if he were looking at the ceiling, but his eyes were closed. He rubbed his forehead with his fingertips then dropped his hands and nodded his head. "What you've been told is pretty much the truth."

"Pretty much?"

"Well, 110 men died when the furnace that was used to circulate the air in the mine somehow caught the breaker on fire. The breaker had been built directly above the shaft, and when it burned, it crashed down into the shaft, effectively blocking the only way out."

"And was that my father's fault?"

"Some say so. He did nothing illegal, mind you, though several laws have been passed since then. Breakers are no longer permitted directly above the shaft of a mine. And all mines are required to have more than one way out. At the time, those things were not required, but most mine owners provided a second way out simply for the safety of their men."

"So, you're saying that he did nothing that would allow him to be charged with a crime, but that he should have taken it upon himself to provide another route of escape in the event of an accident."

"That's what some folks think."

"What do you think?"

He looked at the floor seemingly reluctant to answer her question.

"Dr. Farley?" she prompted.

He looked up at her and said, "Loralee, I'm in the business of saving lives, of easing human suffering. To me, there is no monetary bottom line. I measure my success by the people I can help, not by the amount of money I can make. And, as you can see," he said, holding out his hands to his sides, "my surroundings reflect that. I live above this office in a room as plain as this one. I live alone, because I've never had the time for a wife or family."

"So you're saying my father's lifestyle, my lifestyle, is wrong."

"Absolutely not. That's not what I'm saying. If I had more money, I'd live in a nicer place. I'd have a nicer office, with the very latest medical instruments. I'd dress in fancy clothes and own beautiful carriages and go to big parties. I'd do all those same things that you do."

She sat still, sensing that he had more to say. Knowing that the ax was going to fall.

Dr. Farley sat down next to her in a straight backed wooden chair and took her hands in his own. "But if I had all that money, I would certainly have provided for the safety of my employees. And that means that I would have had at least one other way for them to get out of that hole."

There it was. The evidence that proved her father guilty. Jesse had been right.

She sat for a minute, letting the information sink in. Abruptly, she stood up. "Well, there you have it."

"Now, mind, he didn't break any laws."

"No, no. I understand that. He didn't break any laws, but he did do something that was very wrong," she said, fighting to keep back the tears that threatened to spill.

"I'm sorry if I've upset you."

"No," she said, putting on an artificially cheerful face. "I asked. I wanted to know. And now I do."

"And does knowing change anything?"

She thought about that for a while before answering. She thought about Jesse's words. *Your father killed my father.* She thought about standing beneath the towering oaks while he brought her thrill after thrill with his hands, with his mouth. And she thought about the way his smile turned to ice when he heard her last name.

Did his words change anything?

"Unfortunately, Dr. Farley, knowing changes everything." She turned and made her way to the front door, where a line of patients had already formed out on the sidewalk.

She could heal their wounds. She could ease their pain. But nowhere in her training had she learned how to fix a broken heart.

Because of her father's greed, Jesse's father had been stolen from him. It was a loss that had obviously caused Jesse a lot of pain.

And as Loralee thought about the shattered look in Jesse's eyes, she shared that pain.

She felt every bit of it as her heart broke into a million pieces.

Across town, someone else was only just waking.

Charles propped himself up on one elbow, careful not to disturb her. He wanted to watch Abby sleeping for just a few minutes more.

It wasn't fair. He'd loved her ever since his body had begun to tell him that he would someday love a woman. She'd been his friend, his lover, his obsession. She should have been sleeping in *his* bed every night. She should be married to a man who would worship her, not shackled to an old man more than three times her age.

He reached out and ran his fingers through the locks of dark auburn hair that tumbled over Abby's shoulders and onto both her pillow and his. He closed his eyes and let his free hand roam down miles of bare back, over lushly curving hips and between soft, welcoming thighs.

She curled against him like a contented cat, coming awake slowly, stretching first one leg, then the other. Her eyes fluttered open, and she saw him watching her, and she smiled, pressing her backside more firmly against him.

"It's good to wake up with you," she murmured, her voice all husky from sleep.

"Mmm hmm." He couldn't seem to tear his gaze away from her face. She looked so happy. So perfectly happy. His hand stilled on her hip. The air caught in his lungs as he imagined her husband touching her this way. It wasn't fair that Zachary got to be the man married to Abby, when Charles was the man who loved her.

But, despite that love, Charles would marry another woman. Would, in fact, spend this very afternoon with Edward Vander, his future father-in-law.

Charles despised Loralee Vander, and he despised himself for being so weak. He should have run off with Abby when he'd had the chance. He should have been strong enough to choose his love for her over his love of money. But he hadn't been that strong, and now she was married to someone else.

"It's not fair, Abby."

"What's not fair?"

He blinked his eyes and looked down at her, hating himself for letting Zachary Tyler intrude on the precious time they had together. Zachary was out of town for a few days, and Charles and Abby had decided to take advantage of his absence. Abby had a separate entrance directly into her suite of rooms. So it was easy for them to spend nights together without the household staff any the wiser.

"What's not fair, Charles?" she asked again.

He held back from speaking the words, knowing that it was his choice that had made it so, but in the end he lost the battle with his will, and he said the words that he felt needed saying.

"It isn't fair that he sleeps with you in this bed every night. It should be me."

"I agree. It should be you." She rolled onto her back and reached up to caress his cheek. "He doesn't sleep in this bed *every* night. In fact, he rarely sleeps in here. Zachary prefers the privacy of his own bed."

Charles watched her as she spoke, and her acceptance of the situation infuriated him. "How can you lay there, and say that as though it's of no consequence?"

"It is of no consequence, Charles. My marriage to Zachary has absolutely nothing to do with my feelings for you. It is a completely separate facet of my life. Just as your marriage to Loralee Vander will be a separate facet of your life. It won't intrude on what we share."

"How can you be so sure of that?," he shouted in frustration. "Doesn't it drive you crazy? Doesn't it keep you awake nights? Knowing that we *could* be together . . . if only—"

"But we're not, Charles. We're not," she said firmly. "This is my life," she said, gesturing with her hand. "This is my home. This is where I live, where I dream, where I cry." As if to demonstrate that the words she spoke were true, her eyes filled with tears, and, again, she reached out to stroke Charles's face. "I've accepted what has to be because I cannot change it," she whispered. "You, however, have the power that I lack. Embrace it, or change it, Charles. Embrace it, or change it."

He jerked away from her touch climbing out of the bed and stepping into his pants. "You think I wouldn't love to change it? Do you think the knowledge that I *can* change it doesn't haunt me night and day?" He shoved his fingers through his hair and paced around the bed, glaring at Abby, who sat with the sheets clutched to her chest.

She waited until he had calmed a bit before she spoke. "I've told you before, Charles. I would walk away from this in a minute.''

''And what could I offer you if you did? A reputation tarnished beyond repair? A husband without two cents to his name? Your family plunged back into poverty? I can't do it, Abigail! I can't do it.'' He stopped pacing and stood before her with his head hung low, the hopelessness of their situation washing over him.

She watched him warily. ''Do you think your father will ever change his mind?'' She smiled coyly. ''I have no intentions of living with that old man forever. I've been putting away money since the day we got married. Another two or three years . . .''

Charles looked at her sadly. ''If you do that, you'll prove to my father that everything he ever thought about you was true. He'd have just cause for cutting me off from the family fortune because you married your first husband for his money. And he'll never believe that you aren't marrying me for the same reason.''

Abby climbed to her knees, still covering herself with the sheet. ''But we won't need his money, Charles! We'll have my money!'' She sat down, a slow smile tugging at the corners of her mouth. ''I know things about my husband, Charles. Things that he wouldn't want to become public knowledge.'' Her voice dropped to a sexy whisper. ''Believe me, he'll pay whatever I demand. That, combined with what I've already—''

''It's not the same, Abby! I'd never be able to hold my head up in this town again!''

He spoke the words before he could think, and he watched the pain leap into her eyes.

He reached his hand toward her. ''No, Abby, I didn't mean—''

''It's your pride, Charles! It's your goddamned pride that's keeping us apart!'' She abandoned the sheet and climbed out of the bed, advancing on him wearing fury and nothing else.

"It's not—''

"It is!'' she screamed, pounding her fists against his bare chest. "It is. You would be ashamed to claim me as your wife. It's *you* who sees me as tarnished!''

"I don't, Abby—''

"What was I supposed to do?'' she said, tears running freely down her face. "I couldn't wait forever for you to change your father's mind! Offers like Zachary's don't come along every day for a girl like me!''

Charles looked at her, something about the way she said those words sending off alarm bells in his head. Not proposals. Offers. "What did he offer you, Abby?''

"It's none of your goddamned business, Charles!'' She screamed the words at him, her anger, suppressed for so long, growing with every breath she took. "What it comes down to is this: He wanted me. You did not.'' She leveled murderous eyes on him, daring him to meet her taunts.

Charles felt no anger towards Abby. It was all directed at Zachary Tyler, and if the man had been present, Charles would have gladly strangled him.

Calmly, he bent and picked his shirt up off the floor. He slipped his arms into it and buttoned it almost to the top. He put on his socks and shoes. He draped his jacket over his arm. Still, Abby had not altered her pose. She glared at him. And he deserved every bit of her contempt, he knew. But he had to leave, now. Before she said something that he wouldn't be able to shake from his mind. Before she slipped and told him any more about Zachary's "offer.''

"I have to go.''

"Fine. Go.''

"I'll get in touch with you somehow.''

"You always do.''

"Please don't be mad, Abby. I hate to see you upset.''

She chuckled and shook her head. "You know what, Charles? I hate a lot of things. Not the least of which is you." She advanced a step toward him, anger clearly visible in her eyes. "Slither from my bed, sneak out of my house, and go back to your polite company where you can hold your head up with pride." She looked him up and down, the expression on her face proving that she meant every word she was saying. "I can't stand the sight of you."

He listened silently, and, knowing that she had every right to hate him, he walked out of her bedroom and back into his miserable life.

Jesse relieved both firemen. In the midst of an early heat wave, with outside temperatures hovering in the mid-nineties for days, the temperature next to the steam engine's twin fireboxes had proven to be too much for several of Valley Railroad's best firemen. In an attempt to prevent even more from succumbing to the heat, Stephen had set in motion a temporary, emergency rotating schedule, which allowed each fireman a five-minute break each hour. They were replaced by other employees, who were grateful when their five-minute stint as fireman had ended.

A good fireman could move more than two tons of coal in less than thirty minutes, and as Jesse shoveled with a vengeance, he was among the best. He barely noticed the sweat as it ran down his back between his shoulder blades. He scarcely felt the burn in his arms from the effort he forced upon them. He took no note of his labored breathing as he worked in steady rhythm. *Push, throw, push, throw.*

He'd volunteered to cover the lunch break and had sent the two men off together, leaving him to cover both fireboxes for the next twenty minutes. He worked like a man possessed, relishing the punishment he heaped upon his traitorous body.

How could he have felt such all-consuming passion for the

daughter of Edward Vander? He'd hated the man since he was five years old. He'd sworn to himself, years ago, that someday he would see him pay for the accident that had taken his father's life. And now, even after knowing who she really was, he couldn't stop his body from hardening at the thought of her mouth under his. He couldn't stop the ache that refused to allow him sleep. He couldn't stop his mind from deluging him with images of Loralee. Her eyes closed and her head tossed back as he kissed her neck. Her small hand over his as he touched her breasts.

"Damn it!" he cursed, as pictures of Loralee crowded his head. He flung the shovel into the coal and plunged his fingers through his wet hair, willing himself, yet again, to forget about her.

"Jesse?"

He turned to find John watching him, questioning his uncharacteristic outburst of anger.

Jesse stared him down, almost daring him to challenge the violent behavior. But John only stood there, staring back, until Jesse was forced to look away, swearing softly.

He pulled the shovel out of the coal and began working again, this time, at a more reasonable pace. John picked up the other shovel and moved in next to his brother, matching load for load. Side by side they worked, grown men lost in their own thoughts of the long-ago family that had ceased to be.

Tuesday afternoon, Loralee pulled Dr. Farley's rig into Drifton. Somehow, the sight of the town affected her in ways it never had before.

Drifton was a coal company town. At one end was the breaker, which filled the entire town with the sound of coal rushing down the chutes. The houses, about seventy-five of them, stood on three streets lined up like the rungs of a ladder in front of the breaker. The superintendent lived on First Street.

Those who lived on the last street, looked out their back door to the entrance of the mine itself.

That's where Loralee headed. Many of the coal companies provided medical care for their employees in the form of a company doctor. Payments for visits were deducted from the following week's meager pay check. For some families, a minor illness could reduce them to destitution.

Dr. Farley, and most of the other independent doctors, operated on a sliding scale. Patients paid what they could afford. Often, they could only afford a penny or two. And, sometimes, that penny couldn't be scrounged up until weeks later. So, rather than pay the inflated prices of the company doctors, they waited out most illnesses until one of the independents came through.

There weren't many visitors to Drifton, and the young children playing in the dirt streets would see to it that the grown-ups were informed of Loralee's arrival.

The houses were nothing more than rickety shacks. Front yards had been plowed up into gardens which overflowed with vegetables to be put up for the winter. At the first house where she stopped, a goat had been tied to a post. It had devoured its small patch of grass till nothing remained but scraggly roots.

Loralee's chest tightened, and her eyes filled with tears. Though her father had forbidden her to visit any of the company towns Vander Holdings owned, she knew that they could not be much better than this. It was because of men like her father that these people were forced to live in conditions that could only be described as horrific. Meanwhile, Loralee could not remember ever wanting for anything a day in her life. When she thought back to her childhood, she remembered the many pretty dresses she had worn. Often she wore them only once or twice before they were outgrown. What had happened to all those dresses?

She looked down at the children who had gathered beside

Doc's horse. They wore dirty, tattered clothing and no shoes. And still, they smiled up at her.

"Do any of your mamas need to see the doctor?" she asked, as she tied the horse to a fence post.

"Miss Loralee!"

Loralee looked up and saw an elderly woman on the porch a house down. "Hello, Mrs. Carr. How are you today?" She pulled her bag over the side of the wagon and set it on the street beside her.

"Not good, not good."

And so began Loralee's visit to Drifton. She'd already visited nine houses and treated ailments from "red-tops" (blisters on the fingertips of new breaker boys. Until their skin hardened, it would swell, crack and bleed) to morning sickness. She had just entered the tenth house, to check on a case of chickenpox, which had run rampant through the patch three weeks earlier, when a young boy, seven or eight burst through the door.

"Ma! Ma, come quick!" he shouted, breathing heavily after his sprint across the silt bank.

"What happened?" Mary Boyle asked, jumping up and setting her four-year-old on the floor in front of Loralee.

"It's Al! He's stuck, and they says they're gonna cut his arm off!"

"Oh, God, no!" the woman cried, rushing for the door.

"Wait!" Loralee said, reaching for her bag. "Who's Al?"

"My oldest boy—"

"He's a spragger," the young boy interrupted. "You better come quick! They already sent for the doctor!"

"No!" Loralee said, grabbing the woman's arm. "Let me go. Maybe I can get down there," Loralee said, already out the door. "Take me to him," she said to the little boy.

They ran quickly across mounds of slate and silt, till they reached the entrance to the mine, no more than a hundred and fifty feet from the Boyles' back door.

"He's down there," the boy said, pointing to the gaping black hole in the earth. "They won't let me go down."

Loralee nodded. She had never been down a mine before. She didn't know if they would allow her down, since she was a woman, and the company already had their own doctor. But she wasn't going to let them cut off that boy's arm until she was sure it was the only way to save his life. She made her way toward the group of men gathered at the mine's entrance.

"Excuse me," she said, to anyone who would answer her. "Has the doctor arrived yet?"

"Doctor ain't comin'."

"What do you mean, he's not coming?"

"Went into town for supplies. Boy'll be dead by the time he gets back." The man who was speaking stood looking down into the hole, not even bothering to glance her way.

"What! You're just going to let him bleed to death?"

"I ain't cuttin' him free!" He turned to look at her. "Who else is gonna do it?"

"Me!" She shifted her bag from one hand to the other. "I work with Dr. Farley. I'll do it."

"We can't let you down there!"

"Why not?"

"Well, you're a woman, for one thing!"

"What's that got to do with anything? Do any of you men want to be the one to go down there and cut that boy's arm off?"

Around her, the group of work-worn men looked away.

"Get me down there!" she shouted.

"Let her go, Harry," one of the men said. "Boy's in pain down there."

"Yeah, Harry. What if it was your boy? You'd want someone to help him."

Harry, who seemed to be the man in charge, looked her over. "All right. You wanna try it, go ahead and try it." He walked toward the shaft, and Loralee followed. "Gimme a lamp!" He shouted. One of the men volunteered his own cap, with the tiny kerosene lamp attached to the front of it.

Harry slapped it down on Loralee's head. "Ever been in a mine before?"

"No."

"It's dark. And wet. Your dress'll be ruined."

"I don't care about the dress! I care about the boy!"

"I'll go with you," he said, lighting his own lamp. "It's like a maze. You'd get lost in a minute."

She nodded. Her throat was dry. She was going into a mine, and despite her insistence that she wanted to go, the thought of being lowered into the earth terrified her.

Harry climbed into the basket and helped Loralee over the side.

"Let it go!" he shouted, and the makeshift elevator began its descent.

Around her, the air grew murky and damp, but Loralee kept her thoughts focused on the spragger who'd gotten "stuck." Spraggers were young men whose job it was to slow the cars full of coal as they rolled along the rails. They did this by jabbing a sharp stick, a "sprag," between the fast-moving wheels of the coal car and the tracks it rolled upon. It was one of the most dangerous jobs in the mines, and countless young men had lost fingers, hands, and even whole arms as a result of the all-too-frequent accidents.

"You got the stomach for this kind of thing?" Harry asked.

"I guess I'll find out."

"He'll be a-screamin'."

"Not for long he won't," Loralee said. "I've got chloroform."

"Chloroform won't help him."

"Who told you that?" Loralee asked.

"The regular doctor never uses it. Says it won't help with that kind of pain."

"What does he use?"

"Nothin'. Just cuts 'till the pain gets to be too much. Eventually, the kid'll pass out."

"Oh, my God! That's barbaric!" Her stomach churned at the thought of the pain so many men must have suffered at the hands of this "doctor."

"He doesn't seem to think so."

"And just where did he go to school? Who trained him?" Loralee asked, knowing, even as she did, that Harry would have no way of knowing those things.

"Din't go to school nowhere, far as I know. Trained with someone out of town."

The basket reached the bottom and landed against the floor of the mine with a thump. There were three men waiting anxiously at the bottom.

"Where's the doctor? Who's she?" one of them asked. "My boy needs a doctor!"

"I am a doctor," Loralee said. "The company doctor is not available. I've come down to help your son."

"But you're a woman!"

"Yes, I am," Loralee said calmly. "I'm a very well-educated, medically trained woman. Would you like me to leave, or would you like me to take care of your son?" This wasn't the first time her qualifications had been questioned because of her gender, and she waited while the impact of her words sank in.

The man hesitated only a few seconds. "Come on. He's this way."

She followed behind the three men, Harry by her side, holding her elbow. Water trickled down the walls and flowed across the floor. Some areas were merely damp, but most were completely covered with an inch or more of water. Loralee sloshed through it, trying to ignore the feel of the icy water as it seeped through her work boots.

"How far back is he?" she asked.

" 'Bout a quarter mile," Al's father answered. "You'll hear him soon."

Loralee prayed that Al had already passed out. The thought of the young man suffering was almost too much to bear. She hoped she didn't pass out herself when they finally reached him.

They walked through corridors that were about six feet high and six feet wide. Every so often, they'd pass a small inlet, a sort of room, where one man, maybe two would be working to fill a coal car.

Loralee heard what sounded like a far-off rumbling. "What was that?"

"Blasting."

"They're still blasting? Even with a man hurt?"

"Coal gotta keep movin'," Harry said. "These men get paid by how many cars they fill. Can't afford to stop work just because somebody's been injured. Besides, it happens all the time. They're used to it."

"Used to it?" Loralee asked. How could anyone ever get used to working in these conditions? "How deep are we?" she asked.

" 'Bout thirteen hundred feet."

"Thirteen hundred feet," she repeated. She looked up at the black ceiling above her. There were tons and tons of earth pressing down above her. She looked away.

"In here, missy," Mr. Boyle said. He opened a wooden door, and Loralee heard the screaming. Ahead, there was a bright spot, where several people had gathered, and the light from their lamps appeared blinding in this otherwise black world.

"Get the doctor!" the young man screamed. "Get me out!"

Loralee pushed her guides out of the way and ran the last few feet. She dropped to her knees beside the young man whose arm was caught between the wheels of the car.

"Al?" she said, opening her bag while she tried to assess

the situation, "My name is Loralee. I'm going to get you out of here."

"Where's the doctor?" Al asked. His eyes were wide with fear. Loralee knew from the words spoken outside, that he feared he'd be left to die.

"Your regular doctor wasn't available. I work with Doctor Farley. I'm going to give you some chloroform," she said, dripping a few drops of liquid onto a cloth. "I'll hold it over your nose, and you breathe deeply. It'll stop the pain."

"I don't want you to cut my arm off!" he shouted.

"I don't want that either," she said, clamping the cloth over his face. "Breathe."

Over her fingers, Al looked into her eyes. He breathed in deeply, staring at her until his head slumped sideways.

"He's asleep," she said, discarding the cloth. "I need some more light over here!"

The men rushed forward, and Loralee flattened herself against the floor. She wiggled until she could see behind the wheel where Al's hand was caught.

"Oh, thank God," she muttered.

"What? What do you see?" Al's father leaned forward.

"He's lost his fourth and fifth fingers, but he's still got a hand with three fingers left. His shirt sleeve has got his hand bound up against the wheel. It's holding it so tightly, it probably actually helped, by slowing down the bleeding." She wriggled out of her spot on the floor and sat up to reach into her bag. She pulled out a bottle and set it on the wet floor. The bandages, she set on her belly so they wouldn't get wet.

"All right," she said, lying back onto the floor, "I'm going to cut his sleeve free of the wheel. When I do, lift him away from the car. Try not to let his hand touch the floor. Ready?" she asked, scissors poised. "One, two three . . . okay, lift him!"

Al's father and Harry lifted the sleeping boy and another man held the wounded hand above the ground. Loralee sat up and slid toward him. She opened the bottle of peroxide and poured it over the missing fingers. Al never moved.

She poured some onto her own hands and rubbed them together. Only then did she reach for the bandages. "Hold his arm, but don't touch his hand! I need to wrap it, then we'll get him out of here."

She wrapped the hand, which, miraculously, was bleeding very little, and stood up. "All right. Who can carry him out of here?"

"I'll do it," Harry said.

"I want to go with my boy," Al's father said.

"Stay," Harry said. "You already lost Al's wages. You can't afford to lose yours, too. I'll see to it that he gets home."

Mr. Boyle was obviously torn. Loralee reached out and touched his sleeve. "I'll take good care of him. He'll be resting when you get home tonight."

The man looked at his son, slung over Harry's shoulder. "He's gonna be all right?"

"He's going to be fine," Loralee said. "He still has three fingers on that hand. He'll learn to work around that."

The man nodded and wiped his hands in his pants. "Thank you, missy. Thank you for savin' his arm."

Loralee smiled. "You're welcome."

She followed Harry through the dark tunnels, marveling that he managed to know where he was going when every one of the passageways looked exactly the same to her. They climbed into the basket and were lifted to the top.

"Harry?"

He looked at her, and, through the flickering lamp light, she could see his eyes.

"Would that doctor really have cut an arm off without using chloroform?"

"Does it all the time."

They reached the surface, and Harry looked away. Loralee blinked in the sunny brightness. Mary Boyle came rushing from the crowd. "Al! Oh, God! Al!" She turned to Loralee. "Is he dead? Oh, God—"

"No, Mary! He's not dead," she said, climbing over the side of the basket. "He's just sleeping. Lost two fingers, but he'll be fine."

"Oh, thank God," the woman cried, burying her face in the shoulder of her four-year-old, whom she was holding clutched to her chest.

"I can see your house from here. I'll carry him home," Harry said.

"I'll catch up to you," Loralee said. He raised a hand as he turned to go.

Loralee turned and looked back toward the opening of the shaft. Thirteen hundred feet worth of dirt and rock and coal had been suspended above her head. She looked down at her dress, which was soaking wet and covered with coal dirt.

Miners worked surrounded by those dark, damp, dangerous conditions every day.

And Jesse's father had died under those conditions.

Loralee shuddered, though the temperature was well over ninety degrees. She'd been into a coal mine and survived.

How many others would not?

"How long until you can convince your father that you should come to work for me full-time?" Edward asked Charles.

It was late Tuesday afternoon, and they sat in Edward's private office, papers and ledgers and books littering the table around them. Charles had spent the day being introduced to the workings of Vander Holdings.

"My father was fortunate enough to have six sons and only one daughter," Charles said. "He has plenty of help with the business. He won't even miss me."

"Well, I'd like to see you start as soon as possible. There's a lot to learn, and I see no reason to wait until after the wedding

to begin. Besides, those goddamn union organizers are buzzin'
around my men like flies on horseshit. And I'll be damned if
I'll cow down to those ignorant miners just because they call
themselves a union. I need help keeping the whole lot of them
in their place. That's where I figured I could use you.''

Charles smiled again. ''What, exactly, did you want me to
do?''

Edward looked into Charles's eyes, recognizing him for the
bootlicker that he was. ''Whatever needs to be done.''

Charles wisely kept his face blank. There'd been several
supposedly ''random'' fires and shootings in the past few
months. Except they weren't random at all. In every case, the
victims had been known union sympathizers. The warning was
out there for all to heed.

Charles cleared his throat and sat back in his chair, looking
his future father-in-law directly in the eyes. ''A man has to
protect his livelihood. You've worked hard to build Vander
Holdings into the company it is today. No one should be permitted to jeopardize that.''

Edward almost smiled. Almost, but not quite. So, he'd judged
correctly. Charles could be counted on to stand firmly in
Edward's camp.

''It's good to know that you feel that way.'' Edward eyed
him for several seconds before looking away and slapping the
ledger in front of him shut. ''Well, I think we've covered
enough for one day. It's almost dinnertime, in any case.''

Charles stood up, adjusting his pants and rolling down the
sleeves of his white shirt. ''I'll speak to my father and get a
firm date on when I can start here. Of course, I'll need to clear
up some of my responsibilities at Korwin Investments before
I leave.''

''Of course.''

Charles reached for his jacket and slipped it on, extending
his hand toward Edward as he did. ''Edward. I'm sure I'll be
seeing you within the next few days.''

Edward shook his hand. "Let me know when you can spare another day over here."

"Will do." He opened the door and stepped out, leaving Edward standing in the middle of his office, watching him go.

Charles may not have been Edward's first choice for Loralee's husband, but he was beginning to think that he might be the ideal man for the job after all. He had an ego like nobody's business. It wouldn't be difficult to persuade him that the Vander lifestyle, indeed their very livelihood, depended upon keeping the unions out of Vander Holdings. And, as part of the family, he would be expected to do his part toward that end.

Edward retrieved his own jacket from the back of the thickly padded chair behind his desk. Business could sometimes be such a messy affair. Perhaps it was time to draw young Charles into the flock. Test his mettle.

He closed all the books on his desk, put them into the safe, and locked it. He was the only person who had ever known the combination to that safe. His financial records were strictly off-limits to everyone in his employ. That would be changing.

He checked his watch, locked his office door and left the building, not saying a word to anyone as he left. Several people called out, "Have a good night, sir," or, "See you in the morning, sir." They needn't have bothered; he barely registered their existence as he made his way outside and into the waiting carriage that would take him home.

He spent the fifteen-minute ride thinking about the perfect way to embroil Charles in the family business. Yes, it was important that he knew the legitimate workings of Vander Holdings. But it was just as important that he learn, very simply, the way things were.

Certain practices, though not necessarily illegal, were frowned upon. Robbing pillars was thought to increase the likelihood of a cave-in. And yet, mining coal from the large blocks that had been left behind to support the overhead burden was common practice. Everyone did it, and even the mine inspectors looked the other way. And many activities were flat-out against the law. The hiring of young boys, for instance, to work in the breakers. Some of the children he'd seen climbing the steps to his own breakers looked barely more than five or six years old. Illegal, yes. But that didn't stop anyone from doing it.

Charles needed some grooming, that was all. He'd been accustomed to working with the wealthy, the elite. He didn't know what it was like to employ immigrants, most of whom could not speak a word of English. He didn't understand how to handle such people.

Edward thought about the man he had chosen to be his son-in-law. Despite Loralee's claims that Charles had been ''forceful'' with her, Edward was now more certain than ever that he'd chosen exactly the right man for the job.

It was true. Charles *was* spoiled. He *had* been sheltered. He had no idea what would be expected of him at Vander Holdings.

The carriage pulled onto the cobbled driveway of the Vander home, and Edward smiled as he looked out the window at the life he had built for himself. The Vander mansion was the biggest on the street. The biggest and the best.

Charles might be a bit naïve about the business dealings that were necessary to achieve such a lifestyle.

But he was smart. He'd learn.

CHAPTER NINE

Word of Loralee's foray into the mines spread, and, within days, she'd been summoned to help at another accident. A cave-in, this time. Two men, a miner and his laborer, nearly buried alive by the coal above their heads that had been shaken loose by nearby blasting. Their bodies were bloodied and twisted, but by the time they'd been dug free and hoisted to the surface, they were still whole, which, Loralee had learned, was the goal of nearly every accident victim.

It seemed that the practice of simply lopping off limbs that had been trapped beneath piles of coal, between fallen timbers or crushed beneath the weight of a fallen car was common practice. No matter that most of these amputations could be avoided.

If Loralee had ever doubted her desire to become a doctor, the trips down into the mines restored her determination. It was clear that miners were badly treated. What little medical care they received was marginal at best, downright damaging at worst. It was no wonder they were deathly afraid of doctors.

Loralee visited a different patch town every day. She'd gotten used to seeing chicken coops next to the backdoor and clothes-lines strung between the porch posts. And it no longer seemed odd to her to see a train track running through yards, sometimes even squeezed between houses. But before that night three weeks ago, she'd never imagined Jesse growing up in such conditions. Now ... well, now it seemed she couldn't stop thinking about it.

It had been exactly three weeks since Loralee had last seen Jesse. In spite of her efforts to keep busy, he was never far from her mind. She had sent a note to his home, asking that he talk with her. It had been returned, unread.

Jesse didn't want to discuss their problem, and so she had begun to focus on another.

Charles.

After her father's last outburst and refusal to cancel the wedding, she'd been too frightened to bring it up again. Suppose he responded by moving the wedding date even closer?

She most certainly could not have that happening. It took a few days to come up with a plan, and to store up enough courage to go through with it, but now, she was ready. In just a few hours, she'd be free of Charles for good.

The day before, she had sent a note to Charles, requesting that he reserve his lunch hour for her. She needed to discuss the wedding. Having already been informed of the change in date by Edward, he sent an immediate return. Yes, they had best settle the plans for the wedding. He would wait for her in his office and they could walk to Memorial Park to eat their lunch.

Loralee had no intention of lunching in the park with him. She planned on breaking their engagement in plain view of his father, his brothers, and Suzanne, who was coming along for moral support. Surely, he would not threaten her physically with so many people looking on.

She'd arranged with Dr. Farley to have the afternoon off,

and, at eleven-thirty, a half-hour earlier than usual, they closed the office.

The dress she was wearing was a lightweight calico of light blue background with tiny yellow flowers. She slipped her apron off her shoulders and examined the dress, and found that, luckily, it was still clean.

She untied her braid and brushed her hair, the tight plait leaving it even wavier than usual. She donned a wide-brimmed straw hat and tied the yellow ribbon beneath her chin. Ready.

Loralee paced the waiting room, watching through the front window for the first glimpse of Suzanne. At eleven-forty-five, she spotted her and hurried out the back entrance, and around the side of the building.

"I'm ready," Loralee said breathlessly.

The girls walked slowly toward Broad and Church Streets, where the offices of Korwin Investment Services was located. Loralee had arranged to meet Charles at noon. There was no avoiding it any longer.

"What do you suppose he'll say?" Suzanne asked.

"I have no idea," Loralee said flatly. "He thinks I'm coming to work out the details of our wedding. How he'll react when I break our engagement is anyone's guess."

"I can't believe you're really going to do it!"

Loralee looked at her friend. "Well, I am. And I want you by my side as though we're stuck together at the shoulder with paste. I mean it," she said when Suzanne laughed. "I need someone nearby to catch me in the event I drop over from fright."

"You'll be fine," Suzanne said, wrapping her arm around Loralee. "You are one of the bravest people I know. And I'd be willing to bet that, when word of this gets out, there'll be a whole rash of broken engagements across this town. You'll give every woman who's being forced into marriage with a man she does not love the courage to stand up and say I won't do it!"

Loralee smiled, in spite of the jitters that were causing her hands to shake. "I'm not looking to be anyone's inspiration. I just want to avoid a lifetime of misery."

They stepped up to the doorway, and Suzanne said, "Okay. Let's do it!"

With one last deep, fortifying breath, Loralee turned the knob, and the door swung open, announcing their arrival with the gentle chime of small brass bells. Everyone in the place looked toward the door.

"Loralee!" Thomas Korwin said, dropping a sheet of paper he had been looking at onto a nearby desk. He stepped forward, reaching for her hand. "It's so good to see you." He bent forward and kissed her hand. "And Miss Becker," he said, offering the same kiss to Suzanne. "To what do we owe this lovely interruption?" He smiled a genuinely happy smile, and Loralee felt the first pang of guilt for what she was about to do. Charles's family had always been more than cordial, they'd been downright friendly. It struck her suddenly that what she was about to do was not very nice.

Then she looked up and saw Charles looking at Suzanne. His animosity toward Loralee's closest friend was written clearly on his face. And she thought, Charles does not deserve to be treated nicely.

"I've come to see Charles," she said, trying to smile the best she could. "Would it be all right if we went over to his desk to talk with him for a few minutes?"

"Certainly," Thomas Korwin said. "But it's almost lunch time. Why don't I get him for you, and he can take you two ladies out to lunch?"

"Oh, that's very nice of you, Mr. Korwin, but really, I can't stay for lunch anyway. I only need to speak to him briefly."

"All right then," he said, swinging a hinged, mid-thigh-high wooden door open for her to pass through. "Take your time."

"This won't take long," she said, her heart hammering so hard she was sure everyone in the room could hear it. Suzanne stayed dutifully beside her, smiling at each of Charles's brothers in turn as they passed by their desks on the way to the back of the room, where Charles sat.

He stood up as they approached. "What is *she* doing here?" he asked quietly.

"We're going to do some shopping," Loralee said.

"I thought we were going to talk about the wedding. I don't want to do that with her in between us."

"You won't need to," she said. She held out her hand and placed the gold engagement brooch he had given to her on his desk. She'd never worn it.

He looked down at it. "What's this?" he asked, his eyebrows raised as he waited for her explanation.

Loralee took a deep breath, drawing on every bit of strength and will she possessed. "I'm calling off our wedding, Charles. This is the brooch you gave to me after the announcement of our engagement. I wouldn't feel right keeping it."

"Calling off the wedding?" he asked incredulously. "Does Edward know about this?"

Loralee dropped her gaze to the floor, knowing even as she did so, that she had given him his answer. "No, he doesn't know. But I'm sure he will, as soon as you can find him and tell him."

She looked up and saw him smiling, ridiculing her. It was the same look he'd worn that night in the carriage after she'd danced with Jesse. And she knew then that she was right to do this in front of a room full of people. Charles would have used privacy against her.

"You know he'll never let you do this, Loralee."

His smile mocked her. He was so certain that Loralee would be his that her announcement only amused him. He didn't even bother to ask why she was doing it.

"He has no choice, Charles. This is my life," she said, pressing a hand to her heart. "I will live it as I see fit. And my plans do not include marriage to a man I do not love."

And then, in what was the ultimate insult, he laughed. Loud, raucous laughter filled the building, so loud that everyone turned to look.

But Loralee wasn't embarrassed. She was free.

"Good-bye, Charles," she said, turning and walking between the other desks. Suzanne stayed glued to her side, just as she had promised.

At the doorway, Charles's father was standing, watching his son with a look of confusion on his face. Loralee reached out and rested her hand on his arm. "I'm so sorry," she said. She glanced back at Charles, who was still standing. He mouthed the words *You'll be back.*

Suddenly, Loralee couldn't stop herself from smiling. And even though she had been taught that a lady never shouts across a room, she called out, "Not in this lifetime, Charles!"

And with that, her days as the future Mrs. Charles Korwin officially ended.

"She did *what?*" Edward bellowed. He jumped up out of his chair and stood behind his desk with both hands resting on it as though he needed help to remain standing. Just as Loralee had known he would do, Charles had rushed to Edward's office immediately. Not even a half hour had passed since she'd delivered her message.

"You heard me, Edward," Charles said. "She marched right into our office and announced to everyone there that she would not marry me."

"We'll just see about that," Edward said, growing red in the face. "She might be a reluctant bride, but a bride she will be! A woman her age should have been married years ago. Twenty-two," he said, almost to himself as he began pacing the small room. "Should've had her settled down the day she turned eighteen."

"I think you'll find her a little more than reluctant," Charles said, knowing that he was fanning the flames of Edward's anger. "When I asked her whether or not she had spoken to you about calling off the wedding, she informed me that there's nothing you can do to force her into marriage."

Edward stopped his pacing. "She said that?" he asked quietly.

"Yes, sir, she did."

Edward clamped his mouth shut and stood still, staring intently at the floor. "My daughter underestimates me," he said softly.

Charles watched the quiet resolve settle over Edward's features. He felt his lips twitching and had to struggle to keep from smiling as he wondered exactly how Loralee would be punished! His gray eyes glittered as he thought about the way he would have handled Loralee if she were already living under his rule. Oh, the thrill of teaching that headstrong woman to bend to his will! The thought of it excited him enough to really want to be married to Loralee.

Edward just nodded his head. With the gold engagement brooch clutched firmly in his hand, Charles turned and left, playing the part of a heartbroken jilted lover expertly.

Five seconds out the door and he made a decision. He turned the carriage toward home instead of toward his office. No one would expect him to work today, anyway. Not after the pain he'd been through. He smiled to himself as he pulled up to the carriage house behind the Korwin home.

He left the rig there with the stable boy and took off on foot through the alley, cutting across streets and yards as he went. His destination was only a few blocks away, and he wanted to arrive as unobtrusively as possible. He slipped a key from his pocket into the back gate and let himself into the estate, carefully walking among the trees and hedges so as not to be noticed.

With a different key, he unlocked the French doors that led from the secluded patio into Abby's private suite of rooms. Quickly, he checked the rooms. All empty.

The tiny clock on Abby's dressing table chimed softly. It was two-thirty. He'd have plenty of time to satisfy his lust and have both himself and Abby back at their respective dinner tables with no one the wiser to their little rendezvous.

Charles was alone in his lover's bedroom. A smile tugged at the corner of his mouth. He turned slowly, eyeing each drawer in turn. Which one? Which one?

At the dressing table he pulled out a long, skinny drawer with a brush, a mirror and a button hook lying in it. Hmm. Not much. Slowly, he slid the drawer closed.

The center drawer of the bureau was better. Stockings. Pair after pair of silk stockings, folded flat and resting between layers of scented tissue paper. He selected a black pair and draped them across the foot of the bed.

The room suddenly felt warm, and he took off his jacket, removed his tie and loosened his collar. Then he rolled up his sleeves and stepped into Abby's closet. He filtered through dozens of gowns, all of them tight-fitting and low-cut, until he found what he was looking for. A section of undergarments and sheer nightclothes.

Smiling, he rifled through his lover's belongings, choosing the items he was in the mood to see her wear. A black corset that cinched her waist tightly, pushing her ample breasts up so high that they spilled over the top. The stockings, already on the bed. And over it all, a filmy black wrap that reached the floor, yet hid nothing.

Charles had just finished making his selections when he heard someone enter the room. He stood perfectly still.

A woman stepped into the room and closed the door with a bang. She kicked off her shoes and swore softly. Charles smiled. Abby.

He stepped out of the closet, her clothing in his arms. She gasped when she saw him and pressed a hand to her heart, but said nothing. Her gaze dropped to the clothing he held in his arms, and she smiled slowly. A deliciously wicked smile.

Charles was relieved. Only three days had passed since they'd argued, but already she had forgiven him. She turned and walked to the door, locking them into total privacy.

Abby took his hand and led him to her bed. She reached up and cradled his face in her hands. "I've missed you," she said.

He settled his hand on her waist. "Show me how much."

Hours later, when the sun had fallen behind the trees and long shadows stretched across the lawn, the edge of a lace curtain moved ever so slightly. But the man slipping out through the back gates never even noticed.

Edward walked into the house and went directly upstairs, to the bedroom he shared with his wife. It was late and he was hot. Loralee would just have to wait for his reprimand until he was good and ready to give it. He opened the bedroom door and found his personal valet waiting with a bowl of steaming water and clean, hot towels, as usual.

"Good evening, sir," he said, reaching out to remove Edward's coat.

"Good evening, Gibbons." Gibbons had been his valet for over twenty years, and he was the only member of the household staff that ever received a response to his greetings. He was also the only one ever called by name.

"It's warm today," the valet said—an understatement, amid the near hundred-degree weather. "There's a pitcher of ice water on the table." He stepped into the huge closet, hung the jacket and brushed it before placing it with the others. Then, he removed a lighter weight gray dinner jacket and a pair of black and gray striped trousers.

Edward unbuttoned his top button and stopped to pour a glass of ice water. He drank thirstily from it, refilling it twice. He stood with his feet spread, looking at the enormous four-poster bed that dominated the entire room. He still stood there, the glass in his hand, staring at the bed when Gibbons stepped back into the room.

"Would you like a shave, sir?"

Edward blinked his eyes and snapped out of his daydreams. Did he really want a run-in with Loralee after the day he'd had? He ran a hand up his cheek. Stubble.

He made a quick decision, tossed back the rest of the water in his glass and set it on the table next to the pitcher. "Yes, I would, Gibbons. And when you're finished, bring me fresh water and a clean set of undergarments as well. And tell the stable boy that I want a carriage after all, but I'll take the shay. I won't be needing a driver."

"Very well, sir," Gibbons said, knowing, after so many years what those instructions meant.

Edward Vander would be spending the evening with his mistress.

Abby's bedroom door opened, and she looked up from the mirror where she was dressing for another evening of entertaining.

Zachary walked in and looked at her maid, but said nothing. The woman dropped the brush she had been using to fix Abby's hair and fled the room, closing the door tightly behind her.

He stood staring at her for so long that Abby started to shake. Now what did he want her to do?

"It happened again, Abby, didn't it?"

He knew! Shock ran through her as the realization of what that meant began to sink in.

"You, above all, should know that these very walls have eyes and ears. I may be old," he said, "but I am not stupid."

He knew. She sat staring straight ahead. There was nothing she could say.

"Look at me," he said softly.

Immediately, she raised her eyes to his.

"Take those clothes off."

"I can't. I need Claire—"

"Well, then, get Claire back in here."

Abby sat there, too terrified to speak.

"Claire!" he bellowed, and the woman hurried back into the room so quickly, Abby thought she must surely have been waiting outside the door for his call. "My wife needs your help to prepare." He didn't say what she was being prepared for. Neither woman asked. "Undress her."

Zachary stood straight and tall beside the door. And Abby scrambled to do his bidding, lest his desires have more time to warp.

She didn't care so much what he did to her. She'd stopped caring long ago. But, that the entire household staff knew what she allowed her body to be subjected to, that was what she condemned him for.

Claire hurried to unbutton the dress and untie the corset. When Abby stood wearing only lace pantaloons, he said simply, "Those, too."

Abby pulled the string at her waist, and they dropped to the floor.

When Claire made a move as though to leave, he said, "I'll need a pail of water, make sure it's hot, and the lye soap."

"Yes, sir."

"Oh, and the stiffest scrub brush in the house."

Claire had been moving toward the door, but at his words, her footsteps faltered. She looked at Abby, standing naked in the middle of the room, and dropped her gaze quickly to the floor. "Yes, sir," she said quietly, as she turned away and left the room.

Abby stood there, her arms hanging at her sides, knowing what was about to happen, and powerless to stop it.

Zachary removed his coat and rolled up his sleeves.

She was scared. And though she hated herself for it, she began to whimper.

"Now, love, you know why I have to do this, don't you?" he asked softly. "Don't you?" He reached up to caress Abby's face with his knurled, old hands.

She turned away from him.

Claire came back into the room bearing the steaming bucket and a heavy blanket. She draped the blanket across the bed and left, with one lingering look at her mistress.

"Lie on the bed, Abby."

Hesitating would only make it worse, she knew. She climbed up onto the bed.

He dipped the brush into the water and rubbed the harsh lye soap against the bristles.

"Open your legs."

She did as he requested and began to pray, searching for a place to rest her mind while her husband desecrated her body, all in the name of "cleansing" her of her infidelities.

The scalding water dripped onto her tender skin, and before she could even register the burn, he ravaged the coarse bristles against her most delicate skin.

He scrubbed and scrubbed, and Abby bit back her screams until she could stand it no more.

"Please! Zachary, please stop!" she screamed, her hands clutching at the blanket.

The scrubbing stopped immediately. Pale pink water ran onto the blanket beneath her.

"You know why I have to do this, don't you? Don't you?" he asked again when she didn't answer.

"Yes," she whispered, tears running from the corners of her eyes down the sides of her face and into her hair.

"You haven't honored our agreement, Abby. And for that you must be punished, as well as cleansed. Now, open." He lifted the bucket of hot, lye-laced water, and when she spread her knees, he poured it on her slowly, allowing it plenty of time to seep inside her body, where it would kill the seed of whomever his wife had pleasured. He pushed his finger inside her, swiping it thoroughly against the walls of her body. He withdrew it and dipped it into the remaining water in the bucket, then dried his hands on Abby's bedding.

She dropped her legs and lay still, trying to find a way to endure the physical pain, as well as the humiliation.

Rolling down his sleeves, Zachary said, "You would be wise to consider the consequences of your actions. Our guests will be here in an hour. Dress."

And without another word, he turned and left the room.

CHAPTER TEN

"Oh, look, Loralee! Aren't they pretty?" Suzanne said, holding out a fistful of ribbons.

It was Saturday afternoon, and the girls had been window shopping since noon. They'd stopped at Evans' General Store to pick up a few things for Fiona and had already been browsing the aisles for close to a half hour.

Loralee looked up to where Suzanne was standing with the ribbons trailing toward the floor. She reached out and pulled a strand of white lace interwoven with pink ribbon from Suzanne's hand. "I love this one." She added the pink and white ribbon to the growing pile in her arms. "Before I look at anything else, let me get the things Mother asked for so I don't forget. She needs some embroidery thread."

She found the tiny spools of thread and chose the colors her mother had specified. She walked to the counter where the writing paper was found and selected several sheets with pretty designs for Fiona to use when writing to her sisters. She added two new pairs of white stockings to the top of her heaping arms and decided to carry her purchases back to the counter before she dropped them all.

She turned and stepped into the aisle and slammed headlong into Jesse Sinclair.

"Pardon me, miss. I—"

"Oh! I'm so sorr-"

They stood still as statues. Around them, tiny spools of thread hit the floor and spun in every direction. The writing paper drifted to their feet. The ribbon clung to the splintery edge of a wooden shelf. The only thing either one of them had managed to catch was one pair of ladies' stockings. Each.

Loralee looked down and found herself holding a pair of unmentionables in her right hand. She whipped her arm behind her back so fast it nearly came out of the socket.

Jesse was holding the other pair. Awkwardly, he held them out to her. "Uh . . . I think these are—"

Her hand shot out and yanked the darned things right out of his grasp. She could die! She could just die!

She kept her eyes glued to the toes of his worn boots. Maybe he would just go away. Just walk away and let her nurse her embarrassment in peace. She waited patiently for his feet to start moving.

She waited. And waited.

She should have known better than to think he'd make things any easier for her. Those boots weren't moving. Slowly, her eyes drifted upwards, up over soft, worn denim. Jeans that had, long ago, molded themselves to his shape. Loralee's mouth went dry.

He shuffled his weight from one foot to the other, as if settling in, to allow her a good, hard look. With knowledge that he was watching her discomfort she met his stare, locking on his pale blue eyes. His smirk wiped away all traces of her embarrassment, replacing it with indignation. How dare he mock her!

"Get a good look, Miss Vander?" he asked, his voice soft

and seductive. He smiled at her and slowly scrutinized every curve of her body, all the way down the front of her dress and back up again.

Loralee's eyes widened. "Don't you dare look at me like that!"

"Why not, Miss *Vander*? You seemed to enjoy my touch. My gaze can't be all that unpleasant." The words were whispered, silky soft.

Like lightning, her hand shot out, and she slapped his face, hard enough that within seconds, it had raised to a red welt. He lifted his fingers to his cheek, touching the imprint her hand had left.

"I-I'm sorry," she stammered. "I shouldn't . . . I'm sorry," she repeated.

The fire in his eyes leapt out at her, and he leaned forward as though to take a step toward her. Loralee watched his face and knew the precise moment when the knowledge of who she was once again took control of him. She watched him rein in his volatile emotions and replace them with a mask of indifference.

But his eyes, his beautiful, expressive eyes, were beyond his control. They were hard as ice. And he leveled them on her and said, "Don't be."

He turned and walked out, and Loralee was filled with relief that he was gone. Her hands shook, and her legs felt weak. And, for reasons that she did not understand, she cried.

Ten minutes later, Jesse marched into the stable and flung open the stall of his best stallion. Majesty, with his black coat and temperament to match, was the most powerful animal Jesse had ever ridden. He saddled up and was riding away from the house in minutes. He rode east on Diamond, heading toward Stockton. He followed the road until he came to a railroad crossing, and, turning, he started down the bed.

The ground was level, and Majesty took to it well, running

effortlessly for miles, at speeds that would have left a lesser animal winded. Jesse pushed him, and Majesty responded immediately, picking up speed and racing along miles of railroad track.

In the distance, Jesse heard the bellow of an approaching train, and he eased the pressure on the stallion until they reached a slow trot. He called softly, "Whoa, whoa, boy," until they were standing still.

Jesse knew this stretch of track. They were on a slight downward grade, and the train would be traveling at about thirty miles per hour by the time it reached them. The next stop was a little over ten miles away, and the engineer wouldn't begin to slow down until he approached it.

The ground trembled as the steam engine drew closer, and Majesty began to prance nervously. "Whoa, boy, it's okay," Jesse said, leaning forward to brush the animal's strong neck. "Pretty soon, Majesty. You gonna show me what you got? Hmm? You gonna show me?" He patted the horse, and he stilled almost instantly, despite the increasing vibrations as the train drew near.

Jesse smiled at the horse's reaction. He'd never once led Majesty into danger, and the animal trusted him, even when his instincts told him not to.

The engineer would spot them soon, and Jesse anticipated this, leaning low against Majesty's neck, speaking to him softly and reassuring him that everything was okay. He held the reins tightly, prepared, in case the animal spooked.

The engineer saw them, and as was customary, blew the whistle in warning of his approach. The sound ripped through the air, but Majesty did little more than prance. Jesse stroked his neck gently, waiting, waiting.

And then the engine was beside them, an enormous thing, roaring past so fast that Jesse could barely count the cars. He waited until the last car had passed them, then he dug his heels into Majesty's sides.

"Hya, hya!" he called loudly, and the horse took off, picking up speed as the train sped away from them. The distance between them increased, then slowly decreased as Majesty broke into his stride. Jesse rode low, urging the animal on, and in no more than a few minutes, they had almost reached the last car.

Jesse rode that horse for all he was worth. They reached the last car and passed it, but Jesse didn't let up. One by one, they passed every car until the only one that remained was the engine. With all he had, Majesty ran, his hooves pounding the ground mercilessly. He knew now what his rider wanted him to do, and Jesse felt him stretch to the limit, nose to nose with the massive steel horse beside him. And with a burst of energy, Majesty pulled ahead, not content to win by a hair, and kept on going, until the sound of the engine grew dimmer. Only then did he slow.

"Yahoo, Majesty! We did it!" Jesse cried, his own blood pumping hard. He slid from the saddle almost before the horse had stopped and walked around to stroke the stallion's nose. Majesty nuzzled into Jesse's shoulder and stomped his feet, still worked up from the race he had just won.

As the train passed, Jesse laughed and waved to the engineer who was smiling and shaking his head. Feeling somewhat purged of his anger, Jesse turned and started to lead the horse home.

"Come on, boy. Let's go." He stroked the animal's wet coat then climbed back into the saddle and rode easily, giving Majesty a proper cooling down.

Almost immediately his thoughts turned to Loralee. That woman drove him crazy! He simply could not trust himself to be around her. She'd slapped him with every bit of might she possessed. And, God help him, if he didn't almost grab her and kiss her breathless right there in the middle of Evans' General Store!

The ride back into town passed quickly, and he was home

before he knew it. He led Majesty into the stable, removed the saddle and hung it, and on his way back, scooped out a bucket of oats.

"There you go, boy. Dessert." He patted the horse's neck and began brushing the ebony coat. He didn't stop until it was gleaming. And not for one second did thoughts of Loralee Vander leave his mind.

He walked back to the house and settled into the library, hoping that the work he had piled up for himself would, at the very least, distract him.

It didn't. It unnerved him; it agitated him; it disturbed him. But Loralee was still firmly embedded in his thoughts when his brother knocked on the door an hour later.

"Hey, brub," John said, poking his head around the door. "You busy?"

"Always busy." But at least now he was smiling. It had been a long time since John had called him by the nickname he'd been stuck with for years. Brub. Shortened from "brubber," Johnny's babyhood pronunciation of the word brother.

"Let's go out tonight," John said eagerly.

"Can't."

"You haven't been out in weeks."

"I'm tired, John. I've been working night and day to help out with Dad's rotations, and with this heat wave hanging on the way it has been, it doesn't look like I'll get a break until after Labor Day."

"By then I'll be back at school. I thought I'd have one last night on the town with my brother before heading back. I won't be home again until Christmas, you know."

"I know." Jesse looked at his brother and, once again, saw the eyes of the little five-year-old boy, begging to tag along with his big "brubber". Jesse never had been able to deny him anything. He sighed and tossed his pen on to the desk. He wouldn't be getting any more work done tonight. "What time do you want to leave?"

"You'll go?" John asked, his eyes lighting up, just like they had when he was a kid.

Jesse chuckled. "I'll go. You know, it's not that I don't want to spend time with you. It just . . . there's so much work. Stephen's running himself ragged trying to see to it that none of the workers are hurt by this heat. I can't let him do it all alone."

John stared, and his smile faded to something a little more cynical. "Very noble of you, Jess. But I think there's another reason altogether."

Jesse's eyes hardened, and his chest tightened. "What do you mean?"

John looked down at his brother as though assessing him thoroughly. He pulled a chair up to the other side of the desk. Sitting down, he captured Jesse's gaze, and held it.

"Jesse, you're my brother. We share the same blood. My mother was your mother, my father was your father. There is nothing that you have to keep from me. There is nothing you could do, nothing in this world, that would make me think less of you. I know why you're working so hard. I know why you're punishing yourself. And I know that it's not going to work."

Jesse looked away, embarrassed that his emotions were so apparent. "Why did it have to be her?" he asked softly.

"I don't know. But it's not going to go away, no matter how much coal you shovel."

Jesse leaned back into the leather upholstered chair and looked off into the distance. "This is not just a physical attraction. If it was just that, she'd be easily forgotten. It's that . . . when she's near me, I feel . . ." He closed his eyes, searching for the right word. "Whole. I feel whole. And when she moves out of my arms, it's like ripping away a part of myself." He looked back at John, his expression pained. "I barely even know her, but when I look into her eyes . . . it's like our souls have known each other forever."

"Aw, Jess," John said, "you have to get beyond the past."

"I can't."

"You have to."

"I can't!" he exclaimed, shoving away from the desk to pace nervously in front of the windows. "When I think about what we lost because of Edward Vander, my blood boils! A mother. A father. Two sisters. I can't do it, Johnny! I'd never be able to live with myself."

The minutes ticked by, while both men thought about what had been said. Finally, John stood up, concern for his brother written clearly on his face. "I guess you have to do what you feel is right. You know I'll stand behind you, whatever your choice."

"Thanks, John."

Jesse leaned back, his arms braced against the edge of the windowsill, and watched as John walked toward the doorway. He stopped just before reaching it and turned around.

"You know, we've grown up watching the love that Stephen and Elizabeth share. I think we've both come to expect that out of life. The sad thing is that love like theirs is so uncommon." He looked up into Jesse's eyes. "I know if I found it, I'd hold onto it with both hands, and there's not a man alive who could persuade me to let go." He paused as thought he wanted to say something else but had changed his mind. Then he said softly, "I'll meet you downstairs at nine."

He turned and left, closing the door softly behind him.

Jesse stood gripping the windowsill, his brother's words bouncing around inside his head. He *had* found it. Loralee was the one, and he knew it. Jesse'd been with enough women to know the difference between love and lust. And this was definitely not just about lust.

But it didn't matter. He couldn't have her. What he'd told John was true. He'd never be able to live with himself.

His dark mood had grown positively black. He was hardly in the mood for a party, but, hell, if he had to go, he might as well make the best of it. He'd park himself at a table and find a waiter who'd keep his glass full for a few hours. Sooner or later someone was bound to start looking good.

That's what he'd do. He'd drown his sorrows in wine and women.

He *would* have a good time tonight. He *would* dance with other women. And he would *not* let Loralee into his thoughts.

He walked straight to the liquor cabinet and pulled out a bottle of brandy and a glass. He would *not* think about Loralee Vander.

He repeated that thought with the first shot. He said it out loud with the second. By the time he had reached the third, he realized that the only way he could possibly succeed in wiping her from his thoughts was to simply wipe away *all* thought.

He poured once more, and swallowed.

Fiona was sitting with her needlework resting idly in her lap when she heard the clatter of hooves on the cobblestone drive. A carriage pulled to the front door, stopped briefly, then pulled away. It was nine forty-five, and Loralee had left with Suzanne and her parents not a half hour earlier. Perhaps she'd forgotten something. Who else could it be?

Edward had left the house early this morning. He hadn't even waited long enough for breakfast to be served, and if it wasn't for the fact that it was Saturday night, Fiona would have been wondering where he was.

The front door swung open, and a very drunk Edward stumbled in.

"Edward!" Fiona said, placing her work carefully in the basket that sat on the floor. She stood up and hurried to her husband, who turned so quickly at the sound of her voice that he almost toppled over.

"Here, Edward, why don't we sit down," she said, leading him toward the sofa. He dropped into it the way a deer hits the ground after it's been shot. Thud. Then nothing.

Fiona panicked. She wasn't sure what to do with this man. Edward sober and mean, she could handle. She'd had years of experience with him.

Her husband picked up one of her hands, holding it between his own, as he had when they were courting. "Where could she be?" he asked, holding her fingers to his mouth and covering them with slobbery kisses.

Thinking he meant Loralee, and wondering how he knew that she was not home, Fiona asked, "What do you mean, Edward?"

He looked up at her with tear-filled eyes. "Lily. Where could she be? I looked everywhere I could think. You don't think she's . . ." His voice trailed off.

Fiona felt her heart hammering against her chest, heard the blood rushing through her veins. Lily! After all these years, she finally had a name. Lily. "Edward, I don't know anyone named Lily," she said.

He looked at her as though she must be confused. Then, suddenly, understanding dawned in his eyes. "No. No, I guess you don't." He collapsed sideways onto the sofa, and lay snoring on the cushions.

The town's elite knew the end of summer was near, and they'd taken advantage of the few remaining weekends. There were parties scheduled for every Friday and Saturday night clear through to Labor Day.

As was usual, Loralee was attending this one with Suzanne and her parents. The girls had just stopped for a glass of cool lemonade when Suzanne muttered, "Oh, my goodness, oh, my goodness . . ." Her eyes were wide as she gazed across the room.

"What?" Loralee asked, looking over her shoulder.

Not ten feet away stood Jesse, his blue eyes fixed intently on Loralee. Her breath caught in her throat, and she reached up and touched trembling fingertips to the exposed skin of her neck, as though to free the air that was trapped there by his penetrating gaze.

His eyes followed her movement and swept down her neck, over her bare skin and lingered on her breasts. She felt the heat of his stare, felt it as surely as if he had run his warm hands over her. Then he looked back into her eyes and smiled. That cocky little smile that told her he'd enjoyed the show.

"Why, that arrogant, pig-headed—" she said, advancing toward him.

"Loralee!" Suzanne's hand shot out and grabbed her elbow. "I think you better stay here."

"Did you see what he did? Did you see how he looked at me?" She turned her back toward him. "Honestly, that man makes my blood boil! I could just—"

"Okay, okay," Suzanne interrupted, holding up one hand. "I get the picture."

Neither one of them noticed Jesse moving toward them until he spoke.

"Good evening, Miss Becker. Miss Vander." He kept his eyes glued to Loralee.

"Mr. Sinclair," Suzanne said with a smile. "How nice to see you again."

"Thank you." He looked at Suzanne. "You're looking lovely tonight, Miss Becker. That shade of blue suits you."

"Why, thank you," she said.

"And, Miss Vander," he said, turning glassy eyes back to Loralee. He looked boldly to the deep cleavage she was showing. "That gown is a real eye-catcher." The words rumbled deep in his throat, their meaning perfectly clear.

Loralee caught herself an instant before she slapped his face. It took every bit of restraint that she possessed, but she would *not* make a spectacle of herself.

"May I see you outside on the front porch, Mr. Sinclair? I believe we have some unfinished business, and I think it would be wise to conduct it where we might find some privacy.'' Her voice, which shook with rage inside her head, slipped out of her mouth sounding controlled, low, and *very* seductive.

Jesse glanced at Suzanne as though she might offer some explanation for Loralee's outrageous behavior. But Suzanne was staring at her friend like she had just seen a demon. Well-bred young ladies did *not* invite men outside for *privacy*!

He looked at Loralee and smiled. ''With pleasure, Miss Vander. Lead the way.''

She turned on her heel and moved through the crowded room so fast that if Jesse glanced away, he just might lose her in the crowd. The brandy he'd consumed wasn't helping. He knew in which direction he wanted to go, but he was having a difficult time getting his legs to cooperate. It had been years since he'd drunk this much, and he'd forgotten how much he disliked the way his sense of control fled with his sobriety.

Loralee reached the front door and swung the screen door wide open, letting it slam behind her so that it almost hit him in the face. He cleared his throat and blinked his eyes and tried to prepare for the confrontation before him. Jesse was in no state to do battle with her, and he knew it.

He had barely stepped onto the porch when she turned on him. ''I spoke to my father about the accusations you flung upon him. For your information, Mr. Sinclair, Vander Holdings no longer even owns the property to which you referred. It was sold a long time ago. And, though I am loath to say the words—''

''Did he, or did he not, own that property in 1869?''

''Yes, but—''

''It makes no difference to me what he did with the land after the accident. The only thing that matters is that my father was killed by your father's greed.''

''He did nothing illegal—''

''Did he tell you that?'' He advanced another step toward her, and she stepped back a bit. ''All right, I'll grant you that.

What he did was not illegal at the time. It was, however, wrong. Having a second opening was considered standard practice! Other mine owners did it. They didn't wait for the government to make a law *forcing* them to do it. They did it because it was the right thing to do.'' He laughed derisively and shook his head. ''Loralee, you are so naive. Edward Vander cares about Edward Vander. What's it going to take for you to realize that?''

Loralee stood less than a foot away from him. Jesse looked down into her eyes and wished for the thousandth time that her father was anyone other than Edward Vander. He wanted to touch her so badly that his fingers twitched. But he couldn't. And, in order to distract himself, he threw another taunt at her. ''I gather you never knew your father was a killer?''

She stood silently for a few seconds, and then looked away, and he had his answer.

''You are such a spoiled, little rich girl.''

Loralee's head shot up. ''I am not spoiled, and I am *not* a little girl.''

''Oh, *really*.'' He knew he would regret it later. Hell, he regretted it even before he moved. But he was hurting, and his body was begging for just one touch, just one more sweet taste . . .

In one easy motion, Jesse wrapped his arm around her waist and pulled her flush against his length. His other hand dove into the mass of disheveled curls that tumbled over her shoulders. He tilted her head back and bent forward to meet her.

His mouth claimed hers, hastily, greedily. No gentle exploration, no teasing temptation in this kiss. Jesse knew what he wanted, and he moved right in and took it.

Nothing less than total possession.

Loralee opened her mouth to him, more, he knew, from shock than anything else, and Jesse took advantage of it. He kissed her as though he had to make the memory of it last for all time.

His mind had lost the ability to control the will of his body, which was straining to reach its own goal despite the amount of alcohol he'd consumed. Jesse's need for her was too great, and he reveled in the pleasure of her. He wound his finger around the ribbon that was threaded through her hair.

"This is madness." He heard the words and recognized his own voice, but couldn't recall having spoken. He held Loralee tighter.

She'd been responding to his kisses from the beginning, but, suddenly, she broke away. "Jesse, stop." Her breathing was labored, and Jesse could see that the last thing she wanted to do was stop.

"This is ridiculous," she said, laughing nervously and backing a step away from him. She held a hand against her heart and fought to control her breathing. "I came out here to apologize to you, not to—" She stopped abruptly and shook her head. "This has to stop." She touched delicate fingers to her reddened lips.

Jesse was still breathing heavily, and, as she spoke, he let his gaze wander freely over her. Finally, her words seeped in to his alcohol-dulled brain. "Apologize for what?"

Loralee looked up at him for several seconds, then closed her eyes and shook her head. "The last time we spoke . . . the things you said . . . I . . ." She sighed and looked away, as though she was disgusted with herself for stumbling over her words. She snapped her head up and said, "You were right. I spoke to several people, and I found out some things about my father that I wish I had never known. He was wrong. And I'm sorry."

It was a shocking revelation. Jesse had never expected either an admission of guilt or an apology. He'd thought about this moment for years, wished for it, and now, here it was. Somehow, Jesse had always thought he'd feel more satisfaction at hearing those words. It had cost Loralee deeply to speak them, and as Jesse watched her struggle with it, he felt his anger slowly melting away.

"I'm sorry, Jesse. I know it doesn't mean anything, but—"

"It does mean something." Her apology had doused his passion like a bucket full of cold water, but it took a minute for his body to catch up to his mind. When it had, he turned toward her. He watched her carefully, his feelings for her having changed in the past few minutes into something he wasn't sure he recognized.

Loralee was an honorable person. She was apologizing for something that wasn't even her fault, just because she knew that her father had been wrong. Right now, Jesse couldn't think of anyone, man or woman, that he admired more, as he stood and watched Loralee's obvious distress over what had happened so many years ago. He knew he couldn't leave things this way between them.

"Loralee, I . . . I just want you to know that I don't hold you responsible for what happened to my father. But I will always hold Edward Vander accountable for it. I don't think it's something that I can get past." He looked away. "I think it would be best if I just stay away from you. It seems to me that anything beyond a polite greeting would be too much temptation. And a relationship between us can go nowhere."

She listened quietly then nodded her head. She hesitated a few seconds then said, "I guess I should go back inside." She *knew* she should go back inside. And still, she stood before him, reluctant to move.

Jesse studied her, wondering why fate was so cruel. She was easily the prettiest woman he'd ever seen. She was definitely the feistiest.

Finally, he nodded. "I guess so. I'll wait a few minutes."

She stood looking at him for a long time, as if she wanted to postpone their separation until the very last minute. "Do you think it would be possible to consider ourselves . . . no longer enemies?"

Jesse stood slumped against the side of the house. His reactions were slow, he knew, dulled by the liquor he'd consumed in an effort to forget this beautiful woman. He smiled and boosted himself upright, fighting the urge to pull her back into his arms. Holding out his hand, he said, "No longer enemies."

She didn't even hesitate one second. She put her tiny hand in his and grasped it in a firm handshake. "No longer enemies." It was only after the handshake that she hesitated. When the silence between them became uncomfortable, she said, "Well," then turned and walked slowly up the path and around the corner into the house.

Feisty, most definitely.

He shoved his hands into his pockets and watched her go. Why did she stir such strong feelings in him?

Out of the corner of his eye, something white caught his attention. There, in the grass, was the pink and white ribbon she'd bought just that morning at Evans' General Store. The moonlight shone off of it as though it were actually radiating the light itself, instead of just reflecting it.

He saw her as she had been after he'd knocked into her, holding that pair of white stockings, spools of thread, sheets of paper and the hair ribbon falling all around her. Jesse bent and picked it up, rubbing it between his forefinger and thumb. He held it to his face and breathed deeply the scent of honeysuckle, the same scent he'd smelled and tasted on her neck.

Cursing softly, he thrust the ribbon into his pocket. Closing his eyes and shaking his head, he said, "Jesse, what have you done to yourself?"

He waited another minute before returning to the party, the ribbon in his pocket a constant reminder of the purgatory into which he'd cast himself.

CHAPTER ELEVEN

Loralee thought the silence would kill her.

She sat across the breakfast table from her father, carefully scooping the sections of grapefruit into her mouth. This was the first Loralee had seen of him in two days. Did he even know that she had seen Charles on Friday?

Edward looked awful. There were circles beneath his eyes, and his skin had a strange greenish cast to it. And, though he held a stack of papers in his left hand, he didn't seem to be reading them. He was distracted. Loralee was sure that she was the cause of it.

She couldn't take the quiet anymore, and so, with as much confidence as she could muster, she spoke. "Papa," she said, waiting for him to look up at her, "have you spoken to Charles?"

He nodded his head. "Yes, Loralee, I have."

"Then you know that I returned the engagement brooch to him?"

"He told me that. He's very upset."

Edward was in an exceptionally calm mood this morning, and encouraged by this, Loralee rushed to pour out the whole story. "Papa, I'm very sorry that he's upset. But I can't marry him. Please understand that."

He pushed back his chair and stood up. "I'll be going out of town for a few days. I have some business to take care of."

"But, Edward," Fiona said, holding her toast poised midway to her mouth, "you didn't mention anything about a trip. How long will you be gone?"

"I'll be gone as long as it takes, Fiona." He straightened the papers, put them in a folder and tucked it under his arm. He walked away from the table, but at the doorway turned to look back at his wife and daughter. He said nothing, just stood there looking at the two women as though evaluating something about them. Then he turned and walked out.

"What on earth . . ." Fiona watched her husband leave their home. "He's taken leave of his senses," she muttered quietly. "He's gone quite mad over her . . . going to find her, that's where he's going . . ."

"Going to find who?"

Fiona looked up as though she was surprised to find her daughter still in the room. "Excuse me, please, Loralee." She set her white linen napkin on the table and stood up slowly. She wandered out of the room and into the foyer, then climbed the steps as if in a daze.

Loralee listened to her mother's slow footsteps. A heavy door closed, and then there was silence.

"My family has gone insane," she said to herself. Her father knew about her act of defiance and had said nothing. Her mother mumbled to herself as though no one was in the room. If this wasn't odd behavior, Loralee didn't know what was.

She thought about being with Jesse last night. Since when had overwhelming anger led her straight to frantic, almost desperate kissing?

She had enough to do trying to figure out her own strange

conduct, Loralee thought, as she hurried up the stairs to her room. Her parents could take care of themselves.

Edward climbed into the shiny, black carriage and pulled away from the house, not even bothering to look back.

Lily had disappeared. They'd argued on Friday, and when he had gone to see her on Saturday night, as he had been doing every Saturday night for the last ten years, she was gone.

He'd panicked, searching through the rooms of the small house he'd bought for her. In her bedroom, the scent of her perfume still lingered. She'd taken most of her clothing, some of her collectibles, and all of her jewelry. She wasn't planning on coming back.

Edward had gone straight to the liquor cabinet, where he found a bottle of his favorite Scotch. Lily knew his favorite everything. He could stop by anytime, day or night, and find his favorite drink waiting. She'd have his favorite candies in the crystal bowl by the door. She'd put on his favorite dress. She'd have the cook prepare his favorite meal. And, if he asked her very nicely, and maybe brought her a new piece of jewelry, she'd take off that favorite dress and do to him his favorite thing.

Lily was the perfect mistress. Edward had found her when she was just sixteen. She'd never had the attentions of another man, and she thought that the sun rose and set on Edward Vander.

And so she should have! He'd been good to her, goddamn it! He'd set her up in the house she wanted. He dressed her in fine silks and satins. She owned more jewelry than his wife!

Everything was fine until last year, when Lily turned twenty-five. She wanted a husband, she'd said. She wanted children someday. And she did not plan to wait around for him forever. Divorce Fiona, she'd cried. Marry me instead!

Marry her? Everyone in town knew that she was his mistress.

She was kept in fine style in exchange for the use of her body. She was really nothing more than a high-class whore. He'd never *marry* her!

But he'd not said that to Lily. No, he'd told her that it was complicated, getting divorced when you had as much money as he did. Be patient, he'd said. Someday you'll have everything you want.

It had worked, for a while. She'd stopped her complaining and started behaving like a mistress should—always available—always willing—always satisfying.

And then two weeks ago, she'd announced that she was pregnant. This was a trap.

Edward ordered her to get rid of it. He'd even offered to send a doctor right to her house. It would be taken care of, and, unbeknownst to her, she could be fixed to assure that it never happened again.

But Lily had flown into a rage, and Edward left her to cool off for a few days. But the next time he came to her, she was still standing her ground: divorce Fiona and marry me. So he'd gone away again, leaving her alone for nearly a week.

And the next time he knocked on her door, she was gone. No note, no trace. Gone.

And Edward had never realized that he loved her until she was no longer there to love.

So, here he was, taking off to find his mistress. She might be carrying his son! And, if the baby was born and it turned out to be a boy, maybe he *would* divorce Fiona and marry Lily. Or maybe he'd just take the baby and get rid of both Lily and Fiona. But in any case, he'd have his boy! Finally, after all these years, a son!

He rode north. The trip to Scranton would take the whole day. And if Lily hadn't returned there to be with her family, he'd have to figure out where to try next.

He felt better to be doing something. He'd find Lily. He'd bring her back.

And with her, his son.

Jesse rolled over and buried his head beneath the pillow. The light pouring in through the windows was blinding, and with his eyes feeling like they'd been rubbed with sandpaper, his head throbbing like it would soon explode, and his mouth as dry as a wad of cotton, he'd as soon have stayed in bed all day as face the sunny morning.

Why had he been so stupid as to think that an endless flow of whiskey would make him feel any better? He hadn't consumed so much alcohol in years, and, like every hangover sufferer, he vowed never to do it again.

He had decided to stay in bed, when an ungodly pounding sounded from the door.

"Come in, come in! Just stop that noise!" he yelled.

Stephen Sinclair opened the door to Jesse's bedroom and stuck his head in, following the path of discarded shoes and wrinkled clothing that led to the lump in the bed. He smiled and shook his head, and boomed, "Well, I'm glad to see you made it home all right!"

Jesse scrambled from beneath the blankets, one hand on his head the other held out to Stephen. "Please, please, Dad, quiet, please." Slowly he eased himself back down onto the pillow, wincing as though he were laying atop shards of glass. With a huge sigh he closed his bleary eyes.

Stephen glanced around the room and saw the desk chair, with the suit jacket Jesse'd been wearing the night before dangling from the back and hanging down onto the floor. He walked to the closet and removed a hanger, draped the jacket over it and hung it on the iron rod inside. Then he pulled the chair over to the side of the bed where Jesse lay motionless.

"Late night," Stephen said quietly.

"Very."

"John came with us to church this morning. He isn't looking nearly as bad as you."

"Mmm."

Stephen looked at his eldest son and shook his head. "Here, sit up. Take these," he said reaching into his pocket for two white tablets. He poured a glass of water.

Jesse pushed himself up on one elbow, popped both tablets into his mouth and washed them down with a gulp of water. He handed the glass back to his father. "Thanks." He lowered himself back onto the pillows. "What time is it?"

"Twelve-thirty. Your mother insisted that I come in to check on you. Make sure you're still among the living."

"Barely." He pushed another pillow behind his head and tried to open his eyes.

"You look like hell."

"I feel like hell."

Stephen leaned back into the chair and propped his feet up on the bed. "Well. Come on."

Jesse tried to focus his eyes. "What?"

"Who is she, and what happened?"

Jesse tried to smile. "You know me too well."

Stephen shrugged. "I can't imagine any other reason for you to do this to yourself. So, who is she? Is it the girl from your birthday party? What was her name?" He squinted as though trying to remember.

Jesse ran a shaky hand through tangled, sandy hair. "That's the girl, all right. Unfortunately, it's her name that's the problem."

"I'm not following you," Stephen said, obviously confused. "Her name is the problem?"

"Didn't John tell you about any of this?"

"Should he have?" Stephen asked. "I just assumed you had a woman on your mind. But I didn't realize you were going to go out and hammer the hell out of your body because of it.''

Jesse's voice was little more than a whisper. "Why did it have to be her?''

"Why not her? Who is she?''

Jesse closed his eyes and held a hand to his head, pressing strong fingers to his temples. "Her name is Loralee Vander. Her father is Edward Vander.''

Stephen raised his eyebrows. "Edward Vander.'' He spoke the name calmly, almost as though it held no significance for him. Several seconds passed while he seemed to carefully consider this news. He looked his son straight in the eye. "Well. That does complicate things, doesn't it?''

"I can't do it. I can't forgive him. And I can't stay away from her.'' He sat up, leaning back against the headboard. "God knows, I've tried, but I . . . can't.''

"And she knows . . . your situation?''

"She knows.''

"But you want her anyway.''

Jesse hung his head and looked at his hands in his lap. "I want her anyway,'' he admitted.

"Then you've got some big decisions to make.''

Jesse looked toward the window, squinting at the bright light. "I am obsessed with this girl. I've never met anyone like her. She's beautiful and opinionated and sassy as all hell. She's soft and innocent, she's fiery and passionate, and,'' he said, rubbing his cheek and smiling with the memory, "she's got one hell of a strong right arm.''

Stephen raised his eyebrows. "She hits?''

Jesse smiled and slowly nodded his head. "I deserved it.'' He paused, staring down into the sheets. "She's done something that no other woman has ever done. She's gotten into my blood, and I don't know how to get her out.''

"Maybe you can't. Maybe you're not supposed to.''

"What do you mean?'' Jesse asked.

Stephen pulled his feet from the bed and planted them on the floor. He leaned forward, resting his elbows on his knees. "Jesse, you were five years old when your father died. I have loved you as my son for twenty years now. And I always hoped you would get over the bitterness you feel toward Edward Vander. Johnny has."

"Johnny was just a baby! He doesn't remember ..." He flung back the covers and jumped out of bed, trying to ignore the pounding in his head. He picked a pair of jeans off the floor and thrust his feet into them. He grabbed his white shirt from the night before and pushed his arms through the wrinkled sleeves and stood there, with the unbuttoned shirt hanging over his jeans, the unfastened cuffs flopping over his wrists.

"I know you loved your father, Jesse—"

"I did love my father, but it's not just that! It's that Edward Vander never had to pay for what he did. My mother died of a broken heart. My sisters ... Where are they? Two women who share the same blood as me, the same as John, and I haven't seen them in twenty years! Where do they live? Are they even alive? Do they have children? Am I an uncle?" He rattled off the questions that had plagued him for a lifetime.

"I can't stand the thought that every trace of Samuel Fedosh's life could so easily be wiped out! The man was alive for, what, thirty years?" he asked, opening his eyes wide. "And then, one day, he just vanishes off the face of the earth. Actually, he vanished *into* the earth. And every person who meant something to him scattered. It's as though he was never even here," he said quietly. "I can't stand the thought of that." He turned away and stood at the window with his hands on his hips, his feet spread, his outburst hanging there between them. The minutes ticked by in silence.

Stephen stood and put his hand on Jesse's shoulder. "Jesse, I'm sorry. I tried—"

Jesse spun around and pulled his father into a tight embrace. It was a gesture that took both of them by surprise, but one which Jesse needed to offer. "No, Stephen. I'm sorry. You *are* my father. I am so grateful to have been taken in by you and Elizabeth. And I'm so grateful that you were able to keep Johnny and me together." He held on to the man who had made him who he was today. He couldn't bear to think that Stephen did not know how much he was loved.

Jesse stepped back. "I love you, and I love Mother, more than any other people on this earth. In all honesty, I scarcely remember my other family. I have difficulty remembering what my life was like before you came into it."

"You had a happy family. Your parents loved each other. When we took you in, we talked with the minister, the neighbors. They all thought of you as a happy family. Poor, but happy."

"Poor." Jesse hung his head and stared at his bare feet. Feet that rested upon a fine carpet, in a room that was solely his. His own private room in a twenty-room mansion. Stephen and Elizabeth had plucked him from the ashes of a family destroyed by death and unbearable hardship and transplanted him here, in a family blessed by wealth, happiness and abundant love. He had no right to wallow in self-pity and even less right to let Stephen think he wasn't grateful for the way his life had turned out. "Maybe you're right. Maybe I have been hanging on to this bitterness for too long."

"Hatred serves no purpose, Jesse. It has a way of turning on you, of leaving you old and hard and lonely. I wouldn't want to see that happen to you."

Jesse looked up and nodded, shaking the hair out of his eyes and examining the face of the man who had spent the last twenty years molding his son's character into something he could be proud of. "I couldn't have asked for a better father."

Stephen smiled. "I couldn't have asked for a better compliment."

The two men stood face to face, slightly embarrassed about

the way they had let all their feelings out. They had always been close, but never more so than now.

"So you think this is some kind of test for me. A lesson to teach me how to forgive."

"Maybe. I don't think you should walk away from feelings as strong as you seem to have for her. And I don't think you should try drowning yourself in whiskey."

Jesse chuckled. "Believe me, I won't try that again. God, I suffer when I drink."

They stood in easy silence, thinking about all that had been said. The path to forgiveness would not be an easy one for Jesse. He knew that. But armed with the support of his father, for the first time in his life, he began to think it might be possible.

"So, you think I should make my intentions known?"

"How else can you get to know her?"

"I should call on her? Court her?"

"If she'll have you."

Jesse looked at Stephen then let out a big breath of air. "I can't believe I'm doing this," he said, walking to the window and looking down on the grounds below. "I can't believe I'm actually considering doing this."

Stephen walked up behind him and slapped both of his hands down onto shoulders that long ago had grown wider than his own. He squeezed with gentle affection. "I can't believe it's taken you so long."

Then, much more quietly than he had arrived, he walked out, leaving Jesse alone with only his thoughts of Loralee to keep him company.

CHAPTER TWELVE

Mondays at Dr. Farley's office were always busy, but this Monday they had so many patients that they'd decided to spend the whole day in the office, and it seemed to Loralee that most of them had been injured in mining accidents. Was it just that Loralee was more aware of their plight since she had learned how Jesse's father had died?

As the day wore on, she found herself growing distracted by the thought. First, there were three young boys, none of them older than ten, who showed up with dirty bandages on their hands. She cleaned their wounds and re-wrapped them, listening as they swapped stories of the breaker accidents that had caused their injuries. It seemed that the worse the accident, the prouder they were to have survived it. She wondered if any of them worked for her father.

And then, an hour or so later, a young man, maybe fourteen or fifteen, walked in with a stump where his arm should have been. She couldn't stop looking at it. She looked up at his face, and was embarrassed to have been caught staring. He said, "I'm a spragger. Or, I was."

And in the corner, still waiting to be seen, was a man, maybe forty or forty-five at most. His spine was bent forward till he was nearly folded in half, and he coughed continually, spitting into a rag he kept in his back pocket. As he wiped his mouth, she saw that he was missing a finger. And the ones he had were twisted and misshapen.

A miner. Perpetually slumped over, until his bones simply grew that way. And the rattly cough was probably bringing up the coal dust he swallowed every day.

Something in her stomach flopped over, and she realized with a sickening feeling, that the people in this room, and thousands of others like them, toiled day after day in her father's mines. Did he still treat them as abominably as he had treated the men who worked for him in Avondale?

Dr. Farley pulled the blue curtain aside, and Loralee jumped, sending a bottle of cough syrup crashing to the ground.

He looked up at her, and she closed her eyes. "I'm sorry. I'll clean it up." She turned to leave and he stopped her with a hand on her arm.

"What's wrong?"

"Nothing! Really, I—"

"Loralee. You've been dropping things and forgetting things all day. And, I swear I caught you close to tears a couple of times. What is it?"

She sighed, and, once again, had to fight back tears.

"See?" he said, pointing at her. "There you go again."

She wiped her eyes and took a breath, trying to clear her head. "I keep thinking about what happened to those men. Every time I turn around it's another mining accident. I just can't stand it!" She walked to the back of the examining room and got a rag to clean up the spilt cough syrup.

"Sounds to me like you need a break. Why don't you leave early?"

"But you'll be swamped by yourself."

"I was swamped before you started here. I'll manage one more day." He put his hand on her shoulder and squeezed. "You've been through a lot in these past few weeks. I know you have some thinking to do. Why don't you go do it?"

She wanted to go so badly, but she hated to abandon him. "Are you sure?"

"Go."

She smiled at him. "Thank you so much," she said, slipping her apron over her head. "I'll go out the back way."

"See you in the morning." He stepped out into the cramped waiting room and called out, "Mrs. Temprovich?"

Loralee grabbed her black bag and left. Doc was right. She did need to get away. She walked along Broad Street and turned onto Wyoming.

Since she'd be walking right past her seamstress's shop, Loralee decided to stop in to pick up some aprons she'd ordered. The woman behind the counter wrapped them in brown paper bundles and stacked them precariously in Loralee's arms. Carefully, she eased out the door, assuring the woman all the while that she could manage. Fifteen feet down the sidewalk, and Loralee began to wonder. Carrying her heavy bag and all the packages sure did make it difficult to navigate.

She turned a corner and almost ran smack into Jesse Sinclair on his way out of the barber shop.

"Loralee—"

"Jesse—"

They stood on the street staring at each other, both of them speechless.

Jesse recovered first. "I wonder what the chances are of running down the same person twice in one week."

Loralee smiled. "Actually, this time, *I* almost ran *you* down."

"You're right," he said with a smile. "You know, I don't

remember ever knocking anyone over before. But, put the two of us together, and we sure do get clumsy.''

He was teasing her! She raised one pale eyebrow. ''Well, I don't know about that,'' she said softly, thinking of their kisses. They'd been anything but clumsy. This was the first time she'd ever flirted with a man, and before she could stop it, she blushed.

He chuckled low in his throat, and said, ''I love it when a woman blushes.''

It was one of the first things he had said to her the night they first met. She remembered and looked up at him, her gaze colliding with that penetrating, pale blue stare he had perfected.

She reacted the way most people did. She was captured, and she could not look away, could not even blink, until he released her. The seconds ticked by, and the air around them seemed suddenly very warm.

Jesse looked down at the packages in her arms, and the spell was broken. ''Been doing some shopping?''

She shifted the wrapped aprons, and the paper crinkled as she moved it. ''Some.''

He hesitated, then nodded toward the bundles in her arms. ''Need help with those?''

She stared at him, wondering if she had heard him correctly. ''Oh. I, uh . . .'' At just that moment, the top package began to slip. She made a grab for it and, in the process, dropped all the others.

Once again, they stood with all her purchases scattered on the ground around them.

''I'll take that as a yes,'' Jess said, bending to retrieve her things. He set everything on a pile, then stood, lifting the entire thing up with him.

''Oh,'' Loralee said, blinking her eyes rapidly. What could she say? He was already holding all of her aprons in his arms. ''Well, thank you very much, but I don't want to put you to any trouble—''

''It's no trouble.'' He looked down at her with those blue

eyes, waiting until she stopped fidgeting and stood staring back at him. "Were you on your way home?"

"Yes, yes I was." This man had an incredible effect on her! Even now, standing on the sidewalk while people darted around them, she could feel her pulse quicken. Her mouth felt dry, and she licked her lips and tried to think of something to say. But, for what might possibly have been the very first time in her life, she was speechless. So she just stood there, looking at Jesse and blushing furiously.

"Then I'll walk with you and carry these."

"Oh," she shook her head, "really, Jesse, no. You don't have to do that."

"I know I don't have to. I want to." And with that he turned and started walking slowly in the direction of the Vander mansion.

Loralee scampered to catch up to him, and they walked along in silence. What would they do when they reached her house? Shouldn't she invite him in? No, of course not. Offer him a cold drink? Sit on the front porch with him? She couldn't do any of those things.

Silently, Loralee walked next to Jesse, praying that she'd be able to follow his lead, when the time came.

"Don't you take a carriage when you go shopping?"

"I wasn't planning on shopping, actually. I left work early."

"Playin' hooky?"

"Sort of. What about you? Why aren't you at work?"

"Playin' hooky."

She giggled. "Better watch you don't get fired."

"Nah. I know the boss."

They walked along, their footsteps clicking against the sidewalk. He was wearing jeans again. Jeans and a soft, blue flannel shirt. No one would ever guess that he was the son of one of the wealthiest men in the state.

"I heard about your broken engagement," he said.

"Oh, really?" How did he hear about that? And why would he have brought it up?

"I didn't know you were engaged." That's why.

"I was. Briefly."

"To Charles Korwin, as I understand."

Her heart was hammering! This conversation was most inappropriate! "Yes. My father thought we'd make a good match. I, however, did not."

"I'm glad to hear that."

"Why?" she asked, stopping suddenly.

He turned around to look at her, but continued walking backwards. "Because you're too much woman for a man like Korwin to handle." Then he turned his back to her and kept walking, his boots pounding out a slow, steady beat.

Loralee stared at his back. Why did he care whom she married? And what, exactly, did he mean when he said too much woman to *handle?*

She hurried to catch up to him, and they reached Diamond Avenue and turned toward her house. Some of the trees had already started to turn colors. And as the sun filtered down on them through the subtly changing leaves, Loralee was aware that something between her and Jesse was also changing. His steps slowed, as though he was not all that anxious to reach their destination. At the front gate, Loralee said, "Thank you, Jesse, for carrying my packages."

"I *can* behave like a gentleman, you know. Though, I wouldn't blame you if you didn't believe me. I haven't exactly been on my best behavior when I've been in your presence," he said, settling the bundles in her outstretched arms. "Got 'em all?"

"I think so," she said, shifting her head so she could see him around the mountain of brown paper in her arms. She hesitated, wondering what else she should say.

"Well, I'll be going, then. Be careful you don't fall with all of those,'' he said, indicating the aprons stacked in front of her face.

"I will. I mean, I won't." She laughed and tried again. "What I mean is, no, I won't fall, and yes, I will be careful."

He smiled.

She smiled.

Finally, Jesse broke the awkward silence. "Well, then. 'Bye, Loralee."

" 'Bye, Jesse."

They stood there, with the past pushing its way between them as surely as the afternoon shadow of her father's house which fell on the pavement beneath their feet.

Jesse turned and walked slowly away, and Loralee watched him go. The distance between them stretched until he reached the end of their property. And when he was almost out of her sight, he turned back and looked at her. He raised a hand in farewell, and then disappeared around the corner.

Loralee stood outside on the sidewalk for a long time. Why she should feel so sad at Jesse's leaving, she didn't know. But as she turned around and headed up the walkway, sadness weighed down on her like a heavy cloak.

Did he feel it, too, she wondered?

She climbed the front steps and opened the door to her father's house. She could never have invited him in. But still . . . She closed the door, shutting herself off from the world outside.

And, from the other side of the wrought-iron fence that surrounded her father's perfectly groomed property, a sad young man, in jeans and a blue flannel shirt, watched.

Charles stood at the window of the front parlor watching Loralee and Jesse Sinclair standing on the sidewalk. He put a stack of packages into her arms, and she leaned over to peek around at him. How dare she stand there in plain view of—

"Is something wrong, Charles?" Fiona said, interrupting his murderous thoughts. "You look flushed." She held a wooden embroidery hoop in one hand and a needle threaded with blue embroidery floss in the other.

"Everything is fine," he said, turning back toward the window. Fine, except for the fact that he was watching the rich little bitch he was supposed to marry, flirting with another man. He looked back to the spot where they had been standing, but both Jesse and Loralee were gone. Just then, the front door opened.

Fiona set her work down in a bleached wicker basket and said, "That's probably Loralee now. Excuse me, please, while I check." She breezed past Charles with her head held high.

Snooty bitch! She'd almost refused to let him into the house. He'd had to practically beg just to get over the threshold. She'd finally agreed to let him speak with Loralee for a few minutes, but only on the condition that she, personally, chaperone their visit.

He heard the sound of their voices wafting into the front parlor from the foyer. He strained, but couldn't make out any words. Suddenly, Loralee burst into the room, followed closely by Fiona.

"What do you want, Charles?" she demanded rudely.

"Well, I-I only wanted . . . to see how you're doing," he said, playing the contrite fiancé to perfection. "I miss you. I want to put this silly misunderstanding behind us."

"Misunderstanding?" Loralee asked, her eyes wide. "I returned your engagement brooch. I told you that I did not want to marry you. In fact," she said, growing haughtier by the minute, "I believe I said that I *would not* marry you and that *nothing* would change my mind about that. I understand that perfectly. What, precisely, did you not understand?" She set her packages down on the velvet-covered sofa and stood facing him with her hands on her hips.

He'd like to slap that self-righteous smirk right off her pretty little face! She spoke to him as if he was an imbecile! How *dare* she take that tone with him!

Think of the money, Charles. Think of the money!

Charles took a deep breath and let it out slowly. "Loralee, I simply meant that—" He looked up and found Fiona watching them and making no pretense of it. He snapped his mouth shut, his patience for this entire situation growing thin. He would not beg for the attentions of a woman! *But, the money . . .*

She was ridiculing him! Making him look like a fool! The fraying thread by which he held his temper snapped, and he reached out and grabbed Loralee by the arms, shaking her. "Loralee, I've had about all I can take of your behav-"

"Charles!" Fiona exclaimed, "Let go of her this instant!" She reached up and wrapped her hands around one of his arms.

"Stay out of this!" he thundered, trying to shake Fiona off, though he still held Loralee by the upper arms. Charles could feel the anger taking control of him, and even the thought of the Vander money wasn't enough to stop it.

The sight of Loralee's mother cowering in fear only heightened the sense of excitement he was beginning to feel.

"Charles, let go of me, or, so help me God, I'll scream! Is that what you want?" Loralee asked, struggling against his hold.

"Shut up!" He dragged her toward the sofa, thinking, even as he did, that he'd never be able to talk his way out of this. She'd ruined everything!

He pulled her down next to him, wanting only to frighten her, to pay her back for the way she had ruined his plans. "Stupid bitch!" he yelled, yanking her arms behind her back. "Did you think I'd simply let you walk away?"

"Let go of me!" Loralee shouted, fighting against him with everything she had.

He reached up and wrapped her hair around his fingers. "You ruined everything, Loralee," he said, pulling her hair harder with each word that he spoke. "You just had to cozy up to that Sinclair bastard, didn't you? Didn't you? Couldn't have saved a little of that for me, could you?'' He glared at Loralee, and he could see that her anger was beginning to turn to fear.

''Didn't mind when *he* touched you this way did you? You liked it. You wanted more!'' He looked up and saw Fiona on the floor moving toward them. He yanked Loralee to her feet and twisted her around so that she was standing with her back pressed against the front of him. He clamped a hand over her mouth, and said, ''Get up, Fiona! Get up off the floor!''

Fiona stood slowly, obviously afraid of him. He loved the feeling. He glanced around the room and saw a small door. ''Get in there,'' he said, dragging Loralee with him as he moved toward the closet. ''Unless you'd like to watch, that is.'' Fiona stopped moving. Loralee clawed at his hand, trying to pry it loose. ''Would you like to watch while I make sure no other man will ever want your daughter?''

His masquerade as the perfect husband-to-be was over. He knew it, and the anger he felt at having his plan thwarted pumped the blood through his veins until he couldn't think of anything except revenge.

He opened the door. ''Get in—Aauugghh!'' he screamed, pulling his hand away from Loralee's mouth. She'd bitten his finger! He let go of her and clamped his hands together, squeezing tightly. Blood trickled out from between his fingers, running down his wrist and soaking into the cuff of his white shirt.

''Help!'' Loralee screamed, running for the door that led out into the foyer. ''Help!''

Charles's hand reached her just in time. He grabbed onto the back of her dress, and pulled so hard that it tore away from her, exposing one shoulder. ''Shut up!'' he said. ''Will you just shut up!''

The door opened, and in rushed Anna. ''Madam, is something—oh! Get away from her!'' she cried, reaching out and grabbing the nearest thing her fingers touched. She smashed a porcelain vase over Charles's head. "Gibbons! Marta! Gibbons, get in here!" she screamed at the top of her lungs.

Anna's intrusion jolted Charles out of his violently angry state. He looked at Loralee, her torn dress momentarily distracting him, and Fiona, who was still standing beside the closet, took advantage of every second.

She ran toward the fireplace and lifted the iron poker, advancing furiously on Charles. "Get out!" she screamed, holding the poker like a baseball bat. "Get out, or I'll kill you myself."

Silence blanketed the room. Fiona took a step closer, tightening her grip on the poker. And no one in the room ever doubted that she meant every word she said.

Charles held up his hands, as if he was surrendering. "Fiona, there's no need to—"

"Get out," Fiona whispered. "And don't ever come near her again."

The floor thundered with the sound of approaching footsteps.

Charles moved warily toward the door. He threw one more hateful look at Loralee and slipped out of the room and out of the house just as Gibbons, Marta, and the entire household staff converged in the foyer. They rushed into the front parlor to find Loralee, her clothes in shreds, while their mistress stood beside her, holding the fireplace poker as though she intended to use it.

"Marta," Fiona barked, "take her upstairs." She still held the poker, and the entire staff stood staring at her as though she'd lost her mind. Finally, she lowered it. "Gibbons, please put this where it belongs." He rushed forward to take the makeshift weapon from her shaking hands.

Fiona waited for the chatter to die down. "None of you are to leave this room. Is that clear?"

They stood like statues. Shock was robbing them of speech.

"Is that clear?" she asked again.

Gibbons stepped forward. "Yes, madam. We understand perfectly."

She took a deep breath and let it out slowly, looking each one of them directly in the eye. Then, without another word, she turned and hurried up the steps, stopping only long enough to lock the front door.

Loralee cried wretchedly, more from relief that it was over than from anything else.

"There, there, miss. It's over. All over, and you're safe."

"He's insane, Marta!" To think that her father had wanted her to marry that man!

Fiona knocked lightly on the door and let herself in. "Loralee," she said, rushing to her daughter. "Are you all right? Did he hurt you?" She rested her hands on Loralee's shoulders and held her at arm's length, scanning quickly for any sign of injury.

"I'm fine, Mother," Loralee said, wiping at her eyes. "Do you see? Do you see how mean he is?"

"I know," Fiona said, eyes downcast.

"That," she said, pointing toward the door, "was the man Papa chose to marry me!" She jumped up off the bed, and shrugged the torn dress back up over her shoulder. She was so angry, she was shaking.

"You're right. Marriage to Charles would have been a big mistake."

"A mistake? It would have been a nightmare! I don't want that man near me ever again. And if Papa—"

"We'll talk to your father when he gets home," Fiona said. "Marta, get some hot water up here."

"Of course, Ma'am." She hurried from the room.

Fiona watched her go then said, "Thank God you weren't hurt."

Loralee sighed. "Scared half out of my mind, but not hurt."

Fiona, reached out and hugged her daughter. "I have the

entire staff waiting for me downstairs.'' She stepped back. ''Will you be all right?''

Loralee nodded, and Fiona made a move to leave.

''Mother?''

Fiona turned, waiting.

''Would you really have used that poker?''

Her mother didn't hesitate one second. ''Absolutely.''

Another dinner with no one but Zachary to talk to. Abby fastened the ruby and diamond necklace and turned to look at it in the mirror. Why he insisted that she dress for dinners alone as though she was attending a royal ball was beyond her. It was ridiculous!

She examined the gemstones in the glass. They really—

Abby jumped. Charles was on the patio! She'd seen him in the mirror!

She rushed to the French doors. ''What are you doing here?'' she whispered. ''Oh, Charles, you're bleeding!''

''Can I come in?''

''It's almost dinner time!'' she hissed. ''I can't ...'' She spun around and looked at the clock. ''Oh, God, Charles, what happened?'' He was a wreck.

''I need you, Abby. I really need you.'' He stood there with his shoulders slumped and his hair disheveled and blood on his shirt. And he needed her.

Without further thought, she said, ''Come in,'' She locked the door and checked to make sure the windows were completely covered. ''You shouldn't be here.''

''I didn't know where else to go.''

He sounded like a lost little kid. Abby almost thought that he was going to cry.

''Oh, Charles,'' she said, ''come here.'' She held her arms open for him, and he went willingly into them.

"My hand is still bleeding," he said, holding it away from her.

"What happened?" She reached for his hand and looked at it, wincing when she saw the torn flesh. "Oh, Charles, what happened?"

"It's a long story. Can you get out of dinner tonight? I really need you, Abby. I don't know what I'll do if—"

"Don't even say it! Stay here. I'll be right back." Abby slipped out of the room and hurried downstairs to Zachary's study. She'd never done this before. She stood outside the door, torn in two by what she was about to do.

She had to do it. She had no choice. Softly, she knocked and then let herself in. "I'm sorry to bother you," she said to her husband. "I . . ." She closed her eyes and tried to stop herself from crying. She couldn't do this! She couldn't!

"Is there a problem, Abigail?"

She kept her eyes closed. *Please forgive me, Charles. I can't endure it again. I'm so sorry.* "I won't be down for dinner. I . . ." She tried, but could not go on. Tears formed in her eyes, and when she blinked, they rolled down her cheeks. Damn him! Damn him to hell for what he was making her do!

"I understand completely, Abby. There's no need to be so upset." He spoke gently, as though he truly did understand.

God, how she hated him!

Without another word, she turned and left the room. She'd just betrayed her best friend. She felt as if Zachary had ripped her heart out and stomped all over it.

She rushed back to her bedroom, desperate to hold the only man she had ever loved. "Charles!" she cried, running into his arms.

"Abby, your dress—"

"Damn the dress! I don't care. Put your arms around me. Quickly! We don't have much time," They clung together, and, with her head turned away from him, Abby clenched her eyes shut. "I love you so much. I love you, Charles. I love you . . ." *This much, at least, is pure. This . . . this is for real.*

"I love you, too, Abby."

Hearing him say it only made what she was about to do hurt worse. Abby opened her eyes and looked up at a picture on the wall. It moved. So slightly that, if she hadn't been watching for it, she would never have seen it. Immediately, she dropped her arms from around Charles and led him to the bed. She unbuttoned his shirt and turned around so that he could undo her buttons and hooks.

When she was completely naked, wearing nothing but the ruby and diamond necklace, she lay down on the bed and pulled Charles on top of her. He pushed inside, and Abby bit down on her lip to keep from crying out. It was done. There was no going back.

She had just allowed Zachary to take the only good thing she'd ever had in her life.

And when it was over, and Charles had gone, Abby sat on her bed. Waiting. Dying inside, piece by agonizing piece. In a few minutes, Zachary opened the door. He walked to a chair in the corner of the room and sat down.

Abby got up and walked to him. Her heart was dead.

She dropped to her knees and fulfilled her part of their bargain.

CHAPTER
THIRTEEN

Jesse walked past Dr. Farley's office for the third time in a half hour. There was no doubt in his mind that Loralee Vander was the woman he wanted. He wanted her in his arms, he wanted her in his bed, he wanted her across the dinner table from him fifty years from now.

It was Friday, four days since Jesse had carried her packages home. They'd called a very delicate truce, but could they keep it up? It seemed that each and every encounter was another chance for confrontation.

On the other hand, hadn't Jesse just said he was going to begin calling on her? Hadn't he agreed that it was time he start letting go of the past?

That she stepped right into his path, literally, had taken him by surprise. And the entire time they were together, Jesse tried to think about nothing except the fact that he and Loralee were attracted to one another. He wanted her, and he suspected she wanted him. What difference did it make who her father was?

He turned around at the end of the block and stood looking

back at the door to the building where she worked. Could he walk in there and let her know just how much he wanted her? Would the loyalty that he felt toward Samuel Fedosh allow that?

Jesse stared at that door until his vision blurred. He blinked and turned away, swearing softly to himself.

He walked quickly, before he had a chance to change his mind. He had to get away from her, and if he walked any faster, he would have been running. He kept up the pace until he was halfway across town. Far enough away that he could trust himself to slow down.

It *did* matter. No matter what Jesse told himself, it did matter that Loralee's father was Edward Vander. Jesse would never be able to get over that, and he might just as well start accepting that now. The past would forever stand between them.

Jesse climbed the steps of the train station and stood on the platform looking out across the town that lay between him and Loralee. He might as well have had his body pressed right up against hers. The distance that separated them did nothing to lessen the desire he felt for her.

How far? How far would he have to run to put himself beyond the reach of temptation?

A whistle blew, and Jesse looked down the tracks at an approaching train. He watched it for a few seconds then turned and went into the building.

It didn't matter how far he ran. There wasn't a place on this earth far enough away to make him forget about Loralee Vander.

With the weight of that knowledge nearly crushing him, he went back to work.

Loralee had one more stop to make before heading home for the weekend. She walked quickly, and, in ten minutes, she was knocking at the O'Toole door. Kathleen opened it and smiled.

"Loralee! What a nice surprise!"

She stepped into the kitchen with a hug for her hostess. "I thought I'd better—"

Her breath caught in her throat. Jesse was sitting at the table.

Loralee dropped her arm from around Kathleen's shoulder. "Hello. We just can't seem to stay away from each other," she teased. She turned to Kathleen and said, "We've bumped into each other several times this week."

"Must be followin' the same stars," Kathleen said.

With a smile, Loralee turned to Jesse, who was staring at her like he'd never before met her in his life.

He pushed the tin plate back and stood up. "The pie was great, Kathleen. Thanks." He walked around the table and stood by the door. "I have to get going. You take care of yourself."

"I will, Jesse. 'Bye."

" 'Bye." He turned to Loralee and, with a quick nod, said, "Miss Vander." Then he turned and was out the door, leaving Loralee staring after him.

"He's such a nice—"

"*What* was that all about?" Loralee interrupted.

"What do y' mean?"

Loralee held her hand out toward the door. "I thought we were finally on pretty friendly terms! And, now he's back to calling me Miss Vander?"

"I—I don't know—"

In spite of her anger, Loralee smiled and rolled her eyes. "Men. I wish I understood them better."

"Never gonna happen. God made it this way between men and women for a reason. It's part of nature. No one'll ever really understand it."

Loralee sighed. "I suppose you're right. I don't even understand my own feelings. How in the world can I hope to understand his?''

"Well, whether or not Jesse was happy to see you, I sure am." Kathleen leaned forward and whispered, "Things are startin' to happen."

Instantly, Loralee was all business. "What do you mean? Are you having pains?" She bent down for her bag and opened it to remove a stethoscope. She held the bell-shaped instrument against Kathleen's stomach, listing for, and finding, the baby's strong, steady heartbeat.

"No, no," the reluctant patient said, holding up her hands. "No pains yet, so stop babyin' me!"

"Well, then, what do you mean when you say that things are starting to happen?"

"Well, y' know, I've done this before. And the baby, the baby lays a certain way. It feels different now—I can't explain how—but, if I had t' guess, I'd say the baby has moved. I can't think of any other way to tell y'."

Loralee nodded. She let out a long, relieved breath. "All right. I'd say your baby has moved into position to be born. The head's got to come out first, and he's probably worked himself into that pos-"

"He?" Kathleen interrupted. "Do y' think it's a boy?" Her eyes were wide, and she had stopped rocking.

Loralee smiled. "I really have no idea." She shrugged. Kathleen wilted, as though she had expected Loralee to have some supernatural knowledge of her unborn baby's gender. "Sorry. Do *you* have any feelings? Some mothers have premonitions of—"

"I don't know what that word is."

"Premonition? It's like . . ." Loralee squinted, trying to find the easiest way to explain something that was, basically, unexplainable. "Did you ever have a really strong feeling about something, and then it happened? Without any knowledge, you just get a . . . a feeling in your gut that you know something that's about to happen. Before it actually does.''

Kathleen nodded. ''Oh. I know that feeling. We call it *iomas*. But no, I don't have it now. I'll tell y' a secret, though.'' She leaned forward and whispered, ''I'm hopin' fer another little girl.''

Loralee smiled. ''I'll tell you a secret, too.'' She whispered back, ''So am I.''

They laughed, and Loralee knew they were both thinking about Maggie. They were still sitting, lost in their own thoughts, when Colin walked in.

''Loralee! Good to see y','' he said with a hug.

''It's good to see you, too, Colin, but, goodness! I didn't realize it was this late. I really must go.''

''Don't let me chase y'.''

''You're not,'' she said, placing her stethoscope back in her bag. ''But I really do have to go.'' She stood up. ''Kathleen, you let me know if anything starts to happen. I want to be here when this baby is born.''

''I know, I know. If it's anythin' like when Maggie was born, Colin'll have plenty o' time to fetch y'.'' She pushed against the arms of the rocking chair and struggled to get up. When she did, she waddled to her husband's side.

''You make sure,'' Loralee said, pointing at Colin.

''I will. I want y' here ever' bit as much, maybe even more than y' want to be here.''

Loralee laughed and tucked a stray strand of hair behind her ear. ''You take care of yourself, and I'll be back near the end of next week.''

''We'll be here,'' Kathleen said, patting her tummy. ''And remember, if y' look hard enough fer somethin' t' be rotten, yer likely to find it t' be rotten.''

Loralee rolled her eyes, and Colin looked at both of them as if wondering whether they were talking about some secret *woman thing*. He must have decided he'd be better off not knowing, because he didn't say another word. Loralee stepped off the porch, and behind her, the door closed.

She turned toward home, making a promise to herself right then and there that if she *did* find anything rotten, she'd get rid of it once and for all!

Edward marched into the dining room and sat down as though he had never left. It didn't occur to him that he should offer some sort of explanation to his wife and daughter for his nearly week-long absence.

Something had happened while he was gone. He didn't know what it was, but the staff, even his treasured Gibbons, was watching him as though they expected to see some sort of a show.

When Edward lost his temper, there was usually hell to pay. Though the staff performed their duties efficiently, they seemed to be waiting to see just how high he would blow.

They ate in silence. Edward watched Loralee as she cut up a small piece of roast beef into tiny bits. Then she cut the bits into small shreds. She pushed the food around with her fork, and spent a lot of time cutting, but Edward had yet to see her actually eat anything.

Fiona, on the other hand, was eating as though she'd been starved for days. She was a tiny woman, but she had cleaned her plate three times already, and she showed no signs of slowing down. Where she was putting it all, Edward couldn't imagine.

By dessert, he'd had enough. "All right. Someone tell me what's going on."

They eyed each other nervously. Loralee, Fiona and, had he imagined it, Anna? The serving girl dropped a fistful of silverware, as if even *she* knew their secret.

"All right! That's it! Loralee, Fiona, in my study." He

stood and stomped into his private office, leaving his wife and daughter to scamper along behind him.

"Close the door," he ordered, watching them as they stood in front of his desk like two errant school children. "Out with it. Fiona?"

The woman turned absolutely white. "I . . ." She turned to look at Loralee. "We . . . there was a . . ." She let out a breath of air and stared down at the floor as though that was all she was going to say about *that*.

Edward raised his eyebrows. "That's it?" When Fiona did not respond he turned to his daughter. "Loralee? Perhaps you can shed some light on your mother's eloquent explanation for the unusual atmosphere in this house?"

Neither of them looked at all eager to enlighten him. In fact, they looked like they'd rather be anywhere else in the world than where they were right now.

Edward leaned back in his chair and settled down to wait.

Jesse rolled over, yanking the covers up over his shoulder as he did. It was well after one o'clock in the morning, and, though he was exhausted, sleep wouldn't come.

How could he sleep when his conscience was still berating him for the way he'd treated Loralee earlier?

He'd seen, when she turned around and found him at the O'Toole table, the way her face brightened. And when she'd teased him about how often they'd been running into each other, it was obvious that she'd expected him to tease back.

They'd flirted before. Loralee was better at it than she realized, and it had been difficult for Jesse to hide his true feelings when she'd obviously wanted to play.

But Loralee wasn't one of those girls that Jesse wanted to play with to pass the time. He wanted so much more than that, but he couldn't have it.

Jesse told himself that he'd been cool toward Loralee for

her own good. A woman didn't flirt with a man unless she had *some* interest in him. She'd be better off to forget about him right now. He had done what he did with Loralee's best interests in mind.

Jesse sat up and punched his pillow into a different shape. He had to get some sleep. If only he could think about any other woman than Loralee Vander.

That's it! He opened his eyes. That's what he had to do! He had to find another woman. Not another perfect woman, of course. *Any* woman. Or, better yet, a whole string of women! Jesse stacked his hands beneath his head and smiled.

What a relief! He'd go out tomorrow night, and he'd find *someone* to occupy his time. Why, soon he'd forget all about Loralee!

Suddenly, he was very sleepy. He yawned and closed his eyes.

Tomorrow, his life would get back to normal.

CHAPTER
FOURTEEN

"Is he looking?"

Suzanne looked over Loralee's shoulder toward Jesse. "No, he's not."

"Why not?" Loralee demanded. "You said this would work."

"It will work," Suzanne said. "The whole plan depends upon him seeing you over and over. It isn't meant to happen instantly."

Earlier in the day, while Loralee was lamenting Jesse's sudden aversion to her, Suzanne had struck upon a plan of action. Go to every party in town, she'd said. Be seen with other men, dancing, flirting and having a grand old time. Sooner or later, Jesse's jealousy would get the best of him, and he'd make his move.

Loralee hadn't liked the idea then any more than she did now. But Suzanne, and her mother, who was an incurable romantic who loved to match make, had persuaded her to give it a try. Mrs. Becker was in control of the entire plan. Everything, from the parties they'd attend, to Loralee's wardrobe, to the way she styled her hair. And she was sure that, given time, it would work.

"You've got to get out on the dance floor, dear," Mrs. Becker said. "Remember what we talked about earlier."

"Earlier?" Loralee panicked. Mrs. Becker had begun "training" her student as soon as Suzanne had pitched her plan, and Loralee's head was swimming with more rules and tricks and ploys designed to get a man to sit up and take notice than she had ever imagined there could be.

"Oh, Lord!" Loralee rolled her eyes. "All right, here goes." She glanced at the faces of the men across the room, and when she found Bill Oberman looking at her, she smiled then demurely looked away. A few seconds later, she looked back up and found him still watching her. She smiled again. Bill was a good-looking man whose father's family had owned and operated the local ice plant forever. Not two minutes later, he was by her side, asking for a dance.

Loralee spun around the dance floor with Bill, trying desperately to remember the do's and don'ts of this ridiculous game. When the dance ended, he returned her to Mrs. Becker's side.

"That was good, Loralee," she said covertly. "Jesse couldn't take his eyes off of you. And he drained *two* glasses in the short time you were out there!"

"Really?"

"Really— Oops, here he goes. He's going to ask, he's going to ask . . . Marion Henley. Ooooh, good choice, Mr. Sinclair."

"What do you mean? She's the prettiest girl here!"

"Exactly. He's going right for the heavy artillery." She looked Loralee in the eye and said, "He needs something powerful to take his mind off of you."

Loralee was dumbfounded. "How do you and Suzanne know all this stuff?"

"I learned it from my mother, who learned it from her

mother. And I've taught Suzanne. The question is, why don't *you* know it?''

''Well . . . *my* mother rarely leaves the house, and when she does, it's certainly not to attend a party. So, where would I have learned all of this?'' she said.

''Where, indeed. Your mother has been remiss in her responsibilities. A woman needs to know these sorts of things. In any case—oh!— Here comes Jimmy Sherkens. And he's got his eye on you! Remember to smile,'' she whispered, just as Jimmy stopped before Loralee.

''Good evening, Mrs. Becker. Miss Vander.''

''James.'' Mrs. Becker said. ''How is your dear grandmother?''

''She's improved a little, thank you.''

''I'm glad to hear it. How old is she, now?''

''She just turned eighty-seven.''

''Eighty-seven! Isn't that marvelous!''

James smiled at Loralee and said, ''May I have the honor of the next dance?''

Loralee glanced quickly at Mrs. Becker, and he quickly added, ''With your permission, of course, Mrs. Becker.''

''Permission granted.''

James led her out onto the floor where they stayed through three dances! He was a very good dancer, and Loralee found that she was genuinely enjoying herself. She was almost sad to say good-bye when he delivered her back into the protective custody of Suzanne's mother.

''That was wonderful!'' Mrs. Becker whispered. ''The way you were smiling at him was just perfect.''

''James is very nice,'' Loralee said.

''He is, isn't he? I wish he would ask Suzanne to dance.''

''Where is she anyway?''

''You two have been giving me a run for my money. Why, one of you no sooner gets back and the other is already leaving!

I'm having a hard time keeping track of you both and Mr. Sinclair, too.''

"Have you seen anything?" Loralee whispered.

"I've seen plenty. He's playing right into your hands, Loralee. He's only been asking the very prettiest girls to dance, though he barely looks their way at all. His eyes have been on you the entire time.''

"Really?" This made Loralee nervous. What if she did something wrong?

"Really. Oh, here comes another one. Smile, dear!"

And this is the way the night continued. By the end of the evening, Loralee's feet ached from all the nonstop dancing.

They had decided to leave at midnight. Loralee was out on the floor for what would be her final dance of the night. When it ended, she found Suzanne already standing beside her mother.

"I thought that song was never going to end!" Suzanne said, as the three ladies walked to their waiting carriage. Mr. Becker had gone off to play cards with the men. His wife would send the carriage back to retrieve him after all the women had been safely deposited at home.

"Me, too. I just about—"

"Guess who I danced with," Suzanne said, grabbing her friend's arm.

"Who?"

"Probably the only guy you didn't dance with."

"Jesse?" Loralee felt the blood rush to her cheeks.

"Jesse."

Mrs. Becker was helped up into the carriage. Before Suzanne stepped up, she whispered in Loralee's ear, "I absolutely must speak to you in private!"

"Why?"

"Because, that's why," she whispered. "Oh! Mother, I dropped a glove!"

"A glove? Suzanne, you shouldn't have taken your gloves off yet!"

"I was so warm, I took them off on the porch. I must have dropped it there. I'll go back and look."

"Don't dawdle!"

"I won't. Loralee, come with me," she said, turning her friend back toward the house. They walked with their heads bent, as though they were truly looking for something lost.

"What is so important?" Loralee hissed.

"I have to ask you, please don't be offended."

"I won't." Loralee was alarmed. "What?"

"When you danced with Jesse, did he ever . . . well, he had his hand on my waist, of course, but, well, you know he has big hands, and . . . well, he, I mean, maybe I imagined it, I don't know—"

"Will you just—spit—it—out!"

Suzanne took a deep breath and stopped walking. "He had his hands, well, his fingers were spread against me, and his— oh, I don't know! It just seemed—"

"Suzanne! Your mother is waiting!" They were all the way to the porch by now, and Suzanne looked down and—lo and behold!—there was a glove on the ground. She snatched it up and the two girls turned back toward the waiting carriage.

"What did he do?" Loralee asked.

"His fingers brushed against me!" Suzanne blurted out.

Loralee stared at her blankly, then understanding dawned. "Oh!"

"He did it on purpose, Loralee, I'm sure of it! He knew I would come running right to you."

"That snake!"

"Loralee, I think he's a little better at this game than we realized."

"I can't believe the nerve! My very best friend!"

"Maybe this wasn't such a good idea after all," Suzanne said.

"No! It's the perfect idea!" By now they had reached the carriage, and as Suzanne went to climb in, Loralee said, "If he wants to turn this into some kind of a contest, by God, that's exactly what I'll do!''

Suzanne put her foot back on the ground. ''You don't mean—''

''What I mean is this.'' She leaned closer. ''The next party we attend, some lucky gentlemen will be rewarded a few kisses. Look at it as payment for his part in this charade.''

''Payment! Loralee, that makes it sound like—''

''It makes it sound like exactly what it is. Jesse doesn't want me? Well, that's fine! My mouth is part of the package, and if he's not interested, I'll find someone else who is! A few kisses are a small enough price to pay to watch him suffer!''

Loralee stepped into the carriage and said, ''And who knows? I've never really kissed another man, not by choice, anyway. I might just enjoy it!''

Jesse pulled her closer.

He already had his tongue in her mouth and his hand on her breast, and still she didn't stop him. How much would she allow?

She wasn't completely inexperienced. But neither was she an expert. She followed willingly the way he led, but there was none of the passion he'd shared with Loralee.

Loralee! Even while he ravaged this girl's mouth, even while he pressed against her, he couldn't keep thoughts of Loralee from invading.

Damn her! She'd danced with almost every man in the place. And that dress!

Jesse's breathing quickened as he thought about the way her dress clung to her shoulders, as though the slightest touch would send it to a puddle on the floor. He broke away from the girl's mouth and pressed kisses down her neck, across her shoulders . . . She moaned and let her head fall back. Her hair brushed his hands.

And, *what* did Loralee think she was doing with hair that looked like that! He'd watched her dancing and flirting and tossing that mass of tumbling curls outrageously. She looked like she'd just crawled out from a good tumble in the hay! Whatever was she thinking to go out looking like that? And it hadn't helped matters any that Johnny'd looked at her and said, "Wow."

The girl beside him reached up and pulled his head toward her breasts, and that's when Jesse knew he'd gone far enough. He pulled away.

"Look, I'm sorry. I never should have—"

"Don't be." She reached toward him as though to pull him into another embrace, but he caught her hand and held it tightly between his own.

"It's very late," he said. "You'd better go in." And before she could protest further, he was up and out of the carriage, holding up his hand to assist her.

She hesitated a second then put her hand in his and gracefully stepped down from the carriage. Nothing like the way Loralee hauled herself over the side and jumped.

"Damn it!" he said.

"What!" She held a hand to her heart as though his language was going to stop it from beating right then and there!

Jesse hadn't meant to speak out loud. "Oh . . . I'm sorry. It's just that . . . it's so late. You'd better go right in," he said, hoping that she would think he had cursed from the frustration of being separated from her.

It worked. She smiled and said, "Thank you for a lovely evening." And with a quick kiss on his cheek, she was gone.

Jesse climbed back into the carriage, relieved, if somewhat annoyed, to be alone with his thoughts of Loralee.

CHAPTER FIFTEEN

Autumn came early to Pennsylvania this year, and the trees were already well on their way to the brilliant reds, oranges and yellows that were Mother Nature's last hurrah before the bone-chilling winds of winter set in.

It was Saturday evening. Loralee took a detour on the way home from work just so she could walk through Memorial Park to enjoy her favorite season while it lasted.

It had been an exhausting week. It seemed, lately, like the crowd in the waiting room never diminished in size, regardless of how quickly Doc and Loralee worked. And the calls to the patches, which were growing by leaps and bounds, took longer each day.

Today she'd visited Stockton. And, though there hadn't been anyone who was seriously ill, the visit took all day.

She'd held a three-year-old boy in the tub while his mother scrubbed his head, first with kerosene then with the special soap that would kill lice. He'd kicked and fought until Loralee was not only soaking wet, but bruised and scratched as well.

She'd spread salve on the burned hand of a little girl who had touched a hot pot while trying to "help" her Mama. She showed the mother the proper way to wrap the hand and left plenty of bandages so that the dressing could be changed daily.

She'd dropped off a tonic from Dr. Farley for a newborn with colic.

She'd delivered drops for a little girl with an earache.

She'd been informed of two women who were soon expecting to give birth, and she stopped at both homes to encourage them to call on the doctor when their time came. Often newborns died because of problems that could have been avoided, if only a doctor had been there. This issue had become one of Loralee's personal crusades, and she preached it whenever she got the chance. Still, most women opted to have their husbands or their mothers deliver their babies.

And, then, when she was finally on her way out of Stockton, a little boy fell out of a tree and broke his arm. So she drove both the little boy and his hysterical mother into Doc's office to have the arm set and plastered.

It had been quite a day, but now that it was over, Loralee was beginning to revive at the thought of seeing Jesse again. Ever since last weekend, and Suzanne's shocking revelation, Loralee hadn't been able to think about anything other than besting Jesse at his own game. Suzanne had been right. He'd only done what he did to shock Loralee. And he had succeeded.

And now she needed to think of some way she could shock him back without damaging her own reputation.

Loralee didn't normally work on Saturdays. But because she had left work early last Monday, she had decided to come in and work at least part of the day in order to catch up. Part of the day had turned into the whole day, and now, here she was, arriving home at nearly six o'clock with Suzanne and her parents coming to pick her up at eight-thirty.

She had only two and a half hours to make herself irresistible. As she stepped into the front door of her home, she caught a glimpse of herself in the foyer mirror. Her hair had come loose, and straggles of it hung around her face. Her eyes had dark circles beneath them from the restless nights she'd spent worrying about Jesse, and as she reached up to brush a smudge of dirt off her cheek, she noticed that she needed a manicure desperately.

Irresistible? For that, she'd need a small miracle. What she had was two and a half hours. She'd settle for mildly attractive.

She ran up the stairs to her room, taking them two at a time.

Jesse walked into the room slowly, giving himself a chance to take in the situation. He wanted to find a suitable woman and leave with her. It hadn't worked last weekend. Maybe this time it would.

He *had* to do this. There was no other way to wipe Loralee's memory out of his mind. And after the catastrophe in his carriage last weekend, he wasn't even sure that *this* would work. When had he ever turned down a woman who was obviously willing? Never, as far as he could remember.

The people of Hazleton reveled in a good party. It was only the second week in September, and though the weather had cooled considerably, winter was far off. Still, the town's upper class were spending their weekends socializing as though they were going to be housebound for the next eight months. The wives competed, each one bent on throwing the most extravagant affair possible.

It wasn't an easy task. Virtually every party was arranged to provide entertainment for three distinct groups of people. The main party, where the musicians were located, was the point through which everyone entered. It was the place where everyone put in an appearance, thanked the hosts for inviting them, and made the obligatory greetings among the other guests.

But, once those tasks were completed, husbands left their wives in order to visit the gaming room, where there would be cards, gambling, cigars, and all other sorts of vices that women simply could not be subjected to. The women, for the most part, retired to a separate room, where they could visit with their friends and talk openly, without the worry of being overheard by someone's husband.

The main party, with the music and dancing, was provided as a way for single people to meet. Of course, those women who brought unmarried daughters, stayed nearby, in order to chaperone. And, while the young ladies sometimes mingled in the ladies' private sitting room, and the young men often partook of the male camaraderie in the gaming room, for the most part, the three groups stuck to their own ground.

Jesse had long ago tired of the effort these affairs required. He'd been attending these parties from the time he was eighteen. And, like all eighteen-year-old boys, he'd become addicted to the constant contact with beautiful young women that the festivities provided. But as his experience increased, he developed a kind of sixth sense that told him which women were a sure thing and which women weren't. And at that point, all the fun had gone out of it.

Jesse had found himself going from woman to woman so quickly that even his father had warned him to watch his step. It seemed he had gotten quite a reputation as a ladies' man, and Stephen did not, he said, want to see his son trapped into a marriage he didn't want because of his careless disregard for the women he slept with.

That had opened Jesse's eyes, and for the past few years, he'd been more discriminating. The strange part was that after a constant diet of women, it hadn't been that difficult to go without. It had taken a while for Jesse to figure it out, but, right before his recent birthday bash, he'd finally admitted it to himself: He wanted a wife.

He wanted a woman to love, not just to lust after. He wanted a woman who loved him, not just the social standing that his money could give her. He wanted someone with whom he could build a lifelong relationship. He wanted to make babies, and surround himself with his own warm, loving family.

He wanted Loralee Vander.

He pushed that thought out of his head and began to look around the room. He got a drink, emptied the glass, then got another and started to mingle in the crowd. It wouldn't take long, he knew.

There seemed to be an awful lot of unescorted women at this party. And, for some reason, there didn't appear to be very many men. Jesse moved around the room slowly, sipping at his drink.

From the corner of the room, even over the music, came a burst of uproarious male laughter. Jesse smiled, and sauntered in that direction, wondering what all the fuss was about. Probably some off-color jokes, he guessed.

He approached the group and tried to make his way toward the main attraction when, among all the dark suits, he saw a flash of bright color, something between pink and orange. There was a woman in there!

He leaned forward and nearly dropped his drink. Loralee was in the center of the adoring crowd. She was speaking softly, as though she had just revealed some ancient secret, and suddenly the crowd burst into laughter again.

"No, wait! There's more," she said. And again, she started with the whispering.

Her listeners were hanging on every word. They were riveted. As she spoke, she animatedly waved her small hands to describe whatever it was she was describing.

Jesse could feel the anger boiling up inside, and he spun and stormed away from the crowd, knowing, even as he did so, that all eyes were on him. He couldn't even manage to put on a front in the name of this ridiculous competition the two of them were engaged in. What did she think she was doing? People were going to talk!

Jesse flung back the rest of his drink, got another, and took

a seat, glowering at her group of admirers. What did she think
all those men were after, anyway? They weren't drooling all
over her because she could spin a good yarn!

She was flaunting herself in front of the entire town, and
sooner or later, she would be made to pay the price. Didn't
she realize that?

The tightly knit group of men broke apart, and Loralee
emerged on the arm of Nick Bennet, whose father owned the
Hazleton Sentinel, the local daily paper. He spun her around
the dance floor and Jesse never took his eyes off of them.

Did Nick *really* need to hold her that close? Good God, he
was practically breathing down her neck!

And *where* had Loralee found these dresses she'd been wearing? This one was a deep shade of pinkish-orange that was
almost, but not quite, red. And if the color wasn't brazen
enough, the cut of the thing should have been illegal! The front
was sufficiently modest, but as Nick twirled her close enough
that her skirts brushed Jesse's shoes, he noticed that the dress
had no back! None!

And, once again, her hair had that tousled, just-rolled-out-
of-bed thing going, which only served to showcase that nearly
her entire back was bare.

Jesse fumed as he watched them. He finished his drink, got
up for another and sat back down to find that Nick's hand was
now resting on Loralee's bare back!

"Damn it the hell, who does he think he is?" Jesse's voice
came out low and gravely, and though he hadn't actually been
talking to anybody, hadn't even meant to speak out loud, someone sitting next to him chuckled.

Jesse looked over to see Jimmy Sherkens smirking at him.
Jesse and Jimmy had gone to school together ever since first
grade.

"What's the matter, Jess," Jimmy said, "Finally found one
you can't have?"

Though Jesse had always thought of Jimmy as a friend, he

had an almost uncontrollable urge to bash his face in for that remark.

Without a word, Jesse got up and walked to Rita Santaro. He bent down and whispered something in her ear, and she smiled. She set her glass down on a tray, and Jesse escorted her out of the party and into the privacy of his carriage.

CHAPTER SIXTEEN

The water from the pump was icy cold. Loralee filled Dr. Farley's glass and her own and went inside to eat lunch. Doc was already sitting at a small table that was pushed against the wall in the tiny corridor that led from the examining room to the back of the building.

Loralee set one glass beside him, the other on her side of the table. "Goodness, I'm hungry," she said, digging into the small package that held a ham sandwich with mustard, an apple and four cookies. Two of these she took out and immediately gave to Doc.

"Where are you off to today?" he asked, sprinkling salt on a hard-boiled egg.

"Audenreid. You?"

"Drifton."

They ate in silence for a few minutes, relaxing before the second part of their day began. "How's Mrs. O'Toole?" Doc asked.

"Good. She's got about a week to go, but it could be any time."

"Are you nervous?"

Loralee grimaced. "A little bit." Colin and Kathleen had specifically requested that Loralee deliver the baby.

"You know what to do. You'll be fine."

"I know. I keep telling myself that. And if everything goes the way it's supposed to, I will be fine. I just hope I'm prepared in the event there's some kind of surprise." She hadn't ever delivered a baby by herself, although she'd assisted Doc several times.

"Chances are, everything will happen just the way the book says it should. If you want me to come along, though, I will."

"I know, but I have to do it by myself sooner or later. It might as well be now."

"Good. So that's settled." He dug into the cookies. "Mmm. Oatmeal Raisin."

"You know, ever since I told our cook that they were your favorite, she's been making them quite often. I think she has a crush on you!"

Doc laughed. "Aw, go on."

Loralee smiled. "I think she does!"

"You don't know what you're talking about," he said. But his face had turned brilliant red, right to the roots of his hair.

"I think I might have stumbled onto something here," Loralee teased.

"All right! I called on her once, a few weeks back."

"What?" Loralee asked, nearly popping out of her seat. "I was only kidding! Did you really?"

"Yes, I really did. She's very nice, and I'm taking her to Father Mathew's parade." He said it all in one big rush, obviously anxious to move away from the topic of his love life.

"What?"

"Got a problem with your hearing, girl?" He stood up and

cleared away his things from the small table. Loralee watched, dumbfounded. How had she not known about this?

"You gonna sit there all day?"

"No, sir," she said, jumping up.

"Good. Lock the door when you leave." And with that, he was gone.

Doc Farley was taking their cook to the Temperance Day Parade, the biggest social event of the year! Loralee wondered what the woman would look like dressed in anything but the black dress and enormous white apron that Fiona insisted all her staff wear.

With that thought, Loralee remembered that she was to stop in at her seamstress's shop on her way home from work for a fitting on this weekend's dress. She straightened the room, then left in the shay.

Mrs. Becker thought everything was moving along perfectly. Which was a good thing, because this weekend's parties and next weekend's parade would mark the end of the social season in Hazleton. Oh, there would be get-togethers here and there, but not the steady round of elaborate entertaining that most of the town's elite so enjoyed during the summer months.

Saturday was important, Loralee thought as she rode toward Audenreid. Mrs. Becker kept saying third time's a charm. And Saturday would be the third weekend of what Suzanne had taken to calling Project Annihilate: Jesse!

Loralee was going to a lot of time and trouble to impress Jesse. She sighed and clicked the reins, and the horse picked up speed.

She thought about the dress she was going to wear tomorrow night and the reaction it would get. There was no going back now. She had nothing else to wear that would work. She sighed again and shook her head.

Jesse had better be worth it.

* * *

"Is it working?"

Jesse looked up from the paper in front of him. "Is what working?" It was almost eleven o'clock on Wednesday night, and he'd been in the library ever since dinner.

Stephen pointed to the stack of papers in front of Jesse. "That. Have you forgotten about her, yet?"

Jesse stared at his father then blinked several times before looking away. "Is it that easy to see?" he asked quietly.

"Yes. It is."

"There *is* a lot of work, you know," Jesse said, gesturing toward the mess on the desk.

"I know. There's always been a lot of work. But there's never been so much of it that I've had to bury myself in it for weeks at a time."

"I'm not doing that."

"You're not?" Stephen lifted his eyebrows and waited, until Jesse finally looked away. He *had* been burying himself, and he knew it.

"Whatever happened to forgiving? Whatever happened to letting go of the past?" Stephen asked.

"I tried that." Jesse said, pushing away from the desk. He leaned back in the chair and threaded his fingers together across his stomach. "It didn't work."

"Jesse you've been nursing this grudge for twenty years! Forgiving isn't going to happen overnight!"

"Yeah, well I don't think it's going to happen at all!" He jumped up out of the chair and stormed toward the door, then spun around when he reached it. "Let me ask you something. Why are you so determined to convince me that Loralee Vander is the only girl in the world for me?"

When Stephen would have spoken, Jesse interrupted. "Let me tell you something, Dad. There are a lot of girls out there.

And I've been with quite a few. And I haven't found any one of them that can do anything different from any other!''

The silence stretched out between them. Jesse and Stephen had rarely disagreed about anything, let alone argued about it. To have done so now only emphasized how important the issue was, to both of them.

"I taught you to respect women," Stephen said softly.

The subtle reprimand was all that was needed. The fight went out of Jesse, and he sighed and hung his head. "I know you did. I know." He looked up at his father, and the pressures of the last few weeks suddenly seemed unbearable. "I don't know how to get through this."

"Have you talked to Loralee?"

"I've talked to her, yes. But we haven't talked about . . . . this thing that stands between us."

"I think you have to."

Jesse nodded. He was embarrassed about his previous outburst. He certainly hadn't needed to brag about his experience with women to his father.

He shoved his hands into the pockets of his jeans. "I just want you to know," he said, "I have never done anything with any woman that would bring shame to this family. I've been with a lot of women. But I have *always* been a gentleman. And, yes. You *did* teach me that."

He turned and retreated to his room, and things with Stephen were set back to right.

Charles sat slumped against the bar at one of the nicer gentlemen's clubs in town. The bartender glared at him, and he tried to sit up straighter. He had to remember that he was not in a saloon. Patrons here were not expected to get sloppy drunk night after night. They were not expected to get sloppy drunk ever.

Well! That's because they'd never had a rich little bitch ruin their life! When a thing like that happened, a man deserved to get good and drunk.

Charles deserved this drink, he told himself, as he drained his glass and pushed it toward the bartender for a refill.

Ruined! That's what he was. And it was all Loralee Vander's fault.

Loralee Vander. He couldn't even stand the thought of her name. That stupid bitch had destroyed his life!

She'd tossed him away, and not one week later she was back on the market. She was out every weekend, from what Charles heard. And she was having the time of her life without him. She was hitting two and three parties a night, and the men were practically fighting over her. That's what he'd heard.

Loralee was thrilled to be rid of him. Thrilled to be getting so much attention from so many men. Whore! She hadn't been thrilled to have any of *his* attentions.

What she needed was to share some of Charles's misery! Yeah, that's it. Maybe he should throw her a little bit of the misery she had caused. Let her know how it feels to be ruined.

Charles stood up, and searched through his pockets for some money. His fingers weren't working so well, and neither were his eyes. He pulled out a wad of bills and struggled to count them, but he couldn't seem to separate them. Damn it! They were stuck together! God-damned money!

He threw the wadded up bills on the bar and stumbled out into the night, happy to have finally made a decision about Loralee.

Some misery! That's what she needed. Misery loves company!

Charles stepped out onto the street. He looked up and down. Now, what the hell street was this? He walked a few feet in one direction, then abruptly stopped and turned back the other way.

Misery loves company! I heard there's this party Saturday night . . .

"Mr. Korwin! Mr. Korwin!"

At the sound of someone shouting his name, he turned so quickly he almost toppled over.

"Buck! What'r you doin' here, Buck?"

"I brought you here, sir. I think we should go home."

"Yer abslutly right! We should go home!" His father's driver helped him into the carriage. "I always liked you, Buck. Yer a good man," he said as he collapsed onto the seat.

"Thank you, sir."

"Oh! Buck! Wait, wait," he said as the man tried to close the door. "I got this great idea, Buck. I think maybe you an' me, we can make it work."

"Maybe so, sir," Buck said, deftly tucking Charles' arms and legs out of the way of the door before he slammed it shut.

"See, there's this party Saturday night, Buck . . ."

But the driver never heard him. Which was just as well, because not thirty seconds from the time the carriage was pulled away from the curb, Charles had passed out.

CHAPTER
SEVENTEEN

"You look beautiful tonight."

Loralee smiled. "Thank you." Nick Bennet had been paying quite a bit of attention to Loralee these past few weeks, and it was beginning to worry her. Yes, she needed the attention for her plan to work, but she was starting to feel very guilty about what she was doing. She really wasn't interested in anything beyond friendship with any of the men she'd been spending time with.

The song ended, and Nick asked, "Would you like a glass of punch?"

"Oh, yes," Loralee said gratefully.

He took her arm and led her toward a table where a waiter was serving punch. "Am I wearing you out, Miss Vander?" he teased, handing her a glass.

"Oh, no," she said, sipping from her glass. "Not wearing me out, just drying me out." She laughed. "I'm so thirsty I could drink that whole bowlful."

Nick smiled down at her. "You really do look stunning."

"Thank you." She looked down at the dress she was wearing. It was pink, so pale it looked almost white, and the fabric was a soft, flowing silk that floated around Loralee as she moved. The bodice was fitted, to accentuate her tightly cinched waist, and the skirt was ruffle upon fluffy ruffle. She wore her fullest petticoat beneath it.

The dress had a high neck, almost like a little tube that softly folded upon itself and stacked itself up all the way to her chin. The sleeves were long and loose, but banded tightly at the wrist. Every inch of her fair skin was covered. But the sleeves were made of the sheerest chiffon Loralee had ever seen. And her entire arm, from her shoulder to her wrist, could be seen right through the fabric.

She looked up at Nick, and knew she was blushing. "I was a little worried about the dress," she admitted. "You see, I didn't choose it. It was ordered for me."

Nick looked at the dress, and his eyes lingered on her arms. Loralee felt naked. "I think whoever ordered this dress for you should do all of your ordering from now on." He looked into Loralee's eyes. "There isn't a man in this room who's been able to keep his eyes off of you all night." His voice was deep and husky.

Loralee looked away. What should she say? She cursed her own stupidity for allowing Mrs. Becker to talk her into such an impossibly shocking dress.

"I've embarrassed you," Nick said. "I only meant it as a compliment, Loralee. You truly are breathtaking."

"Thank you, Nick."

"Would you like to dance again?"

"Yes. Yes I would," she said, a bit too eagerly, she knew, but at least dancing would get them off of the topic of her nearly transparent dress!

They spun around the dance floor flawlessly. Nick was a good dancer, and they moved in perfect synchronicity, chatting easily, until Loralee saw Jesse watching them from the edge of the dance floor. She lost both the thread of the conversation and her footing.

"Oh! Oh, I'm so sorry, I don't know ... I just ... What were you saying?" she asked, trying desperately not to think about the fact that Jesse's eyes were on her.

"So, he's here then."

Loralee looked at Nick, confused by his words. "Who?"

"Jesse Sinclair, of course."

Loralee felt as though Nick had squeezed the breath out of her. "I-I don't know." How did he know? How did he know!

"Loralee, it's all right. Everybody knows what's going on."

"What do you mean everybody knows? Everybody knows what?" She was beginning to get hysterical. Oh, what had she done?

"It's just that the rest of us have been watching," he said as though it was no big deal at all. "It's easy to see that your dancing with another man drives Jesse insane. We all know that. We'd have to be blind not to know it. In fact, the way he glares at us, we've been taking bets on which one of us is going to wind up with a broken nose for it." He glanced up at Jesse as they spun past him. "Right now," Nick whispered in her ear, "I'd put all your money on me."

Loralee was absolutely mortified. "Nick, I'm so sorry—"

"Don't be. It's been fun. In fact," he said, looking into her eyes, "we can even make it more interesting, if you like."

And before she knew what had happened, just as they breezed past Jesse for the second time, Nick leaned over and gave Loralee a quick kiss. On the mouth! It was over before she knew it, and so flawlessly timed that it had been apparent to no one else but Jesse.

"He saw," Nick said, with a smile. "Take a good look at my nice straight nose, because I don't think it's going to look like this for long."

"Don't you dare get in a fight over me!"

"Well, I did kiss you."

''I don't care! You don't deserve to have your face beaten to a pulp for it!''

''I think Jesse would—''

''Jesse has nothing to say about this! Nothing whatsoever! Until such time as Mr. Sinclair wishes to do something to change it, he has no say over whom I spend my time with.'' She was worked up now, and Nick obviously didn't know what to do with her. ''And if I want to dance with someone else, or kiss someone else, or whatever! Well, I will!'' She was completely flustered.

The song ended, and Nick said, ''I think I should take you back to Mrs. Becker.''

''Certainly, Nicholas, if you think that's best,'' she said, haughtily. How dare he imply that she should censor her actions to please Jesse Sinclair! Obviously, Nick Bennet, nice though he was, was not the kind of man for Loralee.

Loralee needed someone who would praise her for her independence. Someone who would encourage her desire for autonomy, not try to suppress it or direct it. She needed a man who would stand up to her, who would treat her as an equal, not someone who would pack her safely away when she became too outspoken.

Loralee needed Jesse.

She needed him desperately. Needed his arms around her, needed his sharp wit and quick intelligence, needed his strong sense of right and wrong. She needed everything about him.

''Thank you for the dances, Loralee,'' Nick said, as he left her in Mrs. Becker's care.

''And good luck. Mrs. Becker,'' he said with a nod of his head.

''What was that all about?''

''Oh, Mrs. Becker, I'm sorry. I need to—I need to freshen up.''

''But Loralee, Suzanne is still on the dance floor. Just wait a few minutes—''

"I can't. I need to get out of here." The embarrassment that everyone in the room knew what she had been attempting to do with Jesse was just too much to bear. "I'll be in the ladies' sitting room. I'll wait there for you." She turned and headed in that direction before Suzanne's mother could protest.

She rushed from the room toward the door which led down a small hallway and into the private room reserved for the ladies.

"Well, well, well. If it isn't my fiancée."

Loralee looked up into Charles's glassy eyes. He'd obviously been drinking to excess. She turned to go back into the ballroom, but his hand shot out, and he wrapped his fingers around her arm.

"Where'r you runnin' off to, little lady? Don' you have a little lovin' for your man?" He leaned forward as though to kiss her and Loralee shoved him away with her free hand.

"Charles, let go of me, this instant!"

"No, see, I'm not gonna do that. I'm gonna do what I shoulda done long ago—"

"Charles, so help me, I'll scream!" The bravery was pure pretense. She was terrified! He squeezed her arm mercilessly.

"No you won'." He pulled her roughly against his chest. "Well, maybe you will. Maybe you will be screamin' by the time I get done with you." He laughed.

He was insane! With a strength she didn't know she possessed, she slapped him with her free hand. Hard enough that he let go of her arm from the shock. Loralee turned and ran full speed down the hall and Charles took off after her. She turned the corner and—

"Oh!" She slammed full force into Jesse's chest.

"Hey," he said, and his arms went up to steady her. Charles smacked into Loralee's back, and she squirmed trying to get away from him.

"Get him away from me! Get him away from me!" Her

voice came out sounding hysterical. She scrambled to avoid Charles.

"All right, relax, relax," Jesse said, pulling her arm and setting her behind his right shoulder. He held up his hand to stop Charles when he would have followed her. "Is there some problem here?" he asked Charles.

"No problem at all, Sinclair. 'S none of yer concern. Go back inside."

Loralee clung to Jesse's sleeve. "Don't leave me alone with him!" she begged.

Jesse looked over his shoulder at her. "I won't."

"C'mon, Sinclair, get away from her! 'S has nothin' to do with you. Loralee and I need to settle a little score, don' we sugar?" Charles leaned sideways to wink at Loralee. She ducked further behind Jesse.

"All right, Charles. I think you ought to leave now, before you get thrown out. The lady isn't interested." Jesse stopped him with a hand on the shoulder.

Charles looked down at the hand then back up at Jesse. "An' who's gonna throw me out? You?" He laughed so hard he almost fell over.

Jesse turned to Loralee and said. "Don't move." He grabbed Charles by the lapels of his jacket and propelled him to the main doors, where a uniformed footman stood. "Get him out of here."

Charles stumbled as Jesse let go of him. "I'm not through with you yet!" he yelled. The footman tooted on a whistle, and immediately, another man in uniform was there to help. They carted Charles away from the door, and all the while he shouted. "You hear me, Loralee? I'll find you, honey! I'll find you wherever you go! It's not over yet . . ."

Loralee stood against the wall, paralyzed with fear. He had come after her again! And this time he'd done it in the middle of a party. He was getting braver and braver. Or crazier and crazier. If Jesse hadn't come along—

"Are you all right?"

She jumped and backed herself against the wall, but it wasn't Charles beside her. It was Jesse. It was only Jesse.

Loralee couldn't bear the fear she was feeling. She was afraid, and on top of that, she was humiliated that she had let someone else see her terror. She burst into tears.

"Hey, hey, it's all right," Jesse said, reaching to pull her gently into his arms. "You're okay, Loralee. You're safe." He pulled her against his chest with one arm and cradled the back of her head with his other hand.

She clung to him and sobbed so hard she could barely breathe. "I'm not safe! Didn't you hear him? He'll do it again! He'll try it again!"

Jesse held her tighter. "He won't, honey. It was just the whiskey talkin—"

"No!" She pushed away from him. "He wasn't drunk the last—" She cut herself off, but not before enough of her thought got out that Jesse was able to understand.

He stared at her. Loralee could read each emotion as it flashed across his face. First shock. And then rage. "He's done this before?" he whispered.

Loralee looked into Jesse's eyes, and she knew that it would do no good to lie. She looked away.

"Oh, my God. Oh, my God." He pulled Loralee back into his arms and held her. She could feel his chest rising and falling against her ear as though he had just run a race. "He's threatened you like that before?"

She kept her cheek pressed against his chest. She was safe with Jesse. She could tell him. "Threatened me. And more."

"You've got to get out of here. Let's get you home."

Loralee backed up. "I came with Suzanne. I can't go home with you."

Jesse paused. "Get Suzanne. I'll take both of you home."

Loralee just stood there. She was afraid to walk back into

the ballroom by herself. She was actually afraid to leave Jesse's side. She looked up at him, and her eyes filled with tears.

Jesse took one look at her face and reached for her hand. "Come on." He led Loralee back into the ballroom to the spot where Mrs. Becker was standing.

He tapped her on the arm, and when she looked up at him, he leaned over and whispered something in her ear.

Loralee watched as Suzanne's mother listened intently. The woman raised her eyebrows and leaned sideways to examine Loralee. She looked back at Jesse and nodded. He said, "Thank you."

He turned toward Loralee and said, "Stay here with Mrs. Becker. She'll tell you what we're going to do. I'll see you in a few minutes." Then he turned and walked away from her, and Loralee was filled with fear.

Mrs. Becker put her arm around Loralee and eased her toward the edge of the dance floor. "I should never have let you go alone!"

"It wasn't your fault. Charles is—"

"Charles is a brute! And we're not going to let him anywhere near you. Now look at me."

Loralee looked into Mrs. Becker's caring eyes. "Are you one hundred percent sure you feel safe riding alone with Jesse?"

"Alone? But I thought—"

"He asked permission to take you home. And I gave it. I thought you might need a little time alone to discuss—things. But if you aren't comfortable—"

"No! It's not that," Loralee said. She hung her head for a moment then looked back up at Mrs. Becker. "Jesse would never do anything to hurt me. Never. I know it in my heart."

Mrs. Becker hesitated a moment then said. "All right. You'll be riding to our house with us. From there, Mr. Sinclair will escort you home."

Loralee raised her eyebrows. "When did this happen?"

"That young man of yours has a certain way about him.

He's concerned about your reputation, and suggested the idea himself. I'm sure he's already left, and he probably made sure that quite a few people know that he left—alone.''

"Oh.''

Mrs. Becker smiled with satisfaction. "Fait accompli.'' She put an arm around Loralee, and said, "Now, if I could just get my daughter to cooperate the way you did, I would be a truly happy woman.''

Loralee smiled back. "Thank you.''

"My pleasure, dearest. My pleasure.''

The door to his coach was opened, and Loralee was quickly ushered inside. The driver pulled out immediately. He'd been instructed to drive around town and to keep driving until Jesse gave the signal, at which point they would return the lady to her front doorstep.

She settled herself on the seat beside Jesse.

"Make yourself comfortable. We're going to ride for a while.''

She looked at him as though she was surprised. "Oh.''

"You don't want to? I can take you right home, if that's what you'd prefer. I just thought . . . we might talk.''

She didn't even hesitate. "Yes. We should talk.''

Jesse's heart was hammering. She was here, in his carriage, in complete privacy. And he wanted to touch her so much it nearly killed him not to. But he knew that was the last thing she needed, after what had happened with Charles.

"Are you sure you're all right?''

She nodded, but rubbed her arm where Charles had been holding her. "I'm fine.''

"Let me see your arm.''

"It's fine, really,'' she said, still rubbing the spot.

He looked at her arm. It was completely visible through the sleeve of her dress, and so were the four bruises that Charles's fingers had left in her soft skin. Jesse felt a rage building up inside him like none he'd ever felt before. He hated men who bullied women. It was the biggest sign of weakness a man could show, and Jesse could never understand why some men felt such a need to do it.

He reached out and touched the bruises. "I'm so sorry."

At his touch, Loralee completely collapsed. She dropped her head into her hands and cried her eyes out.

Jesse slid over and wrapped his arm around her, and she turned toward him and rested her head against his chest. "It's okay, honey. You're safe now." He held her head in the palm of his hand and rubbed his fingers slowly in her hair.

"Is it because you broke off the engagement?"

"No! He was nasty even before that. That's what gave me the courage to call it off." She sat back and looked at Jesse and swiped at her eyes with the tips of her fingers. "Did you know I did it myself? I didn't get my father's permission or even tell him I was going to do it. I just . . . I just marched in there and did it."

"Pretty brave."

She shook her head. "No. Not brave. Desperate."

"Why did you agree to the marriage in the first place?"

"I didn't! Charles and my father arranged the whole thing. No one even asked me," she said, holding her hand to her chest.

Her father. Jesse went completely still. Her father had promised her in marriage to a man who terrified her. It seemed Edward Vander had no more regard for his own flesh and blood than he did for those he employed.

Jesse looked at her sitting there, and she looked so small, so vulnerable. She made every instinct to protect that he possessed come screaming to the surface. He wanted to take care of this woman.

"Loralee," he cleared his throat and tried to start again. "I want . . ." He let out his breath and looked away. What did he want? The seconds ticked by while he sat there wondering what to say.

She reached out and slipped her hand into his, and Jesse felt a thrill shoot through him at her touch. She was giving him a hint.

"This game we've been playing is over," he said. "I'm not going to keep trying to forget about you. Because nothing works. Believe me, I've tried everything, and . . . it's not going to go away, and it doesn't matter how many other women I dance with, or how many other men you flirt with, it's just not going to go away."

She looked down at her lap. "I was so mad at you that day at Kathleen's. You walked out of that house as though you couldn't stand the sight of me. I just," she shook her head, "I just wanted to get back at you some way." She looked up at him. "I wanted to make sure you were really sorry that you walked away from me."

"It worked. I thought I was going to go out of my mind with jealousy."

He squeezed Loralee's fingers. "I guess it was foolish— what we did."

She smiled, "Now what do we do?"

"Now," he knocked on the front of the carriage to signal the driver, "we go home, and we think about what we're getting ourselves into."

She looked up at him, and her eyes were wide. She nodded. "We should think about it carefully."

God, she was beautiful.

"It might be difficult," she said.

The carriage rolled to a stop and Jesse reached up to brush his fingers along the side of her face. "It will be difficult," he said softly. "But staying away from you is impossible."

He felt the carriage rock as the driver hopped off, and he anticipated the opening door a second before it happened. He lowered his hand and said, "Good night."

Loralee looked at the waiting coachman, then back at Jesse. With a small smile she said, "Good night. And thank you."

She held out her hand and the coachman helped her down and closed the door behind her. He waited until she had put herself safely behind closed doors before he pulled away.

Jesse slouched down into the seat and rubbed his eyes. It had been one hell of a night.

He couldn't forget the fear in Loralee as she struggled to get away from the man she was to have wed. What in God's name had Charles done to her? She was not a timid woman. It would take something significant to put that kind of fear into her. Jesse felt the rage building up again, and he almost wished he'd floored Korwin while he had the chance.

The coachman pulled into the Sinclair drive, and Jesse sat up. The door opened and he jumped down. "Thank you, Bartol. Good night."

"Good night, sir."

Jesse moved carefully through the darkened house. In his room, he turned on the gas light and began undressing.

Loralee Vander. Could he really do this?

With his collar unbuttoned and his shirt tails pulled out of his pants, he walked to a desk in the corner of the room. He opened a drawer and dug around until he found what he was looking for. He walked back to the bed and dropped down onto the side of it and rested his elbows against his knees.

In his hands he held a tiny, carved wooden boat, a toy from his childhood, made by Sam Fedosh. His father had touched this wood. He'd shaped it and smoothed it with his own hands. Jesse ran his fingers over the simple toy. His father.

Had he died peacefully, Jesse wondered. Was he truly watching him from above, as Jesse had always believed? Did he marvel at the privileged upbringing his sons had enjoyed?

He tried to remember his mother, but, sadly, he could barely picture her face. Jesse tried to take comfort in the knowledge that, wherever Sam and Mary were, they were together.

He wondered about the two younger sisters that had been separated from him and Johnny. Had they been able to grow up together? Were they married by now? Were they happy? Did they know that they had two brothers? Jesse had been the oldest, and even he had trouble remembering things from so long ago. They were younger. Maybe they'd never even been told that they were adopted.

He stood up and put the boat away. He couldn't change the fact that Samuel Fedosh had died. He couldn't change the fact that Loralee's father was responsible for that death.

What he could do was continue the legacy that Sam and Mary had given to him. They'd had the capacity to give love in abundance. They'd passed on that ability to love to their son. And now, Jesse had been given the chance to feel what his parents had felt for one another.

With Loralee Vander. How could he turn away from the same feelings that his own father had embraced? What did it matter who her father was?

He was in love with Loralee Vander and had been since the first day he'd laid eyes on her.

Jesse undressed and crawled into bed. And, for the first time in weeks, he slept peacefully.

Charles stumbled through the gate and dropped the key into his pocket. He moved through the garden carelessly, certain that no one would see him at this late hour, not caring, even if they did.

His fall from grace was now complete.

Somebody had to pay for this! It was all Loralee's fault, and, Charles swore, by the time it was all said and done, she'd pay for what she'd done to him!

He stepped up onto the patio and looked in through the French doors. The room was dark. He had a key, but Abby might be frightened if she woke to find someone in her room. He knocked on the glass.

She didn't move. He knocked a little harder. C'mon, Abby. One more time. He knocked hard enough that she finally woke up.

She came to the door and opened it a crack.

"Charles? What are you doing here?" She rubbed her eyes. "What time is it?"

"I don't know. Let me in."

"What? Let you in? What's wrong with you?"

"Nothin's wrong with me. Please. Pleeeease let me in?"

Abby blinked her eyes hard. "You're drunk."

"I am not!"

"You are, too. Go home, Charles."

"C'mon, Abbyyy. Pleeeease."

"Listen," she said, growing aggravated, "It's late, I'm tired, you're drunk. Go home!" She closed the door, and Charles heard the lock slip into place.

He rested his head against the side of the house. Only, he was too drunk to gauge distance, and instead of resting it against the house, he banged it against the house.

"God damn it!" he said, reaching up to touch the spot on his forehead that had slammed into the brick. His fingers came away wet.

"God damn it!" he said again.

He turned and, with great difficulty, found his way home. He stumbled through the darkened house, bumping and banging into things as he went.

"Shhhh!" he said out loud to himself.

He crawled up the steps and opened the door to his room. His bed. His wonderful, wonderful bed.

He fell into it, fully clothed, and passed out.

CHAPTER EIGHTEEN

Loralee was half a block away when she saw him—head down, and pacing a hole in the sidewalk in front of Dr. Farley's office. Jesse. Her footsteps faltered and her heart went wild at the sight of him.

She walked toward him, and he looked up, and the last few feet of her journey were made while they stared into each other's eyes and felt the bond between them tightening.

When, at last, she stood about two feet away from him, she stopped, and Jesse smiled. "You look pretty in the morning."

Within Loralee, something welled. Was it desire? Anticipation? His words were innocent, yet incredibly intimate. They were words that a man might say to a lover. A husband to a wife.

Loralee stood there, smiling like an idiot, she was sure.

"Aren't you going to say anything?" he asked.

Her smile widened into a grin, and she shrugged. "Hello?"

"That's all I get? Hello?"

Loralee laughed. "I can't help it. I'm dumb struck in your presence."

It was Jesse's turn to laugh. "Yeah, right. I'd be willing to bet you've never been dumb struck by anyone in your entire life. Seems to me, you always manage to find *something* to say."

"In the interest of harmony, I'm attempting to change my evil ways." She batted her eyelashes at him.

Jesse smiled and reached for her hand. "Don't you dare change anything."

He was teasing, but his message was serious, and it went straight to her heart. For the first time in her life, Loralee had found a man who wouldn't try to mold her into something she was not.

"I wasn't sure how else to get ahold of you," he said.

"Doc's office is a safe bet. I'm here more often than not."

"I was wondering if you'd like to have lunch with me tomorrow," he asked.

"Lunch?"

"Yeah, lunch. You know, that meal we eat at noon?" He smiled at her.

She crinkled her nose at him. "Smarty-pants." She looked off into the distance. "Let's see, tomorrow is Tuesday, and I'll probably be heading out to Eckley, which means . . ." What time would she have to leave? By one, definitely. She gnawed at her bottom lip. "Yes, tomorrow would be fine, if we can meet at, say, eleven forty-five?"

"That would be perfect. How about if I meet you over at Memorial Park? I'll wait on the bench under the big oak tree."

"All right. Tomorrow it is." She had a date with Jesse Sinclair!

He backed up a step. "I'd better let you get to work."

"Yes, me, too. I mean, you, too." She rolled her eyes, and he laughed. "What I mean is, I'd better let you get to work, too."

"I'll bring lunch. You bring a blanket."

He turned and walked away, and Loralee hurried into the building. She felt like dancing around the room. Would she ever get over the thrill of the way he looked at her, as if he would be perfectly content to do it for the rest of his life?

With a smile, she breezed into the exam room and found Doc already there. She let out a long sigh, and he raised his bushy eyebrows in question, but Loralee just smiled and turned away.

CHAPTER NINETEEN

At twelve noon, Trinity Lutheran's bells began to ring.

Jesse sat on the bench in the park, and with each minute that passed, his heart fell a little further toward the pit of his stomach. She wasn't coming. She wasn't coming, and it hurt like hell. He stood up and reached for the basket he'd tucked under the bench.

"Jesse! Jesse, wait!"

He looked up and saw Loralee running toward him, and he felt something catch in his heart. He watched her run, with her blond hair flying out behind her, just as he was sure it had when she was a little girl.

"Wait!"

He held up his hand, and called, "Slow down! You'll fall!"

She didn't slow down. Loralee ran faster than he would've thought those small feet could carry her. And she didn't stop until she stood before him. She thrust the blanket into his arms and collapsed onto the bench.

"Oh, Lord." She was breathing heavily, and she held a hand to her heart. "Let me catch my breath."

She closed her eyes and tried to slow her breathing, and Jesse thought *This is what she'll look like after I've made love to her.*

Now, *where* had that come from? He looked over his shoulder as though he'd find someone standing there who had whispered it into his ear.

"I thought you'd be gone. We had a . . . an emergency . . . and Doc needed me to stay. I thought I'd never make it in time."

"I thought you weren't coming. I thought you changed your mind."

"Changed my mind?" She said it as though she thought he must surely have gone insane. She stood up and reached for his hands, and said, "I've never felt so sure about anything in my life."

Jesse looked into Loralee's eyes and knew that she was telling the absolute, heart-felt truth. She was positively certain about the choice she'd made. The fact that Jesse was not made him feel very guilty.

"You don't feel any hesitation? Any doubt?"

"Doubt that I should be with you? No. Do you?" She sat back down on the bench, and Jesse slid in place beside her.

"Not doubt, exactly. I just . . ." He reached for her hand and debated the wisdom of what he was about to say. He wanted to explain what he was feeling. He wanted her to understand the fear that told him that a relationship between the two of them could never work out.

On the other hand, he felt something for Loralee that he'd never felt before, and he wanted her to know that, too.

The only way to do it was to just say the words, and pray that she'd understand.

"I've been with a lot of women," he said bluntly. "I know what lust feels like. But—"

"Lust?" she interrupted. "Is that what this is?" She looked at him as though boldly challenging him to deny it.

"Well . . ." Jesse looked down into his lap. How did a man talk about a thing like this with the woman he loved? "It's part of it. It's a big part of it."

She hesitated. "How big is big? Because if that's all there is—"

"No," he said, nodding his head and opening his eyes wide. "That's not all it is. That's what I'm trying to explain, and obviously, I'm not doing a very good job."

"Try again." She was watching him, and waiting for him to make her world right again. His words had confused and scared her.

Jesse sighed and looked up at the sky as if it might somehow give him the right answers. "I know what lust feels like. And it's very easily dealt with."

He turned and looked at her. "Lust doesn't keep you awake at night. It doesn't make you feel that everything you've come to believe about yourself is suddenly a lie. It doesn't make you question your entire life."

She blinked her eyes slowly and licked her lips. "What you feel for me makes you do that?"

He was baring his soul before this woman. And Jesse was man enough to admit to himself that it scared the hell out of him. "Yes." He watched Loralee's face for a reaction. But she just sat perfectly still, staring at him with those wide, green eyes. He reached for her hand. "And, even knowing that, I wonder how we can ever hope to make this work."

Loralee squeezed his hand. Her eyes were bright with tears. "Oh, Jesse. We'll find a way. I know we will." She leaned toward him, looking into his eyes as though she was looking into his soul. "We have to," she whispered.

Their lips were only inches apart. Jesse looked at her for a few seconds then pulled her toward him. He pressed his mouth against hers and almost drowned in the feelings that spilled over him. He wanted this woman. They *would* find a way.

He wrapped an arm around her waist and pressed her body to his chest. Loralee gasped, surprised, Jesse knew, by the intensity of his need for her.

With a groan, he separated himself and sat back against the bench. Loralee sat there as if dazed. Jesse took a deep breath and let it out slowly. "We're right out on the street," he whispered, with a laugh, trying to break the tension. "See?" he asked. "See what you make me do?"

"Me? I am completely innocent!"

Her words, with their double meaning, shot right through him, and he reached for her and pulled her close. "Yes," Jesse said, looking into her fiery eyes. "You are. And I love it."

She blushed and looked down into her lap. "We should never be alone."

"How about a parade?"

She looked up, obviously confused. "What?"

"A parade. There'd be lots of people at a parade."

"Yes," she said. "There would be. What are you talking about?"

Jesse laughed. "The Temperance Day parade is this weekend. Let me take you."

Her eyes widened. "To the parade? But . . . what if—"

"What if someone sees us together?" he asked, knowing exactly what she was thinking. "Loralee, sooner or later, everyone is going to find out. I don't want to hide away like we're doing something wrong."

"But, the parade?" She stared at him. "It's the social event of the year for the entire region. Practically for the whole state!"

"You don't want to be seen with me?"

"No! No, that's not it. It's just . . ." She closed her eyes and held her breath. And when, at last, she released it, she looked at him, and said, "Are you sure?"

"Is that a yes?"

She smiled. "We might regret this."

"Never."

She hesitated, but she was smiling so hard, he already knew what her answer would be. "All right. It's a yes."

The sound of silverware clanking against china had never been deafeningly loud before. Loralee poked at the food on her plate and tried not to let her jangled nerves get the best of her.

Dinner in the Vander household was never a particularly joyous occasion, but tonight, it was downright stilted. Loralee looked surreptitiously at her parents. She had the strangest feeling that she was not the only one with a secret.

Edward wiped his mouth with a linen napkin and cleared his throat. Uh-oh, Loralee thought, here we go. The big announcement.

"Loralee, I've decided to arrange a meeting between you and Walter Conti."

Loralee knitted her brows together. "Walter Conti? What in heaven's name for?"

"Walter is in the market for a wife. I think both our families would benefit from a union between the two of you."

"What? In the market ... Are you out of your mind?" Loralee threw her napkin on the table. "Walter is at almost twice my age!"

"So? His family is—"

"So? *So?*" Loralee couldn't believe that her father would actually try to arrange another marriage for her, after the way the last fiasco had ended.

"Will you calm down? I could have this discussion with Walter, you know, and merely inform you of the results. I thought this way—"

"This way is wrong, Papa! I will not marry someone simply because the *union* makes good business sense!"

Edward's face turned red, and Loralee knew she was in for a fight. She didn't care! She'd fight until her dying day before she allowed her father to marry her off to a man she did not love!

"You have nothing to say about this, Loralee! It is a father's prerogative to choose his daughter's husband. It's been—"

"Not this daughter!" Loralee said, laying her hand across her chest. "I have told you before, and I will tell you again, *I will choose my own husband!*"

"And *who* would you choose? Who?" Edward's eyes looked about ready to bug right out of his head.

"Well, I don't know!"

"You're so wrapped up in your *work,* you don't even have time for a man to call on you! How would you ever entice one into marrying you?"

"I can't find anyone on my own? For your information, I was invited to the Temperance Day parade this very morning!"

"Who? Who invited you?"

Loralee straightened her shoulders and said, "Jesse Sinclair!"

Fiona muttered, "Oh, dear God."

Loralee thought to herself that she had never before seen her father react in quite this way. If she didn't know better, she would swear he was going to physically explode. Just— Bam!—explode. He began to shake, tiny tremors that rocked his entire body, and Loralee wondered why he was fighting so hard to hold in his rage.

"I don't ever want to hear that name in this house again. Is that clear?" Even his voice shook with the effort of restraining his anger.

"Why, Papa?" she asked, wondering, even as she said the words, what was possessing her to provoke him. "Is it guilt? Is it that you can't stand the guilt of what you did?"

Edward sprang out of his chair and lunged at his daughter. He grabbed her by her shoulders and hauled her to her feet. Loralee screamed.

"Edward, stop!" Fiona was on her feet. "Stop!" She pulled at his arm, but it didn't even slow him down.

"Let go of me!" Loralee screamed. "Let go!"

"If I *ever* hear that name spoken in this house again, I'll kill him! Do you hear me? I'll *kill* the son of a bitch!"

His voice thundered through the house, and Loralee stopped her struggle. He meant it. He would kill Jesse! She snapped her mouth closed, horrified by what she'd done.

Edward stepped back and glared at Loralee. He turned and stormed out of the house, and Fiona rushed forward to wrap her arms around her daughter.

"What have you done, Loralee? What have you done?"

Loralee leaned against her mother, too numb to think.

"I've had enough of it, Charles," Thomas Korwin said. "The drinking the fighting, everything! Why, if your mother was still alive . . ."

Charles sat in his father's study being scolded like a child. It was the final insult.

". . . working, and get on with your life! You can't . . ."

Charles stood up. "You're right, Pop. I can't live like this anymore."

"Well, it's about time!" Thomas slapped his hand on Charles's shoulder. "I knew I could get through to you."

"I guess you were right all along."

"I'll speak to your brothers in the morning. You know, they're not as sure about you as I am. They'll take some convincing."

Charles nodded. His mind was spinning, but at the same time, he felt sluggish.

". . . Monday, then?"

"What? Monday? Yeah. Yeah, Monday would be fine."

"All right, then."

He walked to the door and turned to look at his father. Charles had been a disappointment. He knew that. "I'm sorry, Pop."

"It's okay, Charles. Let's try to put it behind us."

"That's what I want, too. I'll try my best."

"That's all I can ask for."

With a sigh, Charles turned and walked out, hoping that this time, he'd get it right.

CHAPTER TWENTY

Fiona sat in the front parlor working on her needlepoint. After so many years of practice, her fingers moved of their own accord. Her mind wandered elsewhere.

She knew where Loralee had gone. Fiona didn't believe that nonsense about a fund-raiser for one minute. And if Edward did, well, if Edward believed it, then he was not as bright as Fiona had always believed him to be.

Their daughter had run off to meet Jesse Sinclair. Fiona recognized all the signs of her own early love affair with Edward. She'd learned to lie so well it became second nature. She would've said anything, done anything, to be alone with Edward Vander.

Now, twenty-five years later, the thought of being alone with her husband . . . well, she no longer thought about being alone with her husband. She glanced at the clock; it was almost nine-thirty. If she was going to act, it would be best to do it now, before Loralee arrived back home. She folded the pillowcase she was working on and placed it in the basket at her feet.

Do you want your daughter to endure a loveless marriage, Fiona? Doesn't she belong with a man who will cherish her? Doesn't she deserve happiness?

These thoughts spurred her on, and Fiona gathered every bit of strength she possessed and marched right up to the door to Edward's study. She knocked twice, opened the door and walked in, not even waiting for an invitation.

Edward was at his desk with the *Hazleton Sentinel* spread out in front of him. He wasn't working, and still, he felt the need to separate himself from his wife.

"Yes, Fiona? What is it?" He drummed his fingers impatiently on the desk as though she had disturbed some important task to which he was anxious to return. She stared at his fingers, suddenly paralyzed with fear. "What do you want?" Edward shouted. Fiona jumped.

She blurted out her thoughts before she lost her courage. "I don't think you should try to arrange another marriage for Loralee. I think you should let her choose her own husband." There! She'd done it.

"Oh really?" The drumming had stopped, and Edward fixed her with a look that would frighten the devil himself.

She'd already opened her mouth. She might as well finish it. "Really. And if she chooses Jesse Sinclair, I think we should both learn to live with it."

Fiona watched Edward's face as it began its transformation from boredom to outright anger. He stood up and advanced toward his wife. She backed up a step.

"And just who are you to tell me what I should do?"

"I'm your wife, Edward. And I know first hand what it's like to be stuck in a marriage where there is no love."

Edward's face turned red. "Love?" he asked contemptuously. "Fiona, I can barely stand the sight of you!"

"I know that, Edward." She spoke calmly, almost sadly. "And I know that if you love anyone at all, it's Lily."

With the last of her bravery, she said, "Tell me, Edward.

Do you wish for your daughter to be submitted to the same humiliation that I have borne all these years? Would you have your daughter treated the way you have treated me?''

She'd pushed too far. Edward's fury reached the boiling point. ''I treat you the way I treat all my property, Fiona. I own you! You are mine to do with as I see fit.''

''And how do you see fit to treat me? When was the last time you gave me the least bit of attention? Can you even remember?'' she asked, with tears in her eyes. Where had the man she married gone?

''You want my attentions, Fiona?'' he asked, snapping out his hand and latching onto her wrist. ''Is that what you want?'' He pulled her to the wall and turned her so that her back was pressed up against it.

''I didn't mean—''

''I'll give you all the attention you deserve, Fiona.'' His voice dripped with contempt for her. No, it was more than contempt. It was hatred.

Fiona was terrified that her words had sparked such a response in him. ''Edward, I only wanted you to think about what you're doing!''

Neither of them heard Loralee sneak in through the front door.

She closed the door quietly behind her. The front parlor was lit, but the entire house seemed empty. Loralee looked at the clock. It was almost ten. The staff would have already retired for the night. She breathed a sigh of relief and stepped gingerly across the foyer toward the stairs. That's when she heard it.

''Edward, please!''

Her mother's voice, coming from her father's study. Loralee froze.

Were they arguing over her, Loralee wondered? Was her mother interceding on her daughter's behalf? She approached the door and listened carefully.

''Edward, stop! You don't need to do this!''

Loralee's nerves jangled. Something was terribly wrong. Her mother sounded frantic!

Loralee stood rooted to the spot. What was he doing to her? She reached toward the doorknob. Her mother had saved her. Shouldn't she do the same?

Loralee wanted to run. Tears ran down over her cheeks as she listened to her father's words.

"Do you know—how many women—I've pleasured myself with since I—married you? Dozens, Fiona. Dozens."

Loralee could hear her mother's sobs.

Loralee dropped her hand from the doorknob she'd been clutching and flew up the steps. She was hiding behind her own door by the time her mother hurried past.

With her eyes blurred by tears, Loralee undressed and fell into bed. She fell into a troubled sleep, tormented by the sounds of her mother's anguished cries.

CHAPTER
TWENTY-ONE

Jesse was late.

He'd been held up at work, and as he rushed to their meeting spot, his heart thumped with the anticipation of seeing Loralee again.

Jesse rounded the corner, and from a block away, he saw her waiting on their bench. He picked up his pace and didn't stop until he reached her.

"Sorry I'm late."

She looked up at him, and, immediately, Jesse sensed a change in her. "What's wrong?"

Loralee looked away.

Jesse sat down beside her, and reached for her hand. And she jumped. The hair on the back of his neck stood up, and his nerves screamed a warning. *Save yourself!*

He pushed the thought away and said, "Are you all right?"

"I'm fine." She stood up as though she had somewhere she had to get to, then looked at him and sat back down. Jesse reached for her hand and she bolted.

"I'm sorry, but I can't stay."

"Can't stay? Why not?"

"I just can't. I-I have to go back . . . I shouldn't have . . ."

"You shouldn't have what?" Jesse stood up and took a step toward her. And she looked at him like a rabbit that's just been cornered. Absolutely terrified and frantic for a way out.

"I'm so sorry, Jesse—"

"For what? You keep saying that. Just tell me what it is!"

She seemed like she wanted to say something but couldn't. "I . . . I can't," she said, looking away from him.

"Can't what?" He put his hand on her shoulder, and she jerked away from him as though he'd burned her. "Loralee—"

"I have to go!"

He watched her run across the leaf-strewn grass. "I'll wait for you tonight!" he called. She didn't stop. Didn't even slow down.

Was this the same woman he'd been with last night? Something had happened to change her. Jesse was turning to walk away when he realized what it was .

It wasn't something. It was some *one*.

Edward. Her father had gotten to her! Anger flared up in Jesse at the thought of Edward Vander once again taking away someone he loved. What right did he have to keep Jesse from Loralee? They loved each other!

Jesse's feet pounded the ground as he stomped back to work. Edward had ripped out Jesse's heart once.

He'd be damned if he'd let the bastard do it again.

The October wind whipped through the streets, tearing dry, faded leaves from the branches of trees whose bark had turned gray with the certain approach of winter. Brown leaves swirled around Loralee's feet as she walked home from work, but she scarcely noticed them. The temperature had dropped, and goose-bumps puckered her skin, an early harbinger of the bone-chilling cold that was to follow.

Through the front gate, into the house and up the stairs to her room. Her feet moved her forward despite the fact that she dreaded anything that would put her in her father's company. Dinner would most certainly do that. Still, she changed her clothes, fixed her hair and walked down the stairs to the dining room.

Fiona was alone at the table, and when Loralee saw her, she walked around to her Mother's side and hugged her. "Oh, Mother."

"Loralee," Fiona said, obviously surprised by her daughter's unusual show of emotion. She reached up and removed Loralee's arms from around her neck. The sound of the front door closing drifted into the room, and Fiona said, "Please sit down. Your father is home."

Loralee dropped her arms to her sides and sighed, near tears. When had hugging her mother become taboo? Clearly, the show of affection was unsettling to Fiona. If such a simple gesture was too intimate for comfort, how must she have felt to have her most private places violated. Loralee's heart ached as she thought about what her mother had been forced to bear.

Edward strode into the room, and Fiona immediately turned to Anna, who stood guard at the door to the hallway which led to the kitchen. She tugged on the tasseled bell-pull which signaled the servers waiting in the kitchen that the meal was to begin.

Edward sat down just as the first girl hurried into the room with small bowls of soup. "Fiona, Loralee."

Neither woman responded, and Edward didn't seem to mind. He opened the newspaper and scanned it while slurping his soup.

Loralee looked from her mother to her father and back again. The silence between them was normal. Fiona was eating her soup, seemingly unruffled.

"Fiona," Edward said, without looking up. "Says here William Brady's mother died. Send flowers, will you?"

"Of course."

"Oh, and you wanted to donate to the Ladies' Temperance Society. I left the money with Gibbons. He'll take care of it when they come to collect."

"Thank you, Edward."

Thank you, Edward? Loralee's mind was spinning. How could her mother possibly have said thank you, for whatever reason, to the very man who not even twenty-four hours earlier . . .

"Don't let them talk you into pouring out any of that whiskey," he said, gesturing toward the front parlor, where he kept the liquor cabinet. "They want their donation, and they can have it. But my whiskey is my business."

"Of course, Edward."

The waiters were removing the soup bowls and replacing them with dinner plates.

"Are you finished, miss?"

Loralee glanced at the young man standing beside her. "Uh . . . yes. Thank you." He took her untouched soup bowl and replaced it with a steaming plate.

Didn't Fiona realize how outraged she should have been, Loralee thought? Could they both be acting as though nothing out of the ordinary had happened because nothing out of the ordinary really *had* happened? Was cruelty an accepted thing inside the bonds of marriage? Was it not only acceptable, but *expected?*

It couldn't be! But what other explanation was there? Was that what Loralee had to look forward to if she married?

She couldn't take that chance. She'd not been able to break it off with Jesse this afternoon, but she'd do it tonight.

She looked again from her mother to her father, and suddenly, she hated them both. She hated Fiona for spending all those years grooming her in the gentle social graces that would eventually attract a husband. And she hated her father. For proving to her that, when it came to husbands, gentleness had nothing to do with it.

Fog had settled down over Hazleton, and the dampness it brought with it chilled Jesse to the bone. He stood on the corner with his hands shoved into the pockets of his coat. It was nearly eight o'clock, and he'd already been waiting for a half hour. Would she come?

Did she really believe that Edward would come after Jesse? A threat like that might be enough to make her stay away. But even Jesse didn't believe that her father was capable of cold-blooded murder.

He looked toward the red stone house where she lived. The front door opened, and Jesse watched as Loralee hurried down the path and out onto the sidewalk.

She'd come. At least she had come.

He looked around the corner at her so that she would know he was there, but instead of continuing on her way beside him, she came to an abrupt stop.

"Hello," he said, reaching for her hand.

She backed up a step and wrapped her shawl more tightly around her shoulders.

"What's wrong?"

"I'm not going to the park."

"Why not?"

She backed up another step and glanced toward the house, and Jesse had the eerie feeling that they were being watched.

"Jesse, I can't see you anymore," she blurted. "I can't see you ever again." She turned as though to run back to the house, and Jesse reached out and grabbed her arm.

"Wait—"

"*Nooooo!!!*"

Loralee let out a scream and jerked her arm away. She ran

back to the house and left Jesse standing on the sidewalk, so shocked, he barely moved.

Jesse stared long after the slam of the front door had stopped echoing. The woman he loved had just fled in terror from his touch.

Once again, Jesse's anger flared. He started on his way home, cursing himself for having fallen in love with the one woman it seemed he could never have.

He wanted her, God-damn it! And he'd have her if it took till his dying day to get her. Some one had set out a challenge for him, and he didn't believe for one minute that it was Loralee.

The lights had been out for an hour. And still, Charles waited. He reached into his pocket and rubbed the key to Abby's room as though it was an amulet that would aid him on his mission.

How many times had he used that key to go to Abby? Charles pushed the troublesome thought away and tried to stay focused. It was important that the entire plan was carried out. He couldn't allow it to be thwarted before completion. That would be disastrous.

It was time. Charles unlocked the door and slipped inside, then quietly closed and locked the door behind himself.

Abby was in bed. Charles could see the lump beneath the blankets on the bed where they had so many times made love. He refused to think of it as anything else.

As he approached the bed, Charles reached into his pocket and pulled out a gun. He touched her on the shoulder, and she came awake easily, as though she had just dozed off.

"Shhhh," he said, lifting the gun just enough so that she would see it.

She did. She scrambled to sit up. "What are you doing?" she whispered.

"Where is Zachary's room?"

Charles waited for her response. Would it be what he

expected? She stared at Charles, glanced at the gun, and said, "Follow me."

Good girl! She'd assumed precisely what Charles had wanted her to.

The two of them stepped out into the hallway and moved past two doors before stopping at the third.

"This is it."

"You do exactly what I tell you. Okay?"

Abby swallowed and nodded. "Okay."

"When he wakes up, hustle him out of that bed. I want to get this over with."

She nodded again.

Charles went into the room first and moved around to the far side of the bed. He looked up at Abby one more time then poked Zachary with the barrel of the gun. "Get up, old man."

He came awake slowly, as though he wasn't sure where he was. "What'r you . . ."

"Get up."

"C'mon, Zachary, get up," Abby said. She reached out to help him to his feet.

Charles waved the gun at both of them. "Back to Abby's room."

"What?" she asked. "Why do we—"

"Because I said so, that's why. Move." He waved the gun again, and Abby took her husband's arm and led him down the hall and into her bedroom.

"Abby, light the lamp."

She reached up and lit the gas lamp, never questioning Charles's directions.

"Sit on the floor. Both of you."

"Charles—"

"Abby, please. Just sit."

She looked at him then turned and helped her husband ease himself onto the floor. Charles pulled the chair from the corner of the room until it was directly facing the two of them. He sat about eight feet away from them, far enough that any false moves on their part could be put to a stop, and close enough that Charles, who hadn't very often handled firearms, wouldn't miss his mark.

He leaned forward, bracing his elbows on his knees, and, with the gun pointed right at them, he said, "Okay, Abby. Talk."

Her gaze flew from Charles to Zachary and back again. "I don't know what—"

"You told me once that he made you an offer," Charles said, tipping the gun in Zachary's direction. "I want to know exactly what you meant by that." Charles's voice was silky soft.

Abby looked at Zachary, and he said, "Go on. Tell him."

"Charles, I don't know if—"

"Listen to your husband, Abigail. Tell me."

Abby's eyes widened, and for the first time, Charles could see that she was afraid. This wasn't turning out to be what she had expected. She looked down at the gun in his hand.

"I have to hear it, Abby. I *need* to hear it."

She nodded her head as though she understood what he meant. Then, she told him. She told him how Zachary had approached her at the millinery shop where she'd been working for years. She told him how he'd befriended her, and how he'd given her a taste of wealth by buying her gifts so expensive she had to hide them from her family.

And when Abby's hunger for the better things in life had started to gnaw at her, he'd made his proposal. If Abby agreed to marry him, she would get all of his money when he died. She never even had to share her bed with him.

"Didn't you think that was too good to be true?" Charles asked.

"He told me that I could take as many lovers as I wanted."

Charles hadn't thought he could feel any more pain, but he'd been wrong. "You had other lovers? I wasn't the only one?"

"No, you weren't the only one."

"Bastard!" Charles's chest was heaving. He held out a hand to Abby. "C'mon—I want you away from him." He kicked Zachary in the gut hard enough that he spit up blood. But it didn't stop the old man.

"The perfect whore. Every man she wanted. Including the last one, a week or two ago—"

"Zachary, don't!" Abby shouted.

"D'ya wanna know who it was?" Zachary taunted. "Wanna know?"

Abby pulled as though to let go of Charles's hand. "Please! I'm begging you!" Charles held fast to her hand. He looked at Abby's face. She was wild. Who was it, he wondered, that she was so desperate to keep him from hearing the name. If there really had been that many men, there were bound to be some that Charles knew. What made this particular man any different?

Abby spun around to face him. "Charles, don't! It doesn't matter! It doesn't matter who any of them were! You are the only man—"

"Who was it?" Charles asked turning toward Zachary.

The old bastard smiled. "Your father."

"*Aaaggghhh!!!*" Abby fought against Charles's hand, which had gone limp. She broke free, and she pummeled her husband with her fists. "I hope you burn in hell!"

"I'll be there soon enough, I think." He winked at her as though they shared some secret then turned back to Charles. "Your father always thought she was a whore after your money. Just in case he might change his mind after I was gone from this world, I gave him a chance to find out for sure. Couldn't have the two of you spending my money, now could I? Letting your father bed my wife was the perfect way to ensure that that never happened."

Charles struggled to remain standing. His own father!

He held up the gun and fired, and Zachary slumped forward.

Abby jumped and, staring at her husband's body, she backed away. She looked up at Charles. "I'll stand beside you in any court of law. You shot him in self-defense. He was jealous of our childhood friendship." She had the whole thing figured out. She reached up and wrapped her arms around Charles's neck.

His father had lain with her. Charles reached up and peeled her arms away. "I loved you Abby. I loved you so much. And it hurt so bad when you married him."

"I know it did. I'm sorry. I shouldn't—"

"I'm sorry, too. I'm so sorry." And he raised the gun and fired a second shot. The force of the bullet sent her flying backward onto the bed. She lay looking up at him with unseeing eyes.

Charles waited only a few seconds to make sure they were both dead before he lifted the gun again and joined Abby on the other side.

CHAPTER
TWENTY-TWO

Dr. Farley had just opened the front door a few minutes earlier, and already the waiting room was filled.

"Another busy day," Loralee said to Doc. That was good. Maybe the work could keep her from thinking about her broken heart.

"Might as well get to it, then. Send in the first one."

Loralee walked out into the front room and picked up the sheet of paper where she had written the names of the patients as they walked in. "Mr. Adams? You're first." She looked up, waiting for him to make his way out of the crowd.

"Mr. Adams?" she called, a bit louder this time.

The gossip must have been juicy this morning because nearly every patient was huddled in a circle, and Mr. Adams appeared to be one of the principal characters telling the story.

She approached the group and rested her hand on Matthew Adams's shoulder. "We're ready for you."

"Did y' hear, missy?" he asked, obviously thrilled to be the one spreading the word.

"Hear what?"

"Was a murder last night!"

"Murder!" Loralee's heart jumped.

"Din't ya hear?" a young boy asked. "Ol' Man Tyler and his wife! Shot dead!"

"Zachary and Abigail Tyler?" she asked. Oh, Lord, no.

"Not only them," added a woman with a baby on her hip. "A young man found with 'em." She leaned closer to Loralee as though she was about to reveal a deep secret. "I heard it was 'er lover."

Loralee's mind was reeling. Lover? But *Charles* was having an affair with Abby!

"I know who it was," boasted a second woman. "One o' them Korwin boys, I heard. The baby o' the bunch."

"He killed them?" Loralee asked, trying to slow her breathing. "Charles killed them both?"

"Not only them, Missy," Matthew Adams said, eager to add more wood to the fire. "Turned the gun on 'imself, too. Three o' them. All dead."

Loralee felt the room begin to spin. "Doc!" she called out. "Dr. Farley!" The world was beginning to close in on her.

"What's wrong? Loralee!" Doc shouted.

The sound of his voice shouting her name was the last thing she heard before she slid to the ground.

It was Friday night, and Jesse was at home working. Or, trying to work.

By now, everyone had heard the story of the lover's triangle, double murder/suicide that had taken place the night before. The story had come out after the police had been summoned by Abigail Tyler's maid. It seemed that Mrs. Tyler and Charles Korwin had been involved in a long-time affair. Most of the staff knew about it, as did her husband Zachary.

No one knew, however, what had finally driven Mrs. Tyler's

lover to kill her and her husband and then turn the gun on himself. Some speculated that it was the recent end of his brief engagement to Miss Loralee Vander, heiress to the prosperous Vander Holdings coal company, that finally pushed him over the edge.

Jesse thought to himself that Charles had been over the edge long before that. To think that Loralee had been engaged to that man nearly drove Jesse insane.

He couldn't stop thinking about the night Charles had accosted Loralee and how terrified she'd been. Who knew what he had been capable of doing? Jesse began to wonder why Loralee had insisted that she could not see him any longer.

Was it possible that Charles had forced himself on her? The way she had begged Jesse not to leave her alone with him. And, later, the way she had screamed when Jesse touched her arm.

Could it be?

"Hey."

Jesse looked up and found Stephen standing in the open doorway.

Could Charles have done such a thing? Jesse blinked, and let out a huge breath.

"What's going on? You look like you're in the middle of something critical."

Jesse paced the room, and his heart hammered. And with each step he took, he became more and more convinced that Charles was in some way responsible for Loralee's strange behavior.

He looked at his father, and wondered whether Stephen would think he was grasping at straws. "I want to ask you something," Jesse said, closing the door.

Stephen looked at the door, looked at Jesse and raised his eyebrows. "Must be serious."

"It is serious."

"What is it?" Stephen asked, sitting down in one of the leather-upholstered chairs in front of the enormous desk.

Jesse moved around the room, unable to stand still. With his back to Stephen, he said, "Loralee says she can't see me anymore."

"Why?"

"No idea."

"She offered no explanations?"

"None at all. When she turned to go, I reached out to stop her. I only wanted to talk to her. But when I touched her sleeve, she screamed." Jesse widened his eyes. "And I do mean she *screamed,* at the top of her lungs."

Stephen looked at his son, obviously puzzled. "She screamed?"

"Yup." Jesse shook his head. "I was so shocked by it, that I just stood there, and she ran back into the house."

"Where were you?"

"We were right on the sidewalk, on the corner of their property. We were in no way secluded; she was in absolutely no danger. Also last night, Charles Korwin, the man she was supposed to have married, killed his lover, her husband and himself."

"And . . . ?"

"And I'm wondering if Loralee's fright had anything to do with Charles. Last weekend he threatened her. He scared her half to death, and Loralee is not a timid woman."

"Did she say anything to explain it?"

Jesse hesitated. "After Charles had been removed from the premises, she was still insisting that he would come after her, and I was trying to calm her down. I thought it was just the whiskey talking. I really didn't think he meant anything he'd said. And then she slipped and said something about the 'last time.' "

"He'd done this before?"

"Apparently so. I asked her, and she wouldn't answer, but she didn't deny it."

Stephen thought about all that Jesse had told him. "So, you think he did something to her, and frightened her so badly that when you grabbed her arm, she thought you were going to do the same?"

"Do you think that's possible? Or is this a real stretch?"

"Well, Charles killed himself and two other people. I'd say anything is possible."

"That's what I thought."

"Now what do you do? Will she even talk to you?"

"I don't know. We were supposed to go to the parade next weekend. It was going to be our first public date." Jesse paced around the room, restless. "If that bastard so much as touched her—"

"I know, Jess." Stephen stood up and rested his hand on Jesse's shoulder. "I know. And, if he wasn't already dead, I'd be standing in line right behind you. And if John wasn't already back at school, he'd be right behind me."

Jesse grunted. "The Sinclair men. Coming to the aid of a woman wronged."

"You got it."

Jesse took a deep breath. "It's a good thing he's already dead. Because feeling the way I do, I wouldn't be able to stop until all three of us ended up in jail."

Stephen smiled. "That's my boy. Protect what's yours."

"But, is she still mine to protect?"

"I think what you've got to do is make sure that she is. Give it everything you've got, and don't stop until you've got that ring on her finger."

Jesse looked at his father and nodded. There was nothing else to say.

*   *   *

Fiona watched her daughter sleeping. Dr. Farley had sedated Loralee when he'd brought her home. She'd been totally irrational, and frightened half out of her mind.

Not that Fiona blamed her. Learning that the man you were supposed to have married was capable of murder would have been enough to send even the most imperturbable woman into a fit of hysterics.

It was well after five o'clock, and the room was growing dim. Loralee had been asleep the whole day. There was a soft knock at the door, and Fiona stood to open it. It was Dr. Farley.

"How is she?"

"She's been sleeping the whole time."

"Good. That's what she needs." He moved to the side of the bed and looked down at Loralee. "Her mind is hard at work trying to figure out this terrible thing that happened. It's important to keep her asleep awhile so she can come to grips with this trauma."

"You think she'll be all right when she wakes up?"

"It might take her a few days to get back on her feet, but I'm sure she'll be fine."

"Will she sleep all night?"

"She will after I give her this," he said, opening his bag. "Tell me," he said as he filled the syringe, "do you know what she was ranting about?"

"I have no idea."

Dr. Farley looked up at her as though he wasn't quite convinced. "Strange." He reached into his bag and pulled out a bottle and a small envelope. "I'm going to leave you with these pills. They're the same medicine that's in the injection, but not as strong. Give them to her two at a time every four hours from the time she wakes up in the morning until nightfall. And then no more after that."

"What will they do?"

"They'll keep her drowsy enough that she'll nap off and on throughout most of the day tomorrow. But she will be awake

for part of the day. Which is what we want. She has to start
thinking about what happened and why it upset her so much.
The pills will be a good transition for Sunday, when she won't
be medicated at all.''

"I see."

He packed up his bag and walked to the door. "I'll stop in
on Sunday."

"Thank you, Doctor."

Fiona watched him walk to the stairs, and then she closed
the door.

She went back to the chair beside the bed and sat down,
listening to her daughter's deep, even breathing.

Sleep, child, she thought, reaching out to hold Loralee's hand
in her own. There'll be time enough to face the demons when
you wake.

CHAPTER
TWENTY-THREE

Loralee opened her eyes on Monday morning to find sunlight pouring through the windows. The small clock on her dressing table read nine-thirty. She should have been at work a half hour ago. She rolled over and pulled the covers up to her neck.

Yesterday, when Doc had visited, she'd told him that she wasn't sure when she'd be back. And he'd answered that he expected her on Monday morning, same as always.

But, things would never be the same as always again. Loralee knew that now. Before, she'd been happy with her work. So happy, she hadn't needed anything else in her life. That was before Jesse. Now, there was an emptiness, a void she'd never even noticed. And she knew that that void would be with her for the rest of her life.

Loralee would go back to work. She would have her friends. And that would be that. It had been enough before. It would be enough again.

She threw the covers back and padded across the floor to stand in front of the window. Below her, Diamond Avenue had come to life. Carts and carriages rolled past, women with baskets on their arms haggled over prices with the vendors and delivery men ran from house to wealthy house, dropping off everything from milk to dry goods to fifty-pound bags of oats for the horses.

All the activity was a little overwhelming to someone who had spent the last three days sleeping. She *would* pick up her life again. She would.

But not today. She crawled back into the bed and closed her eyes.

When Dr. Farley opened the front door on Monday morning, Jesse was waiting.

"Well, look at what we have here."

"Hey, Doc. She here yet?"

"Not yet. Don't know if she's going to be, either."

"What do you mean?" Jesse asked, stepping up into the building. He followed Doc into the back room and stood in the doorway, watching him prepare for his day.

"Well, here's the thing. I went to see her yesterday, and she told me that she's not sure when she'll be back."

"What? Why?" Jesse was surprised to hear that. Loralee loved her work! He figured she'd be burying herself in it.

"I don't know why. There's nothing physically wrong with her. There's no reason why she can't be back today. But if she's not here by now, I'd guess she isn't coming."

"That's no good for her," Jesse said, shaking his head. "All she'll do is sit in that house and think about what happened."

"I can see how that might be disturbing, but Loralee was way, way beyond disturbed."

"How so?"

Doc pulled out a drawer and removed several small instruments which he placed on a clean white cloth that was spread over a small table. "You haven't seen her since?"

Jesse looked down. "Uh, no. A few days ago, Loralee decided that we shouldn't see each other anymore."

"Why?"

Jesse shrugged. "I don't know. I thought maybe you'd be able to shed a little light on that. Have you noticed anything unusual about her lately?"

Doc stopped to think. "You know, we spend a lot of time together, Loralee and I. I can usually tell when something is bothering her, and last week, was one of those times. But, to be honest, I attributed it to the fact that you two were seeing each other. Few weeks back she asked me some questions about Avondale. I thought her preoccupation of the past few days was because of you. I thought she was worried about how it would all work out, with Edward Vander being her father and all."

"So there was something bothering her even before the murders."

"Definitely."

Jesse looked up at Dr. Farley, wondering if it would be a breach of Loralee's trust to mention his suspicions about Charles. "Doc, I want to ask you something, but it's just a theory. Please don't ever mention it to Loralee."

Doc walked over and pulled the blue curtain across the doorway. Several patients had arrived, and even though it wasn't much, the drape did offer a modicum of privacy. "Doctors are bound by confidentiality, you know."

"I'm not here as a patient."

"Maybe not. But Loralee is a friend and colleague. If you have some idea that might explain what's troubling her, I'd like to hear about it."

Jesse stared at Doc Farley and knew that he could be trusted. "Do you think it's possible that Charles might have . . . forced himself on her?"

Doc raised his eyebrows. "Well, I suppose when you're

dealing with someone as unstable as he obviously was, anything is possible. Why would you think that?''

''Several reasons, but mostly the unreasonable fear she had of him, and also her abrupt refusal to see me again.''

Doc took his glasses off and wiped the lenses with the vest he was wearing. ''She was real upset on Friday, I'll tell you that.''

''Did she say anything?''

''As a matter of fact, she did, though I didn't understand it at the time. But, if what you suspect is true, it makes sense.''

''What did she say?'' Jesse's heart was pounding. This might be the answer.

''Now, mind, she was pretty irrational. But she kept talking about passion.''

''Passion?'' This was it.

''Kept saying how passion led to violence.''

Jesse looked down at the floor. ''That's it.''

''You think so?''

He nodded ''I can't stay away from her,'' Jesse said, baring his soul. ''I love that girl.''

Doc smiled. ''I know you do. I love her, too. And I think that, maybe, between the two of us, we can get through to her.''

''How?''

''Let me think on it a little. I've got a room full of patients out there, and no assistant, so I have to get to work. But stop back in tonight, after five. Maybe by then, we'll have thought of something.''

Jesse stuck out his hand. ''I'll do that. Thanks, Doc.''

Dr. Farley shook Jesse's hand and said, ''See you later.''

Jesse worked himself through the crowd that had assembled in the few short minutes he'd been speaking with Doc.

He stepped out into the cool air and turned in the direction of the train station. He'd figure this out. And when he did, he wasn't going to waste one minute of time before he asked Loralee to marry him.

He'd finally found The One. Now, all he had to do was convince the girl.

Loralee looked out the window and watched as Dr. Farley walked up the path. He'd be wanting to see why she hadn't gone to work. She turned away from the window and sat down at her desk. She'd been up and dressed for hours, but still hadn't ventured from her room.

Doc knocked. "Loralee?"

"Come in, Doc."

He walked in, all out of breath. "Thank goodness you're up. How're you feeling?" He wedged himself into a small upholstered chair in the corner.

"I'm sorry I didn't come in today."

"It's okay," he said, waving off her apology. "Just make sure you get in there tomorrow. I think you might have a baby to deliver."

Her head shot up. "Kathleen?"

"Yup. I thought I'd better stop in on her today since you didn't have the chance to see her this weekend. She's starting to get some pains—nothing regular, but I'm thinking it'll be soon."

Loralee jumped out of the chair. "Oh, my." She paced around the room fanning her face with her hand.

"Take it easy. You know what to do."

She nodded. "I know I do, but knowing what to do and actually doing it are two very different things. I knew what to do the first time I stitched someone up, too, and look how that turned out."

She'd been so afraid to poke the needle into the patient's skin, that the man had finally shouted, "Will ya just do it, woman, or hand over the needle and I'll do it myself!" She'd finally gathered the courage to do it, but not before Doc had given her a small glass of "tonic to calm the nerves" that tasted suspiciously like very strong whiskey.

"You did fine. And just think, when you finish up with this job, there'll be a whole new life because of it."

Loralee's eyes filled with tears. She nodded. "I know."

"Kathleen will be the one doing all the work. You just have to help her along."

She took a deep breath and let it out slowly. "I know."

"Well, if you know, what are you so nervous about?" he teased.

She smiled. "Now, *that,* I don't know."

"All right, girl. Help me out of this vise grip you call a chair," he said, struggling to stand.

It was good to be around Doc. He put things into perspective like no one else Loralee knew. She squeezed between the wall and the chair and leaned down on the arm rests. "Now, stand."

He did, and with a little twisting, they managed to remove the chair from his backside.

"Lord, that was an ordeal," he said, straightening his tie. "See you in the morning?" he asked hopefully.

Loralee smiled and looked away, embarrassed that she had let her personal problems keep her away even this long. She nodded. "See you in the morning."

Doc hugged her and left the room. Loralee took a deep breath and squared her shoulders. Kathleen was depending on her.

She walked to the mirror and stood looking at herself. She would *not* let Charles take this away from her. She'd dreamed about being a doctor since she was a little girl. Now, the dream was within her grasp.

Loralee had stood up to her father to get where she was today. She wasn't about to let a few unpleasant memories stand in her way. She had a career to pursue.

She took a deep breath and let it out slowly. A patient needed her.

Loralee Vander was back among the living.

CHAPTER
TWENTY-FOUR

"Funny thing about babies. Can't hurry 'em up."

"I guess not," Loralee said, closing her notebook and packing it into her bag. It was Tuesday afternoon, and she'd been out to visit with Kathleen, but there was no baby as of yet. "I sure do wish it would get here already because I'm a nervous wreck. By the time it decides to grace us with its arrival, I'll need some of that nerve tonic of yours."

"Help yourself. There's more where that came from."

"Where? In your liquor cabinet?" she teased.

"Liquor?" Doc asked with mock horror. "What do you take me for, girl?"

"I take you for the kind of man who knows when a shot of whiskey can do the most good," she said, facing him with her hands on her hips.

He smiled. "You got me."

"I knew it," she said turning away. "Can't fool me." She wrapped her shawl around her shoulders, picked up her bag and stepped toward the back door. "I'll see you tomorrow."

"Loralee?"

She turned. "Hmm?"

Doc smiled at her. "It's good to have you back."

She returned the smile. "It's good to be back. Thanks for giving me the little shove I needed. 'Bye." She stepped out of the building feeling good. Actually feeling good! And then she rounded the corner and saw Jesse waiting for her.

Loralee just stood there, staring at him, and aching inside.

"Hey, Loralee." He leaned against the red brick, one booted foot braced on the wall beneath him.

"Hey, Jesse." This hurt worse than she ever thought it could. Maybe someday, she'd get over the pain of seeing him, but right now, Loralee thought she couldn't have hurt worse if she was dying.

"I miss you."

Loralee looked down at the ground. She couldn't do this. She couldn't stand here and talk to him as though her entire life hadn't been changed because of him. "I have to go," she said.

"Wait."

The foot came down off the wall and he walked towards her, slowly, as though he was afraid any sudden movement might spook her. It was as though he was approaching a wounded animal, she thought. He stopped and stood about three feet away from her. "Loralee," he whispered, taking another step toward her. He reached toward her face. "Please don't do this."

The second his fingertips touched her cheek, she flinched. "Jesse," she said, as the tears welled up in her eyes. "Don't do this to me. You have no idea how hard this is!"

"Explain it to me."

"I can't!" she shouted.

"All right. All right," he said, backing up a step. "You promised to go to the parade with me on Saturday."

She looked up and shook her head. "Oh, no, I can't do that."

"But you promised."

She blinked her eyes, searching for some way out. "I-I know I did, but that was—"

"That was what?" he interrupted. "I didn't realize that a promise was conditional!"

Loralee sighed and looked away. This wasn't going to accomplish anything. "I can't go," she said. She turned to walk away, but Jesse moved around to block her path.

"I want to know what happened," he said. His voice was low, and Loralee could see a muscle twitch in his jaw. She looked into his eyes.

That was a mistake. She'd forgotten the way he could trap her in his gaze. She stood there, unable to look away, and the tears came again.

"Jesse, please . . ." she whispered. "Can't you just let it go?"

His gaze didn't waver. Jesse stared into her eyes like he was looking at her very soul. He moved backwards a step and said, "No. I can't."

Then he blinked and the spell was broken. He turned and walked away.

Loralee wiped her tears away and started walking toward home. She would get over this.

Making herself fall out of love with Jesse Sinclair would not kill her.

Then why, she asked herself, do I feel like I'm already dead?

"Oh, honey, what happened?" Suzanne asked, wrapping her arms around Loralee.

"So much, I don't even know where to start."

"You should've sent for me!" Suzanne admonished. She'd come at Mrs. Vander's request. "Start at the beginning. And don't leave anything out." She looked into Loralee's red eyes. "I mean it. Good and bad. I want to hear it all."

Loralee closed her eyes, and Suzanne knew that she was debating about telling her.

"Loralee," she said softly, "I will do whatever I can to help you. But you have to trust me. I promise, I won't judge you, no matter what you tell me."

Loralee hesitated, then nodded her head. "All right. There are a lot of things, though. A lot of . . ." her glance skittered away, ". . . very upsetting things."

"That's all right. I can take it," Suzanne said, climbing onto the bed. Loralee waited a few seconds and then followed suit.

"All right. I'll start with Jesse."

"Oooo, something good," Suzanne said, rubbing the palms of her hands together in anticipation.

Loralee smiled.

"Do tell."

"Well, the whole week after he took me home from that party, I was meeting him for lunch in Memorial Park—"

"You weren't!"

"—and then sneaking out of the house after dinner and meeting him there again."

Suzanne's eyes opened so wide from the shock, she was surprised they didn't fall right out of her head.

"Did he take you in the woods?"

Loralee stared. "You *knew* about those woods?"

"Of course I knew. Didn't you?"

"No!"

"Oh. Well, you know now!"

"Thanks a lot! Anyway," she said, rolling her eyes, "we kissed. A lot. A real lot."

"How does he kiss?" Suzanne asked, leaning forward.

Loralee closed her eyes. "I can't even tell you how he made me feel."

"I *knew* he'd be a good kisser!"

Loralee blushed. "You have to swear never to speak a word of this!"

"I swear," Suzanne answered, crossing her heart with her finger.

Loralee seemed to consider this carefully. "All right, but I mean it! Not a word!"

"Loralee, whatever did you do?"

"Well, as I said, we kissed a lot. And, well, I don't know if you've ever been kissed by a really good kisser—"

"His brother John wasn't bad."

"Suzanne!"

She shrugged. "Well, he wasn't! He was actually quite good at it. Maybe it's a family trait."

"And, how would you know a thing like that?"

"Not important, here. We're talking about your problems, or lack thereof, if Jesse is such a good kisser."

"No," Loralee said, "you don't understand. That *was* the problem. He makes me feel so . . . I just . . . I . . ." she squirmed around, trying to impart the sense of frustration she'd felt.

"Okay, yes. I know exactly what you mean," Suzanne said, nodding.

"All right. So then, I start to notice that every time we get to a certain . . . level, shall I say, he'd say he had to stop."

"Well, of course he had to stop!"

Loralee rolled her eyes. "Well, I know that, but . . . it was as though something had taken control of him—"

"That was you," Suzanne interrupted.

"What?"

"It was you. You had taken control of him."

Loralee looked back at Suzanne, obviously perplexed. "Honestly, Loralee, how can you be so smart about some things and so dumb about others?"

Loralee's eyes widened, and she shrugged. "I don't know! I don't have anyone to teach me. Your mother seems to know just about everything there is to know when it comes to men! But my mother? Well, you can imagine."

Suzanne dropped her face into her hands. "It's like starting first grade all over again,'' she muttered. She raised her head. "Look. The same things Jesse was making you feel, you were making him feel. And for the same reason that you knew he had to stop, he knew he had to stop. And, well, sometimes it can be very difficult to stop, even when you both know you should.''

"Passion?''

"Yes!'' Suzanne said, pointing at Loralee. "Passion. It sometimes wants to take control of the situation. Wouldn't you say?''

"Yes, yes I would! And *that's* where the problem comes in. Passion is a *horrible, awful* thing!''

"What?'' Suzanne asked. "What are you talking about? Passion is wonderful!''

"No, Suzanne, you're wrong,'' Loralee said, shaking her head as though she was about to impart some grave news.

"Why? What . . . ? I don't understand. What happened?''

Loralee folded her hands in her lap and sat looking down at her fingers as she squeezed them and released them. Squeezed them and released them.

Suzanne reached out and touched her sleeve. "What happened?''

Loralee looked up. "Charles and Abigail Tyler were having an affair. Do you see where passion led Charles? Do you?''

Suzanne shook her head. "Oh, no, Loralee. You can't think that all men—''

"They are!'' Her eyes were filling with tears, and she blinked rapidly to keep from crying. "Right after I broke the engagement, Charles came to my home, and with my mother in the very same room with us, he . . . he . . .'' Loralee closed her eyes. "He had every intention of . . .'' She stopped.

Suzanne was speechless. "I-I don't know what to say. I didn't know—''

"Of course you didn't know! I didn't want anyone to know.

So, you see, it wasn't just one case of passion leading to violence. With Charles, it seemed to be a set pattern.''

"Yes! With Charles," Suzanne repeated. "Charles obviously had some serious problems. Most men aren't like that."

"No?" Loralee asked, raising her eyebrows. "All right. I have something else to tell you. And it isn't about Charles."

"Jesse? Surely—"

"No, not Jesse."

Loralee was silent for so long that Suzanne finally said, "Who, Loralee?"

She closed her eyes. "I don't even know if I can tell you this. It's so horrible."

Suzanne reached out and held her friend's hand. "Loralee, listen to me. If you don't want to tell me, that's fine. But if you need to get this off your chest, rest assured, I will take this secret to my grave." She held Loralee's gaze. "I mean it."

Loralee nodded, and the tears she had been trying to hold back finally spilled over. "You know I said that I had been sneaking out to see Jesse at night?"

"Yes?"

"Well, one night, when I came back home, it was late. Everyone had retired for the night. Except my parents. They were in my father's study, and they were fighting. I thought they were fighting about me, and when I heard their voices, I stopped outside the door to listen."

She stopped talking, as though that was the end of her story, but Suzanne knew there was more, and she waited, giving Loralee time to work it out.

"They were fighting horribly. Papa said . . . some of the nastiest, most hurtful things I have ever heard anyone say. Ever. And he was saying those things to my mother."

"Oh, Loralee. I'm so sorry you had to hear that. But all couples fight. And everybody says things that they later regret—"

"You don't understand," Loralee interrupted. "He wanted to-to . . . he wanted to completely destroy her sense of self-worth. He wanted to take away every shred of dignity she had. He wanted her to feel worthless, and low, and dirty."

Tears filled Suzanne's eyes at the thought of Loralee's mother being degraded.

"Do you see now why I can't be with Jesse anymore? This is what men do, Suzanne."

Suzanne reached out for Loralee's hands. "Loralee, you're wrong. That is *not* how men are. It's not."

"But—"

"No! Listen to me. Charles might have been that way, and your father might be that way, and I'm sure there are other men who are that way. But Charles was downright mean! Does it really surprise you that he'd do something like that? And your father! I'm sorry to say it, Loralee, but your father has always treated your mother despicably!"

"But how do I know? How can I be sure? If that ever happened to me, I would die! I would not be able to live with it. It's better to avoid the chance of it ever happening."

"By avoiding the chance that you might find love?" Suzanne shouted. "Don't you understand what you're doing? You're convicting Jesse of a crime he did not commit! He did nothing to hurt you, did he?"

Loralee shook her head. "No, but—"

"But nothing! He loves you Loralee! He wants to be with you every bit as much as you want to be with him. He wouldn't do anything to hurt you."

Loralee sat clutching her hands together again. "But, how do I *know?* How can I be sure of that? As far as I can see, passion makes men angry and mean."

"Not all men, Loralee. Passion can just as easily lead to love. Look at my parents," Suzanne said. "Have you ever seen a woman more pampered, more cherished by her husband than my mother? Why do you think I haven't met anyone I want to marry, yet? I'll tell you why. Because I want a husband who will love me the way my father loves my mother.''

Loralee looked up, and the doubt she was feeling was written clearly on her face. ''You think they really love each other? I mean, really, really, love each other?''

''I don't think it. I know it.''

''And you don't think he'd ever—''

''I'll tell you a secret,'' Suzanne said, lowering her voice. ''My mother has told me . . . things.''

''What kind of things?''

''Things that *you* probably already know about. I mean, you *are* going to be a doctor. You do know better than most women how the human body works.''

''Oh. Those kinds of things.''

''Yes.''

''But the things I know, have more to do with . . . logistics. I know what goes where and the order things happen, but I don't know anything at all about the feelings I get when Jesse kisses me. I don't know anything about those at all.''

''I do.''

Loralee looked at her friend, and it was clear that she was worrying about how Suzanne had managed to learn such things.

''I know about those things because my mother told me.''

''What did she say?'' Loralee sat forward, eager to hear.

''She said—don't tell your mother about this, Loralee, okay?''

''My mother? My mother would drop over dead if I so much as hinted at anything at all having to do with kissing.''

Suzanne nodded her head. ''All right. My mother had to tell me about a lot of things that you already know. But she went on to tell me more. About . . . love. Making love.'' Suzanne sat forward. ''It's a good thing,'' she whispered. ''She said it's a very, very good thing.''

Loralee's eyes were like saucers. ''She said that?''

Suzanne nodded. ''She did. She also said that in order for

it to be good, the man and the woman have to have a genuine love and respect for one another. Without that . . .'' Suzanne shrugged.

"Without that, you have a relationship like mine and Charles's.''

"Exactly.''

Loralee sat still for a minute. "I think Jesse has a genuine respect for me.''

"I'm sure of it,'' Suzanne said.

"Are you sure your mother isn't just—''

"I'm sure. She was pretty specific.''

Loralee's eyes widened, and she nodded. "Oh.''

"Loralee, just give him a chance,'' Suzanne said, reaching out for her friend's hand. "Give your heart a chance.''

Loralee looked at Suzanne for a long time. She was obviously torn.

"It might be the best thing that ever happens to you.'' What else could Suzanne say to convince her?

Loralee sighed. "I'll think about it.''

Suzanne smiled with relief. She leaned forward and wrapped her arms around her friend. "You won't be sorry, Loralee. I just know you won't be sorry.''

CHAPTER TWENTY-FIVE

"I don't know what Charles did to her, Jesse," Elizabeth said. "The point is, whatever it was, it struck fear into her. That's why she's acting like she's afraid of you. Because she *is* afraid of you."

Elizabeth had received a visit from Suzanne Becker. It seemed that Miss Becker was worried that Jesse had given up on Loralee. And, while she hadn't given any details, Suzanne had said enough to let Elizabeth piece the story together.

Jesse was pacing the floor of his father's office, and looking like he was about to start climbing the walls.

"So help me, God, if he so much as—"

"Jesse, the man is dead. Let it go," Elizabeth said. "What you have to do now is try to approach Loralee. But you have to remember to do it in a way that isn't going to frighten her. Don't get too close, don't move too fast and *don't* try to get her alone!" She reached out and rubbed her son's arm. "This might take some time."

"Time, I've got. It's Loralee that I need."

He looked so sad. Elizabeth went to him and wrapped her arms around him. "I love you so much," she said.

He rested his chin on top of her head. "I love you, too."

"She'd make an awfully nice daughter-in-law."

Jesse laughed and pushed her away. "Okay, that's enough. Go, and let me—"

Stephen opened the door, and said, "Don't go taking off anywhere, Jess. I need you." He walked around his desk and pulled out a train schedule.

"What's going on?"

Stephen held up one finger, busily scanning the paper in front of him. "I'm going to need you to fill in."

"For who?"

"Colin." Stephen looked up from the paper where he was scribbling and smiled. "It's baby time."

Elizabeth drew in her breath. "Oh, my goodness!"

"Kathleen sent one of the neighbor boys down to fetch Colin. Said to take his time, things are moving slow, but Colin took off down the street almost before he brought the train to a stop!"

Jesse laughed. "I guess a man deserves to get a little excited at the thought of his child being born."

"I guess so. I'll need you to finish out his shift."

"Sure," Jesse said, moving around to read over Stephen's shoulder. "Where is he?"

"He's on 482. Has two more runs left. Next one's . . ." Stephen looked up at the clock on his desk, "in twelve minutes."

"Okay," Jesse said, grabbing his cap. "Gotta go. See you, Mom." He gave Elizabeth a quick peck on the cheek.

"Did you see that?" she asked her husband.

"What?"

"My twenty-five-year-old son still kisses me good-bye."

"You want some kisses?" He winked at her. "I've got kisses."

She rolled her eyes. "Stephen!"

"What did I say?" He held his hands out to his side, trying, but failing to look innocent.

"Now I know where they get it from. Your boys have learned from you." She leaned over and said. "Do you know what that means?"

"No, what?"

Elizabeth smiled and lowered her eyelids. "It means that if Jesse plays his cards right, Loralee Vander is going to be one very happy girl."

"And what do I have to do with that?"

Elizabeth leaned forward and, in the privacy of Stephen's office, felt safe to nibble on his ear. "You have everything to do with that. You are the best husband in the world. And your sons have learned by watching you."

Stephen smiled. "Thank you."

"No," Elizabeth said, flirting shamelessly, "thank *you.*"

"Not yet, Kathleen," Loralee said. She went to the pan of boiled water she'd just prepared and scrubbed her hands. Again. Dr. Farley was a firm believer in germ theory, and he'd taught Loralee that there was no such thing as too much hand washing.

"Oh, Lord, I don' know how much more o' this I can take," Kathleen said, panting her way through yet another contraction. She'd been laboring already for close to ten hours, and though the pains had been steady and strong for the past three, she'd not made any progress.

"I have chloroform," Loralee said. "I can use it if you want, but it sometimes slows things down."

"No, no. I don' want this to take any longer than it has to." She struggled to sit up on the bed. "Help me walk."

Loralee wrapped her arm around Kathleen's waist and moved the curtain aside. Colin, who'd been sitting near the stove, jumped up.

"What's wrong?" he asked.

"Nothing's wrong," Loralee assured him. "Things just aren't moving along as quickly as your wife would like," she teased. "She thought a little walk might help."

"Colin hold-ohh!" Kathleen stopped in her tracks, clutching Loralee's arm on one side and her husband's on the other, as another contraction took hold of her.

"Easy, Kathleen. Breathe, now. Come on, breathe," Loralee coached. "That's a girl," she said, as the pain began to ebb. "Now, take a big breath."

Kathleen did as she was instructed, and the three of them moved around the cramped kitchen as much as they possibly could. Colin pushed the table to the wall, and rolled up the rag rug so that his wife's shuffling feet wouldn't get caught on its fringed edges. He propped a window open when she complained that it was too hot. He gave her sips of water when she was thirsty. He rubbed her back between pains.

And still, at the end of an hour, after Loralee had once again examined her, Kathleen had not progressed any further.

Loralee was worried. It was almost nine o'clock at night, and the labor had begun midmorning. After that amount of time, especially with a second pregnancy, this baby should be ready to be born. But if things kept on at this pace, they'd be here all night.

"Kathleen, listen to me," Loralee said. "You've still got a ways to go. I think you should take some chloroform so you can get a little bit of rest before the pushing begins. By the time it wears off, you might be ready."

The pains were coming faster now, about every two minutes with a duration of almost a minute and a half. The thirty-second breaks weren't nearly enough to let Kathleen catch her breath before another one came.

"No. I don't want it! It'll only make this agony longer!" Her hair, which had been tightly braided, had worked its way loose, and damp strands clung to her face. Colin reached out and brushed it away.

"Are y' sure, Kathy?" he asked. "Take it, if it'll make it any easier."

"No."

She was gripped by another pain, and Loralee shouted, "No pushing! No pushing!" Kathleen ignored her. "Kathleen, look at me!" She grabbed the woman's face and turned it to look into her eyes. "You can't push yet. You'll hurt yourself! Breathe. Breathe. That's it." She turned to Colin who was standing by the side of the bed looking helpless. "Colin, help your wife breathe."

He leaned over and did just as Loralee was doing. "Keep looking into her eyes," she said. "Keep her focused on you."

The contraction ended, and Kathleen's head dropped back against the pillow. She slept. For a few glorious seconds, she slept.

"Colin, I really think she should take that chloroform."

"She doesn't want it."

"I know, but she's not going to have any strength left when it comes time to push."

His wife stirred, and he glanced at Loralee. "Not yet. Give her a bit more time."

They gave her an hour, and at ten o'clock, when Loralee examined her, Kathleen had moved ahead. Not enough to begin pushing, but enough that everyone was satisfied to let nature take its course a little while longer.

Loralee left Colin with his wife and went outside to the pump to get more fresh water to heat. She was carrying two buckets back inside when a rider stopped in front of the house. She watched as a man slid from the back of his horse and tied him at the hitching rail.

He turned to face her. It was Jesse!

"Hey."

"Hey," she said with a nervous smile. She set both buckets on the ground and dried her hands in her apron.

"Do we have a baby?" he asked.

She shook her head. "Not yet."

"Not yet?" he glanced toward the house. "This is taking long, isn't it?"

"Too long, I think."

He stepped toward her. "Problems?"

"No, not yet. But she's exhausted. I don't know how much longer she can keep this up, and she won't let me give her any chloroform."

"Who's inside?"

"Just me and Colin."

"No other women?"

"Nope." Usually, a woman was attended by family members during childbirth, whether or not a doctor was present. Often mothers, sisters, aunts and grandmothers had more say over which treatments were used and which were rejected than the attending physician. But Kathleen and Colin had come to America and left their families behind in Ireland. And Kathleen didn't know any of the neighbor women well enough to ask for help with something as intimate as childbirth.

"I'd better get back in."

Jesse nodded. "Do you need anything?"

Loralee looked to the house, then back at Jesse. This was it. He was asking to approach her. She swallowed, and said, "When I dump these in the reservoir, I could use another two buckets full. It seems like there's never enough hot water."

"You got it," he said, reaching for the full buckets. "In fact, you just get back in there with her, and I'll empty these for you."

"Oh, thank you, Jesse." She ran a hand over her forehead, pushing away the few blond curls that had worked themselves loose.

"No problem. I'll keep it full."

She nodded. ''Okay.''

He followed her into the house, and emptied the buckets while Loralee went behind the curtain to Kathleen.

''How's she doing?'' she asked Colin.

''She wants to push. I been talkin' 'er out of it, but she's a stubborn thing, y' know?''

Loralee smiled. ''Yes. I know.''

Kathleen woke up and started to push as another pain came crashing down on her. ''No, Kathy, look at me! Look! Breathe, girl. Breathe! That's it. Good, good.''

Loralee watched Colin, and was grateful to have him there. Kathleen let him guide her, and because of that, when the contraction ended, and their patient was once again sleeping, Loralee looked at the watch which hung around her neck, and said, ''I'll wait until ten-thirty to check her again, and if she's still not ready, I want to use the chloroform.''

Colin's head shot up. ''She said no! She—''

''Colin listen! I'll just give her enough to let her sleep for about fifteen minutes. That's all. She needs a break, or she'll never be able to push!''

He looked down at his wife, who was moaning and coming awake as another pain began. He shook his head. ''You think it's for the best?''

''I do.''

Kathleen's back came up off the bed, and this time, as the pain peaked, she screamed. A long, agonized scream that sent her husband over the edge.

''For God's sake, do something!'' he shouted. ''Oh, God, oh, God . . .'' He left Kathleen's side and paced around the room breathing too fast.

Loralee thought that if she didn't do something soon, she'd wind up with two patients, one in the bed, and one on the floor.

''Colin go out and see if the water has boiled. If it has, rinse the pan and fill it so I can scrub my hands.''

He looked at Kathleen. ''But . . .''

"I'll take care of her," Loralee said, shooshing him out. "Jesse's filling the reservoir. The water in the kettle should have boiled by now."

"Jesse's here?" Colin asked, walking out of the makeshift bedroom and into the kitchen. Loralee closed the curtain behind him and rushed to Kathleen, who was awake and in the clutches of another pain.

"Ohhhh, Loooord!" she screamed. "I can't! I can't!"

"Kathleen, listen!" Loralee shouted. "I'm going to scrub my hands. We're going to see where things stand."

She nodded, too winded to speak. Loralee waited until she was once again sleeping before she left the room.

"Colin, she's sleeping. I'm going to scrub."

"I'll watch her," he said, going back into the bedroom.

"Is this enough water?" Jesse asked. The pan was half full.

Loralee looked into it. "That's fine," she said. She squatted down in front of a second pan, which was on the floor. She poured some liquid from a bottle into the pan and used a small brush to scrub her nails.

"What is that?" Jesse asked. "It smells like turpentine."

"It is turpentine." She scrubbed thoroughly, well past her wrists, then dropped the brush back in the pan and moved to the hot water. Again she scrubbed, this time using a different brush and yellow soap.

"Why all the washing?" Jesse asked.

"Some doctors believe that childbed fever is caused by germs. Germs that doctors unknowingly carry from their hands to the mother when doing an examination." She looked at her fingers the whole time, scrubbing until her skin was red. "Since learning about the benefits of disinfecting, Dr. Farley hasn't lost a single woman to the fever."

"Really?" Jesse said, obviously impressed. It was a sad fact of life, but childbirth carried with it many hazards.

"Really. He's been keeping records of births in and around Hazleton. Actually, he includes every woman he hears of who's delivered a baby, whether he attends or not. Do you know that one out of every five women dies either during childbirth or afterwards, as a result of complications?''

"Oh, my God!'' he said. "One out of every five?''

She nodded her head. "It's frightening. That's why so many women make funeral plans when they find out they're expecting.''

Jesse stood holding both buckets with a look on his face that could only be described as horror. "My mother died after having John,'' he said quietly.

"Oh, Jesse—''

"NO!!! Nooooo!!!!''

At the sound of Kathleen's screams, Loralee dunked her hands into the steaming water and rinsed the soap off.

"Would you get the curtain?'' she asked, holding her wet hands up in front of her.

Jesse set down the buckets and held the draped piece of cloth aside. When she had entered the room, he closed it.

"What happened?'' she asked Colin.

He shook his head. "She's gettin' harder and harder to handle.''

Loralee moved to the side of the bed, and with one hand, moved the sheet that was draped over Kathleen. With the other, she checked her progress. *Please, God, please.*

Loralee sighed and closed her eyes. "Not yet,'' she said quietly.

"Use the chloroform,'' Colin said. "I can't stand to see 'er in such pain. Use it.''

Loralee nodded. "I'll get it. You help her through this next pain, and when she drifts off to sleep, we'll give it to her. Otherwise, she might fight it.''

Colin nodded. It was clear that he was terrified of losing Kathleen. Loralee said, "I'll be right back. She's waking up,'' and went back out into the kitchen. She washed her hands in the soapy water again, and walked to the pantry. She opened a door and removed a drinking glass.

"What are you doing?" Jesse asked.

Loralee took a wad of cotton, pushed it into the bottom of the glass, and poured a few drops of clear liquid onto it. She hurried to cover the glass with the palm of her hand. "I'm giving her some chloroform. This is taking too long."

She went back into the bedroom just as Colin was saying, "Good girl. Rest, now."

The second Kathleen's head fell back onto the pillow, Loralee stepped forward and held the glass over her nose. She watched as the woman's chest rose and fell, and when she had counted five breaths, she removed the glass.

"Let's see if that's enough." She reached out and rested her hand on the sheet that covered Kathleen's abdomen. "Here it comes," she said, as the flesh beneath her hand grew rock hard. "Oh, boy, that's a good one. Here," she said, motioning to Colin, "feel."

He stepped forward and tentatively rested his hand on his wife's belly. "It's so hard!"

"That's the contraction. Her uterus is contracting. Now, feel," she said. "It's passing."

Colin looked up at Loralee. "It's amazin'. An' she slept through it!"

Loralee smiled. "Yes. She slept through it. That's exactly what we want. She should sleep for at least fifteen minutes, maybe even a little longer, at the dose I gave her." She still held the glass. "Come on. Let's take a break."

"Can we leave her?" he asked.

"We'll hear her when it starts to wear off." She put her hand on Colin's shoulder. "She'll be fine, Colin."

He looked back at his wife, who was sleeping peacefully. "All right. I guess I could sit for a spell."

They walked into the kitchen and found Jesse pouring coffee. "I hope you don't mind, Colin. I thought you might need a cup of coffee, and since you seemed a little bit busy, I made it myself.''

"Ah, Jesse, how'd ya know? A good cup o' Irish coffee is just what I need.''

"Well, this isn't Irish.''

"Not yet it's not,'' Colin said, opening the pantry door and reaching to the back for a bottle of whiskey. He added a healthy amount to his own mug and set the bottle on the table. "Help yerself,'' he said, swallowing a gulp.

Loralee smiled. "No thank you. I'll just take a little cream and sugar in mine.'' She reached for one of the mugs and fixed it to her liking. "Mmm. Good coffee.''

"Thanks,'' Jesse said. "How's she doing?''

"Stuff's amazin','' Colin said. "Knocked 'er right out.''

"Sounds like she's having a hard time,'' Jesse said.

"No harder than last time,'' Colin said, sipping at his drink. "Maggie gave her a hell of a time.'' He sat staring at the floor for a few seconds, and Loralee knew he was thinking about the daughter he had lost.

"Well,'' he said, tossing back the last of his coffee. "I think I'll check on the missus. Jesse, how 'bout a refill? And make it strong.''

Jesse smiled and stood up. "You got it, Colin.'' He poured the mug full of coffee, added a dose of whiskey, looked at Loralee questioningly, then shrugged and added a little more.

"Jesse!'' she admonished.

He laughed. "The man deserves it.'' He carried it to the bedroom and knocked on the frame. "Here you go, Colin.''

He held the drink out and Colin reached for it. "Thanks.''

Jesse turned and found Loralee staring at him. "What?''

She hesitated a few seconds then said, "I was just wondering . . . why are you here? I mean, I'm glad you're here. I need you here. I don't think Colin and I could handle this by ourselves. But,'' she lowered her voice to a whisper, "why are you here?''

He looked at her from across the room for a few seconds then moved toward her and sat down at the table. "I'm not sure, exactly. I finished Colin's shift for him, and I was thinking about you the whole time." He looked into her eyes the entire time he spoke. "I knew you'd be here. I rode past, thinking that you'd probably have finished up long before, but when I saw Doc's rig out front, I knew you were still here. I knew you'd be busy, but I guess I was worried that you might need help and be too proud to ask for it."

She smiled and looked down. "I guess you were right."

"You're doing a great job."

"I haven't actually done anything yet."

"Sure you have. Delivering a baby is not easy. Sometimes just having someone there who knows what to do can make all the difference in the world."

"You say that like you're speaking from experience," she teased.

He hesitated. "I am, actually."

Her head shot up. "What? You've helped deliver a baby before?"

He nodded, and with his face completely blank, said, "My brother John."

Loralee felt her heart jump right up into her throat. Her eyes filled with tears, and she said, "Oh, Jesse. You were barely more than a baby yourself."

"I was five."

"Five?" she said, reaching out to touch his hand. "You must have been terrified. Wasn't anyone else there?"

"My sisters. One was two. One was three."

"You have sisters?" she asked, surprised that she hadn't heard about them before.

"I had sisters." He looked down at where her hand was resting across his knuckles, and it was only then that Loralee realized she had touched him. She fought the urge to pull her hand away and watched as he turned his fingers so that he ended up holding her tiny, reddened hand in his own. "We were separated after my mother died. I've never seen them again. I don't know where they live, or even if they're still alive."

Loralee pressed her lips together and looked away. She would cry if she looked at him, she knew it. "I'm so sorry," she whispered.

"I know you are. I am, too."

She looked down at the tablecloth and tried to hold herself together. Jesse had suffered so much. He'd lost so much because of her father. How could she blame him for hating the man? And yet, he was trying to get over that hatred, trying to put the past behind him so that he could have a future with her.

And she'd turned him away.

Suzanne was right. Jesse was not at all like her father or Charles. Jesse was caring and considerate. Jesse was fair and honorable. He was strong and protective. And he loved her.

She looked up at him. "Jesse, I'm so sorry about the other night. I don't know what ever possessed me to scream and run away from you like that. You did nothing wrong, and I'm sorry I treated you that way. You didn't deserve it."

She looked into his blue eyes the entire time she was talking. He held her hand between his own and rubbed it. She felt him struggle with the desire to pull her closer.

"I love you, Loralee. I would never do anything to hurt you."

"I know you wouldn't. It wasn't really you, it was just . . . I can't say what it was. What I can say is that I understand now that my thinking was . . . It was all wrong." She looked away and lowered her voice. "I'm afraid. Getting closer to you . . . that way . . . it frightens me."

"I know," he said, twining his fingers with hers. "I know it does. But I promise you," he said with a squeeze of her hand, "you do not have to be afraid of me. Have I ever hurt you?"

"No."

"Have I ever forced you to do anything you didn't want to do?"

"No."

He paused. "I never will. No matter what happens between us. No matter how far this relationship goes. I will always listen when you say no."

She lifted her teary eyes to his. "I want to believe that."

"Believe it. I will never hurt you, Loralee. Never."

"Loralee?" Colin called from the bedroom. "I think she's wakin' up."

She stood and wiped at her eyes quickly. Jesse sat back in his chair.

She leaned over, and said, "I'm so glad you're here. Please stay." She didn't wait for him to answer before turning to go back into the bedroom. She pulled the curtain closed behind her and took a deep breath to clear her head.

Kathleen was indeed waking up. She got through one more contraction on the fringes of sleep, but by the time the next one came, she was fully awake.

"All right, Kathleen," Loralee said with a smile, "you're doing great. How do you feel?"

She didn't seem to realize that she'd been asleep for nearly thirty minutes. "I feel ready to get this baby out," she said between breaths.

Loralee and Colin looked at each other and laughed. "I'm going to go scrub one more time, and we'll see how things are moving along. Colin, help her through these next few."

Loralee repeated the whole disinfecting process, hoping that it would be the last time. And this time, when she examined Kathleen, she found her ready to begin pushing.

"All right, Kathleen," she said, "this is what we've been waiting for! Ready?"

"I'm way past ready," she said, excited now that the time was here.

Loralee helped Kathleen through another contraction, and when it had ended, she somehow managed to get her up and out of bed, stripped, washed and covered with a clean gown.

"The sheets are over there," she said to Colin, nodding toward a folded pile on the bureau. He quickly, if inexpertly, spread them over the bed.

"I have to push!" Kathleen cried, hanging onto Loralee's arm while a contraction ripped through her.

"Go ahead," Loralee said, "push! Push with all you've got, Kathleen!"

Kathleen pushed so hard, that, as Loralee reached beneath her to help ease her off the floor, she felt the baby's head.

"Oh, God!" Loralee shouted. "It's coming! It's coming right now!"

Kathleen was oblivious to them. Nature had taken over, and she instinctively knew what had to be done. She had to get that baby out, and she pushed until she was red in the face and gasping for air, and she seemed much calmer and in control than she had all day.

"Here it comes, here it comes!" Loralee called from her spot on the floor. "Head . . . shoulders . . . ah! It's here!" She turned the baby over and said, "It's a girl! It's a girl!"

Kathleen cried out, and Colin's eyes filled with tears.

"A girl," Kathleen said with a smile. "I wanted a girl."

"So did I, sweetheart. So did I."

Loralee was busy at work, clamping the cord, severing the child from her mother, wrapping her in a blanket. As soon as the cord was cut, the baby let out a strong cry. It was the most beautiful sound Loralee had ever heard.

There wasn't a dry eye in the house, not even on the other side of the curtain.

Loralee handed the baby to Colin, and said, "Here you go, Papa. Hold your daughter while I tend to her mother."

Colin held out his arms, and Loralee laid the baby gently against him. Loralee looked at her and smiled.

Truly, life was a miracle.

"Can you believe that?" Jesse said, as they walked away from the house. He lifted Loralee's bag easily into Doc's rig.

"It's amazing. I don't think I'll ever get over the magic of it, even if I do it a thousand times."

They'd finished up, and with little Glenna Margaret suckling at her mother's breast, and most of the house put back to order, Loralee and Jesse had taken their leave.

It was well after one o'clock in the morning, but still, they hesitated to part.

"Thank you, Jesse. I don't know what we would have done without you."

"What a thing to see," he said, thinking of the way Colin had bathed the newborn child. "A father with his child. You know, everyone always thinks about mothers and children. Fathers," he waved his hand, "yeah, they're around somewhere, earning a living, providing. But to see a father, loving his child. It's a wonderful thing."

She nodded. "I don't think I'll ever get over the amount of strength it takes to have a baby. Men always say that women are weak—"

"Not this man!" Jesse interrupted. "There is *no way* I could ever go through that. Kathleen may be smaller than me, but she's a hell of a lot stronger than me."

"Ah, if only we could get all men thinking that way," Loralee said teasingly, "the world would be a better place."

He smiled. "The world already is a better place." He pointed to the house. "That baby in there? She'll make it a better place. And every other baby you deliver, they'll make it a better place. Things will change, Loralee. If only one woman out of a hundred has the determination you do, things will change.''

''Well, thank you, Jesse. I don't think you could have given me a better compliment if you tried for a year.'' She smiled at him.

''You're an inspiration. You go after the things you want, and you don't let anyone stop you.'' He reached out and held her by her wrists. ''I'm going to follow your lead. I know what I want. I want you. And I'm going to do everything I can to get you.''

''Oh, Jesse, this is going to be so hard.''

''I know.'' He leaned forward and kissed her on her forehead. ''The parade is tomorrow. I know you'll be too tired to go, but I still want to see you.''

''When?''

''How about after it's over? It's supposed to be ending around four. I could meet you after dinner. Just to talk?''

''All right. Seven-thirty?''

''Good. We have to face your father.''

''I know,'' she said, looking down at the ground. ''You don't know how I dread it.''

''No, but I know how I dread it. Now go home and get some rest. I'll see you tomorrow.''

He helped her up into Doc's carriage. ''Where should I meet you?'' she asked.

Jesse thought about saying Memorial Park, but then remembered his mother warning him to take things slow. He'd never be able to keep his hands off of her if they were alone.

''I think downtown is going to be busy tomorrow, well into the night. How about if I meet you in front of Hazleton House and we take a walk through all the hubbub?''

She smiled down at him. ''That sounds good.'' And then, with no warning, she was besieged by an enormous yawn.

''All right, that's my signal,'' Jesse said. ''I love you!'' he called as he turned away.

She turned and looked at him over her shoulder with a shy smile.

Jesse took a deep breath. Tomorrow would be a day of tests. Could he really stand face to face with Edward Vander? Could he really put the past firmly in the past?

"I can try like hell," he said to himself. And then, urging the horse into a gallop, he raced toward home.

CHAPTER
TWENTY-SIX

Celebrations didn't come often in Hazleton. When one did, the entire town turned out to take part in it. And so it was with the annual Union of Father Mathew Catholic Temperance Society's parade.

The Temperance Society wasn't actually temperate at all. They advocated complete abstinence from alcohol. So it was somewhat ironic that this town full of immigrants, whose only social life consisted of time spent in barrooms, would turn out in such numbers in support of a group who desired to make their sole source of entertainment illegal.

The parade had ended sometime around four o'clock, and Jesse, who had come downtown with his father, was wandering through the crowd. Around him, children chased each other, bands played, housewives gossiped and far-flung families, reunited for this one day event, visited. But Jesse scarcely noticed the thrum created by the nearly ten thousand attendees.

All he could think about was the fact that this very night, he'd be facing Edward Vander for the first time. After twenty years of hatred, Jesse would step forward and ask this man for his daughter's hand in marriage. If Edward had been hating the Sinclairs the whole time, how would he respond? How would Jesse himself respond, if their situations were reversed, he wondered?

He stopped to watch a group of young children dancing to the sounds of a gypsy band. They were dark-haired and dusky-skinned and dressed in brightly colored, ornately patterned clothing. The little girls whirled around, their skirts spinning faster and faster, creating a brilliant and constantly changing kaleidoscope of color. The boys moved among them, jumping and leaping, flipping and rolling as the onlookers clapped in time to the driving music.

He watched for a few minutes, mesmerized by the rhythmic repetitions of the dance. From the sidelines, an old woman called out instructions in a language Jesse guessed to be Hungarian. She motioned with fingers that had long ago lost the ability to straighten, but the children, moving as one, easily interpreted her meaning. The song ended amid much applause. With great flourish, the dancers bowed and rushed forward into the welcoming arms of mamas and papas.

Jesse turned away. The streets were teeming with people, and still, it was easy to pick out the different ethnic groups. He passed an alley and saw a group of Italian men playing boccie while a gathering of Irish watched. It wasn't just the fair skin and red hair that gave them away as being Irish. It was also the flask they covertly passed among themselves, willing, if only for this one day a year, to claim they abstained, but unwilling to actually do it.

The Dutch, with their tell-tale sing-song dialect, the Poles with their notoriously greasy, spicy foods, the Welsh, from whom Jesse himself had inherited his love of sweets.

Hazleton truly was a melting-pot, populated by the need for laborers to work the mines and dig the coal that was fueling the world's entire machinery. It was exciting to be a part of what people were calling history in the making. It seemed that every day one heard of new, time-saving inventions that replaced the labors of men, freeing them from the chains of back-breaking work that had held them captive since the beginning of time.

Most of those inventions required some sort of energy to run, and energy came from coal. Ironically, the people who fed those machines still worked in the dark, abysmal conditions they had ever since the first outcropping of anthracite in Hazleton was discovered in 1826 by John Fitzgerald. Miners provided the fuel for the industrial revolution, and, in the process, because of men like Edward Vander, they were thrust into the clutches of poverty.

As Jesse walked through the streets watching the celebrants, the class divisions stood out in stark contrast. In Hazleton, there were very poor people, and there were very rich people. Not many in between.

If more employers followed the lead set by Stephen and a few generous others, workers would be paid a fair wage for a fair day's work. Employers would enjoy greater loyalty. Production would increase and so would self-esteem. Families could plan for their future, instead of living day by day.

But so far, that dream remained just that. A dream. The reality, for most residents of Hazleton, was a daily struggle for survival. So, it only made sense that, given a chance to relax and have fun, people would come out in droves, even though the cause was one they didn't espouse.

Jesse walked toward the train station. People had come from all over—Wilkes-Barre and Scranton to the north and the Lehigh Valley to the south—and the station would be busy. The day of Father Mathew's annual celebration was an event second to none, and space on the excursion trains was always severely limited.

"Jesse! Over here!"

At the sound of Stephen's voice, Jesse turned. He found his

father standing next to Asa Packer, owner of the Lehigh Valley Railroad.

"Hey, Dad. Mr. Packer," he said, holding out his hand, "how're you today?"

"I was having a good ol' time until a few minutes ago." Asa was responsible for much of the growth of Pennsylvania, and when he spoke, people listened. He was a razor-sharp businessman, a generous philanthropist and the richest man in the state. He was also the founder of Lehigh University, and Jesse had seen a lot of him during his years away at school.

"What happened?" Jesse asked turning to wave as an old friend thumped his shoulder in passing.

"What happened is one of my engineers was just arrested for public drunkenness and carted off in the paddy wagon. I've got almost two hundred people to get to Mauch Chunk and no one to take 'em there."

"Why don't you take them yourself?" Stephen asked. "Pretend it's the old days, before you lived in that fancy house overlooking Millionaire's Row."

Asa laughed. "It'd be fun, wouldn't it? Except we weren't planning on going back tonight. My wife has relatives in Hazleton, and we plan on staying with them a day or two." He shrugged and shook his head. "Ah, well, she'll just have to visit another time."

"I'll do it," Jesse said.

Asa turned to look at him. "You would?"

"Sure. If I can hitch a ride on a returning train and get back here by seven-thirty." Jesse smiled and said, "I'm meeting a certain young lady."

Asa laughed. "Well, I wouldn't dream of keeping you from your . . . young lady. Let's get you on one of these sections ready to pull out." He turned to Stephen, and said, "Stephen, excuse us for a minute."

"Take your time. Jesse, I'll see you later," he called.

Jesse was already on his way to the trains, and he raised his hand in farewell. He was only too glad to have something to do for the next few hours. And with talk of Asa's being considered as a candidate for the Presidential nomination, Jesse was quick to realize that a favor given to Asa Packer might someday be a very handy thing.

They did some shuffling of schedules, moved a few men around, and Jesse was in line and waiting to pull out, the seventh in an eight-section, eighty-seven car train.

"Hey, Brody," Jesse said, as he climbed aboard. Brody Sencavage was a fireman—and a good one, too. He'd worked for Stephen years before, but had left when he and his family moved back to Mauch Chunk to be closer to his ailing parents.

"Hey, Jess! What are you doing here?" He pulled a bandanna from his back pocket and used it to mop his face.

"Favor for Mr. Packer. He found himself unexpectedly short by one engineer."

"Let me guess. Patrick Iam."

Jesse laughed. "Good guess."

Brody went back to his shoveling, and Jesse watched for the signal to turn. He loved to operate trains, loved the way he held all that power in his control. He felt it, harnessed and eager, as it shimmied its way up through his legs.

There was a mandatory ten-minute span between trains, and Jesse kept his eyes on the signal up ahead.

And there it was.

He released the brakes, opened the throttle and felt the engine strain to move forward. There were nine passenger cars behind the coal car, each one filled to capacity. It was a heavy load, and it would take a few minutes to gain momentum. Jesse reached up for the plaited cord and pulled, and the blast from the whistle split the air, letting everyone know of their departure. He sat back, crossed his booted feet and relaxed to enjoy the ride.

They were out of the city and into the woods in minutes. This line was on a slight downward grade, and, as they approached

Weatherly, Jesse let the train pick up some speed. He could see the signal for the next stop. It was white, turned to let him go. The ten minutes between Jesse's train and the one in front of him had passed. He slowed only slightly and, blowing the whistle, kept right on moving through the Weatherly Station.

Jesse approached Mud Run and found the signal turned against him. He closed the throttle, reached for the brake and pulled hard. They were still rolling down hill, and it would take some muscle to stop a train of this size. When he'd slowed to a crawl, he let up on the brake, and at the station, he brought the train to a stop. The signal man displayed red lights on the rear of the train, and the flagman went back with his lantern to warn the eighth section of the delay.

Jesse tapped his foot nervously. "Come on, come on," he muttered to himself.

"You sound like a man in a hurry," Brody said.

"I'm supposed to be meeting someone at seven-thirty."

"Back in Hazleton?"

Jesse nodded. "I'm gonna hop a return in Mauch Chunk."

"Seven-thirty? It'll be close, but you'll make it."

"*If* this signal ever turns," Jesse said.

From behind, he heard the whistle of the eighth section as it approached. He leaned out the window and looked back. They were stopped on a curve, but Jesse could easily see a half mile back. His gaze lifted upwards. Two streams of exhaust. That meant two engines. "Must be a long one," he said.

He watched as the smoke moved nearer and nearer, and suddenly, he realized that the train didn't seem to be slowing down. He turned and looked ahead at the signal. It was still red. He swung his head around to the back and saw the flagman, up on his platform, signal held high, waving his arms frantically.

"Oh, Jesus . . ." Jesse blinked and looked back down the tracks. There it was. The eighth section was approaching at full steam.

"What's wrong?"

"He's not stopping!"

Brody poked his head out the window. "God Almighty!"

Jesse jerked his head back around and released the brake, threw the throttle wide open and the train lurched forward. He turned again to look out the doorway.

"Hang on, Brody, he's gonna hit us!" he cried. He laid on the whistle, and braced himself for the impact he knew was coming.

Jesse's train had barely begun to move when the eighth section barreled into it. He was thrown against the front of the cab where his head slammed into the small window, shattering the glass. He fell back against the door and felt the bone in his left arm snap.

"Oh, God! Oh, my God!" He yelled as he scrambled to stand. That train had *two* engines! And there were people back there! "Brody, you okay?"

Brody pulled himself up from the floor. "My leg . . . it's burned." Hot coals from the fire he'd been tending had spilled out onto him. There was only red, bloody flesh where Brody's left trouser leg should have been.

"Can you stand?"

"Yeah. I don't think anything is broken."

"I've got to see what happened." Jesse was dizzy, but he hauled himself out of the engine cab and dropped down into the dirt, cradling his left arm which dangled uselessly. The air was thick with smoke and screams. And then he saw it.

"Oh, God, no," he said, as he walked to the back of the train. The rear car had been telescoped completely. There was nothing left of it. And nothing left of the people who had been sitting in it.

"Oh, good Lord," Brody said, as he approached the rear of the train.

The cars had been compressed into one another by the overwhelming force of the duel train engines. The flimsy wooden passenger cars had split apart as if they were made of toothpicks.

Cars and pieces of cars had tumbled down the embankment, and steam spewed from the damaged locomotive.

There were bodies everywhere. Some had been thrown from the wreckage, and others lay pinned in it, unable to escape. Several people who had survived the carnage wrought by the collision itself were scalded to death by the hot steam. The burning coals had started the passenger cars on fire, and flames were beginning to leap out.

At the sound of a scream, Jesse sprang into action. "Listen, there's a lot of people to get out of there." Jesse took in the scene and made a quick decision. "Let's start at the front. There might be some uninjured men up there willing to help, and, besides, that's where the fire is spreading the most. We've got to get them out of there fast."

"Let's go."

They made a move, and Jesse groaned.

"What's wrong?" Brody shouted.

"Broke my arm. Heard it snap." He held the arm close to his body and tried to breathe through the pain that was shooting up his shoulder. "Give me your shirt."

Brody shrugged it off, and Jesse held his arm to his chest. "Tie it around me. Bind the arm so it doesn't move."

"Jesse—"

"Just do it! It doesn't hurt as bad if it's not swinging."

Brody extended the arms of his shirt and wrapped it around Jesse. He tied it and stood back. "How's that?"

"Tighter."

He reached out and pulled the arms of his shirt until Jesse said, "That's enough."

Around them, survivors began climbing out of the wreckage. "We need volunteers!" Jesse shouted. "Any men not seriously injured, we need help pulling out the others. Any women who could tend to the victims would be appreciated!"

Thankfully, several men, dazed and bruised, but able to move on their own volition staggered forward, and the rescue mission began.

From the front sections of the train, there were more live bodies than dead. Cuts and scrapes and broken bones accounted for most of the injuries. The smoke pouring out of the burning wreckage hindered the rescuers, who coughed and choked, but worked on.

As the first three cars were emptied, and the rescuers moved toward the back sections, there were few people moving, and they were praying for death.

Jesse helped seven survivors and pulled four bodies out before he fell the first time. He staggered to his feet and looked down at his arm. Brody's shirt was soaked in blood. He reached above his elbow and nearly passed out when his fingers touched a sharp piece of bone. Dropping his good hand to his side, he rushed back into the pile of splintered wood and twisted metal that held the remaining survivors hostage.

He dragged three more bodies and helped two men, injured, but alive, out to the side, where a makeshift hospital of sorts had begun to take shape. The most seriously injured were tended by those whose wounds could wait.

Jesse turned to go back but fell, so dizzy he couldn't get back up. He pushed himself to sitting and tried to stop the world around him from spinning. He was on his knees when Brody came running.

"That's enough, Jesse!" You can't do anymore!"

"I have to! There are still people in there, and the flames are getting closer!"

"You can't!"

"Help me up. Just once more in. I can do one more!" Jesse said. His vision was blurred, and he wondered if he'd be able to stand even if Brody did help him to his feet.

"One more!" Brody said, reaching down to hoist Jesse to standing. "One more, then get over there with the rest of them before I end up dragging you out!'' He turned and stalked toward the wreckage.

Jesse moved forward only with great concentration. It took supreme effort to lift his feet. He stepped over a pile of wood and bent over the body of a woman, her fancy silk dress soaked in blood. Her eyes were open, and Jesse knew instantly that she was dead.

Beside her, a man groaned and Jesse blinked. He was alive! He leaned forward and said, ''Hey, buddy, I'm gonna get you out of here!'' The man was lying face down, and Jesse rolled him over to get a better hold.

And below his feet, the very earth shook. The man looking back at him was Edward Vander.

The recognition dawned in Edward's eyes instantly, and he stared without saying a word. Jesse looked at the face of the man who was responsible for his father's death. The man who had shown no remorse for the damage his greed had caused.

The man who was Loralee's father.

Jesse's vision blurred. There was no time to think. The flames were getting nearer, and the smoke was consuming. He reached down and grabbed the front of Edward's shirt. He boosted the man's back off the floor and squatted down to wrap his one good arm around Edward's chest. Jesse stood, lifting Edward with him.

He'd barely cleared the wreckage when the world began to tilt. In slow motion, he watched himself fall toward to the ground. And with his good arm wrapped around Edward, he had nothing to brace his fall.

He landed with a thud, and after a blinding flash of pain, the world went black.

Loralee was in her bedroom braiding her hair. It was almost dinnertime, and she was already anxious to see Jesse.

She hadn't gotten home last night until almost four in the

morning. And, although she was exhausted, she'd still been awake when the first light of day began creeping up the sky. It was morning by the time she fell asleep, and she'd slept until midafternoon.

She'd helped deliver a baby! A beautiful, healthy baby girl. She still couldn't get over the wonder of it.

And, Jesse! He'd been there almost the whole time. And after working with him for most of the night, she'd come to realize that her fears were completely unfounded. Jesse wasn't at all like her father or Charles, and she wondered, now, how she ever could've thought that he was.

Loralee loved him. She loved him, and she'd hurt him terribly. She intended to start making up for some of that hurt tonight.

From downstairs, she heard a commotion, then her mother calling to her.

"Loralee! Come quick! Loralee!"

"What on earth . . . ?" She jumped up and ran out into the hallway. From the top of the stairs she shouted, "What's wrong?"

And then she saw. On the foyer floor, lying on a makeshift stretcher was her father, twisted and broken. She raced down the stairs.

"Papa!" she shouted, falling to her knees, "Papa, can you hear me?"

Edward opened his eyes, but said nothing.

"Marta, get my bag! It's upstairs!" She looked up at the two men standing above her father. "Go get Dr. Farley. Tell him to come right away!"

"He's not there. All the doctors been called out, 'bout an hour now."

"What?" Loralee asked knitting her brows together. "I don't know what you're talking about. Called out for what?"

"Been a train wreck. Out Mud Run."

"A train wreck!" Loralee looked down at her father. She

ran her fingers gently over his limbs. He had more broken bones than she'd ever seen on one person, and his breathing was labored. A punctured lung filling with blood, she guessed. Her father would not live. With all of her training, there was nothing she could do.

The men who had carried him stood waiting awkwardly. Finally one of them said, "We been takin' the injured to their homes on our wagon. It'll be five cents."

Loralee stared, dumbfounded. This man wanted money from her?

"I'll see to it," Gibbons said. He retreated into Edward's study and returned to drop a few coins in the bedraggled man's outstretched hand.

"Thank you. And, God willin', may your father live."

Loralee watched him leave then turned toward her mother.

"Edward, oh, Edward, what have you done to yourself?" Fiona cried, kneeling beside her husband.

He looked at her. "My fault. I was taking Lily to—" He was racked with a coughing spell.

Loralee said, "Hush, Papa. Don't talk. You'll only weaken yourself."

He looked into Loralee's eyes, and said, "Have to tell you . . . he pulled me out . . . saw my face and pulled me out anyway . . ."

"Who pulled you out? I don't know—"

"Sinclair . . . pulled me out of the train."

"Jesse?" Loralee said, opening her eyes wide. "Jesse pulled you out?"

Edward nodded. "Wanted you to know." His eyes drifted shut, and he said, "Good man." With much effort, he opened his eyes and turned to Fiona. "Sorry. Very sorry."

He closed his eyes again and Fiona said, "No, Edward, don't sleep!"

Loralee rested her hand on her mother's shoulder. "Mother, let him go."

They sat on the floor looking at each other, then down at Edward, who suddenly stopped struggling for breath.

"He's dead." Fiona announced. She sat looking at her husband for several seconds then looked up and said, "We should call the priest."

"Yes," Loralee said. Her eyes filled with tears as she looked down at her father. He hadn't been an easy man to live with, but still . . .

"Gibbons, would you be kind enough to select a suit . . . and-and whatever else—"

"I'll take care of it, madam," Gibbons interrupted. "Marta," he barked toward the woman who was still hovering nearby with Loralee's black bag in her hands, "please assist madam to her room."

"Yes, of course." Marta rushed forward and helped Fiona to her feet. "Here we go, missus, let's get you upstairs."

Fiona walked up the stairs with Marta holding one arm and Loralee the other, though she appeared to need no assistance whatsoever. Halfway up the stairs she called, "Gibbons please take his navy blue suit, not the black. Black is so somber."

"Yes, madam."

Loralee watched her mother warily. Marta helped Fiona into the master suite and said, "Can I get you anything, missus?"

Fiona sat down at a small table near a window. "Yes," she said, turning away from the window, "I believe I'll have a glass of wine."

"Wine?" Marta said the word as though it was a preposterous idea.

"Yes, wine. My husband has just been delivered to my doorstep on the brink of death. My daughter and I have had to watch as the life ebbed out of him. I think I deserve a glass of wine." Fiona looked at Loralee, and said, "Would you like some?"

Surely, her mother must be in shock. "No, thank you, Mother."

Marta excused herself and Loralee asked, "Are you all right?"

"I'm fine," Fiona answered evenly.

"But, Papa—"

"Papa's dead. Yes. I know."

Loralee narrowed her eyes. "But, you seem—"

"Loralee, your father and I had a very strained relationship. You know that as well as I do. I won't go so far as to say I'm happy he's dead, but neither will I squander what's left of my heart grieving for a man I stopped loving long ago. I'll wear black. I'll restrict my outings. But I will not shed one more tear over Edward Vander."

Loralee was shocked.

Marta came back bearing a small silver tray with a full wineglass. She set it down then closed the door behind her.

Loralee watched as her mother raised the glass and drank deeply from it. She could have sworn she saw a smile cross her mother's lips! But it was gone so quickly, she couldn't be sure.

"Mother, who's Lily?"

"Hmm? Oh, I don't know," she said distractedly. "Loralee, I was thinking. You should go to Jesse. If he was on that train, he may have been injured, too—"

Loralee's hands flew to her mouth. "I didn't even think—"

"We'll go now. I'll go with you."

"What?"

Fiona, who rarely left the house for any reason, was offering to accompany Loralee to the Sinclair home?

"Loralee, the young man rescued your father. At the very least, he deserves a thank-you for his efforts. From both of us."

"But, Papa—"

"Your father wanted us to know what happened. Why do

you think he struggled so hard to tell you what Jesse did? Why do you think he told me he was sorry? After all this time, Edward finally realized that he was wrong about a lot of things.''

Loralee considered her mother's words. The fact that Jesse might be wounded made her want to go running to his side. ''All right, we'll go.''

''Of course we will,'' Fiona said, draining her glass. ''We'll have to change first.'' She walked out of the room and from the top of the steps shouted, ''Gibbons, my daughter and I will need a carriage.''

''Certainly, madam. I'll see to it.''

''Thank you.'' She came back into the room and found Loralee in the same spot. She rested her hand on Loralee's shoulder and urged her into the hallway and toward her own room. ''Go change your dress.''

Loralee looked down at her blood-stained dress. She walked to her room and closed the door.

She shrugged out of the soiled dress, put on the one black dress she owned, coiled her hair into a chignon and used a long hat pin to fasten a small black hat adorned with black netting.

She looked in the mirror. On the outside, she looked like a woman in mourning. But on the inside, she felt like a woman liberated.

On his deathbed, her father had given her the one thing she always wanted. Freedom to choose. And she chose Jesse Sinclair.

Loralee's eyes filled with tears. She squeezed them shut and whispered, ''Thank you, Papa.''

And in her heart, she heard, *You're welcome, daughter.*

The Vanders' driver pulled in front of a house he had never before been asked to approach. Fiona and Loralee were helped down, and they walked up the path to the front door. Loralee rang the bell, and the door was whipped open by a short, round man who looked as though he had just run a mile.

"May I help you?"

Loralee thought to herself that perhaps they should be helping him. He was red in the face, breathing heavily and sweating profusely.

"Good evening. My name is Fiona Vander, and this is my daughter Loralee. We would—"

"Loralee?" He asked excitedly. "Loralee Vander?"

"Y-yes, I—"

"Come right this way, Miss Vander. Please, come, come," he said urging them into the house.

He seated them in a sun room and hurried away.

Loralee looked at her mother and raised an eyebrow. Fiona shrugged.

Suddenly, Elizabeth Sinclair burst into the room. "Loralee! Oh, thank heavens!"

She jumped up. "Mrs. Sinclair, this is my mother, Fiona."

Elizabeth held out her hand. "Mrs. Vander."

Loralee couldn't wait for the pleasantries to pass. "How is Jesse? Is he all right?"

"Jesse has a broken arm, quite a few cuts and scrapes, and a temper like you wouldn't believe," Elizabeth said.

"He's okay?"

"Yes. He's upstairs, and he's mad as a hornet."

Loralee held a hand across her heart. "Thank you, God," she whispered.

"We were hoping to see him," Fiona said, coming to her feet. "As I understand it, your son is responsible for pulling my husband out of the wreckage."

"Oh, I'm so sorry! I didn't even think to ask. How is he?"

"Edward died shortly after he was brought home."

"Oh, Mrs. Vander! I'm so sorry."

"I appreciate your condolences, Mrs. Sinclair. It was because of Jesse that Loralee and I were able to share some very important last words with Edward before he died. I would like to thank Jesse for his efforts.''

"Oh," Elizabeth seemed confused. "Y-you want to speak to him now?''

"If that's possible.''

"Of course. Actually, I think seeing you will be just the thing Jesse needs. He's been asking for you ever since he woke up.''

"Asking for me? Really?''

Elizabeth let out a great gust of air. "Actually, he's been demanding that the doctor let him out of bed so that he could go to meet you. He seemed to think you would be waiting for him somewhere, and he gave Dr. Harding quite a difficult time. He finally gave him a sedative.''

"Dr. Harding treated him?''

Elizabeth led them out of the room and up the stairs. "From what I understand, the doctors that were dispatched to the scene returned the wounded to their homes in groups. Apparently, Dr. Harding was unfortunate enough to get Jesse in his group. My son can be quite persistent.''

Loralee smiled. "Actually," she said, turning to face her mother, "Jesse and I *were* supposed to meet. We were going to come to Papa tonight to tell him that we want to be together. Jesse wanted to face him and make it clear that Papa could not stand in our way any longer.''

"Oh, Loralee," Fiona said, reaching for her daughter's hand.

They stopped outside a door, and Elizabeth said, "Let me just check to make sure he's decent.'' She slipped through the door and closed it, and Loralee and Fiona waited in the hallway for her.

"That's one fine young man you chose," Fiona said quietly.

"Thank you," Loralee said with a small smile. "I didn't really choose him. In fact, we pretty much wanted nothing to do with each other, but . . .''

Fiona smiled and reached up to lay her hand on Loralee's cheek. "But Cupid had other plans for the two of you."

"It would seem that way." Loralee sighed. "I love him, . Mother. I love him so much."

"I know you do."

Elizabeth opened the door. "You can come in."

Loralee smiled and rushed through the doorway. Jesse was sitting in the bed. His left arm, in a cast, was propped on a pile of pillows beside him.

"Hey," he said.

Loralee rushed forward and wrapped her arms around him. "Oh, Jesse!"

"Ow, ow," he said.

"Oh," she said, backing away and wiping at her nose, "I'm sorry." Seeing him here and realizing how close she had come to losing him, brought tears to her eyes. She leaned over and rested her head on his shoulder.

Using his good arm, he patted her back. "Listen," he said, "I know we didn't talk to your father yet, but I don't want to wait any longer to say this."

She lifted her head, and he looked into her eyes. "I want to marry you, Loralee Vander. I want to marry you. I love you, and I don't want to wait any longer. I'll talk to your father, and I'll make him understand—"

"Jesse," Loralee said, and the tears in her eyes slowly ran down her cheeks. "My father died."

His eyes widened. "What? But—"

"A few minutes after he was brought home, he died." She reached up and wiped the tears away.

"Oh, Loralee, I-I don't know what to say."

"I do," Fiona said, from the doorway where she had been standing. She held out her hand. "I'm Fiona Vander, Loralee's mother. I take it you're Jesse."

Jesse reached out to squeeze her hand. "Yes."

"We want to thank you for pulling Edward out of that wreckage."

Jesse's eyes flashed to his mother, who only shook her head. "How did you know?" he asked.

Fiona smiled. "Edward told us."

"He *told* you?"

She nodded. "He did. I want you to know, that because of you, because of what you did, Edward had the chance to make peace with us before he died. We couldn't have done that if not for you."

Fiona leaned forward and kissed Jesse on the cheek. Her eyes were filled with tears. "Thank you for that."

Jesse squeezed Fiona's hand.

"I just wish it hadn't taken arriving on death's doorstep for Edward to finally show signs of becoming half the man you already are," she said.

Loralee watched with tear-filled eyes. Jesse looked at his mother, then back to Fiona, "It's time to forgive. It's long past time," he said. He turned to Loralee. "What about you?"

"Me?" she asked with her eyes wide. "What about me?"

Jesse smiled, that teasing, cocky smile she'd come to love. "I'd get down on one knee, but I don't think I'd be able to get back up again. So this will have to do." He reached for her hand and said, "I love you, Loralee. Will you marry me?"

"Marry you?" Loralee felt as if time had stopped, and everything in the universe was waiting for her answer.

"Yes. Marry me."

She hesitated a few seconds and looked down at her hands. "I don't want to give up the practice of medicine," she said softly.

"I'm not asking you to."

She looked up at him. "You're not?"

He shook his head. "You're a healer, Loralee. I know how much you love your work. I would never ask you to give that up."

Loralee looked down at their joined hands and smiled. She leaned forward, and, with both their mothers watching, kissed him full on the mouth. She leaned back and looked into his beautiful blue eyes. ''In that case, nothing could stop me.''

CHAPTER
TWENTY-SEVEN

"This was, without a doubt, the absolute best Thanksgiving I've ever had," Jesse said to his bride.

It was their wedding day. The bride and groom had opted for a small, private ceremony followed by Thanksgiving dinner, served at the Sinclair home. The guests included Stephen, Elizabeth and Fiona, Suzanne and John, who had served as witnesses, and Mr. and Mrs. Becker.

Beneath the table, Jesse rested his hand on Loralee's knee. Her eyes widened slightly and she sat up straighter, as though trying to appear perfectly respectable while her husband's fingers crept up the inside of her thigh.

"What room will you be doing next?" Elizabeth asked.

"I'm not sure," Fiona said, pausing to think. "Loralee's room, maybe. Or maybe the dining room." She waved her hand. "Oh, I don't know. The master suite will probably take all winter to finish, at the pace things are moving."

Jesse looked at his newly acquired mother-in-law. The changes in her these past few weeks were unbelievable, and

Jesse found himself admiring her more with each passing day. Finally, he was able to figure out where Loralee had gotten all her spunk. Fiona Vander was a little spitfire!

From the beginning, she'd treated Jesse as though he was already family, as though she expected to see his face at her dinner table more often than not. She asked his opinion on everything from finances to furniture.

After the accident at Mud Run, which claimed the lives of sixty-four people, Edward Vander had been buried, and with him, the sense of sufferance that always seemed to hang over his household.

Fiona, though she wore the traditional black of mourning, had never been as cheerful. She was active in her household, excited about Loralee's wedding, and able, it seemed, to keep the offices of Vander Holdings up and running, until such time that Edward's will could be read and his final plans carried out. She hadn't so much as touched a single strand of embroidery thread in the weeks after Edward's death.

She'd had numerous meetings with both bankers and lawyers, during which she'd managed to extract the basic information she needed in order to continue operations of her husband's business.

She made sure that every employee was informed of the status of his job. The official statement was, "Vander Holdings will continue in operation in accordance with past policy until such time that new management takes effect."

Meanwhile, she attacked the home front with a vengeance. After encouraging the staff to help themselves to anything of Edward's that had been marked for disposal, she had the remnants boxed and stacked in the office of Vander Holdings. On payday, the employees were told to take anything that caught their eye. By the end of the day, all the boxes were empty.

Fiona went through Edward's home office herself. There seemed to be very little of anything that pertained to the business. There were books and maps and some personal correspondence (these letters, Fiona burned), but almost nothing went into the pile to be moved to her husband's downtown office.

The books she kept. The rest of the room she had stripped bare. She hired carpenters to come in and remove the shelves, the furniture and anything else that reminded her of her husband. They cut holes in the walls and installed enormous floor-to-ceiling leaded-glass windows. They repaired plaster, sanded and refinished the floors and papered the walls.

Fiona brought out boxes and boxes of samplers she'd completed over the years and had them framed. Jesse had helped her hang them on every available wall, sizes and styles mixed to create a warm, welcoming look.

She bought new furniture. Pretty, delicate furniture covered in fabric in various shades of yellow. She had more samplers sewn into throw pillows, which she trimmed with fringe and tossed on every chair.

When the room was sunny and bright and exactly to her liking, Fiona began on the master suite.

The bankers came calling, warning her that she was spending carelessly. The lawyers sent letters, advising that her allowance had been exceeded. Fiona prepared her own statements in which she tallied up both her and Loralee's personal allowances as well as those for household expenses through the years. From that figure, she deducted expenditures (amounts which, due to Edward's meticulous bookkeeping, were easy to find). The balance, which it would take several *years* of careless spending to deplete, spoke for itself. The lawyers and bankers left her alone.

All in all, Jesse thought the change in her was astonishing.

"I don't think I ever ate so much in my life," Stephen said, sitting back and patting his stomach. "I can't move."

"You say that every Thanksgiving," Elizabeth teased.

"Well, this time, I mean it. You're going to have to roll me away from the table."

The chatter around the table was friendly and light. Fiona

and Elizabeth ganged up on Stephen, Suzanne flirted shamelessly with John, who, Jesse noticed, was looking at her with puppy-dog eyes, and the Beckers sat back and watched it all. Jesse had the feeling Mrs. Becker felt personally responsible for the marriage.

The butler walked into the room and bent to whisper something to Fiona, who wiped her mouth and stood up. "Excuse me for one moment, please." She followed him out into the foyer.

Jesse looked at Loralee, who shrugged, and said, "I have no idea."

Fiona was back in a few minutes, bearing a thick white envelope. She stood beside the table and said, "I have something I'd like Jesse to read."

"Me?"

Fiona smiled. "You're the only Jesse here," she teased.

Elizabeth stood up, and said, "Let's retire to the parlor."

Fiona stood to the side and waited until her host and hostess had passed before she followed them out of the room.

"What is this all about?" Jesse whispered to Loralee.

"I don't know. She didn't mention anything to me."

They all found places to sit, except Fiona, who stood facing the small gathering.

"I only found out about this a few days ago," she said, fumbling with the envelope. "Of course, I wanted to say something right away, but the lawyers insisted that to do so would jeopardize the legal standing of the document." She walked to Jesse and held out the envelope. "Jesse, would you please read the section I have marked? Out loud, please."

Jesse glanced toward his father, then reached out and took the package from Fiona's hands. He pulled a thick bundle of papers from the envelope and unfolded it. "Last Wi-" his head shot up to Fiona, who only smiled and said, "Go on."

He cleared his throat and looked down at the papers in his

hands. Why did she want him to do this? "Last Will and Testament of Edward Joseph Vander."

"Papa's Will?" Loralee asked. "Oh, Mother, I don't think we should—"

"Be patient, Loralee," Fiona said. "Jesse, go ahead. Read the section I had marked. It's on the third page."

Jesse hesitated then flipped through the first two pages. There was a small pencil mark in the left hand margin. Why in the world did Fiona want him to do this? And why did she want it done right now? He took a deep breath and began reading. "My entire business, operating under the name Vander Holdings, all property owned by me and used for the business, all moneys collected by the company, all accounts held in such name, these I leave to my daughter, Loralee Vander." Jesse paused and looked up at Loralee, who was staring at him as though waiting to hear the bad news.

He looked down and began reading again. "However, in the event she marries—" Jesse stopped. Would Edward have been cruel enough to take his empire away from his only child as a way to punish her for having married a man not hand-picked to his liking?

"Go on, Jesse," Fiona said. "Keep reading."

He stared at her for a few seconds then looked back at the page. "In the event that she marries, ownership of all these shall be immediately transferred to—" Jesse's jaw dropped and he looked up at Fiona, who was looking very pleased with herself.

"This can't be right," he said.

"What?" Loralee asked. "What does it say?"

"But, it is right," Fiona said excitedly. "The lawyers have checked into it thoroughly. Edward had this document designed to be unbreakable. There is no way around it." She smiled at him.

"No way around what?" Stephen asked.

"I can't believe this," Jesse muttered to himself.

"Can't believe what?" Elizabeth asked. "Will you please finish? In the event she marries . . . ?"

Jesse looked around the room. He wasn't sure he could even say the words. He looked back down and read, "In the event that she marries, all these shall be immediately transferred to her husband's name, giving him sole ownership and management rights."

Jesse dropped his hand into his lap. He was the sole owner of Vander Holdings.

"My father left his business to you?" Loralee asked. "Why?"

"He didn't leave it, specifically to Jesse Sinclair," Fiona clarified. "He left it to your husband, in the event you married. This document had not been updated in nearly a year. At the time this was written, Edward had no idea who, or even if, you would marry."

"But, if I did marry, he wanted my husband to be in control of the entire business," Loralee said flatly.

"And in control of you," Jesse said. Loralee would have wound up in the same kind of subservient role her mother had been forced to endure all those years.

Jesse wouldn't have it. "Is that lawyer still here?" he asked.

"Yes. I had him wait outside. He has some papers for us to sign."

Jesse stalked to the front door and whipped it open. The man standing on the other side jumped.

"Come in. I need to talk to you."

"Certainly, Mr. Sinclair." The man picked up his case and followed Jesse back into the parlor.

Jesse paced around, obviously agitated. Loralee came to stand by his side. "Are you all right?"

"Hmm? Yes. Fine." He turned toward the lawyer. "Let me see if I have this straight. I own Vander Holdings."

"Yes, Mr. Sinclair. You can see why we felt it prudent to

wait until after the wedding to disclose the contents of Mr. Vander's will.''

"Yes, I certainly can. Is there anything I need to do, or sign, to make this official?''

"As a matter of fact, there are several papers that will need your signature." He opened his briefcase and withdrew a stack of papers.

Jesse looked at Loralee and held out his arm. She stepped into it and he pulled her protectively to his side. She was shaken by this latest turn of events, he knew. It had to be unsettling to her to learn that her father wished her to remain penniless, and therefore, powerless, in any marriage she would have entered into.

The lawyer withdrew a pen and said, "Sign here, please." Jesse signed his name.

"And here . . ."

He signed again.

"And here."

One more time.

"There we go. I can sign as witness, if you like, or someone else may do it."

"You can do it," Jesse said.

The man leaned forward and signed his name. "There. It's official. You, Mr. Jesse Sinclair, are the new owner of Vander Holdings. Congratulations."

Something about the way he said that—congratulations— rankled Jesse. It was as though the company was the prize and Loralee was just the baggage that went with it.

"Thank you. Now, as the owner, I can do anything I want with this company?"

"W-well, y-yes," he said, probably anticipating by Jesse's tone that something was going on.

"Even sell it?"

"If you want to. But, Mr. Sinclair, I would strongly advise

against that. Vander Holdings is an extremely profitable enterprise. Selling it would not be in your best interests.''

''Hmm,'' Jesse said, pausing as though to consider that fact. ''If I did sell it, I could sell it for any amount at all?''

The lawyer was getting nervous. He didn't like the way this conversation was going. ''Well, yes. But, again, Mr. Sinclair, I would *strongly* discourage you from selling. Perhaps—''

''And what would be needed in order to complete a transaction such as this?''

''Oh, there'd be a lot of paperwork involved. It's a big company—''

''The minimum. The bare minimum to make it legal?''

The lawyer was definitely nervous. ''Well, that would be an Agreement of Sale. A paper in which you, as the present owner, and the proposed new owner agree to the terms of the sale.''

''In other words, I, Jesse Sinclair do sell Vander Holdings to so-and-so for the amount of—whatever?''

''In its entirety.''

''Pardon?''

The man waved his hands. ''. . . Vander Holdings, in its entirety . . . ,''

''Okay, Vander Holdings in its entirety. Do you have a blank sheet of paper?''

''Well, oh, Mr. Sinclair, I *strongly*—''

''I know. Do you have a sheet of paper?''

The man fumbled through his case and withdrew a single sheet of paper. Jesse took it from him. ''Thank you. May I?'' he held out his hand and the man handed over the pen.

Jesse leaned forward and jotted a few lines onto the paper. The room was silent. Even the lawyer had stopped babbling.

Jesse stood up and held the paper out to him. ''So this is all it would take? I fill in the blanks and that's it?''

The lawyer swallowed and nodded, as though by not speaking, he wouldn't be held responsible for this terrible mistake. ''Of course, the same documents you just signed would need to be drawn up for the new owner. Deeds, bank statements and so forth. But that can be done at a later date. A signed Agreement of Sale would suffice for now,'' he said resignedly.

''And that's official? Iron-clad?''

''With a witness or two, yes. Iron-clad.''

Jesse smiled. ''Great!'' He turned to Loralee. ''How much money do you have?''

''What?'' she asked, drawing her brows together.

''Money. Do you have any with you?''

''Well, I-I don't know. Some spare change, maybe, but—''

''Go get it.''

''Jesse, what are you doing?''

He smiled at her. ''Listen to your husband. Go get it.''

She hesitated then turned and walked out into the foyer. The butler retrieved a small satin bag, and Loralee pulled the drawstring open. She rooted through it and held out her hand. ''I have one dollar and fifteen cents.''

''Great,'' he said again. He bent over the sheet of paper one more time and scribbled something onto it.

The lawyer, who was reading over his shoulder began to sputter. ''Mr. Sinclair! I *must* advise you *not* to—''

Jesse held the sheet of paper up for him to see. ''Is this legal? Binding? And I mean iron-clad binding.''

The lawyer sighed. ''With signatures and witnesses, yes. Legal. Binding. Unbreakable.''

Jesse smiled. ''Just what I wanted to hear,'' he said, thumping the man on the back so hard he nearly stumbled. Jesse turned to his wife. ''Loralee, I would like to sell Vander Holdings to you for the sum of one dollar and fifteen cents.''

''*What?*'' she cried.

''I would like to sell Vander Holdings-''

''I heard you the first time!'' she shouted. ''Why would you do that?''

''Because it should be yours. I want you to have it.'' He reached out for her hands. ''I don't want you coming into this marriage powerless.'' He looked at Fiona and said, ''And penniless means powerless.'' He smiled at his mother-in-law, and she smiled back. He understood.

''Oh, Jesse.'' Loralee's eyes filled with tears. ''You are the most perfect man.''

He smiled and cocked his head, ''I don't know about that.''

''I do.'' She stood on tiptoe and kissed him on the cheek. ''Here,'' she said, holding out her hand. She dropped the coins into his palm. ''Where do I sign?''

Jesse laughed and picked her up off the ground. He planted a kiss on her and spun her around once before setting her back down.

''You heard the lady,'' Jesse said to the lawyer. ''Where does she sign?''

The man, thoroughly exasperated, thrust the paper toward Loralee. ''Here,'' he said, pointing. ''Don't forget to use your marriage name.''

Loralee smiled and glanced up at her husband before penning *Loralee Vander Sinclair. November 25, 1888.*

She held out the pen to Jesse. He wrote *Jesse Samuel Sinclair. November 25, 1888.*

''I'll need witnesses,'' the lawyer said, disgustedly.

''I'll do it!'' The words were spoken by every person in the room. They all looked around and laughed.

''I only need two, but you can all do it if you want to.'' It was a done deal. Might as well make the clients happy.

They stood in line, and eventually, the Agreement of Sale which transferred ownership from Jesse Sinclair to Loralee Sinclair was witnessed by Stephen Adam Sinclair, Elizabeth Ann Sinclair, Fiona Sarah Vander, John Samuel Sinclair, Suzanne Marie Becker, Robert Lawrence Becker, and Penelope Susan Becker.

That was as iron-clad as one got.

And on the heels of one very frustrated lawyer, Jesse and Loralee took their leave.

Amid hugs and kisses, and thank-you's and good-bye's, the newlyweds ran out the front door and climbed into a waiting carriage.

Jesse looked over at his bride. "I love you," he said.

"I love you, too. And thank you."

Jesse smiled and leaned over for a kiss. "Don't thank me, yet. Later, definitely, but not yet."

His blushing bride giggled and pushed him away.

And it was all he could do to keep his hands to himself for the short ride downtown.

"They make a beautiful couple," Fiona said.

"Yes, they do," Elizabeth answered, as they settled in for one last piece of pie. The Beckers had gone, and Johnny had offered to walk Suzanne home, under the guise of "working off some of the turkey."

"Jesse will be a wonderful husband. I just know it," Fiona said with tears in her eyes. "You've raised a son you can be proud of," she said.

"Oh, thank you," Elizabeth said, dabbing at her own eyes. "Jesse made the job easy. He's . . . well, he's a very special person."

"I was thinking," Stephen said with a smile, "those two are going to make us some fine-looking grandchildren."

"Grandchildren!"

He nodded. "Grandchildren. And by the way they can't even keep their eyes off of each other, I don't think we'll have to wait very long."

"Stephen Sinclair!" Elizabeth said, blushing.

"What did I say?" he asked.

"He's right, Elizabeth," Fiona said. "Just think . . . babies . . ."

Elizabeth softened as she thought about her own children as

babies. She'd never seen Jesse as a baby. "You're right." She reached for her husband's hand. "Oh . . . babies . . ."

"Don't drop me!" Loralee cried as Jesse carried her over the threshold into the most luxurious suite in the Altamont Hotel.

"Drop you? Never." He carried her into the room, closed the door with his foot and set her down beside the bed.

They stood looking at each other, silent while they adjusted to being alone together.

"So," he said, brushing her hair back from her face, "how does it feel to be Loralee Sinclair?"

She rolled her eyes, and said, "Loralee Sinclair. Mrs. Jesse Sinclair." She shook her head. "I can't believe it. I feel . . . I feel . . ." She looked down at his arms wrapped around her. "This feels so right."

He pulled her to his chest. "Ah, Loralee. It is right. You feel perfect in my arms."

"Mmmm."

Jesse leaned down and kissed her. "You looked beautiful today." She was still wearing the white satin sheath she'd worn for the ceremony.

"Thank you."

He rested his hand at her neck and rubbed his thumb along her jaw. "Do you want to change?" he asked quietly.

She stiffened in his arms, but nodded.

"Okay. The bags are in the corner."

"I need help with the buttons," she whispered, looking straight into his chest.

"Oh." He hadn't thought about the buttons. "Well . . . I can help you with that. Buttonhook?"

She pointed to a small traveling bag. "In there."

"All right," he said, rooting through the contents of the

bag. "Buttonhook . . . buttonhook—ah ha!" He held it up. "Buttonhook."

She smiled and presented him with her back.

Jesse's heart suddenly started pounding. He raised the button hook, and found that his hands were shaking. "Uh . . . your hair is . . ."

She reached up and lifted the hair from the nape of her neck, and something deep inside Jesse tightened. He stood looking at her bare neck for so long that she finally twisted around and peeked at him over her shoulder.

He got to work. "Sure are a lot of buttons on this dress."

"Fifty-six."

"Fifty-six? Holy Moses, fifty-six buttons to hold a dress on a tiny thing like you."

"Well, they're not just to hold the dress on."

"Why else would you put them on?" Women sometimes did things that made absolutely no sense.

"Mrs. Stachinski, that's my dressmaker, she says that . . . well, that . . . closely spaced buttons outline the curve of a woman's spine. She says it's very appealing to men."

"Oh." Jesse let his gaze follow the buttons that outlined the curve of his wife's spine and found it very appealing indeed. Women were sometimes so smart.

He finished with the buttons, all the while watching as the thin ribbon of skin that was exposed grew longer and longer. He cleared his throat and held the button hook over Loralee's shoulder.

"Thank you."

"You're welcome. Need anything else?"

"No, that's all."

"All right. I'll wait in the other room." His hand was already on the doorknob when she spoke.

"Jesse?"

He looked up at her.

Her eyes were wide and filled with tears. "I'm really scared."

"Oh, don't be. Please, don't be." He was back beside her in a second. He held her in his arms and rocked her gently. "Just remember what I told you. I will never do anything that you don't want me to do."

She nodded her head against his chest. "I know. But I'm still scared."

"We'll go slow. And if I do my job right, *then* you can thank me."

She chuckled, and the mood was lightened.

"Okay?" he asked leaning back to look into her eyes.

She nodded. "Okay."

He walked into the small sitting room that was attached to the bedroom. There was a well-stocked bar in the corner, a sofa beside it. Jesse kicked off his shoes, shrugged off his jacket and removed his tie. He splashed some brandy into a glass and stood looking down into the amber colored liquid. Loralee should be the one drinking brandy, he thought. Poor thing was terrified.

"Loralee? Would you like a drink? Some wine maybe? Or-Oh, hey! There's champagne!"

"Champagne? Oooo," she called from the other side of the door.

"I guess that's a yes?" he said with a smile.

"Yes, definitely yes."

He got out two champagne flutes and set them on the bar. But no matter how he pulled, the cork was not coming out of that bottle. It wasn't until he held the bottle wedged between his knees that he managed to get the darned thing out, and just as Loralee opened the door.

"Oh!" she cried, as the bubbles foamed out of the bottle and over Jesse's hands. She ran to the bar and held the glasses beneath his fingers, and the champagne dripped off of him and into the glasses. She laughed.

"Lord," he said, with a smile, "you would think I've never opened a bottle of champagne before."

Loralee laughed and held one of the glasses out towards him. "You're sticky."

"I know." He set his glass down and reached for a piece of ice from the bowl beneath the bar. He held it until it melted, and he rubbed his hands with the water. He dried in a small towel, and said, "Good as new."

In all the commotion, one tiny detail had jumped out at him. Loralee's feet were bare. Now, he stopped and took a good look.

She was wearing a long white dressing gown. It buttoned from her neck to the floor, and the long sleeves were tightly tied at her wrists with white ribbon. She'd taken her hair down, and it fell down her back in long, blond waves.

She looked beautiful. He wanted to tear the thing right off of her.

She caught him staring and blushed.

"I love it when my wife blushes," he said.

She smiled, but couldn't look him in the eye.

"Let's make a toast," he said.

"To what?"

"To a lifetime of happiness." He held up his glass, and she touched hers to his.

"To a lifetime of happiness." She took a sip from her glass. "This is good!"

Jesse tipped his glass and emptied it.

"Jesse! It'll make you dizzy!"

He took her arm and pulled her back into the bedroom. "If anything makes me dizzy, it's my wife. My beautiful, sexy wife."

"Jesse!" she said, blushing even more.

"There you go again," he teased. She laughed, and he pulled her into his arms. "I love you very much."

"I love you, too."

She had closed the curtains when she changed, and the room was filled with the murky glow of twilight. Jesse was glad the room was nearly dark. It might make this first time easier for her.

He reached out and rubbed her sleeve between his fingers. "Can I take this off?"

Beneath his fingertips, she tensed. Jesse closed his eyes and racked his brain to think of some way to make this easier.

"Okay," he said, backing a step away from her. "This is what we're going to do." He went to the bed and pulled the covers back. Then he fluffed the pillows and piled them in the center of the bed. "Up you go."

"*What?*"

Jesse smiled. "You, my dear, are entirely too tense. I think you need to have your tootsies rubbed."

She opened her mouth, then closed it. She examined him as though she was trying to figure out a puzzling mystery. "My feet?"

"Your feet. Up." He jerked his head toward the bed and swatted at her behind, and she jumped. Then she smiled and climbed up onto the throne he'd prepared.

"All right, my queen, make yourself comfortable," he said, as he sat at the foot of the bed facing her. With just a little bit of playfulness, he'd relaxed her. She settled into the pillows and folded her hands across her stomach.

Jesse lifted one tiny foot and rested it in his lap. "Are you ticklish?" He ran his fingers from her heel to her toes, and she yanked her foot out of his grasp. "Oooo, I guess you are."

"I am. So don't do that again."

"I won't. Close your eyes."

"Why?"

"Because I said so, that's why. Now, close 'em."

She smiled shyly, and closed her eyes.

"Very good. Now rest your head back. And don't ask why."

She giggled, but obliged him.

Just looking at her made him smile. Being married to Loralee was going to be fun. He could tell already. He wrapped his hand around her foot and kneaded the arch with the heel of his hand.

"Oh, that feels so good," she murmured. "No one ever rubbed my feet before."

"I would hope not!"

"You know what I mean. I never even thought about anybody rubbing my feet. They were just . . . feet."

"Mmmm." He used his thumb and index finger to gently massage the area just above her heel. He suspected that Loralee'd been sensually deprived. She had no idea what she'd been missing. Tonight, Jesse was going to show her, inch by tantalizing inch.

He stayed away from her toes, knowing that she'd be so ticklish she'd be climbing the walls to get away from him. He let his hand move over her ankles, and when she didn't open her eyes, he rubbed her calf until she moaned.

Jesse rested the first foot beside his knee and reached for the other one, repeating each step and moving further up her leg until he was able to touch the back of her knee.

Her dressing gown was pushed up above her knees, and with her legs spread on either side of him, her head tossed back and her eyes closed, she painted an incredibly erotic picture despite the fact that she was covered with white cotton from her neck to her fingertips.

She didn't seem to mind that he was touching her bare legs, so he took a chance.

"Loralee?"

"Hmm?"

"If I take this robe off of you, would you roll over so I can rub your shoulders? You can keep the nightgown on."

"You'll rub my shoulders?" she mumbled.

Jesse smiled. "I'll rub anything you want."

She opened her eyes and lifted one eyebrow, then dropped her head back onto the pillows and said, "You open the buttons. You're good at buttons. And these don't even need a hook."

"You sure?"

"Mmmhmm."

He started from the bottom and worked his way up over her tummy, between her breasts and all the way to her neck. "Geez. How many buttons are on *this* one?" he teased.

"Seventy-two."

"*Seventy-two?*"

"Mmmhmm."

"And what, exactly, is the purpose of seventy-two buttons on a dressing gown?"

"Mrs. Stachinski says it's to give a woman enough time to change her mind."

"Do you want to change your mind?"

"Oh, no. Definitely not if there's rubbing involved."

Jesse couldn't help himself. He laughed. "Oh, there's a lot of rubbing."

"Then get to it," she said, sitting up and slipping her arms out of the sleeves. She flopped onto her stomach so quickly, Jesse couldn't believe that she'd actually done it. But there she was. Lying with her arms lifted to the sides of her head.

He moved up to sit beside her and rested his hands on her back. He moved his whole hand, opened flat, from her shoulders to her waist, where he could feel the edge of her pantaloons. He used his fingertips to press along both sides of her spine.

Jesse massaged her shoulders, and he could feel the tension melting away. It was his guess that she'd never been touched this way, probably not even as a child, when the weight of a parent's hand could be the most comforting, reassuring thing in the world. She'd missed out on a lot of love, but Jesse meant to make up for it.

He knelt and used the weight of his body for pressure as he rubbed his hands against her back. Up through the center, then around and down the sides. Up through the center, then around and down the sides. With each stroke, his fingers crept closer and closer to the fullness at the sides of her breasts. When he finally touched her, she drew in a breath. He did it again, and she said, "Oh, my."

Jesse smiled. His bride was not afraid of him anymore.

He leaned over and kissed the back of her neck. He nudged her chin up and dropped kisses from her ear, under her jaw and down her shoulder until she shuddered.

He came down on one elbow and stretched out beside her. "How do you feel?"

"Mmmm. Like I could get used to this."

Jesse rubbed her back with one hand, and she purred. "Loralee?"

"Hmm?"

He hesitated for a second. "I'm going to undress."

She didn't move.

"Loralee?"

She didn't answer.

He buried his fingers in her hair and pulled gently until she rolled to face him.

She was so small beside him. He looked into her eyes, and said, "I want to make love to my wife."

She stared back at him, then nodded, so slightly, he almost missed it. "Tell me what to do," she whispered.

He leaned down and kissed her cheek. "Do you remember the night of my birthday party?"

"How could I forget?"

"Do you remember when we kissed in the garden?"

She nodded.

"It felt good, didn't it?"

"But that was just kissing."

"Kissing is part of it. Do you remember that feeling?"

She smiled. "I remember it well." She looked away shyly.

"I'm going to undress and get under the covers. You can leave your nightgown on if you want." He knew she wouldn't want it on for long.

"All right." She rolled off the bed, pulled the sheet back,

and rolled back on in one fluid movement. She held the sheet up to her chin.

Jesse sat up with his back to her. He opened his shirt and his pants, stood up and swept everything off, and was beneath the sheet in a matter of seconds.

Three feet of empty space separated them. Jesse moved to Loralee's side of the bed.

"Kiss your husband."

She picked her back up off the bed and kissed him so quickly it was over before he realized it had started.

"Now, kiss me like you mean it." He rested his elbows on either side of her face, and after a few seconds, she reached up and pulled his mouth to hers. Jesse followed her lead. When she opened her mouth, he did the same. When she stroked his tongue, he mimicked her movements. When she held onto him tighter, he wedged his hand beneath her back.

He was against her, and he was naked. There was no hiding what she did to him.

The kiss changed, and suddenly, Jesse was in the lead. He kissed Loralee until she had both arms wrapped around him and she was gasping for air.

"Oh, Jesse . . . this is good," she said.

He rolled into the space between her legs and brushed his lips along her shoulders. Lower, lower, with each stroke, lower. Until he was brushing against the hardness of her nipples through white cotton.

Loralee was breathing heavily, now, and Jesse felt her hands tentatively brush his back. She wanted something, but didn't know what.

He kept up his teasing torture until she opened her legs a little wider and he settled down against her.

"Oh . . ."

"You like?" he asked.

"Oh, yes. I like, but . . . I . . ."

"Do you want your nightgown off?"

She nodded. "Yes. I want it off."

Jesse pushed himself up. "Sit up." She did, and he lifted it over her head and tossed it onto the floor.

He gently pushed her back down, and settled himself in the spot she liked. He filled his hands with her breasts. "Oh, Loralee," he said, closing his eyes.

He molded and shaped them with his hands, and she squirmed restlessly beneath him all the while. He brushed his thumbs over her nipples and her back came away from the bed. He did it again and she groaned. He did it over and over, faster and faster, until she said, "Please, Jesse . . ."

"Please, what?" He leaned so close that his lips brushed the raised peaks as he spoke.

"Yes. Oh, yes. Please."

He opened his mouth on her, drawing her into the warm wetness. Oh, God, this was good. It took every bit of will power Jesse possessed not to crawl inside of her. Inside, where she'd be warm and moist and tight.

"Oh, God, Loralee," he said, kissing her again. She held his head with both hands and pressed against him, aching for something she didn't yet understand.

"Lift your bottom," he said.

She didn't question him this time. She lifted, he slid the pantaloons down her legs and sent them to the floor.

Jesse kissed her neck, her breasts, her belly. And when her breathing was ragged and she was pressed against him, he moved away.

"Oh, no . . . don't—"

"Oh, yes," he said, as his fingers found her ready. He poised above her, and when he entered her, he was looking into her eyes. "Are you okay?"

She nodded.

He leaned forward to kiss her, and when he did, he thrust all the way in. She drew in her breath and tensed beneath him. "I'm sorry," he said. "I'm so sorry. It won't hurt anymore. I promise you, it won't.'' He kissed her and held her face in his hands. ''I love you. Oh, God, Loralee, I didn't even know how much . . . I didn't know.''

She pulled him to her, and they kissed. Jesse let the feeling between them build until she was writhing beneath him.

''Jesse, I-I can't . . . I, oh, I don't know—''

''Feel it, Loralee,'' he said, as he began rhythmically moving. ''Just feel it. See how good we are together? See how right this is?'' He couldn't last much longer. She was wrapped tightly around him, and she was rubbing against him, trying to get to the place she had to go.

''Loralee,'' he said, as he began moving faster. ''Loralee . . .'' Oh, God, How to stop it? How to make himself wait for her? But she felt so damn good.

''Jesse, something's happening—''

''Go with it, honey. Go with it.''

She pressed against him, and a moan started from deep in her throat.

Jesse listened, and with each second that passed, it got harder and harder for him to hold back. Suddenly, she stiffened and then began moving against him. ''Oh, Jess, I . . . ohhhh,'' She wrapped her legs around him, and rocked against him until the shudders passing through her body slowed, then stopped. She held him clasped to her body while she tried to catch her breath.

They lay still for a moment, each one lost in their own thoughts. ''I didn't know,'' she said breathlessly. ''I never knew.''

''Now you do,'' he said. He lifted himself above her and began moving again, drinking in the sight of her beneath him. His wife. Holding him deep inside her body.

The pleasure swept over him like a tidal wave that he tried to hold back. He didn't want to hurt her, but . . .

''Go with it,'' she whispered.

And he was gone. He groaned as he lunged against her. And

his release was fast and furious. He moved until he could move no more, and he dropped down upon her, weak from the effort.

Jesse struggled for breath, and Loralee wrapped her legs and arms around him. When his breathing had slowed, he boosted himself up enough to see into her eyes. He loved this woman more than he ever thought possible. "I never knew," he said. He brushed the gentlest of kisses across her open mouth. "I didn't know it was supposed to be like this."

She smiled up at him. "Now, you know."

She rested her forehead against his chest. "Will it always be like this?"

"Not exactly."

She whipped up her head. "What do you mean?"

He reached up and smoothed her hair out of her eyes. "Sometimes it'll be fast, sometimes it'll be long. Sometimes it will be playful and silly. Sometimes it will be tender and sweet. But the part of me that loves you," he said, touching his chest over his heart, "the thing that makes this an act of love, that part will always be there. Every time. Every single time for the rest of our lives."

She nestled into the hollow in his shoulder and said, "I love you, Jesse."

"I love you, too."

He was feeling sleepy, and by the way Loralee was cuddling up next to him, he guessed she was, too.

She yawned, and said, "Thank you."

Jesse was within an inch of sleep. "What for?" he mumbled.

Loralee wrapped her arm across his chest and hugged him. "A job well done."

And Jesse chuckled. Life with Loralee was definitely going to be fun.

ROMANCE FROM JANELLE TAYLOR